MONTEREY
Memories

GAIL GAYMER MARTIN

BARBOUR
PUBLISHING

Cover photography © Adrian Rahardja

Published by Barbour Publishing, Inc., P.O. Box 719, Uhrichsville, Ohio 44683, www.barbourbooks.com

Our mission is to publish and distribute inspirational products offering exceptional value and biblical encouragement to the masses.

Member of the
Evangelical Christian
Publishers Association

Printed in the United States of America.

 Dear Readers,

I have enjoyed the thrill and blessing of traveling to many parts of the world and through every
state in the union. When I recall the beautiful
landscapes I've witnessed, I can't help but think of
our God creating each mountain and valley, each
forest and desert, each lake and ocean. Besides
Michigan, which is my home and a favorite place
to set my stories, I've had wonderful experiences
in California—where some of my family has lived—traveling from
top to bottom and camping all over the state. Some of my favorite
spots are the central coast of California that offers rolling foothills,
lush farmlands known as "the Salad Bowl," the rocky coasts along
Monterey Peninsula, and the amazing Highway 1.

Monterey Memories features three novels set in this area and cap-
tures the lives of many different people—from migrant workers in
the lettuce fields to wealthy ranch owners. In these books, I wanted
to share the message of God's love and deal with the issue of trust.
Each story dramatizes the importance of trusting God's promises as
well as trusting those we love. Trust is an issue we all struggle with as
Christians, asking the Lord for help in prayer and then continuing to
worry and doubt.

If nothing else touches you in this book, I hope it is Psalm 148:8,
the verse that resonates throughout each story: "Let the morning
bring me word of your unfailing love, for I have put my trust in you."
May God bless you with His promises and touch you with His unfailing love.

Many blessings,
Gail Gaymer Martin

And Baby Makes Five

Dedication

Dedicated to my niece Andrea who lives in Salinas and provided me with great information.

Thanks also to my nephew Joe Fernandez for his medical information, and to Judy Rasmussen at Natividad Medical Center.

Thanks also to those who provided me with the help in the Spanish translations.

Chapter 1

Felisa Carrillo's pain surged down her lower back into her belly. She doubled over in agony while the hot California sun beat across her back. She took deep breaths, controlling the spasms that weakened her knees, and struggled against falling to the lettuce field as the wave of pain raked through her.

"*¿Estás bien?*"

Her coworker's voice wrapped around her, but she couldn't answer. No, she wasn't okay, although Maria's tone alerted Felisa that she knew the answer to her question.

Maria boosted herself from her haunches, dropped the head of lettuce into the basket, and darted to her side. "*¿El bebé está naciendo?*"

When the pain subsided, Felisa lifted her head. "Yes, the baby is coming," she said in Spanish. She looked down the green, even rows to find a place to escape to, but instead her breath left her when she saw a man striding her way. The boss. The owner. She recognized him from other visits to his fields.

"*Déjeme ayudarte,*" Maria said, offering to help her. She slid her arm around Felisa's shoulder, trying to support her.

"*El jefe. El dueño.*" Panic filled Felisa, and she motioned toward the owner, warning Maria of his presence as she tried to pull away. "Maria, you must get back to work," she whispered in Spanish.

"No." Maria's voice snapped with determination.

Felisa slipped from her arms and knelt beside the lettuce, gesturing for her to leave.

Maria finally moved away and crouched farther down the row while Felisa struggled to focus on a plant to avoid drawing the owner's attention. The earthy scent of sun-heated soil and foliage swept over her, causing her stomach to churn. She couldn't get sick now.

As she reached for a lettuce head, another contraction stabbed her. Panic filled her as the man moved closer. She couldn't afford to lose her job, and she sent up a prayer that God would help her bear the pain until he passed. She puffed to control the twisting anguish that seared inside her as the man's shadow fell across her and stopped.

"Are you ill?" His raspy voice hovered above her. "*¿Está usted enferma?*" he repeated.

She didn't look up but only shook her head.

He didn't move.

Tears ballooned in her eyes and escaped to her cheeks. She knew the drop-lets would leave a telltale trail on her dusty skin. She tried to brush them away, but she felt the sticky grime against her fist.

The man lowered his hand and tilted her face upward into the glaring sun. She flinched with his touch and closed her eyes to the brightness, but when she opened them she saw only concern in his eyes. His gaze left her face and lowered to her bulging belly she'd tried to camouflage with an oversized shirt. "Pregnant," he muttered then lifted his gaze to her face. "*¿Está usted embarazada?*"

She tugged at her top to cover her belly and ignored his question, but she felt her face go pale.

"You're in labor." His voice sounded disbelieving, and he bent over her as frustration rattled in his throat. He straightened and scanned the field. "Husband?" he muttered before he turned to her again. "*¿Dónde está su esposo?*"

Felisa's throat knotted. "Dead." *And good riddance,* she added to herself. She immediately became ashamed of her thought, but she knew God understood.

"You speak English." Relief filled his face.

"Yes."

"Your husband is dead?"

Felisa gave a fleeting nod. "Killed."

She watched his head swivel as he studied the field, like he were looking for a body. Finally he turned back to her, seemingly satisfied. "When? What happened?"

She winced, remembering the day she saw Miguel's mangled body. Though she knew some English, under stress she struggled to remember the words. "*Ocho*—eight months ago. *Accidente*—an accident," she corrected. Miguel had been drunk as always, but that day he was dead drunk. Coming out of a barroom, he staggered into the street and was hit by a car. The police called it an accident. She called it freedom.

The man shook his head and drew out a handkerchief to wipe the perspiration from his face. "Do you have family in Salinas?"

"No," she said, feeling another contraction grip her. She coiled into a ball. "No family."

She heard the irritation in his voice.

"You're not having a baby in this field," he said, his voice deepening with emotion. "I'll take you to the hospital."

"No, please," she said, fearing a hospital bill. She barely had enough for food.

"The Natividad Medical Center. It's a hospital. You're not staying here," he said, sounding determined and hitting numbers on his cell phone. "Can you walk?"

He turned his attention to the phone call while she let the last of the pain fade. Could she walk? Determination charged through her. She would. She had to.

The man disconnected, then reached toward her.

"I can walk," she said, pushing her hand against the pungent earth to hoist herself. As she rose, her legs buckled, and he grasped her arm, lifting her to her feet and supporting her along the lettuce rows.

"My truck is this way." He motioned toward the distance.

Felisa felt her knees buckle again, and she stumbled forward. The man scooped her into his arms and carried her, his urgency obvious. His strength gave her a sense of security, and she drew in the smell of the heat radiating from his skin, a clean aroma so different from the workers in the field. His fresh scent mingled with the tangy fragrance of his aftershave.

"Do you think you can make it?" he asked. "By the time I get an ambulance here, we can probably be there." He boosted her more securely against his body.

A wave of pain bore down on her, and she struggled until she could speak. "I'll make it." Yet her voice sounded breathless and insecure. She recoiled with anger at her stupid response. She had no idea if she could make it. What if he had to deliver the baby? As she opened her mouth to retract her statement, Felisa felt the man shift her weight and realized they'd reached his truck.

"Can you stand?" he asked as he lowered his arms.

She nodded, and he braced her against him as he pulled out his keys, then opened the door and lifted her onto the seat. "We'll be there in a few minutes." He eyed her again. "Are you sure you can do this?"

She had little choice. "I'm okay," she answered, praying that God would keep the baby safe until she reached the clinic.

He closed the door, and in a moment the driver's side door opened and he slipped in beside her. The ignition kicked in, and she leaned her head against the leathery seat cushion as the truck bumped and rocked when they pulled away. Her gaze rested on his tanned hands gripping the steering wheel, and she saw concern in his bearing.

A cool breeze washed over her legs—air conditioning, a luxury she and her husband had never been able to afford. She felt blessed her junker car still ran. Sometimes it was not only her transportation but also her bed, more often than she wanted to remember, and now with the baby what would she—

"What's your name?"

His voice jerked her from her thoughts. She eyed his profile. "Felisa Carrillo."

"And you have no family here?"

"None. My parents live near Guadalajara."

"You should go back home."

His blunt comment punctured her. "I can't."

He glanced at her, his hazel eyes flashing a questioning look, but he didn't probe further.

A sudden fear settled over Felisa. What did he want of her? Why had he insisted on taking her to the hospital when so many women had their babies in the fields or outbuildings, anyplace they could find privacy and cover?

She tilted her head to search his face. Determination had settled in his jaw, his lips pressed together, and his hands gripped the wheel with purpose. Would he try to take her child away from her? Would he offer to buy her baby? She'd heard stories of people bargaining for the migrants' children, and they were so poor they would give in to their weakness. She would not, but she had no money to fight a battle, no money to—

Another contraction wracked her, and Felisa bit her lip to keep from screaming. She focused on the cool air of the cab and the soft hum of the engine, letting the pain seep away until she could breathe. She didn't even know the man's name. They'd all referred to him as el dueño, the owner. That was all she knew.

"I'm Chad Garrison," he said as if hearing her thoughts. "I own the farm."

"I know." She brushed her gritty fingers through her hair that matted against her cheek.

"What would you have done if I hadn't come along?"

"I—I. . ." Giving birth in the field was nothing new; yet how could she tell him she would have done what other women had to do?

"You would have had the baby in the field. Do you realize that?"

"Yes," she whispered, wishing she'd had a better plan, but being without a husband, she had no other means.

"Unbelievable," he said, shaking his head as if disgusted. "Don't you realize the danger? How could you think that little of bringing a life into the world?"

Felisa felt dirty and worthless. "I know." Even his shiny new truck seemed more worthy than she felt. She felt more like her old car, which had lost its sheen just as her life had lost its color.

His neck twisted with the speed of a bullet, and his eyes narrowed. She felt like a flyspeck beneath his gaze until his look softened. "I'm sorry. I don't mean to judge you. I suppose you have little choice."

The expression in his eyes broke her heart, as if the danger she was in belonged to him. She studied his face again, his firm chin and lips so full they looked soft and pliable when earlier they had looked rigid and compressed. Felisa didn't respond to his comment. She had nothing to say. She'd made her decisions and married badly. Her life had become one sleazy motel or low-income housing unit after another, and since Miguel's death, it had been even worse. She closed her eyes as the next sudden pain nearly rent her in two.

~

Chad pulled his hand away from the steering wheel and stretched his cramped fingers. He'd gripped the wheel as though he feared for his life. Emptiness hammered in his chest. He glanced at the young Hispanic woman beside him, sorry he'd lost control and snapped at her. Her presence triggered horrific memories that tore through him—memories he'd kept deep inside for the past two years.

Felisa's dark hair clung in ringlets against her damp face. He longed to brush it back to make her more comfortable. Instead he adjusted the air conditioner, but reality told him it was the pain that caused her to perspire and not the heat.

The bright rays came through the window and shone through her dark tresses glinting with streaks of copper, as if they had been bleached by the sun.

He watched a grimace surge across Felisa's face. Another contraction. Chad looked ahead, praying they reached the medical center before the baby came. He'd been foolish not to call for an ambulance; but he figured by the time they arrived it would be too late and the baby would be born in the field. Even cattle had the comfort of hay in the shelter of a barn. This woman deserved that much. The thought of the Christmas story charged through his mind, when Mary birthed Jesus in the covering of a stall.

He watched the speed limit as he hurried down Natividad Road, and when he crossed Laurel Drive, Chad drew in a lengthy breath. Only a few more yards and he could put the young woman into the hands of the medical staff. "We're almost there," he said, hearing relief in his voice.

He took the emergency entrance and pulled up to the door as a medic met him with a wheelchair. Chad jumped from the truck and hurried around to the passenger side where the medic was already helping the woman into the chair.

"Good thing you called. Looks like you got her here just in time," the man said as he lowered the footrest while Felisa raised her feet to the platform. He released the brake and headed inside.

Chad stood for a moment, watching her until she vanished through the doorway. He drew in a breath, turned, and climbed into the truck. He sat for a few seconds, deciding what was right. Chad had nothing to do with this woman and had done his duty. He could leave.

He turned on the ignition and pulled away from the emergency door, but his conscience prickled in his thoughts. She was his employee. What if she ran into a problem? Would she be all right? Would the baby make it through the ordeal? Chad figured Felisa had received no prenatal care. He'd seen that before, and it knotted his chest.

Chad knew what the Lord would have him do. He turned the wheel and pulled into a parking slot, then climbed out and strode toward the entrance. He could at least make sure someone had taken care of her.

The summer heat beat against his shoulders as his boots clicked along the concrete walk. Chad passed the security guard with a nod as the double door swished open. Inside he was greeted with air conditioning and the scent of antiseptic. He strode to the desk and waited until the woman raised her head. "I just brought in Felisa—" Felisa what? He'd already forgotten her last name. "She's in labor. A young Hispan—"

"She's in the back," she said. "You're her husband?"

Her question yanked at his memory. "She's my employee. She has no family here."

"You can wait in the visitor area." She swung her arm toward the hallway. "Mrs. Carrillo is in delivery."

Chad glanced at his watch, remembering the list of jobs he was supposed to do today. "How long will it be?"

She rolled her eyes and shook her head. "Babies come in their own time, sir."

"I realize that." He lowered his head and backed away, irritated with himself and with her. He paused, then turned toward the door, deciding to forget his attempt to be a good Samaritan.

"Sir."

He halted and pivoted toward her.

"Let me call delivery and see how she's doing."

"Thank you." He shoved his hands into his pockets and stepped forward.

She nodded and picked up the telephone while he waited. His mind tumbled with painful memories. Only two years ago he'd waited like this at Salinas Valley Memorial Hospital—the horrible long wait with a horrendous ending.

"She's delivering now, sir. It won't be long."

Her voice pushed its way into Chad's consciousness. "Now?"

"You apparently got here just in time." She motioned again to the waiting room. "Why not wait a few minutes? The doctor will see you shortly."

His mind reeling with memories, Chad forced himself to focus on today. He turned and made his way to the waiting room. Inside, he stopped to pour a cup of strong black coffee from the carafe. Its acrid scent permeated the room. He crumpled into a nearby chair and leaned back his head, wondering how he'd gotten into the mess in the first place. Chad glanced at his watch again, then pulled out his cell phone, punched in the numbers, and waited for an answer.

"Joe," he said, once he connected, "I'm at—" He stopped himself. "I'm on an errand and can't get back for a while. Can you handle things until I get there?"

As he expected, Joe had no problem with his request and didn't ask what was keeping him. He didn't want to lie, but he didn't want to tell the truth. He'd avoided getting familiar with his workers. Their plight ate at his conscience. So many lived in less-than-acceptable housing with little to offer their families, but migratory workers were the backbone of his business. He paid them better than most did and tried to provide temporary housing, although the task was endless and often hopeless.

He closed his eyes, envisioning the lovely young woman now facing a dilemma. How could she work with a new baby? Where would she go? His fingers knotted into fists against the vinyl upholstery. He felt responsible for some reason, angry at the whole situation—her husband dying, her pregnancy, the fact that his own visit to the field this morning had brought her into his life. He could have gone anywhere but that field.

He opened his eyes, his thoughts filled with shame. Where was his compassion? His upbringing? *Lord, You have the answers. I'll put my trust in You. I can't solve these never-ending problems. I place this in Your hands.*

He rose and poured the coffee down the drain, then tucked his hands into his pockets and paced. When he met the eyes of other families waiting, they smiled as if understanding his anxiety, but they didn't understand. He wasn't the father. He shouldn't be involved, but he'd gotten himself into it.

Chad strode to the window and looked out at the beaming sun in the clear blue sky. He wished Felisa's future could be as bright as the heavens.

"Mr. Carrillo?"

Awareness clicked in Chad. *Carrillo.* That was Felisa's last name. He turned to see a physician in green scrubs, a mask dangling around his neck. Heat rose up Chad's face. He pulled his hands from his pockets and strode toward the physician, his hand extended.

The doctor gripped his fingers. "Congratulations! You're the father—"

"I'm not the father."

The physician's eyes widened.

"She's a widow and works for me. I brought her in."

The doctor's handshake loosened, and he stepped back. "She and the baby are fine."

Discomfort settled on Chad's shoulders. "Boy or girl?"

"A boy."

A boy. Chad thought of his twin daughters so lost without their mother, who died delivering Chad's stillborn baby son. The pain seared through his chest. "I'm glad they're okay," he said finally, monitoring the emotion that welled inside him.

"You can see them if you'd like. It will be a few minutes."

"No, I—" *I what? I'm a wimp?* Chad swallowed, hoping to regain his control. "I'd like to see the boy."

"I'll send a nurse in when he's ready."

The doctor backed away, and Chad turned and settled into the chair he'd occupied earlier. A boy. A new life. And what a life the small infant had to face. Reality pressed down upon him like a lead weight as a prayer rose to heaven, begging the Lord to care for this woman and child.

Time dragged, and Chad had second thoughts. He should leave. He'd done his duty as a Christian. He knew she was in good hands for now. Slipping his hand into his pocket, he felt the car keys jingle against his fingers. He wrapped his fist around the keys and pulled them upward.

"Is someone waiting to see the Carrillo baby?"

Chad's head swiveled toward the nurse in the doorway. He didn't have to answer, but his mouth opened. "Yes. Thank you."

He met her in the hallway and followed her down a corridor. Realizing they weren't heading to a nursery, he faltered.

"Is something wrong?"

"No, but I thought—"

"Wait a minute." She held up one finger. "I'll check inside." She strode into the room and came out again. "Mrs. Carrillo is sleeping, but you can see the baby."

His heartbeat slowed. Felisa was sleeping. His throat knotted. It wasn't his place to look at her child, and he couldn't talk to Felisa now; but he wanted to see the boy.

The nurse gave him a questioning look, and he pulled himself together and followed her, his mind swinging from one direction to another. They passed the first bed, then stepped around a curtain. His heart jumped when he saw Felisa, her eyelids closed, her breathing soft. She looked tired, yet beautiful. He forced his attention toward the nurse standing beside a bassinet.

"I'll leave you alone," she said and left the room.

Chad lowered his gaze. He looked into the tiny face of Felisa's beautiful baby with dark, curling hair and creamy bronzed skin. His chest ached as he studied the tiny fingers and black lashes that flickered beneath the bright light.

"Welcome to the world, little boy," he said. "Welcome to harsh reality." He felt the car keys still gripped in his fingers and wished he'd fled instead of seeing this helpless babe who needed so much love and security.

He tore his gaze away and turned his back to the room. Sadness washed over him, and he hurried down the hallway and out into the sunny day. Sunny for him, but not sunny for that beautiful little boy.

Chapter 2

Felisa cradled her son in her arms. Tears of joy rolled down her cheeks until reality set in. What did she have to offer this child God had given her? She worked hard yet got nowhere. She couldn't return to her parents' house in Guadalajara. They had rejoiced each time one of the seven children had left the nest, making one less mouth to feed. They were as bad off as she was. Worse, maybe. She couldn't burden them now with her problem.

She gazed down at her beautiful child and tucked her finger into the baby's palm, feeling his tiny fist curl around it—perfect little fingers, bronzy and soft, a tiny life that had lived inside her during the worst of times. He would grow up to be strong, and, God willing, maybe he would have a better life than she had. Felisa drew in a deep breath, determined her son would succeed where she'd failed. But how? It seemed so hopeless.

She promised herself this boy would never be like his father. Never. She closed her eyes, knowing she couldn't make such a promise. She had no power to make things better. Only God could guide her son's destiny. She bowed her head, asking God to bless her baby and keep him strong in body and faith. Her faith had been what she'd clung to the past year, a faith that had been strengthened by a wise Christian woman who'd taken her under her wing and taught her more about Jesus. She would be grateful forever, because her faith now burned in her heart more brightly.

A sound outside her room caught her attention. Her heart fluttered as she wondered if she had company. Chad Garrison's powerful image filled her mind, but when she looked toward the doorway, an aide entered the room, pushing a cart with carafes of fresh water. Felisa drew up her shoulders and smiled at her son. "We don't need anyone," she whispered. "It's you and me. . .and the heavenly Father. That's all we need."

You and me. Felisa Carrillo and who? She studied the baby's face, his tiny nose and the dark eyelashes that brushed against his soft cheeks. Tears welled in her eyes. *What is your name?* God had written her child's name in the book of life. A deep ache burned in her, wondering what life held in store for her little boy.

She watched the aide straighten her bed table and replace the water, then slip from the room without a word. She lowered her gaze to the tiny features, the soft cuddly form that lay against her body. "You are my son," she whispered. "Only mine. By what name will you be called?" She searched through the list of family names, men she worked beside, but nothing seemed to stir her heart.

In the quiet her thoughts again turned to Chad Garrison. Why had he been so kind? Rarely did the workers ever see the farm owner in the fields. The field managers told the workers what to do and saw that they did it. Had this man acted out of kindness or for some ulterior motive? The thought frightened her.

Her earlier horrible questions returned. Would he allow her to continue to work at his farm without giving him her son? It might be for the best, but she couldn't give away her child. Her mind swirled with fears; yet in her heart she wanted to think he was only being kind. A knot of confusion coiled in her chest and rose to her throat. "Dearest Lord, take care of us," she whispered as tears pooled in her eyes and ran down her cheeks.

Chad looked up from his desk in the field office and saw Joe standing in the doorway.

"So you're back," Joe said, ambling into the room and slumping into a chair.

He cocked his head, hoping to avoid the foreman's questions. He spread his arms, managing a grin. "Looks like it, doesn't it? Here I am."

Joe leaned forward and folded his hands between his knees. "Heard you helped a woman off the field this morning."

"You did, huh?" He kept his eyes focused on his work.

"Right. What's up?"

Chad dropped his pen onto his untidy blotter and leaned back. "You tell me. Sounds like someone already told you the story."

"Mexican woman in labor. That's what I heard."

"Then you heard right."

Joe leaned even closer, questions written on his face.

Trying to avoid eye contact, Chad stared at the ledger, then picked up the pen; yet he feared the interrogation wasn't over.

"And?" Joe's voice punctuated the silence.

Chad tossed the pen onto the desk again. "What do you want to know?"

Joe shrugged. "I don't know. What happened? You've never done that before."

"I've never watched a woman nearly give birth in the field before. I took her to Natividad Medical Center. What did you expect me to do?"

Joe rose from the chair. "Don't bite my head off. I was just curious."

"Curiosity killed the cat."

Joe raised his arms in a hopeless gesture and strode toward the door.

"I'm sorry," Chad said, watching Joe brace his hands against the doorframe for a moment, then turn to face him.

"What's gotten into you, Chad? It's not like you—"

"I know." His head lowered, and he wove through the millions of feelings churning inside him. He regained composure and looked at Joe. "I saw the woman in labor, and I couldn't help but think of—"

"Janie." Joe looked stunned and moved toward him from the doorway, his expression filled with sympathy. "I'm sorry, man. I didn't think. It makes sense that you'd think of your wife." He settled back into the chair. "You did the right thing."

Chad wondered. Now that he'd become tangled in this woman's problem, he couldn't let it go. Distraction followed him home from the hospital while his thoughts drifted again to Felisa's needs. Felisa. He'd never bothered to learn the names of his workers. It made them too real, and now this woman and her baby were too real. "She had a boy."

Joe didn't respond but looked at him, his eyes searching Chad's face as if wondering what he'd gotten himself into.

He felt defensive with Joe's probing look. "I didn't go in to see the woman."

Joe let out a stream of breath as if relieved. "Don't get too involved, Chad. It's a hopeless situation."

Chad heaved back his chair, hearing the scrape of the legs against the wooden floor, and rose, his chest tightening with Joe's reality. "I know. I know, but—"

"You did your good deed. Natividad will take the financial loss, and you can feel good you did that much."

That much. The woman could survive, but that baby boy. What about him?

Joe didn't move, and Chad felt his inquisitive stare.

"Don't you have work to do?" Chad asked, sending an arched brow his way.

"Sure I do. I just thought..." He let the rest of his sentence die as he headed for the door.

Chad waited until he heard the click, then collapsed into the chair and lowered his face in his hands. He knew it wasn't wise, but he had to make sure this woman had a place to go. The hospital wouldn't keep her more than a day or so—just long enough to make sure they were healthy. She'd be sent out to face the world, but not alone. This time with a child. He cringed, knowing what he had to do and knowing he would be sorry.

⌇

Night would soon settle over the city, and Felisa could see streaks of dusky rose spreading across the sky from the setting sun. Soon the city lights would come alive like fireflies at her window. She nestled deeper under the blankets, unaccustomed to air conditioning—such a luxury. Felisa imagined her friends fanning themselves against the heat before the sun vanished and the cooler air drifted into the valley.

She closed her eyes and worried about tomorrow. If she was released, where would she go? She'd missed a day's work and probably two, she guessed. Her pay would be so little, and now she needed things for the baby.

She pictured her child's sweet face, longing to know what he would look like grown up. His father had been a handsome man. That had been her foolish downfall. She should have listened to her friends' warnings, but she'd been so certain, and she never asked the Lord to help her make a godly decision. She'd tripped over her wisdom to marry Miguel. She'd been so young. Sixteen. Felisa hardly knew what marriage was to be, although she'd seen her parents' struggle. Why hadn't she been smart enough to realize what life would hold for her?

Footsteps caught her attention, and when the privacy curtain drew back, her heart skipped a beat. Chad Garrison stepped inside and stopped at the foot of her bed, silent as a stone.

Felisa pushed her hair away from her face, knowing she must look a fright. She had nothing with her to make herself look better. She hadn't even combed her hair that she could remember. Felisa lowered her gaze, unable to look him in the eye. Questions filled her mind. Why was he there? What did he want of her? Panic knotted in her chest.

"How are you?" he asked, his voice raspy but gentle.

"Fine," she said.

She sensed he'd stepped closer and heard the chair shift on the tile floor before he sat beside her hospital bed. "Your boy is a handsome baby."

Her arms wrenched against her chest, wanting to hold her child in her arms, to protect him. She would not give him away—not for any money on earth. "Thank you," she mumbled.

Despite her attempt to cover her fear, her voice sounded cautious. He must have sensed her concern, because he leaned closer and said her name.

Felisa lifted her gaze, afraid of what she'd see, but again she saw only kindness in his soft hazel eyes.

"I want to ask you a few questions. I know this isn't my business, really. You're only an employee. That's it, and all you owe me is a good day's work. But I brought you here, and now I feel. . ."

His voice drifted off, and she studied his face, wondering what he felt. Surely he didn't feel he owed her anything. No other employer had ever provided anything beyond her wage.

His mouth tensed. "I'm concerned about your working in the field with the baby."

"I'm fine. Look at him." She motioned toward the bassinet. "My son's fine. I can work." She felt tears blur her vision. He couldn't fire her. She had no money and nowhere to go. She had—

"I'm not doubting you can work, but you have the baby." He rose and looked at her boy a moment before turning back to her. "Do you have someone to care for him? Where are you living?"

"I have help. Don't worry." She didn't have any earthly help, but she knew where her help came from. A voice rose in her mind. *"My help comes from the Lord."*

"Felisa, where do you live?"

His voice sounded stern, and she lowered her gaze. What could she say that wasn't a lie? "I make out okay."

"That's not what I asked you. It's not just you, but your child. I want to know if you have a home. Are you in the government housing?"

Although she sensed concern in his voice, she didn't want to let down her guard. "No, but I can make do."

"Then where—"

"I rent a motel room," she said then realized she had to tell him the whole truth. "When I can afford one."

"If not, do you stay with someone?"

"I'll ask around. Maybe—"

"You don't sleep in the train or bus station, do you?"

She shook her head, although she knew those who did. "My car. I own a car."

"You live out of your car?"

"Sometimes, but—"

He rose and jammed his hands into his pockets. "I'll make some calls. Do you know when you'll be released?"

"Why?" The question flew from her mouth.

"Why?" He looked confused. "I want to know when you're released so I can—"

"No, not that. Why are you helping me? What do you want?"

He drew back as if she'd slapped him. "I don't want anything. You have a child, and you need a home for the baby."

She eyed him, her suspicion raging. "No one has ever offered me anything. I don't understand."

He shook his head. "You don't need to understand."

But she did. "I don't want to lose my son."

"I don't want you to, either, and you won't. I'll ask at the desk, and I'll talk with you tomorrow."

He turned and stepped toward the curtain; but it opened, and a nurse entered the room pushing a monitor. "Time for your blood pressure," she said. "Do you want to sit up?"

"In a minute," she said, eyeing her employer and wondering if he were leaving.

He didn't move away. Instead he shifted closer to the bassinet and looked down at her child. A mixture of fear and pride waged war inside her. She studied him as he bent lower as if to touch her son.

"Do you mind?" he asked, looking at Felisa over his shoulder.

"No." But she wasn't sure if she minded or not. He'd said kind things to her, but did he mean them?

He brushed the baby's cheek with his finger and smiled.

"Would you like to hold him?" Felisa asked, startled when the words left her.

He glanced from her to the nurse with a questioning look on his face.

"Have a seat," the nurse said, pointing to the chair he'd just vacated.

He sank into the chair, and Felisa wondered if he'd had second thoughts about whether he wanted to hold the baby, but he didn't have time to decline. The nurse lifted the infant from the bassinet and nestled him into Chad's arms, then moved back to Felisa with the blood pressure cuff.

Felisa watched his face flicker with deep emotion. Her pulse tripped, wondering what thoughts were running through his head. She'd thought he had evil on his mind; yet now she sensed something deep and sad stirring inside him, something she would never know, but whatever it was it gave Felisa a feeling of confidence in him. Maybe he was a good man who really wanted to help her.

Chad sat for a moment and watched the nurse pump up the cuff and listen through her stethoscope; then he glanced at Felisa with a mournful smile, holding her son in stiff arms as if he feared he might break.

"You didn't have to hold him," she said, concerned about his discomfort.

"It's fine." He seemed to relax and study the baby again. "He's a good-looking boy already. I think he has your chin and the same large eyes as yours."

Her chin. Her eyes. She had no idea he'd even really looked at her. "Thank you. I pray he's kind and honest. Good looks aren't as important." Miguel burst into her mind, and she wished she'd realized that seven years ago, before she married him.

"That's it," the nurse said, unwrapping the cuff from her arm. "Everything looks good." She grasped the monitor and pushed it past the curtain.

Chad had turned his attention back to the baby. "What's his name?"

Felisa scooted to the edge of the bed and looked over at her sleeping son. "I haven't decided." She looked into Chad's eyes and again saw that faraway look.

"A boy needs a name," Chad said. "Something special for this one."

Something special. Her baby was special. He was her family, part of her being. Felisa's thoughts drifted to her family in Guadalajara, and she was filled with melancholy. "My mother once told me she would have named me Nataniel if I'd been a boy."

"That's a nice name."

"It means gift from God."

Chad lifted his gaze to hers, and her heart flooded with warmth as he brushed his thick finger over the baby's cheek.

"I've decided to name my son Nataniel," she said, feeling more relaxed in her employer's company, "and call him Nate."

"That's a good name. A very good choice." He leaned over the baby. "Welcome to the world, Nataniel."

"Nate," she whispered.

"Nate it is." He rose and settled the baby into her arms. "I need to make some calls. I'll talk with you tomorrow, and I hope you'll have a place to stay."

"Thank you," she said, admiring his tall, lanky frame as he strode across the room.

He gave her a fleeting look and slipped behind the curtain.

Felisa looked down at her son. She pictured her baby in Chad Garrison's arms, and she prayed her instinct about the man had been right. He seemed to be a sensitive person—a kind man. She hoped he wanted only to help her and Nate. Hearing her son's name in her thoughts sent shivers of joy through her. Her child deserved better than she could offer, and if this man could help, she would accept his offer. Just this once.

～

The morning sunlight flickered beneath the blinds of Chad's Corral de Tierra home. He stirred under the sheet and opened one eye to gaze at the alarm clock. Six thirty. He hadn't rested well last night, his mind shifting from Felisa's dilemma to his own emotions, which had been rattled since he'd driven the woman to the hospital.

He yawned but couldn't indulge his desire to sleep. He had work to do. On the way out of the hospital last evening, he'd asked at the desk about Felisa's release. Though they were unsure without a doctor's statement, the nurse calculated today or tomorrow at the latest. The baby and Felisa were both healthy, and without insurance they wouldn't keep the mother and child in the hospital too long, he knew.

Chad shifted his feet from beneath the covering and sat on the edge of the bed. He ran his fingers through his hair, thinking about where to begin. The first thing to do was call the agency regarding housing facilities, units used for migrant workers. The cost was low, and the government facilities always provided daycare. Still, with over 250,000 farm workers in need of housing each year, he knew he couldn't take availability for granted. He could only hope.

After rising, Chad showered, shaved, and headed to the kitchen. The scent of coffee and the fragrant aroma of cinnamon beckoned him down the hallway. He came around the corner in time to see his housekeeper pull a tray of pastries from the oven.

"Good morning," she said, setting the tray on a rack. "You're just in time."

"Thanks, Juanita," he said, grabbing a cup from the rack and filling it with steaming black coffee. He settled onto a kitchen chair, took a cautious sip of the drink, and flipped open his cell phone. He flicked through the address book for the Office of Migrant Services and hit the call button. OMS worked hard to provide inexpensive housing for the vast number of workers who streamed into the area during planting and harvest. He sent up a prayer that they would have housing for Felisa and the baby. Now he could only hope someone was there this early.

Juanita set a plate in front of him with a warm cinnamon pastry and slices of fresh fruit. She walked away, and he heard her hit the toaster button.

"This is enough for today, Juanita," he said, gesturing to the dish in front of him. His stomach felt knotted with his thoughts. When his call connected, he listened to the automated menu list, irritated that finding a human at the end of the line seemed impossible. Finally he hit the zero, and his shoulders relaxed when a human voice responded. "Is Bill Garcia available? This is Chad Garrison of Garrison Farms."

He waited, listening to music strum over the lines, until he heard a hello. "Bill, this is Chad Garrison. I have a favor. I need housing for one of my workers. She just gave birth to a baby at Natividad and should be released either—"

Bill's voice cut into his explanation, and Chad shrank with his abrupt response.

"Nothing? She only needs a small place. She's desperate."

Bill's voice sounded weary, and Chad thought about the time. The guy had probably come in early to catch up on paperwork.

"I see," Chad said. "What about another facility not too far from Salinas? Do you know if—"

Bill's answer snapped through the speaker.

"Nothing. You're sure?" He listened to Bill's comments. He'd heard the story before. The waiting list and the tenant council who worked to fill available spaces. "Thanks anyway, Bill. I'll have to give this some thought."

He closed the cell phone with a flip and set it on the table, discouragement coursing through him. What now? Most low-cost motels were filled, he knew, and even then, what would Felisa do with the baby while she worked? Chad couldn't imagine her bringing the newborn in a baby backpack while trying to pick lettuce. Yet he'd seen that done, too.

Juanita hovered nearby, cleaning the counter from her baking and readying things to pack Chad's lunch. Since he'd hired her she'd been a wonderful, hardworking woman, and she'd put up with the antics of his twins uncomplainingly.

"Are the girls up yet?" Chad asked.

"No. Nanny said she'd hog-tie them if they got up too early. She's losing patience, I'm afraid, just like the others."

Juanita surprised him. She had never been one to gossip, so her comment made an impact on him. He'd noticed the nanny hadn't been the most patient woman. Yet his four-year-olds could try most anyone's patience. He had to bite his tongue many times to keep from yelling at them himself. The words in Proverbs had entered his mind more than once. *"A gentle answer turns away wrath, but a harsh word stirs up anger."* He'd tried to follow God's direction, but he'd nearly failed many times.

"Juanita, you know the area. I'm looking for housing for one of my workers who—"

"I couldn't help but hear you," she said, stopping her work. "I don't know anyplace that has openings. Where has she been living, and what about her husband?"

Her question aroused his emotion. "She's a young widow. From what she told me, her husband died only a month after she conceived. I'm guessing she's been sleeping in her car somewhere."

Juanita shook her head and took a deep breath. "Very sad. Such a difficult life. I'm grateful to my parents that they worked hard and made a good life for us. I'm able to fend for myself."

"You've been blessed, Juanita."

"I can ask around and see if any of the housekeepers in the area know if their employers are looking for help, but I think that's a lost cause." She paused and then gave him an uncomfortable look. "Is she trustworthy?"

He shook his head. "I don't know the woman, but I'd guess she is."

Juanita shrugged. "I'll ask around when I finish up here."

"She'll be released today or tomorrow. That doesn't give much time."

"I'll do my best," she said, opening the refrigerator door.

He studied Juanita. She'd been a faithful employee and worked hard, almost too hard, and never complained. He admired her for that. She deserved a break.

Chapter 3

C had stood outside Felisa's hospital room the next afternoon, amazed. He had sensed the Lord leading him to help her, but he felt overwhelmed by the Lord's request. He felt drawn to her and her needs; yet it set him on edge. People had attitudes. People talked. Joe's criticism came to mind.

Earlier in the day Felisa had called, and he could still hear her tentative voice. She'd called his home first, and Juanita had provided his cell phone number. When he'd answered he'd hoped the call would be good news about housing. Instead it was her soft request. "Can you pick me up? I have no way to get to my car."

Get to my car. Her words pierced his heart, and he'd made his decision at that moment.

He drew in a deep breath and walked through the door into her room. He gave a nod to the patient in the first bed, then stood outside the curtain. "Are you dressed?" he asked.

"I'm ready," she said, her voice as gentle as a breeze rippling the colorful bougainvillea blossoms outside.

He slid the curtain over and stepped inside. Felisa sat on the edge of the bed, dressed in the same clothing he'd brought her in with. What did he expect? Who would bring her clean clothes?

She turned to look at him over her shoulder. "Thank you for coming." Her face looked pale, with worry lines on her forehead.

He walked farther into the room and leaned over the bassinet to look at the tiny boy. Nate. He had a name. Chad's chest tightened, and he forced himself away, trying to repress the memories that flooded his mind. "Do you need to do anything before you leave?" He sat in the same chair he'd used to hold the baby the day before.

She shook her head, then thought better. "I have to wait for a wheelchair."

He motioned toward the call button. "Let's buzz the nurse and tell her you're ready."

Felisa leaned over and signaled the nurse's station. When she finished she rose and straightened her oversized top. "I'm sorry. I don't have any clean clothes with me."

"I should have asked if you needed anything," he said, wondering where she kept her belongings. In her car, he guessed.

She looked pale and frightened, and she wandered to the window, looking

24

out, then turned, walked past the curtain, and peered toward the corridor.

"It'll be a while, Felisa. You might as well sit."

She stopped pacing, looking as jittery as he felt, and he wondered how she would react when she learned he hadn't found a room as he'd promised.

Felisa sank onto the edge of the bed and gazed toward the window. He wondered what she thought of him. She'd already mentioned that no one had ever treated her so well. Chad wondered if she needed his reassurance. He sensed she was looking for his motive. The more he thought about it, the more he knew he needed to say something.

"I've tried to help you, Felisa, but I expect nothing in return. I don't want you to worry that I had any motive other than to help a fellow human being. The Bible says what we do for others we do for Him, and I've tried to live my life that way."

Surprise registered on her face. "You're a Christian?" Her eyes searched his. "I sure am."

He saw her shoulders relax and realized his comment had given her relief. "Did you think I had some other reason?"

She shrugged. "I didn't know. People—people sometimes want—want babies, and I—"

"No. No. I would never have—" He couldn't believe what she'd thought. "Did you really think I wanted to take your son from you?"

"I—I didn't know, but I couldn't imagine what you wanted from me, except. . ."

Her voice faded, and he could only guess the dire thoughts that had filled her mind.

"You have an unusual circumstance without a husband and now a new baby. I wanted to help you. I have two daughters of my own."

"Daughters?" Her dark eyes widened, and he saw a glint of interest that brightened her tense face.

"Two four-year-old girls. They're two handfuls. Maybe four handfuls." He chuckled, although it wasn't always a laughing matter.

Her gaze traveled over his face. "I'm sure they are beautiful children."

"They look like their mother did."

Her face twisted in question. "She is gone away?"

His chest constricted, taking away his breath. "In heaven. Maybe she knows your husband," he added, to make her aware he understood her sorrow.

"No." Her voice darkened. "Miguel is not in heaven. He didn't love Jesus, and he didn't follow His ways."

"You never know, Felisa," he said, sorry he'd mentioned her husband. He wondered if the man's faith was one of the deep regrets he saw in Felisa's eyes.

"I do know," she said. "Miguel will not be in heaven."

Awareness shot through Chad. Miguel had not been a good husband, he guessed. His sadness multiplied. The man had apparently led her into a world of migratory work, then stranded her there by dying. Chad couldn't believe Felisa would choose such a life. She'd mentioned her husband had died in an accident. Her comment made him curious.

The curtain shifted, and a volunteer appeared pushing a wheelchair. "Ready to go home?"

Felisa gave Chad a frantic look and nodded.

His heart ached for her. He glanced around the room, looking for something to carry while the attendant settled her in the chair and then handed her the baby. He saw nothing. No flowers, no luggage, no cards or gifts. Her aloneness made him weak.

As he followed the volunteer along the hallway, the woman paused at the desk and accepted a package. "This is for you and the baby."

Chad took the bag of gifts and mumbled a thank-you as they left. He glanced inside the plastic shopping bag and saw a bundle of diapers, items wrapped in paper and plastic, nothing that concerned him, and yet it did. He'd acted on compassion, and he would not stop now.

When they reached the outside door, Chad paused. "I'll bring the car up for you. Wait here." He took the plastic bag and headed through the door.

⌘

"Is this your first child?" the volunteer asked, gazing down at Nate.

"Yes," Felisa said, thinking, *My first and last.* She couldn't raise children living in this environment, and she had no means to get out of it. She'd dropped out of school. She had no training other than housework. She'd always helped at home, and she could cook, but she had no way to earn a real living.

The volunteer stood behind her, humming a nonsensical tune to pass the time, and Felisa was glad she'd stopped asking questions. She had no answers, and questions would only remind her she would now face the most trying time of her life.

Felisa looked toward the parking lot. She'd hoped her employer would be true to his word, but he hadn't mentioned finding her a place to live. She would have to make do in her car, or maybe she could ask Maria or another worker to take her in until the baby was a couple of months old.

Her head drooped as she faced the truth. She would never ask. Her coworkers were already in overcrowded conditions, and some were worse off than she with no car to call their own. Her pulse tripped when a sleek, deep blue car pulled up to the front door and Chad climbed out. He headed her way and propped the door open while the volunteer rolled her to the car.

"Where's your pickup?" Felisa asked, handing Nate to the volunteer while she rose from the wheelchair.

"Home," he said. Instead of opening the passenger door, he unlatched the back door and set the plastic bag inside.

Felisa felt her jaw drop. A newborn infant seat had been attached to the middle cushion. She stared at it, not knowing what to say. "This was your daughters'?"

"No," he said, "but you can't take Nate onto the highway without one." He gave her a warm smile. "Federally approved."

She couldn't help but smile at his playful expression. Felisa thanked the volunteer and took Nate into her arms. She followed Chad's direction and settled Nate into the seat, facing backward. She smiled at her son, so small and beautiful. He'd been the best little boy. He cried only when he was hungry, and then only a whimper.

"This seat is great," Chad said. "We didn't have this kind for the twins. You don't have to remove the whole thing. See?" He pointed to the base of the infant seat with its special locks. "This part is stationary, and the top comes off as a baby carrier."

With Nate safely settled, Felisa slid into the car while Chad held the door.

"The salesman said this is the most secure seat," he added. "And if the baby's sleeping, he can stay in the carrier without waking up." He closed her door, and she watched him hurry around to the driver's side and open the door. "Another feature is the carrier fits into a stroller with a simple click."

She nearly chuckled at his excitement about the baby carrier until it registered concern. Why had he purchased a new car seat for Nate?

Chad smiled and settled beside her then turned the key in the ignition. "Here we go," he said, shifting into gear and rolling to the driveway.

"I can't thank you enough," she said, trying to squelch her fear. She twisted in her seatbelt to look behind her at the infant seat. "I don't know how I can pay you. I'd hoped to borrow—"

"I don't expect payment, Felisa. You'll need lots of things. A baby is expensive."

She felt her back stiffen. She didn't like charity, and she didn't want to be beholden to anyone. She owed him too much already. "I have things in my car that people gave me. I'll get by."

"In your car?" he said, a look of discomfort on his face.

She sensed she'd hurt his feelings with her comment. "I didn't have a car seat for Nate. I didn't think of that."

"Now you have one," he said. "It's a gift from me."

She mumbled a thank-you and looked out the passenger window, amazed she was riding in this luxurious car heading for her junker. She would be embarrassed when he saw it.

Chad nosed the car onto Natividad Road and made his way through traffic to Highway 68, she assumed, back to the field where she'd left her car. They rode in silence, and she realized he hadn't found her a place to stay or he would have told her by now. No matter, she'd get by. God promised to be her strength and shield. He wouldn't let her down.

"Thank you for looking for housing for me. I know it's not easy. I've made it so far, and I'll be just fine. You've been so kind."

He glanced her way, his hands resting on the wheel without the death grip she'd seen on the way to the hospital. "I'm sorry I couldn't come up with one of the government units or the motels—"

"I know. I tried to find one myself. They're hard to come by, too." She heard sadness in his voice.

"But I've found another solution. I hope you'll be okay with it. It's not exactly what you'd planned."

She'd had no plan, but she was pleased he gave her credit for having one. Living day by day, surviving, was her way of life. As the thought filled her, his words traveled through her mind. "What do you mean another solution?"

"I've found a job for you. A housekeeping job where you can have the baby with you." He glanced at her again as if wanting to see her expression. "Is that okay?"

Okay? It was wonderful. A real house, and housekeeping—she could do that with ease. "That sounds very nice, but where will I—"

"You'll have your own room there."

He'd answered her question before she asked it. She sat stunned. Her own room. A room for Nate and her to live in, in a real house. Yet how had he arranged this? She opened her mouth to ask, then stopped herself. She assumed this was temporary, until she could find something more appropriate for her and Nate, but while she could she would be thrilled to live in a real house.

Felisa recognized the area and knew they were near the field she'd been working when she went into labor. Chad pulled down the road, and she pointed to her junker, its dull, rusted body causing her to cringe.

"This one?" he asked, pulling alongside it.

She nodded, afraid to speak for fear he'd hear the shame in her voice.

"Where are your things?" he asked, stopping in front of her car.

"In the trunk." She dug into her pocket and took out her keys.

He reached across the driver's seat, and she dropped the keys into his hand.

"We'll pick up your car later," he said, closing the door and vanishing behind her view.

In moments she heard the trunk lifting, the rustle of her belongings, and the lid closing. She eyed Nate, who stirred at the sound but never whimpered.

The driver's door opened, and Chad slipped back inside. "Now we're on our way."

He still hadn't given her any details, and she didn't feel right asking. He would tell her about the family in time. She could only pray they were kind people who would be patient with her. She'd been away from housecleaning and cooking for some time, but she would learn their wishes fast.

Tired, Felisa leaned her head against the seat cushion. The scent of leather wrapped around her, and she ran her hand over the smooth upholstery. She closed her eyes, then heard a click, and soft music drifted from the radio. The lull of the music and hum of the engine drew her into a haze. When she opened her eyes again, she was startled to see they were out of Salinas proper and passing the sign for Toro Park. She straightened.

"Did you have a nice nap?"

Chad's quiet voice startled her. "Was I sleeping?" She looked at the dashboard clock and realized she had slept for a number of minutes. "Where are we going?"

"Corral de Tierra."

Her stomach knotted. Rich people lived there. She hadn't thought. She glanced down at her apparel, still dusty from her day's work in the fields. "I should have changed my clothes."

"Don't worry. No one will care. You can take a bath and freshen up when you get there."

She glanced at the street sign as he made a left turn onto Corral de Tierra Road. His confidence confused her. How did he know what the owners expected or allowed? The questions welled inside her. "How do you know these people?"

He hesitated before answering. "Because it's my home, Felisa. My housekeeper needs a break, and I thought you could give her a hand once you're stronger."

She froze. Had she been wrong? Could this be a ploy to get her son after all? Or to entrap her? She'd heard about men doing horrible things.

"I am strong now. I can work the fields. You don't need to give me a—"

"Felisa." His calm voice mingled with the music. "I'm not kidnapping you. I can hear in your voice you're worried. I want nothing from you. I told you that already. My housekeeper is working too hard, and I decided this was God's way to motivate me to action. I've been putting it off. It's a big house with two little girls that make a mess."

Her heart thundered, wanting him to be telling the truth, yet so afraid. She looked around at the expanse of trees and foothills where large sprawling homes nestled amid the rugged landscape. A golf course appeared on her left, its short clipped grass and rolling hills dotted with flags on poles hanging in the hot sun.

"That's the country club," he said, as if reading her thoughts again.

A prayer rose in her mind, a prayer for protection and peace as he veered left. He slowed, and Felisa gazed at the large Spanish-style home with wrought iron work, terra-cotta roof and stucco exterior, the color of a soft coral sunset. The warm hues looked inviting and safe.

"This is home," he said, pulling into the driveway. He pushed a button, and the garage doors rose. Inside was the pickup that had carried her to the hospital and another sedan. He pulled inside and turned off the ignition. After he opened the trunk, he hurried around to Felisa's door and opened it. "You get Nate while I unload the trunk."

She stood for a moment, scanning the huge garage. It was bigger than the inside of any house she'd been in, and she could only imagine the size of the Garrison home. She opened the rear door, but instead of unlatching the carrier, she unbuckled Nate from the car seat and snuggled him against her chest. Feeling his warm body nestle against hers aroused more emotion than she'd ever allowed herself to feel. His mouth made sucking noises as if he were ready to eat, but she needed the privacy of the house.

"You'll eat soon," she said, pressing her cheek against the baby's.

He gave a tiny mewl.

"We'll go this way," Chad said, motioning her toward a door to the rear of the garage.

She followed, and when he opened it, they stepped into an amazing courtyard with an ornate fountain like one in the plaza of a Mexican village. Her gaze traveled along the covered portico and the many doors leading inside. She'd never seen so many doors and windows, had never seen such a huge mansion.

Chad had lifted some of her boxes from the trunk and followed the tile path to one of the doors. He turned the knob, and the door opened. "I'll give you a key to the room," he said, as he stepped back and motioned her to go inside.

She moved forward and then faltered, seeing the huge room. A large bed stood at the center of the wall across from the doorway. She scanned the room, noticing an easy chair and table, a dresser, a nightstand with a lamp beside the bed, and, nearby, a cradle. Tears filled her eyes, and she lowered her head, afraid he would see her crying. She prided herself on being strong and didn't want him to think she was weak.

He crossed the room and rested his hand on the cradle. "I hope you don't mind. It's like new." He rubbed his hand along the wooden footboard. "It belonged to one of the children. I didn't know why I kept it, but I do now." He patted the wood and stepped away, as if the cradle had stirred his memories.

"It's beautiful," she said, inching farther into the room toward the crib— pure white with a clean mattress and a colorful blanket folded at the foot. She'd never seen anything so wonderful.

"We'll have to pick up some linens for it and other baby supplies, but this should do for now."

She swallowed her emotion. "It's too kind of you. I have some blankets and baby clothes in the box." She motioned to the carton he still held in his hand.

He looked surprised that he still held the box, and he hurried to set it on the bed.

Nate gave a soft whimper. "He needs to be fed," she said.

He backed away, nearly tripping over a scatter rug. "I should let you alone. You want to get cleaned up and feed Nate." He swung his arm toward a closed door, then headed toward it. "The bathroom is here."

He swung open the door, and from where she stood Felisa could see a bathtub and sink and no other doors—a private bathroom all her own.

"It's small, but you'll find clean towels and clothes."

Small? She couldn't believe he thought it was little. It looked luxurious to her. "It's just fine." His intense look caused her to flush. "It's more than I had ever imagined."

"This is normally a guest room," he said. "The other door is a closet, and the one there is to a hallway that leads into the other rooms of the house." He turned toward the door, then paused as if having an afterthought. "I'll put the rest of your things outside the door so I don't disturb you."

"Thank you, Mr. Garrison. I don't know what to say."

He shook his head with an endearing grin. "Don't say anything, Felisa." He opened the door to the portico and left her standing in the middle of the room, cuddling Nate to her chest.

〜

Chad stepped outside and sucked in a lengthy breath. That had been more difficult than he'd thought. He'd asked Juanita to bring in the crib. It had been purchased for his new baby but never used. Sorrow rippled through him. He'd been unable to give it away, and now he realized the reason why. It had found a worthwhile purpose. Felisa's glowing smile filled his thoughts. The Bible said to show compassion and to help others, but he realized today he was receiving more than he'd given. The smile and joy on her face paid far more than the cost of the crib or the salary he would pay her for her work.

Chad strode back to his car and pulled out the rest of Felisa's belongings from his trunk, then closed the trunk lid and carried the bag and another carton to her doorway. He left them there and headed inside. As he opened the door he could hear the twins' nanny bellowing at the girls, and he cringed at the sound. Instead of quieting, they only followed her example and screamed louder.

He halted in the doorway of the family room in time to see Faith toss a wooden puzzle at her sister. The pieces scattered across the room and blended with the debris strewn across the carpet. "Girls," he said, using the calmest voice he could.

"Daddy!" Joy screeched, racing into his arms. "Faith hit me with the puzzle."

"She missed," he said, "but it's wrong to throw things."

"I've told them that," Mrs. Drake said. "You'd think they didn't have brains in their heads."

Chad tried not to glare at the woman. She'd been the third replacement in the past two years, and he wanted to give her a chance to succeed. He always avoided addressing issues in front of the girls, but he'd remind her later that they were bright enough to know how to rile her.

"Faith," Chad said, holding his arm open to his daughter, "come here."

"No." She was curled into a ball on the wide sofa.

"Faith, please come here."

"I didn't do it."

"I saw you throw the puzzle, but that's not what I asked you. I asked you to come here." He didn't move but waited.

Finally Faith rolled off the sofa and plopped to the floor. She looked at him with that stubborn look both girls seemed to have as if challenging him. He'd learned not to give in.

"Okay, then I'll just tell Joy the news." He pushed back Joy's hair and spoke softly into her ear. He could see Mrs. Drake staring at him with narrowed eyes and Faith getting more curious by the second.

"Really?" Joy exclaimed, her eyes as wide and blue as her mother's had been.

Chad watched Faith rise from the floor and amble across to his side.

"What news?" she asked.

"First, I need an apology to your sister."

"She hit me first," Faith said.

Joy clung to his neck. "I did not, Daddy."

Chad drew both girls into his arms. "Jesus tells us to ask forgiveness for our sins even if we don't know we did them. So I think you both need to say you're sorry to each other, and then for whatever you might have done today, even if it was an accident, you can both be forgiven."

Both girls shook their heads.

Chad shrugged and let them slide from his arms. "Okay, it's your choice. You can have dinner in your room tonight and miss out on everything."

"Daddy, that's not fair." Both voices blended in one litany.

"No one said it was, but you can make a choice. Dinner in your rooms or say I'm sorry and mean it."

They did a staring standoff until Faith relented. "I'm sorry for throwing the puzzle."

Chad waited a moment to see what Joy would do.

"I'm sorry, too," she said.

Chad pulled them back into his arms. "Now that wasn't so hard, was it?"

"What's the news, Daddy?" Faith asked.

"We have a new housekeeper, and she—"

"Where's Juanita going?" Joy asked.

"Nowhere," he said, "but she needs a vacation, and once the new woman is trained, Juanita can have some time for herself."

Nanny made a disapproving sound, and Chad turned his attention toward her. "Did you want to say something, Mrs. Drake?"

"No, I'm just surprised."

"Perhaps she can give you some help when you're feeling overwhelmed?"

"Overwhelmed? I—I don't need any—I'm just fine with the girls. Thank you."

"Daddy." He felt Joy tugging at his sleeve. "You didn't tell Faith the best part."

"What best part?" Faith whined. "You didn't tell me the best part."

"The housekeeper has a brand-new baby," Chad said.

Mrs. Drake snorted. "Well, I'll be."

Chad turned his attention in her direction. "Mrs. Drake?"

"A newborn?" She drew up her shoulders. "Whose job will that be? I can't imagine—"

"Don't worry about it. Felisa will care for her own child."

"Felisa," she muttered. "You mean she's another—"

"She's a new employee here for the time being. I'll appreciate your giving her a hand learning the ropes." He saw her disapproval in her eyes, but she didn't comment further.

"Can I hold the baby?" Faith asked.

Joy patted his shoulder. "Me, too. I want to hold the baby."

"That will be up to Felisa, but I suspect she'll want the baby to get a little older before she allows anyone to hold him."

"Him?" Joy sounded disappointed.

"Is it a boy?" Faith asked.

Chad gazed at his two look-alike daughters. "A good-looking boy named Nate." Emotion welled in his chest as he pictured the infant. His own son had never had a chance to be held and loved. His own son never had a chance.

Chapter 4

Felisa slipped into a pair of pants and buttoned her blue and white flowered cotton blouse. Nate had fallen asleep in the cradle after he'd been fed, and she'd enjoyed a relaxing bath, a rarity for her instead of a quick shower. She'd found a bottle of sweet-smelling bubble bath and leaned her back against the tub, enjoying the fragrance and the soothing sway of the water over her tired body. Afterward she'd washed her hair and dried it with fluffy large towels that wrapped around her whole body.

She gazed at Nate for a moment as she closed the last buttons on her blouse, then smoothed a pink shade of lipstick over her lips and looked in the mirror. She felt like Cinderella, visited by a fairy godmother. Today had been more than she could ever have dreamed. Still, she monitored her joy, wondering if she'd find some catch—a snag or problem that would make her realize it had been a nightmare and not a dream. So much of her life had been.

Not wanting to stray too far from Nate, she opened the door and stepped out for a moment into the sunlight. The fountain tinkled into the pool, and she moved closer to sit on the rim and allow the sun to dry her hair. With the door open, she knew she could hear Nate if he cried.

A sound came from behind her, and when she glanced over her shoulder she saw Chad, and behind him two identical little girls. Their light brown hair hung in ponytails and bounced as they skipped her way. She remembered his saying the girls were a handful, but at the moment she could see only their sweet innocence.

"*Hola,*" she said, before realizing she'd spoken Spanish.

"Hola," they echoed back to her.

She gave Chad a questioning look.

"Our other housekeeper is Hispanic, too," he said, standing above her.

She rose, then knelt to the girls' level. "What are your names?"

"Joy."

"Faith." The two names almost came out as one.

"From the Bible," Felisa said. "They're very pretty names." She studied the two girls, looking for a clue to their differences but noticed none.

"Faith has a small freckle in the middle of her forehead," Chad said, as if understanding her searching look at his daughters.

Faith pushed away her bangs and grinned.

The grin reminded Felisa of her employer's words—the girls were a handful—and she could see that glint in Faith's eyes.

"Can we see the new baby?" Faith asked, her excitement evident.

Joy jumped beside her and tugged at her blouse. "Please. Can we see him?"

"Girls, don't bug Felisa."

"Please," they sang, dragging the word into a whine.

Felisa rose. "Just for a minute, but you have to be very quiet. He's sleeping."

"We will," they said in chorus.

Both girls tiptoed beside her across the tiles to her door. She opened it farther, and they scooted inside with their father behind them.

The twins ran to the cradle and leaned over the edge. Faith reached in and touched Nate's fingers. Joy followed, patting his cheek.

"He's so tiny," Faith said. The baby grimaced with the sound.

"Girls," Chad whispered, "you said you'd be quiet."

"We are," Faith said, her volume bombarding the room.

Felisa noticed Joy jiggling the crib, and when she looked, Nate had begun to squirm. Felisa covered Joy's hand with hers and pulled it away without saying anything. The girl looked at her with a sweet smile, but Felisa noticed her foot was pushing against the crib legs. "Enough," Felisa said, shooing them toward the door.

Chad shook his head and mumbled he was sorry, but she understood and realized he did have his hands very full. Those girls missed a parent's attention. Chad worked, and their mother was in heaven. They were left all day with hired help—necessary but unfortunate.

"Would you like to see the rest of the house?" Chad asked.

"I would," she said, "but I'm afraid to leave Nate alone."

"We have an intercom system in the house." He stepped inside and showed her the button. "When it's on, any sound in any room will come into the other rooms. We had it installed when the girls were little, and it makes life easier for Juanita and Mrs. Drake, the nanny."

Amazed, Felisa eyed the button. She'd never experienced such a thing.

"You can feel easier now, and we won't be gone long."

She nodded, wondering how the monitor worked. She was nervous about meeting the other servants.

She followed him as the girls raced ahead, their exuberance almost overwhelming. When she stepped inside the vast interior of a ceramic tile foyer, she looked ahead to see a charming breakfast nook set in a bay window looking out to the fountain, and once she'd traveled the nook's length the spacious island kitchen came into view.

"Juanita," Chad said as they entered.

A middle-aged Hispanic woman turned toward him, and when she saw Felisa, her kindly face made her feel welcome. "This must be Felisa." She gave her a friendly nod. "Welcome to the Garrison home."

"Thank you," Felisa said, embarrassed by her gaping as she viewed the modern kitchen. "This is so beautiful."

Juanita looked around as if seeing it in a new light. "It's roomy and a nice place to prepare the family's meals."

Felisa looked at her and then at her employer, her mind swirling with questions. "I don't know my duties. Am I to help with the cooking or only the cleaning?" She settled her gaze on Chad, almost frightened by the modern conveniences that filled the kitchen.

Chad's face flinched with his own confusion. "You'll fill in where needed. I'll let Juanita give you the duties. I want her to have a vacation, and then you'll take care of everything."

She turned her attention to Juanita. Though she'd been pleasant, she wondered if the woman resented her coming here.

"I'll be happy to do that," Juanita said, then turned and gave Felisa a welcoming smile. "I'll show you around after dinner before I leave."

"Leave?" Felisa cringed when she heard her question blurt out into the room, fearing the woman planned to leave on vacation already.

"I live at home," the housekeeper said. "I come early in the morning and go home after dinner."

"I—I didn't know." The response had left Felisa unsettled. She wasn't comfortable being the only employee staying in the home.

"Mrs. Drake, the nanny, lives in the house," Chad said, as if knowing her thoughts. "You'll meet her at dinner. We all eat together, except Juanita, of course."

"Once dinner is on the table, I head home to my family," she said.

The weight lifted from Felisa's shoulders. "You're all so kind. I—"

A small cry stopped her in mid-sentence.

Juanita chuckled. "That's your baby." She pointed to a box attached to the wall. "It's the monitoring system. You must have turned it on."

"I did," Chad said, motioning toward the doorway. "You can go tend to Nate. We'll call you for dinner."

Her heart rose to her throat. She'd be called to dinner. She was invited to sit at his table. The image swirled in her mind. Life had never treated her so kindly.

࿐

Chad watched her hurry away, her slender frame vanishing around the corner, her dark hair falling in kinky waves below her shoulders. He felt his pulse react to the attractive woman, and it startled him. He needed to be careful. Juanita was a motherly figure, and the nanny was an ornery woman he'd thought had good skills with children, but Felisa was lithesome and lovely. Much time had passed since a woman had entered his thoughts. Now one had, and she didn't fit into his world. Yet his emotions didn't seem to care.

He pulled his gaze from the doorway and turned his attention to Juanita. "What do you think?"

She gave him a strange look. "She's had a hard life, I'm sure. She appreciates your help."

"Will this work?"

Juanita shrugged. "We'll see. I'll go easy on her until she adjusts with the new baby, but I hope she'll catch on easily. She seems bright enough. She speaks English well."

"I noticed," he said.

"*Mamá*'s here." The sound came over the intercom. "Come here, *mi niño dulce*."

Chad's chest tightened when he heard Felisa call Nate her sweet boy, though he felt uncomfortable hearing her private thought to her child. He looked at Juanita. "I suppose we'd better tell her to turn off the intercom." He walked to the wall and pressed the button, reminding Felisa to turn off the monitor.

In a moment he heard a click and silence. "I'd better get over to the field. I'll leave her in your care." He jammed his hands into his pockets, aware he didn't want to leave, but knowing he must. "We'll have to pick up her car later, and I'm sure she'll need some things for the baby. Maybe I should—"

His heart rose to his throat as he heard his enthusiasm. Chad hadn't felt motivation like this since before his wife died, and it unsettled him. He stole a glance at Juanita, who'd been eyeing him off and on as she worked at the island making a pie.

"I'll say good-bye to the girls and then be going."

He heard Juanita's good-bye as he made his way into the family room, and though the floor looked as if an earthquake had knocked the contents every which way, the girls weren't there. He retraced his steps, then took the hallway into the bedroom wing. A piercing scream gave him direction, and when he came through the doorway he saw the nanny with her fingers clutched around Joy's arm while the other hand pointed in her face.

"What's the problem?" he said, not happy at what he saw.

"These girls must learn to listen. I've asked them to hang up their clothes, and look." She gestured toward the floor and a chair, which had been strewn with garments.

"That's not too much to ask. Joy, if you want dessert tonight, you'll have this mess cleaned up in five minutes. Juanita's making a pie, and it's probably one of your favorites."

"I think Joy should go without dinner," Mrs. Drake said, having pulled her pointing finger from Joy's face but still grasping her arm.

"We'll talk about this later." He took a step backward, then stopped and leveled his gaze at the nanny. "If you let go of her arm, Joy can begin putting away her clothing."

She released her grasp without a word and crossed her arms over her chest as she watched. Chad stood for a moment, seeing his little four-year-old gathering the garments and dropping them on the bed. He'd made closets with hangers low enough for the girls to reach. He knew they needed to learn tasks, but seeing the look in their nanny's eyes didn't sit well with him. They did need to talk.

He passed Faith's room and saw her sitting in the middle of the floor working a puzzle. She loved puzzles, and, seeing her so quiet for once, he didn't want to disturb her, so he tiptoed past and made his way to the garage, his mind tumbling with thoughts.

Pulling the car keys from his pocket, Chad stood for a moment, aware of the strange sensations reeling through him. Felisa had stirred memories he'd tried to keep in check. She'd stirred the love he'd felt for his wife and for his stillborn child as he watched her with her own son. The tiny bundle of life aroused his paternal feelings, and he didn't know how to handle them.

He dismissed his thoughts, climbed into the truck, and backed out of the garage into the street. As he drove, Felisa's image rose in his mind. He'd watched her gentleness with his girls. She hadn't shown anger when the twins misbehaved by the crib. She'd taken control and guided them away with patience.

His twins. The two matching faces replaced Felisa's image. Maybe he hadn't been a good father. He'd grieved so long for his wife and son that perhaps the girls had sensed it. Had they felt rejected when he sank into his sullen moods? They'd gone through one nanny after another. None had been able to find a way to reach the girls, and he couldn't stay home and do it himself. He had a business—a huge farm to run, his livelihood. It gave them a good life, a very good life, he admitted.

Yet he had to beware. He wanted to turn around and drive back home. He wanted to take Felisa shopping for baby clothes and baby bottles, shopping for all the wonderful things he could afford to lavish on the little boy, but she'd halted him with her comment; she had a carton of used items. How could he insist the child have new things when she had learned to live with hand-me-downs and accepted them with no regrets?

His way of life was so different. Yet he longed to share that life. . .with someone.

↭

Felisa lit the candles in her room and knelt at the side of her bed for her morning prayers. She looked at the picture of Jesus she'd hung on the wall and smiled. He had provided for her as He always had. Knowing she had someone to count on, someone who stood by her side, made all the difference.

After a week in the Garrison home, she'd begun to relax. She'd learned her way around the house, helped Juanita in the kitchen, and felt blessed at the wonderful life God was allowing her to lead. Juanita had been gracious, and only the nanny made her feel out of place. She thanked the Lord for all the gifts she'd received—the good food, the comfortable bed, the friend she'd found in Juanita—and she asked Him to be with her each day.

As the amen faded, Felisa's mind drifted to Chad. She needed to thank the Lord for the gift of an employer who cared. She knew Chad was a Christian, not only by the prayers they said at dinner, but by the faith he showed in his actions.

She knew she was saved by grace through faith, but she also knew the Bible said faith without deeds was dead. Chad Garrison was a man of faith. She had no doubt.

Felisa rose from her knees, blew out the candles, then opened the blinds on her windows. The sun spilled through the window, throwing lines of shade and light on the carpeting. She walked to the crib and looked down at her son, who seemed to be smiling up to her.

"*Te amo*, Nate, my little *muchacho*," she said, expressing her love as she reached down and lifted him against her chest. He'd already eaten, and he looked content. "Want to see the sunlight?" She carried him to the door and pulled it open, letting the warmth float through the screen. She stood there for a moment listening to the splatter of the fountain and nothing more. The hush of this quiet place amazed her. They were far from other neighbors, many blocked from view by the rolling foothills and masses of trees that covered the mountainsides.

Once she'd settled Nate into his carrier chair, she headed for the house. Juanita had been very cooperative and allowed her to work with the baby alongside her. She grabbed a piece of toast from the kitchen and began her tasks for the day, cleaning the master bedroom and bath. She left Nate with Juanita while she gathered her supplies to take to the rooms; then she would return.

The master bedroom amazed her the few times she'd seen it. Felisa set her basket of cleaning equipment on the floor near the door and gazed at the spacious room. The deep brown carpeting spread across the expansive floor, and a wide window looked out to the rich mountain scenery. She gazed at the stone fireplace, a large built-in television, and a bed that could hold five people. She shook her head at the wasted space, but she loved the thought of having all this room for oneself.

Behind the fireplace wall was the bathroom with a large sunken tub. She could only imagine such luxury. A shower stood nearby, and a gigantic closet he could walk into. It could hold so many clothes that it, too, seemed wasted space.

She hurried back to retrieve Nate from Juanita's caring hands, then delved into her work. Pride filled her as she dusted and polished the room, scrubbed the bathroom porcelain, vacuumed the floors, and shined the mirrors. She paused at the wide mirror to study her face. She witnessed the same glow of happiness on her countenance that also burned in her heart.

The thought expanded and then popped like a pin-poked balloon. Once accustomed to this good life, how could she ever go back to the cheap motels and nights in her car? This was a dream world where she didn't belong, and the longer she stayed the worse it would be to go back.

Felisa sank to the tub's edge and put her face into her hands. As much as she longed to stay, she must leave. Nate seemed healthy and happy. He had been a good baby from birth, and she could carry him on her back in a sling and still work the fields. She had to tell her employer. She had to tell him soon.

Tears welled in her eyes. She'd allowed her imagination to grow, and sometimes she even pictured herself as the wife of the manor. Foolish dreams could only hurt her, and she knew his world would reject her as fast as Mrs. Drake had.

Pushing away her meandering thoughts, Felisa worked at her tasks while keeping an eye on Nate. She finished the master bedroom and bath. Then after lunch, she moved into the breakfast nook and the foyer. Keeping the tile shining seemed an eternal job, and the twins popped up everywhere, always underfoot.

Felisa wondered why the nanny didn't have a better understanding of the little girls. She never saw her play with them or read to them. Instead the woman snarled instructions and jerked them to get their attention. She didn't want to see that, and she wondered why the nanny remained employed. When she asked, Juanita said Mrs. Drake was the third nanny in the past two years. Something seemed wrong. Two little girls needed love and attention, not punishment.

Punishment. If anyone should punish, it would be God. Everyone deserved punishment, but instead the Lord granted forgiveness and eternal life. Everyone needed love and security. They needed hope. These two little girls needed the same. If God could forgive His children's sins, then Mrs. Drake should be able to overlook two little precocious girls' antics.

Today Juanita didn't need help with dinner, so Felisa took advantage of the lovely day and pulled a chair from the umbrella table to sit beside the fountain. As she settled with Nate at her side in his carrier and began to sing him a Mexican lullaby, footsteps sounded on the tiles beneath the portico, and the twins came darting toward her.

"Let's play!" Joy shouted.

"We have puzzles," Faith added, dropping pieces as she skittered toward Felisa. The child stopped and scooped up the puzzle pieces, then continued to scurry toward her.

"You should sit at the table," Felisa said, gesturing toward the round table just outside the shade of the covered porch.

"We want to do it here with you and Nate," Joy said, plopping at her feet.

Felisa drew in a lengthy breath, then grinned, knowing her short relaxation had ended. Before she could steer them to the table, Faith had joined Joy on the tiles at her feet, and they'd begun to argue.

"Do you like people hollering at you?" Felisa asked.

Their entangled voices silenced, and two faces tilted up to her.

"No," they both said in unison.

"Then why are you yelling at each other?"

Faith put her hands on her hips. "But we're—"

"You're yelling."

Faith wrinkled her nose. "We don't like Nanny yelling at us."

"I don't like you hollering at me," Joy said, glaring at her sister.

"Do you know why we don't like it?" Felisa asked.

Both girls raised their eyes to her.

"Because everyone likes to be respected, and we can't be respectful when we yell. How do you think we can be respectful?"

Both heads lowered for a moment until Joy raised hers. "We listen?"

"Right," Felisa said, giving her a smile. "We listen to what the other person has to say."

"I listen," Faith said.

Felisa tousled her hair and decided to take the lesson one step further. "But only when you want to. We have to be willing to listen to each other and then ask ourselves if the person has been honest. Jesus wants us to cooperate with one another and to be honest." She picked up one of the puzzles and held it out to them. "Who brought this puzzle outside?"

"I did," Joy said, grasping the puzzle piece and leaping up.

Faith clasped two of them against her chest. "These are mine."

"I see three puzzles. Instead of arguing, you could each work on your own and then trade when you're done, or. . ." She paused to let them think.

Faith flashed her a grin. "Or we could do one at a time and each take turns putting in a piece."

Felisa clapped her hands. "Right. That's a great answer. So which do you want to do?"

"We want you to work the puzzle with us," Joy said, leaning against her as if she were a lamppost.

Felisa slipped her arm around the girl's waist.

Faith tugged at her pant leg. "We'll take turns." She patted her hand against the tiles as if inviting her to join them on the ground.

Looking heavenward, Felisa sent up a little prayer of thanks. Before she could join them a noise caught her attention, and she spotted Mrs. Drake standing in the shadow of the portico, arms akimbo, staring at her with narrowed eyes. The woman didn't like her at all, and she could do nothing to change that. She'd tried.

She turned away and shifted to the tiles beside the girls. They liked her. Juanita liked her, too, and her employer seemed to care. What more did she need?

Chapter 5

C had stepped from the garage into the sunlight. When his eyes adjusted, he paused, looking at the startling sight. Felisa sat on the tiles near the fountain between his daughters, playing a game, and they were so intent, they hadn't seen or heard him arrive. He moved closer and realized they were working jigsaw puzzles. His heart soared at the sight. Normally he arrived home to the girls' voices bellowing their complaints and arguments, but today his ears picked up only their happy voices and playful giggles.

He stood in the distance, watching Felisa with the girls. He heard her soft laughter and tender voice as she spoke to them. He heard Joy beg her to sing them a song, and Felisa shook her head no, but soon her clear voice lifted in an old Mexican folk song he recalled hearing among the field workers. He didn't move, not wanting to break the spell.

When she finished, the girls spoke in soft voices, and he ambled nearer.

"Daddy!" Joy sang out, jumping from her play and dashing toward him. Faith soon followed, and he wrapped his arms around the girls while his gaze lingered on Felisa, who sat where she'd been, smiling up at him.

He clutched the girls' hands in his and guided them back to Felisa, then stood above the carrier, admiring the beautiful boy. "Do you mind?" he asked, gesturing to Nate.

"Not at all," she said.

He crouched and lifted the child into his arms, smiling at the infant's tiny fists flailing in the air. A warm sense of love flooded him. He rose and gazed at his daughters, quiet and happy by Felisa's side, and then again at the baby boy against his chest. The child flung his arm upward, then lowered it and jammed his fist into his mouth.

"He's hungry," Felisa said, seeing Nate suckling at his fingers. "I should take him inside."

She moved beside Chad, and the sweetness of her scent enfolded him. He drew in the aroma, letting it rush through his senses. He gave her a nod, though hating to let the child go. He brushed his lips against the baby's cheek, then nestled him back into the carrier. He glanced at his watch. "It's nearly dinner-time. Can I carry him inside for you?"

"You don't have to," she said, her voice as stirring as a mountain breeze.

"I don't mind," he said, hoisting the carrier into his arms and carrying it toward her door.

The girls rose and scampered along with them and dashed inside as soon as Felisa held open the door.

"Outside, girls," Chad said, setting the carrier beside the crib. "We have to get ready for dinner, and Felisa needs to feed the baby."

"Can we help?" Joy asked, leaning over the carrier and tickling Nate beneath the chin.

"Not this time, Joy," Felisa said, giving the girls a pat. "Soon he'll be older, and then you can—then you could help."

Chad watched her expression change to sadness. What had happened to cause her unhappiness? He lingered for a moment, wanting to ask, but the baby's whimper and the twins' exuberance gave him a nudge. "We'll see you at dinner."

"Thank you," she said, her voice as wistful as her look.

Chad beckoned the girls through the doorway, his emotions tangling with concern.

The girls raced on ahead and nearly ran over Mrs. Drake, who stood in the shadow of the portico watching him.

He studied her as he approached, seeing darkness in her eyes, and he figured he was ready to hear her "bad girls" report he received so often. "Did you want to see me?" he asked.

"I certainly do," she said, her gaze drifting from him toward Felisa's room. "I'm not comfortable with that woman being here. She's trying to undermine my relationship with the twins, and it's making things more difficult for me, Mr. Garrison."

He studied her dire expression, trying to understand her complaint. "What has she done?"

"I try to discipline them, and the next thing I find is her sitting outside with them playing games. Naturally they would rather stay there than do the tasks I ask them to do."

"I'm sorry. I don't understand. I would think you'd be pleased when the girls are amused and not under your feet."

She folded her arms over her chest. "Children need to follow rules. They need discipline, not a playmate."

Chad shook his head. "Joy and Faith are four years old. Do you realize this is the time of life children enjoy playing? I expect them to mind and to do reasonable tasks. They need to learn to hang up their clothes. I support you on that, but I see no harm in their playing outside, and if Felisa is playing with them, I don't mind at all."

"I thought she was the housekeeper. Isn't she supposed to be doing her job?"

"I assume she had finished her work, but I'll check with Juanita."

"Juanita? They're two of a kind. You won't get an honest—"

This time he glared at her. "I have every confidence in Juanita. She's been employed by my family for many years. I'll check with her, and thank you for your concern."

He held his ground while Mrs. Drake stomped away, muttering under her breath.

Chad didn't move. He stood in the silence, pondering what had just occurred. Was it jealousy or true concern? He didn't want the girls to be rude to the nanny; yet he knew they responded better to affection, and they received little from Mrs. Drake.

Guilt slid down his back as he thought of the many hours he spent away from the children when they really needed him. He wished he could put his trust in Joe to keep things moving smoothly while he took a short vacation. Joe had been a hard worker and had done nothing to lose his trust, so why not? Maybe he would take a week off to spend time with the girls. He could even take a day or two and focus on the twins. They could go to the beach in Carmel, and he could stop by his store. He hadn't been there recently, and the trip could serve two purposes.

He pulled back his shoulders, excited about the venture. He wondered if Felisa had ever enjoyed a day in Carmel on the long stretch of white sand. Perhaps she would join them. The thought prickled down his arms. It wasn't appropriate to take her, he supposed—the employer and his housekeeper going out for the day. He tilted his head and looked from beneath the portico to the blue sky. *Lord, help me. My heart is leading me in one direction, and wisdom is leading me in the other. You're both heart and mind—love and wisdom. Help me make sense out of my feelings and lead me in the way I should go.* He whispered an amen into the sunshine, then headed inside to talk with Juanita.

༄

Felisa gazed at Nate waking from his nap, his tiny arms waving above his head at a mobile the twins had given him—one that had been theirs when they were babies. Nate loved the twirling figures that danced above his head when he awakened in the morning or from his naps. Her stomach growled, letting her know she'd better get in to eat dinner now that Nate had awakened. Juanita would be cleaning up and getting ready to go home.

The room felt cool, and Felisa was amazed at how the heat of the day seemed blocked by the stucco walls. She walked to the door and pulled it open to let in the light. Instead she saw two matching faces standing outside looking at the door. Both girls bounced and clapped when they saw her.

"So why this happy greeting?" Felisa asked, curious as to their excitement.

Joy shielded her eyes and pressed her nose against the screen. "Daddy said we could make a piñata tonight."

"Where's Nate?" Faith asked, following Joy's determination to look inside her room.

"He's watching the lovely gift you gave him." She gestured toward the colorful mobile, then addressed Joy's comment. "Do you know how to make a piñata?"

Joy giggled. "No, but you do."

"I thought so," she said, gazing at the two eager faces. "I'll talk to your daddy. We'll make a mess, you know."

"He said we could make it on the porch." Faith pointed to the covered portico.

"I'll still check with him first before I say yes or no."

"Okay," they said in unison, then backed away and scampered toward the house.

Felisa settled Nate into the baby carrier and headed inside. She wanted to talk with Chad, but not about piñatas. With the girls' eagerness, she feared she wouldn't get a moment alone with him.

When she stepped into the back foyer, her heart rose to her throat. Chad was still seated in the breakfast nook, reading the evening paper. She forced herself forward, her emotions torn between running away and running toward him. He gave her the greatest sense of security she'd ever felt, and besides, he made her pulse flutter. She hadn't felt that since she'd first laid eyes on Miguel before she knew his faults. Then her pulse only raced from fear of Miguel's temper and nothing more.

"Hungry?" Chad asked, looking up. "How's the little muchacho?"

"He's a good boy," she said, resting him beside a chair before heading into the kitchen and greeting Juanita.

The housekeeper chuckled. "I'm guessing the girls have already talked to you about their plans."

Felisa grinned. "About making a piñata."

"They've been after me about those things since you talked to them." Juanita handed her a dish and motioned to the food on a warming plate. "Have some dinner."

"*Gracias.*" Felisa lifted a cheese quesadilla from the platter and shifted it onto her plate, then spooned fresh fruit beside it.

"Would you like a cup of coffee?" Juanita motioned toward a mug. "I brewed caffeinated. I think you'll need your energy tonight with the girls."

"You mean making piñatas?"

Juanita gave her a grin and nodded.

Felisa headed toward the breakfast nook, but uncomfortable with imposing on Chad's privacy, she passed him and made her way to the outside umbrella table.

"Where are you going?" Chad asked.

"I thought I'd eat outside. I'll be back for Nate in a minute."

"Sit here. By the time you do all that, your food will be cold." He rose and pulled out a chair for her.

His gaze captured hers, and her heart pounded. His eyes flickered with emotion she hadn't expected, a look so tender and warm it washed through her. She sank to the chair, set her plate on the table, then looked down at Nate. "You're such a good baby."

Chad had folded his paper, and it sat beside him. "Do you mind if I hold him?"

"Go ahead," she said, confused by his preoccupation with her son.

He crouched and unhooked the baby, then lifted him to his chest. "He's growing already, and look at him grin." He tilted the baby toward Felisa.

She chuckled. "I think it's gas."

"That's okay. If I can get a smile, I'll take the gas, too." He settled back into the chair and bent down to kiss the baby's cheek.

Chad's tenderness sent emotion stirring in Felisa's chest. She wished she understood why a rugged, hardworking man showed so much delight in an infant. Usually men seemed to steer clear of babies. She recalled so many who would do anything rather than feed or diaper a child.

She lifted the quesadilla with her fingers. The cheese oozed onto the plate, and when she took a bite, amid the sharp cheddar she tasted the smoky crispness of bacon. She licked her lips and noticed Chad watching her. Her stomach twisted, her food forming a lump. She had this moment, and she needed to use it. "I wanted to talk with you about—"

"The piñata," he said. "I know. I'm sorry, but the girls have been bugging me all evening." He grinned. "Every minute, actually, since they learned you know how to make them. I told them it was your decision if you wanted to do it tonight." He gave her the sweetest, guiltiest grin she'd ever seen while he nestled Nate in his arms and gave him tiny pats as he swayed with him.

Before she could respond, the girls bounded into the room.

"Did you ask him?" Faith asked, jiggling beside her chair.

"I did—"

"Daddy," Joy said, clinging to his arm, "you're always holding Nate." She gave him a questioning look.

"I held you and Faith just like this when you were babies."

"You did?" they both said at the same time.

The girls hovered around him, eating up the attention, and it filled Felisa's heart to see the joy in their faces. This was what they needed—wonderful times with their dad he could show his love and concern for them. She missed that, too, as a girl, but then that was life for many of the children from hardworking families. Too many kids and too little money.

"What about the piñata?" Faith asked again, shifting her focus back to Felisa. "Isn't it late?"

"The sun's still shining," Faith said. "Daddy?"

He grinned at Faith and then at Felisa. "Felisa can spend the evening as she wishes."

"Do you wish to make a piñata?" Joy pleaded.

Felisa burst into laughter. "You girls certainly know how to nag."

"Isn't that part of a woman's charm?" Chad said, his husky voice sending quivers down her back.

"Okay, we'll make a piñata," she said, avoiding his comment, "but they make a mess."

"We'll clean up," Faith said.

"We promise." Joy hung onto her arm.

Chad's voice broke through the girls' exuberance. "And I'll watch Nate. How's that for a deal?"

"Okay," Felisa said, realizing her goal of a private talk had faded away.

Juanita came out to say good-bye as she left for home, so with Chad tending to Nate, Felisa gathered the supplies—flour, water, newspapers, and string—and carried them to the umbrella table. She sent the girls to find a large balloon they said was left over from their last birthday party a couple of months earlier.

When they returned, Felisa drew in a deep breath. "Now you know we can only shape part of it today. It has to dry for a few days before we can make anything."

"Okay," they chimed in.

"Here's what we do." She turned to Chad. "You can blow up this balloon for me, and girls, you can mix the paste." While Chad worked on the balloon, she emptied two cups of flour into a large basin and poured in three cups of water. "Now we need to mix this until it's smooth."

The girls dived into the job, cooperating as she'd never seen them do before. She noticed their father watching, his eyes twinkling with joy at seeing his two mischievous girls working so hard.

Felisa opened the newspaper and tore the sheets into long strips.

"Is this good?" Joy asked.

Felisa dipped her fingers into the pasty substance and gave them a smile. "Good job." She glanced at Chad, who held the balloon pinched between his fingers.

"I can't put a knot in it." He nodded his head toward the baby.

Chuckling, Felisa took the long length of string and knotted it around the balloon; then for good measure she held Nate while Chad knotted the balloon again. With a smile, they traded the balloon for the baby.

"Now it's time to work. What will we make? A star? A burro? A flower?"

"What's a burro?" Joy asked.

"It's a donkey," Chad answered.

Joy curled up her nose. "I want a star."

Faith folded her arms across her chest and yelled, "I want a flower!"

"Hmm?" Felisa said. "We have only one balloon and two votes. Which voice wins? The very loud, mean voice or the soft, happy voice?" She raised an eyebrow at Faith, who squirmed beneath her gaze. "Which voice did we like the best, Daddy?" She turned her gaze to Chad, and her stomach yo-yoed with the look.

"I think the happy voice wins today. We'll make a star."

Faith's lips puckered as if she were going to whine, but she seemed to think for a minute before reacting. "Next time can we do a flower?"

She had used her sweetest voice, and Felisa was filled with relief and happiness. "Yes, we can do that for sure."

༉

Chad's heart swelled as he watched Felisa with his daughters. She knew the right thing to say and seemed to love the girls despite their behavior. He'd noticed them changing since they'd spent time with Felisa. With Mrs. Drake, they attacked each other over every issue, but Felisa knew how to guide them to good decisions. He sent up a prayer, thanking God for her stepping into their lives. She'd brought joy and peace to the house, making it more a home than it had been since Janie had died.

Thinking of Janie, Chad turned his gaze to Nate, wondering how he would have felt holding his own son in his arms, seeing him grow and become a toddler. Years later he would have grown into a young man and one day would have begun to date and would want the family car. A bittersweet grin tugged at his mouth.

He leaned back, surrounded by the scent of baby powder and milk, as he held the tiny infant against his chest. But soon the baby's fragrance was covered by the mixture of flour, water, and wet newspaper the girls had helped prepare.

Felisa amazed him. Her patience with the twins touched his heart, and he made a decision that if Mrs. Drake threatened one more time to leave his employ, he would replace her with Felisa. She seemed to be doing most of the work lately anyway.

He watched the piñata take shape. Layers and layers of pasted paper wrapped around the balloon. The girls' clothing and faces were gooped with the adhesive, but they looked so excited, he couldn't complain.

"That's about it," Felisa said, stepping back and looking at the lumpy newspaper orb. "Now we use this piece of string to hang it outside in the sun where it can dry."

"How long?" Faith asked.

"A couple of days. We'll have to see."

"I can't wait," Joy said, grinning at the misshapen paste ball.

Chad's heart felt light, and an idea flashed in his mind. "Let's say we get you girls ready for bed, and since Mrs. Drake is off tomorrow, we'll all go into Carmel for a trip to the beach."

Felisa glanced his way. "You'll enjoy that." She gave them each a squeeze. "I've never been to the beach at Carmel. I've never really been—"

"Then you'll enjoy it, too," Chad said, watching her expression switch to surprise.

"Me?" She touched her finger to her chest. "But I thought you meant the—"

"You thought wrong. I meant all of us. We'll buy a picnic lunch at my store."

She drew back. "Your store?"

"I have a shop in town that sells sandwiches and grocery items. People love to pick up a lunch and head down to the beach or eat in the park. We'll take chairs to sit on."

"And a blanket," Faith said. "And beach toys."

"We'll take blankets and toys, too." He listened to their exuberance until Nate's cry captured his attention. "What's wrong, Nate?" Chad gave him gentle pats on the back.

"It's his bedtime, and he's hungry, too," Felisa said. "It's past his feeding time."

Chad sent the girls a grin, then rose, gave the crying Nate a tiny squeeze, and handed him to Felisa. "I'll get these two off for bed, and you can take care of this sad fellow."

"Are you sure you want us to go?" She gave him an apologetic look and clutched the crying baby to her chest. "I never know if Nate will be cranky."

Her face filled with question, and her sacrifice touched him. "I've never been surer." He gave her hand a pat, and the touch filled him with longing. The sensation startled him. He knew he cared about Nate and had compassion for Felisa, but today he became aware of his growing feelings. She'd become more to him than a housekeeper and a woman who needed help. Chad realized he needed help, too. He wanted to live again, for himself and for his two sweet girls, who deserved a parent who was truly alive.

Chapter 6

On Saturday Felisa felt excited as Chad parked the car by the white sand and the sparkling blue green water. She slipped Nate into the stroller, still astounded that one baby seat could also be a carrier and a stroller. Chad's gift had been wonderful, but too extravagant. The girls skipped along as they headed toward his store. Chad had pointed it out earlier as they drove down to the ocean, and she'd noticed the nearby park, too.

The walk from the beach was uphill, but she enjoyed the exercise. She glanced into the charming shops with gifts and women's fashion filling the display windows. A nature shop had caught the girls' interest, and Felisa wished she had enough money to go inside and buy the twins a gift. As they passed a luggage store, the scent of leather filled her senses, followed by the aroma of candles drifting through another doorway.

In the next block, she eyed jewelry in the displays, and as she moved farther along the sidewalk, she saw wonderful sparkling gems and shiny gold. Then a quaint quilt-maker's shop came into view. She'd never seen so many people meandering along as if they had no place to go and no care in the world. This was a life she would never know.

Chad pointed ahead, and she looked up and saw the sign: GARRISON'S GROCERIES AND DELI. He nodded when she smiled, and the look on his face made her smile back. Inside the shop, Chad was greeted by the manager and introduced her to a couple of workers behind the counter. He introduced her as Felisa Carrillo, with no mention that she was his housekeeper. She saw one worker give her a questioning look, but she turned her attention to the luncheon meats.

When Chad finished talking, they all chose their sandwiches. She and Chad selected pita bread stuffed with ham, salami, and cheese with shredded lettuce and a special sauce, while the girls wanted plain ham and mustard sandwiches on white bread. Chad grabbed a large bag of potato chips, and the girls picked out their favorite cookies. When he pulled out his wallet, the clerk grinned and motioned him on. He laughed and tucked his wallet back into his pocket. He waved, and they followed him outside into the bright sunshine.

Chad halted on the sidewalk. "We could eat at the park, but I thought—"

"At the beach, Daddy," Faith said, bouncing beside him.

"Please," Joy intoned while she clung to the bag of chips.

He glanced at Felisa, and she gave him a willing nod, happy to return to the white sand and the breeze drifting from the wonderful blue green water. She'd never seen anything so lovely.

The walk back to the beach seemed easier to Felisa, and the closer they came to the ocean the more she felt overjoyed. She drew in deep breaths of salty air and listened to the gulls squawk as they dipped and soared overhead. She eyed the gnarled Monterey pines dotting the beach with their twisted branches. Though they looked dead, she knew they had life. That was how she had felt for so long, dead to the world. Yet God had given her back a life so amazing it made her heart feel as if it would burst.

They stopped at the car for blankets and chairs and to change Nate's diaper. She cuddled him to her side, knowing he'd never remember this day, but she would. Always. When her feet touched the sand, Felisa slipped off her shoes and let her toes sink into the white crystals. Chad gestured to an empty area and opened the chairs while the girls spread out the blankets. They unpacked the sacks holding their lunch, then bowed their heads as Chad prayed. Felisa felt close to God here, just as she felt God's presence in all of nature from every lettuce head to the smoky purple rise of mountains.

"What do you think?" Chad asked, gesturing toward the wide expanse of ocean and beach.

"It's so beautiful. I've never seen anything like this before. I never had the time or the mon—" She stopped herself. This was no time to moan about her lack of finances. No matter how kind, Chad Garrison was her employer, and he might think she was asking for more.

He washed down a bite of sandwich with some soda, then grinned. "I'm glad you're enjoying this. I can't thank you enough for all you've done for us." He tilted his head toward the girls. "You've added something special to our home that's been missing for too long."

She felt herself frown. She couldn't make sense out of that. What could he be missing in that wonderful home?

"You don't understand?" he asked.

She shook her head.

"Laughter, for one."

Laughter? No one had ever thanked her for laughter. What about her housekeeping? "I hope I'm cleaning well enough for you. If I'm missing anything, please let me know. I—"

He reached out and touched her hand. "I have no complaints at all, Felisa. I'm telling you that you're not only working well for us, but you're giving the girls and me so much more than I can ever repay."

The girls and me? She'd given the girls her time, but what had she given him? "Living in your home is gift enough for me. Thank you for trusting in me."

He smiled, but beneath the smile, she sensed he had more to say.

"Can we play now?" Faith asked, wiping her hands on a paper napkin.

"Down by the water?" Joy added.

Chad looked toward the water, then back at the girls. "Okay. Let's go." He sent Felisa a grin and hoisted himself from the chair.

"Goody!" They sprang up and pulled off their bathing-suit covers. They dropped them on the blanket and skittered across the sand to the water's edge with Chad behind them.

Felisa laughed when Faith put one toe in the water and jumped back. Joy did the same when she sank her toe in the water. Felisa couldn't hear what they were saying because of the surf hitting the shore, but she knew they were calling to her that the water was cold.

In minutes they moved back to the damp sand, and the twins began building a castle or a fort—Felisa couldn't tell. But they were busy at their task and working together. She was pleased to see the girls getting along so well lately.

"Look at them," Chad said, returning to his chair. "This has happened since you came." He shifted his gaze to hers. "That's what I mean. You've touched our lives with something special. I look forward to coming from work at night to a home with laughter instead of a house with angry voices."

"I like your girls, Mr. Garrison."

He drew back and eyed her. "Mr. Garrison sounds so strange for some reason. I know it's proper, but when we're alone, would you please call me Chad?"

Her skin prickled with his request. She'd called him Chad in her mind but never aloud. She knew it wasn't right, but she felt so close to him. "I'm not sure that's—"

"Mrs. Drake would be unhappy, I know, but in private she'll never know. I'm not happy with—" He faltered and shook his head. "You'd make me happy by calling me Chad."

Felisa felt her heart in her throat and could only nod. Nate let out a cry and, grateful for his intrusion, she lifted him into her arms and cuddled him against her.

Chad glanced away, then rose. "I'd better see to the girls."

He strode toward them while Felisa remained with Nate in her arms. She'd been stunned to hear his request and his kind words. He'd almost admitted his frustration with Mrs. Drake. She'd seen it on his face, but it wasn't appropriate for him to admit it. Felisa didn't like the woman, either. She seemed more concerned about the children's training than she did about their happiness. The girls needed a balance of both. Discipline and love worked miracles on them. She'd seen that happen today.

Nate let out another cry, this time without letup, and Felisa knew he would want to eat. She'd made the decision earlier to take him into the car when it was time, and when Chad turned to gaze at her, she signaled him where she was going, and he waved. With her feet slipping in the sand, she hurried to the nearby car and climbed into the backseat. Nate was eager for his feeding, and as he nestled in her arms, Felisa gazed out the window and watched Chad with the twins.

Felisa had wanted to see Chad become an active, loving father, and her prayer had been answered. He'd come to life today. He knelt beside the girls, his strong back bent over their attempts to make a sand castle. She could see his firm jaw relax in a smile, and when his head tilted back in laughter, she felt a smile grow on her face. She released a sigh, longing to let her heart open to the emotions that jarred her with awareness. She had to be grateful for Chad's friendship even though it had to be hidden from the others who worked for him.

Chad stood and looked across the water, and Felisa wondered what he was thinking. Perhaps his thoughts were on his work. She knew he had a good business sense. His farm managers had always treated the help well. His wealth was obvious from the look of his home and by the shop here in Carmel. She'd never had an opportunity before to see how the other side lived. Felisa had come to realize that even with money they, too, had their lives stressed with worries and their hearts broken.

Felisa glanced at her watch, wondering when they would leave. The girls had already bugged her on the way to Carmel about finishing the piñata even if it was wet. If awards were given for nagging, Faith especially would win the gold medal. She chuckled, realizing she, too, was anxious to see the results of their handiwork.

Her opportunity to talk with Chad had died with the girls' interruption, and now Felisa didn't want to talk about leaving. She needed to think and pray about it. Chad had made her feel welcome and needed, a feeling she'd never experienced before now. Her son needed good care, and the housekeeper job gave her that opportunity. She would have to remind herself each day that she didn't fit into the Garrison world. She would have to guard her heart.

※

Chad watched the ocean rolling in, the tide tugging at the sand beneath his feet. Life seemed the same sometimes, problems and worries making him lose balance, the beauty in front of him marred by the things that lashed against him like waves on a stormy sea. Today the tide only played games with the sand. The water rolled to shore in rounded waves like corrugated paper.

He listened to his daughters' laughter and saw their contentment in playing together, and he glanced toward his car, where Felisa nursed her beautiful son. His heart filled with God's blessings; yet something inside told him to beware. Hearts could be broken. If the twins became too attached to Felisa, they would be hurt when she left. He jammed his hands into his pockets, admitting he would be hurt as well. Why had his heart turned into mush? Was it because Nate reminded him of his own little boy? Was it the woman whose vulnerable eyes sent shivers down his back? Could it be a little of both?

He turned to see Felisa returning to her chair, her attention focused on the little one in her arms. When she looked up he waved, and she waved back, her smile as bright as the late afternoon sun. He eyed his watch. They needed to head home soon. The sun had begun its slow journey toward its familiar soft coral glow over the horizon, and later, when it vanished beneath the amazing stretch of blue, the breeze would chill.

God gave His children lessons through nature. Even the brightest moment could dim with dark worries and problems. He'd felt in darkness for the past two years. The light had finally broken through his deadened heart. His girls needed him, he knew, and for once he felt ready to admit he needed someone, too.

The following Saturday Felisa rose from her prayers and stretched her arms over her head. She'd had a wonderful time with Chad and the girls a week earlier, and she felt as happy this weekend had arrived, although she'd been disappointed when Chad told her he had to work. Felisa wanted to talk with him. Something inside nudged her to go back to her hard life in the fields. She had prayed every day for God's guidance, and she wasn't sure if it was the Lord prodding her or her own fear.

Since she'd arrived, Felisa sensed Mrs. Drake would do anything, even lie, to get her out of the house, and she also worried about her feelings for Chad. She felt drawn to him. When she watched him with Nate, her heart nearly burst, and though the girls had their moments, she'd grown to love them.

Last Tuesday they'd finished the star piñata, and on Thursday Faith had coerced her into making the other piñata, this one a flower. She'd promised the girls they could finish it today if it had dried. Felisa spent a lot of time with the girls, and she would have thought Mrs. Drake would be grateful she took such good care of them. But the woman saw her as the enemy, trying to turn the twins against their nanny. From all Felisa could tell, the girls weren't fond of the nanny before Felisa had arrived.

With Juanita off for the day, Felisa had prepared breakfast, done the chores, and, later in the afternoon, checked the new piñata. Confident it had dried, she settled the girls around the table to finish it. Once again they were covered with paste and strips of crepe paper, but the twins had so much fun it gave her joy to watch them.

Mrs. Drake had come by, complaining about their noise, and asked how the twins could benefit from making the colorful Mexican toy. Felisa kept calm and told the woman the girls were having fun and that was important. Mrs. Drake had lifted her nose and strutted away, mumbling under her breath.

When the pretty flower piñata had been strung up again to dry, Felisa looked at her watch and decided to clean the mess later. She headed into the kitchen to prepare dinner. Without Juanita, the family was at her mercy for meals. She loved the comfortable kitchen with its wide space and cooking gadgets, a microwave oven, and a refrigerator that actually spit ice cubes from the door. She could only shake her head at the amazing things she'd seen since she came to the Garrison household.

A noise sounded in the yard, and she looked out the window. When Chad walked from the garage and lowered the door, then turned to the girls, happiness filled her. She couldn't resist being part of the greeting, so she lifted Nate in his carrier and followed the girls' chatter to the patio.

"Look, Daddy," Joy said, tugging at her father's arm as she pointed to the piñata hanging from a beam of the portico.

Felisa watched him, looking at their handiwork with pride.

"Wow! You decorated that all by yourselves?"

Joy crinkled her nose. "Felisa helped us."

"But they did most of it," she said. "I just cut out the flower petals."

"I've never seen such a pretty posy," Chad said, opening his arms to the girls.

They rushed in for a big hug and wrapped their arms around his neck while he lifted both of them into the air.

"You girls are getting too heavy," he said, lowering them to the ground. "I'll break my back."

"Pick up Felisa," Faith said. "She didn't get a hug."

"No, she didn't," he said, giving Felisa a grin.

"It was nothing," Felisa said, waving his words away while her pulse tripped through her. "I'd better get inside and fix dinner."

"Give her a hug, Daddy," Joy coaxed, as she maneuvered behind him and pushed him toward Felisa.

Felisa stepped back, her mind whirring while her heart thundered in her ears.

Chad stepped closer and opened his arms, then drew her into them, his manly scent filling her senses. Felisa prayed he couldn't feel her heart hammering against his broad chest. His gaze met hers, a hint of surprise and a glint of pleasure.

A sound came from over his shoulder, and as Chad released her, Felisa leaned around to see Mrs. Drake standing just outside the door beneath the portico. The woman spun around and marched inside the house.

Chad's cheery expression faded to dismay. "I'm sorry," he said.

As if a cold rain had covered the sunshine and dampened their spirits, Felisa felt a chill reel up her back as she watched Chad stride toward the house.

"Girls," she said, wanting to keep them away from the confrontation, "let's clean this table, please. It's going to be dinnertime soon."

Their attention hadn't left the back door, but she clapped her hands and waved toward the mess of newspaper covered with colorful markers, bottles of glue, and leftover strips of crepe paper, its color soaking into the damp paper beneath. As they worked she eyed the door, hoping for Chad to return; but he didn't, and the worry darkened her mood.

"Can we go inside?" Joy asked, as if aware something bad had happened.

"I thought you'd like to help me diaper Nate and get him ready for bed so I can finish dinner." She'd never let the girls help her before, but they'd become gentle with him, and today it seemed a necessity to distract them from their curiosity about Mrs. Drake.

"Can we really?" Faith asked.

"Really," she said, shoving the paper and scraps into a trash can they'd brought from the garage. "You can leave the other things on the table for now."

Her ploy worked. They skipped beside her to her quarters, pulled from the issues going on inside, but Felisa couldn't keep her mind from drifting there. What did Mrs. Drake think? The possibilities filled Felisa's mind and made her flinch.

With a dry diaper and his sleepers on, Nate flailed his arms and jammed his fist into his mouth. Felisa prayed the trouble in the house had ended, because she needed to send the girls on their way and finish dinner. Before she had to make the decision, she heard a rap on the door and raised her head. Chad stood outside, waiting.

"Let your daddy in," she said.

Joy darted to the door and flung the screen open. "Want to see Nate ready for bed?"

"I sure do," he said, "and guess what? You can go and play now until dinner, and bed's early tonight. We have church tomorrow."

Church. Memories of her family's church in Guadalajara filled Felisa's mind. The arched ceiling covered by a beautiful mural, the statues, the candles, and the hard wooden pews where she knelt in prayer. Although she'd been born and raised in that church, she'd always left the service knowing she was a sinner who needed prayers and intercessions for her evil ways.

She'd wondered about Chad's church since she'd arrived. When he came home from worship, he walked through the door whistling a song that seemed so joyful it made her heart ache with the longing to feel that same way. She'd asked Juanita about the song, and she'd said it was a praise hymn. She'd never heard a praise hymn in Guadalajara, at least not one that made her feel like that.

Chad clapped his hands as if shooing the girls out the door like chickens. "Go inside now. We'll be there in a minute."

"Oh, pooey," Faith said.

Chad tapped her on the head. "What's this I hear? After all that fun with Felisa helping you make a piñata, you're going to whine?"

Faith lowered her head. "I'm sorry."

Chad bent down and kissed her cheek, then kissed Joy's.

The girls gave the baby a quick kiss on the cheek; then, to Felisa's surprise, Joy kissed her, too. Not to be outdone, Faith did the same and added a hug. Felisa couldn't help but laugh when Joy returned to give her a hug, too.

"Competition," she said when they'd scampered out the door. She rose from the bed and carried Nate to the crib, then turned on the intercom so she'd hear him in the kitchen.

"In more ways than one," he said, his face losing the smile he'd had for the girls. Felisa knew he was referring to Mrs. Drake.

"What happened?"

He shook his head. "It's not your problem."

She tucked the blanket around Nate, then turned to him. "It is my problem if I caused it."

"You didn't cause any problem. I wasn't aware that she. . ."

"Mrs. Drake?"

He nodded. "Don't worry. She feels very threatened by you and for good reason."

Felisa's back stiffened. "Threatened?" She studied his face. "I've done everything trying to make friends with her. She won't let me."

"She's jealous and prejudiced."

"Prejudiced because I'm Hispanic?" Felisa studied his face.

"Yes, and envious of your time with the twins."

"But she could do things with them, too." Then she thought about what had happened and stepped closer to Chad. Her heart beat in her throat. "She saw me in your arms, didn't she? What did she say?"

He shook his head again. "Nothing that holds any truth."

Felisa realized the time had come to talk. "I should leave. Nate is so healthy, and he's small. I can carry him in a sling on my back with no problem. I'll return to the fields on Monday."

Chad clasped her forearms in each hand. "Who will be the girls' nanny if you leave?"

"I'm used to field work. I've—" His words swung through her mind, then struck her. "What do you mean?"

"Mrs. Drake has threatened to quit numerous times. This time I took her up on the offer. She'll be leaving tomorrow. You can't leave now."

"But—"

His grip softened, and he drew her closer. "I told you earlier today, Felisa, that you've brought joy back into our lives. You've helped me see what the girls need. They need a father who gives them time and attention. Your care for the girls has done wonders. They've changed in the short time you've been here."

"Children need love and caring. . .as well as discipline. That was Mrs. Drake's mistake."

"I see that now," he said.

She felt him quiver. Chad lowered his face toward hers, his eyes hooded, and her chest tightened with anticipation. She waited for the kiss—a kiss she should refuse, but one she wanted so badly.

"Will you stay, Felisa? Please," Chad said, his voice husky and so near—until he bolted backward.

His action startled her, and the tender words left her disappointed yet grateful he'd behaved wisely in his self-control. He could promise her nothing, and she respected that he wouldn't toy with her heart.

"I'll stay until you find someone else."

"Someone else?" His eyes pleaded with her.

"It's best."

"I will find someone else to help Juanita, but I can't replace you."

She held her breath and sent up a prayer, trying to make a wise decision.

"You can have Mrs. Drake's room if you'd like, and I can put the—"

"No. I love my room. It's off the courtyard, and I can see the sun and hear the fountain and—" She swallowed, realizing she'd already answered his request.

"Then you can keep your room. Anything." He studied her face then touched her shoulder. "Will you go to church with us in the morning?"

"Church?" His invitation whirled through her. The vision of his spirit-filled face, the remembrance of the joyful hymn he often whistled, grasped her curiosity. "Is it wise?"

"Mrs. Drake often went with us."

"As their nanny?"

He studied her a moment. "Yes, as their nanny."

"I'll go to worship with you then, and thank you for inviting me." She braced herself against the sensation that rolled up her back. Stand guard, she told herself, then sent up a prayer. *Lord, help me walk the path You've prepared for me. That's all I ask.*

Chapter 7

Felisa stepped inside the church building, her focus jumping from one side of the huge space to the other. She viewed the comfortable seats, the large windows looking out to a garden on one side and the mountains on the other, and a vestibule that brought the outdoors in with large potted plants and light colored wood.

"Look at the church," she whispered in Nate's ear. She hadn't set foot in a church since his birth, and she felt ashamed. Her gaze drifted to the unusual setting—no statues, no vigil candles, no hard pews or tall stained-glass windows. Instead of an altar she saw a raised area where musicians assembled on one side and a group of singers formed on the other. A large screen hung from the center of the ceiling, and her head spun with questions. This was so different from the usual church she attended.

"You're frowning," Chad said, catching her off guard.

"I'm just looking around. I've never seen a church like this before."

A warm grin spread across his face. "Wait until you hear the music. You've never heard anything like it before, either."

Eyeing the band, she guessed Chad was right. An organ or sometimes guitars were what she'd sung to in church.

Felisa held Nate against her chest and followed Chad down the center aisle. About midway, he motioned her to turn into the row, and she shifted down a few seats with the girls after her, and then Chad. As soon as they were seated, the girls opened bags they'd picked up in the vestibule. Each sack was filled with crayons, coloring-book pictures of Jesus, and small toys, all kinds of delights to keep children quiet. Felisa chuckled at her feeble attempt. She'd dropped a few hard candies into her bag, thinking if the girls became restless, she could offer them a treat.

People streamed into the space, filling the seats as the musicians began to play a song she'd never heard but one that lifted her spirit. Some people clapped to the rhythm while others swayed. She bounced Nate in her arms to the beat of the music.

Soon a light flashed across the screen, and words appeared. A small group gathered near the front, the band grew louder, and the people rose, singing the words that continued to change above her head. Felisa didn't know the tune, but it was simple. Chad's deep, rich baritone drifted over her. She envisioned the times he'd come home from church on Sunday, whistling a happy tune. Today she understood why. Joyous voices filled the air, and people lifted their arms toward heaven as if speaking to God. "We praise His holy name." The words soared through her mind, and Felisa recalled these past weeks when she'd praised God in her own quiet way.

The jubilant sound lifted her, and she felt a smile spread on her face, then tears well in her eyes. Tears of joy for God's blessings, tears of sorrow for her past, tears of uncertainty for what the future might hold, and tears of wonder at what God could provide. She glanced at the twins, who were standing on the seats, clapping their hands and singing the simple tune. Her heart filled with pure happiness. Joy beyond measure. She'd heard the phrase. Today she felt that joy permeating her body.

Finally the music resolved, and she settled into the comfortable seat to listen to the prayers and Bible readings. Nate seemed as mesmerized as she was by the happy songs.

A young man, dressed in a suit, stepped to the stand, and the people hushed. His strong voice warmed the room with his message of hope in Jesus. His words settled in Felisa's mind like a glorious rainbow. She'd trusted God, even when things were darkest, and He'd sent her a spectrum of color into her life—her beautiful son, the lovely home, Chad's friendship, and the love of two little impish girls.

The preacher, so different without a cleric's robe, captured Felisa with words she needed to hear. God loved her, He walked beside her each day, and He guided her steps. Guidance was what she needed so badly, God's wisdom and direction. The preacher opened the Bible and began to read from a psalm. *"Let the morning bring me word of your unfailing love, for I have put my trust in you. Show me the way I should go, for to you I lift up my soul."*

"Show me the way I should go, for to you I lift up my soul." She wanted to remember the verse so it would calm her when fears filled her mind and decisions spun in her head like water down a drain. Nate squirmed, and she lifted him higher and kissed his soft cheek. He smelled of powder and baby soap.

Thank You, Jesus, for this gift. She admired her son, then turned her gaze to Chad, whose eyes focused on her. She smiled, and when he winked she felt a flush warm her cheeks. He gave her a hand signal that he'd like to hold Nate, and she kissed her son's cheek, then handed him over to Chad. She watched him cuddle the baby against his broad chest, her son looking so tiny in his arms. Warmth fluttered in her chest, and she pressed her fingers against the spot to calm herself.

Joy wiggled beside her, and she gazed down at the girls, who had turned their attention to Nate in their father's arms. Her heart gave a tug. She would miss them terribly when she had to move away—and she would one day when Chad found a new nanny.

Nanny. A chill rolled down Felisa's back. She'd been uncomfortable with

Mrs. Drake around and even more so yesterday when she'd threatened to quit and Chad had taken her up on her threat. At breakfast the woman's eyes were filled with anger. Felisa had decided to eat toast in her room and not endure the woman's silent contempt. Today was to be Mrs. Drake's last day, and she hoped the woman would be gone by the time they returned home from church. Felisa thanked the Lord, not for herself, but for the twins. They needed someone who loved them.

People rose around her, and Felisa was startled that the service was ending. She'd drifted off in her own thoughts, and she asked God to forgive her. The final hymn stirred Felisa most of all because it was the familiar tune Chad often whistled—"Lord, we lift Your name on high." When the service ended, she would be sure to thank Chad for inviting her to join them. She'd missed attending worship, and though this was so unlike her usual tradition, she loved the fellowship and the happiness that filled the air and her spirit.

♫

Chad pulled into the drive and nosed the car toward the garage. He paused when he saw Mrs. Drake outside, loading her belongings into her trunk. She turned to look at them, her nose raised in a tilt that told him her thoughts.

"You can get out here if you'd like," he said, noticing Felisa's discomfort. "Girls, you can climb out, too. I want to talk with Mrs. Drake for a few moments, and then you can say good-bye."

"I don't want to," Faith said, her old belligerent attitude permeating her words.

"Faith," Chad said, giving her his get-ready-for-a-lecture look.

She lowered her head. "But—"

"Jesus said to be nice to people," Joy said, her motherly tone making Chad grin.

Faith gave her an elbow. "That's not in the Bible."

"Yes, it is," Chad said. "Love your neighbor as yourself."

Faith put her hands on her hips. "But she's not our neighbor."

"Everyone's your neighbor, Faith. We should treat people like we want to be treated even if they don't treat us nicely."

She sat for a moment as if she couldn't get a grip on the idea.

"You know the Golden Rule," Chad said. " 'Do unto others as you would have them do to you.' That means just about the same thing."

"Okay," Faith said, her voice not totally convincing.

Chad looked up and noticed that Felisa had already vanished inside her room with Nate. Joy stood by the car door, and Faith finally climbed out and shut it. The girls hurried off for the house, and Chad squared his shoulders, gathering his thoughts, then pulled into the garage.

"Can I help you, Mrs. Drake?" he said as he stepped out.

"No, thank you." She didn't look his way.

"I have your check." He patted his pocket, glad he'd thought to get it ready. He handed it to her, and she studied it as if calculating for accuracy.

She tucked the check in her pocket, seeming to be satisfied, but she didn't mention the bonus he'd given her.

"I'm sorry you haven't been happy here, Mrs. Drake."

"I was fine until. . ."—she tilted her shoulder toward Felisa's doorway—"until she came along, trying to stir up trouble."

"Felisa didn't stir up any problems. I told you that the other day. She's been very good with the girls. They like her, and—"

"And so do you," she said, her eyes narrowed, "too much, and you call her Felisa. What about Mrs. Carrillo, or did you forget she's married? I find it disgusting."

He drew back from her biting words. "She's a widow." He was stunned by her insinuation. "Nothing inappropriate has gone on in this house, Mrs. Drake. I hope you don't—"

"God sits in judgment, Mr. Garrison. I don't."

She was judging him, and wrongly so. "I think your decision to leave is a good one. You're obviously bitter and prejudiced, and—"

"Prejudiced!" She straightened her back like a flagpole. "Facts are facts. You just don't know the truth."

A scowl weighted his brows, and he stared at the woman, trying to make sense out of her words. "What truth?"

"Never mind." She waved him away. "I'm nearly finished here; then you can wallow in your delusion."

He jammed his fists into his pockets. "Truth? Delusion? You're making no sense."

"I've heard her talk. Look around you, Mr. Garrison. This woman came from an impoverished background. No education. No social skills. Can't you see she's using you? She's after your money and a green card. She's come out and said it."

Green card? What was she talking about? "Felisa has a green card, Mrs. Drake."

"That's what she's told you." She slammed her trunk lid and turned on him. "If you want that kind of lying woman to influence your little girls, that's your sin. I pity you, Mr. Garrison. Lust is a sin, you know."

He heard the door bang and saw the girls heading his way, but the woman didn't wait for the twins or his response. She climbed into her car, slammed her door, then revved the motor and backed from the garage.

Chad held up his hand to hold the twins back from getting run over by the irate woman. He watched her tear off, his heart thundering from her anger and from the sharp words she'd tossed in his face. Could there be some truth to her words? His heart said no, but reality said it was possible. He'd heard horror stories of men and women being duped into falling in love and marrying someone only to learn the love was for money or prestige, but Felisa would never do that to him.

"Where'd she go?" Joy asked, hurrying to him as Mrs. Drake vanished down the driveway and around the corner of the house.

"I guess she had to rush," he said, dazed by the incident and the look of bewilderment on the girls' faces.

"Can we play?" Faith asked, a smile growing on her face.

"Sure. Until lunch."

They skipped off, and he stood looking at the rolling foothills with his heart in his throat. He lived in a lovely setting, amid God's glorious bounty of trees, mountains, and fresh air. He turned and faced his expansive home—the fountain's soft tinkle, the coral stucco and tile roof that offered not only a shelter but luxury as well.

Felisa had, at times, lived in her car. His gaze shifted to the doorway to her room. Inside, he guessed she was feeding Nate, perhaps sitting on the queen-size bed in the well-appointed room. She'd said she'd never seen so much space. She told him once she'd never taken a real bubble bath until she'd come here. He'd had women give him the come-on look after Janie died, and he'd never given one a thought until Felisa. What had drawn her to him?

He needed to think. He knew Mrs. Drake spoke out of anger, and anger didn't always carry truth. Yet he felt like a jury who heard testimony before the judge told them to disregard it. Once a juror heard the witness, how could he forget what he'd heard? He closed his eyes for a moment, letting the sun warm the chill that ran down his back. His feet felt glued to the ground, his stomach knotted, and his breath constricted. He raised his eyes to heaven, gulping at the air, until the feeling passed.

"Lord, You know the truth," he whispered. "It's in Your hands."

⌇

Monday morning Felisa struggled to concentrate. She sensed something had happened before Mrs. Drake had left. Chad had seemed quiet at dinner, except to tell her he'd hired a young woman to help Juanita. She hoped this one was gentler than Mrs. Drake. The girls had mentioned the nanny had gone without a good-bye to them. Felisa wasn't sure if it made the twins sad or relieved.

She'd eyed Chad as they ate, wondering if he regretted the woman's quitting her job or if something else had set him on edge. After dinner he slipped away without making eye contact, and Felisa lingered at the table, trying to make sense out of it.

Had she done something to offend him? Her mind dug back into the past day, but nothing came to mind. She'd thanked him for inviting her to the worship service. She'd truly felt blessed by being there. She'd taken good care of the girls when he stopped to chat with people he knew.

The image tightened in her head. Had someone made a comment about her? She cowered beneath the thought, knowing she didn't fit into Chad's world even as a nanny.

Yet she thought back to their trip home from church when she and Chad had talked as if nothing was wrong. They'd laughed, and she'd mentioned hearing him come home from previous worship services whistling the praise song they'd sung and how it made her feel good inside. He'd given her shoulder a squeeze and said how glad he felt that she enjoyed the service.

She pictured him in church with Nate in his arms. His face had glowed when he held her son, and again the sting of fear rippled to her stomach and churned the small amount of breakfast she'd forced herself to eat. Though she'd tried to push the fear aside, sometimes she imagined that Chad had manipulated the situation to get his hands on her son. The thought slid across her like ice, chilling her to the bone.

Finally she rose and carried her plate and silverware into the kitchen. She scraped and rinsed the dishes and utensils while Juanita loaded the dishwasher.

"You're quiet today."

Juanita's voice startled her, and she jumped.

"Aren't you feeling well?" Juanita asked. "Maybe you had too much sun this weekend."

"No, I'm fine."

Juanita's eyes narrowed as she searched her face. "You're not fine."

Unable to hide anything from Juanita's sharp eyes, she gave a nod. "I'm curious, I guess."

"Curious? I thought you might be upset about Mrs. Drake's leaving."

Felisa's chest constricted. "Why would I be upset?"

"She blames you. I thought you knew that."

"Cha—" She caught herself. "Mr. Garrison said she was jealous that the girls liked me."

Juanita raised her brows, then nodded. "I'm sure that's part of it."

Part of it? What did that mean? She turned toward Juanita but found her heading away. Felisa stood beside the sink with questions roiling in her head.

Juanita returned with the dust mop and dragged it across the floor, never looking up.

Though she wanted to ask, she hesitated. Juanita didn't gossip, and she could get very close mouthed when pressed. Instead Felisa made use of the time to ask the lingering question that had often troubled her. "Why is Mr. Garrison so interested in Nate?" She'd been more careful this time to say *Mr. Garrison*. Her slip had been careless.

Juanita paused and leaned against the dust mop. "He's a kind man, and he likes children."

"But I think it's more than that. He's always wanting to hold Nate and—"

"He has his reasons, but it's his business. It's not my way to gossip about my employer. I hope you understand, Felisa," she said kindly. "He'll tell you if he wants to."

She gave the mop a long push and delved into her task, leaving Felisa with questions dangling in her thoughts but no one to ask. Juanita had made it clear that she'd said enough.

⤳

For a week, uneasiness had weighed on Chad's shoulders. When he looked at Felisa, he saw her questioning, sad eyes. She clung to Nate when he was nearby as if he were an ogre who planned to steal her child. He made no sense out of that; yet he understood her concern. She must have sensed his wariness.

The new girl was working out. Gloria liked the twins and related to Juanita well. Juanita said she was a hard worker and seemed trustworthy. Chad had talked to the pastor before hiring the young woman. She'd recently joined the church and she'd had some personal problems; but the pastor vouched for her, and that was all Chad needed.

On Saturday he took the girls into Salinas to pick up some paperwork he'd left behind in his office. His mind had been everywhere but on his job, and he promised them a trip to a fast-food restaurant where they could play on the plastic slides and tubes, then burrow into the huge mound of colorful plastic balls. They had begged to go there, but he'd avoided it. Greasy food and screaming kids weren't his idea of a relaxing lunch, but he'd finally given in. He needed to spend time with the twins, and at home Felisa was always around. Today he left Felisa behind, and he saw her study him with a question.

They'd spoken to each other during the week, but the conversation was strained. He kept his distance. He'd nearly lost his heart. Since Mrs. Drake's charges against her he'd thought back, trying to find the clues to Felisa's intentions that he might have missed. Mrs. Drake's accusation made little sense when he thought about it. He'd been the one to insist on taking Felisa to the hospital. She'd begged him not to. He'd been the one who had given her the housekeeper job. She'd had no idea of his plans. So if he'd been the one to arrange her stay at the house, when had her goal to trick him been devised?

Chad sat at the small, round table, watching the girls through the restaurant window, and rubbed his temples. He missed his conversations with Felisa. He missed holding Nate, who seemed to grow an inch each day. His dark hair had already grown thick and curly like Felisa's. The boy followed motion with his deep brown eyes. He would be smart like his mother.

His thoughts shifted. Chad knew nothing of Felisa's husband except that he'd been run down by a passing car. He assumed her life had been hard. Migrant workers had to be strong people who could deal with moving from place to place, living in low-income housing, and working in the draining heat of the day. Felisa had stamina. She'd handled the girls with patience and taken over the housekeeping job with skill, and he'd found her to be an excellent cook.

Besides her homemaking skills, Felisa was a beautiful woman with strength of character. He'd come to think of her as honest and trustworthy, a woman of faith. She'd never asked for anything special. Even the day he planned to take them all to the beach, she had assumed he meant only the girls. That didn't sound like a woman on the make to him. He trusted Juanita, and she seemed to like Felisa.

Juanita. Why hadn't she warned him if she'd sensed something awry? She had given him odd looks the past few days, but she'd probably noticed his distraction. Juanita had never been a gossip. She'd always been one to avoid rumors. Still, he couldn't believe Juanita would be aware of Felisa's attempts to manipulate him into marriage and not say something.

Rumors. Gossip. Juanita followed God's Word. The Bible said to slander no one. Had Juanita not told him about Felisa's motives because she thought it wrong to spread rumors? Chad's thoughts wavered in one direction and then another.

His head pounded while Bible verses raced through his mind. A verse from Proverbs struck him. *"He who conceals his hatred has lying lips, and whoever spreads slander is a fool."* He needed to question Juanita. Mrs. Drake had probably been lying. Juanita would tell him the truth if he asked her.

Chad rose and wandered to the door and out into the play area. He stood looking into the tubes and plastic pathways, smiling at his daughters as they waved and called to him. They had become happy children. He'd become a more light-hearted man, a man who could feel again and see a brighter future. How could he think Felisa had plotted to harm him and his family? She'd been a blessing, a gift from the Lord. How could he doubt her?

Chapter 8

Felisa sat outside her room, nestling Nate against her and listening to the quiet. The only sound was the splash of the fountain and an occasional birdcall. She'd weighed her thoughts carefully, and though she still had no idea what had disturbed Chad, she sensed his interest in Nate was from his heart and nothing more.

Chad seemed too tender and too loving to want to take her little boy from her. She winced at the evil thought that had settled into her mind. Chad, a Christian through and through, would no more hurt her than he would hurt Joy or Faith. A chill of loneliness settled over her. Usually she would have gone with Chad to tend to the girls, but today he'd not invited her. She still struggled to recall what she might have done to offend him.

Being the nanny seemed almost a waste of time. She'd been close to the girls before when Mrs. Drake was nanny and she still did chores around the house. Now Gloria had been hired to help Juanita, and Felisa could spend more time with Nate; but she also had more time to think and to brood. The happiness she'd felt for the past weeks had faded like a wilting rose.

Glancing down, she noticed Nate had drifted to sleep. She rose, carried him to his crib, and placed him down for a nap, then set the monitor in case she went inside the house for some reason. From her chair outside, she could hear his cry. She closed the screen door softly and settled again on the chair in the warm sunlight, trying to recapture the contentment she'd felt until the past week.

The crunch of automobile tires sounded around the corner of the house, and she looked up to see Chad's dark blue sedan pull in front of the garage as the door opened. The girls scampered out, each carrying a package. They darted toward her, and her loneliness dissipated.

"Did you have fun?" she asked.

Joy nodded while Faith opened her parcel and pulled out a box. "Look what Daddy bought me."

When Chad's shadow fell at Felisa's feet, she glanced up. His sad eyes glided over her before he walked away into the house.

"Aren't you going to look at my present?" Faith asked, holding the box in front of her.

She pulled her gaze from Chad's retreating back and forced a smile. "Let me see."

Faith opened the box and pulled out wind chimes attached to a brightly painted metal sunflower. "Listen." She held the flower in the air, letting the metal pieces tinkle as they struck one another.

"It's beautiful," Felisa said. "We can hang it on the edge of the portico so it will be stirred by the breeze."

"Will you help me hang it?" she asked.

"We'll need a hammer and nails." Felisa paused. "Maybe your daddy can hang it better. He's taller."

"Okay," she said, skipping off while Joy stood beside her holding her little box in her hands.

"Do you want to see my present?"

"I do," Felisa said, realizing from Joy's expression she felt left out. "What do you have?"

Joy lifted the lid on the box and pulled back the paper. "It's a butterfly."

The colorful metal butterfly with moveable wings hung from a lightweight cord, and though it wouldn't clang, it would certainly sway in the breeze. "I love it, Joy. It's so beautiful."

"Like you," the little girl said, wrenching Felisa's heart.

"Thank you. That's the sweetest thing to say." She held the cord and watched the butterfly flutter on the light breeze. "Is this for your room?"

She shook her head. "It's for outside."

Felisa placed the butterfly back into the box and handed it to Joy. "Your daddy can help you hang this, too."

Joy held the box against her chest and stared at the ground, her toe bouncing from side to side on the patio tiles.

Felisa studied her face. "Is something wrong?"

She shook her head without looking up.

"Did you get into trouble today?"

Joy shook her head again.

"Then why are you so sad?" She tilted her chin upward. "Can I help?"

Joy nodded. "I want you to be my mommy."

Felisa's heart spiraled to her throat and back. "Oh, Joy." She wrapped her arms around the girl. "I'm your nanny. Isn't that almost as good?"

"But someday you'll leave, and then I won't have you anymore." She searched Felisa's eyes, and Joy's expression clasped her heart and twisted it.

She couldn't promise the child she would never leave, because she knew she would. Words clung to her throat. "I'm so honored that you love me so much, Joy. Thank you. I love you, too. Very, very much."

"Then you could be my mommy." Her eyelashes fluttered, and she gave Felisa a questioning look. "I don't remember my real mommy. I was too little."

"I'm sure she loved you very much." Felisa knew that if Joy were her child she would have indeed loved her with all of her being. She held the child closer, wondering why this troubled Joy now. Was it Mrs. Drake's leaving? The child had lost a mother and many nannies. Felisa ached, thinking of the pain she would cause this little girl when she had to go.

She heard the door slam and looked toward the sound. Faith had already cajoled her father into hanging the wind chime. He stood beneath a crossbeam at the edge of the portico, holding the hammer and apparently searching for a place to hang the chime where it would best catch the wind.

She gave Joy a pat. "You'd better get over there so he can hang your butterfly."

Joy rallied and skipped away with her small box clutched in her hands.

Felisa stayed in the chair and watched from a distance. Normally she would have been with the girls, helping decide where the chime should go, but the past days she felt as if she were an outsider.

Chad looked her way, then went back to work, pounding a nail into the wooden beam and hanging the chime. He moved closer to her side of the patio and hung Joy's butterfly. When he stepped away, the lovely creature dipped and fluttered, just as Felisa's heart had done for so long.

He headed back to the house with the girls, and she settled back and closed her eyes. She hated to face dinner, and her mind worked to find a reason why she wouldn't eat at all or would eat in her room. She didn't want to lie, but she just couldn't face him any longer.

"Felisa."

His soft, raspy voice rippled past her ear. She opened her eyes to see Chad standing above her.

"I'm sorry to disturb you," he said, "but I think we should talk."

She shook her head, wondering if she'd fallen asleep and this was only a dream or if it were real. She watched his serious face flicker with emotion and tried to read the meaning. He was letting her go back to the fields as she'd requested. "Talk? You mean—"

"I owe you an apology."

"Apology?" Felisa had never been so surprised.

He gave a fleeting nod. "For my behavior."

She lowered her gaze, watching the shadows from his body shift over her. He'd acted strangely—distant, really—but then so had she. "I—I know I did something wrong, and I've wanted to apologize to you."

"What do you mean you did something wrong?"

She rose, feeling uncomfortable sitting while he stood. "I must have. You've been upset with me."

"What did you do?"

She searched his face. "You tell me, because I don't know."

The stern look cracked into a faint grin. "You did nothing wrong, Felisa. It was me. I listened to rumors and—"

"Rumors?"

"Gossip. Mrs. Drake told me. . ." He motioned to the umbrella table. "Let me get a chair so we can really talk."

She watched him move across the tile surface of the patio, lift the chair, and carry it to her side. When he returned, she sank back into her seat, the muscles of her legs feeling empty of strength. Felisa folded her hands in her lap and waited to learn what Mrs. Drake had told him. She'd rarely spoken to the woman.

Chad leaned forward, resting his elbows on his knees, his hands fidgeting in front of him until he wove his fingers together. He raised his head, his eyes searching hers as if he were struggling to find the words to say. "The Bible tells us not to listen to hearsay, not to spread false rumors, and I failed miserably."

His expression made her ache. "I don't understand."

"I'm ashamed to tell you what I gave credence to."

"Credence?" She didn't know what the word meant.

"What I thought might be a possibility."

"Maybe it doesn't matter." She lowered her gaze and shook her head.

He leaned closer, capturing her hand in his. "It does matter, Felisa. It matters a great deal, because I should know you better. I should have trusted you."

The warmth of his flesh heated her skin and sent electricity surging up her arm. Her mind swirled with his words and her lack of understanding, while her breath seemed to leave her. What had Mrs. Drake said, and why hadn't he told her?

"Mrs. Drake hired on as my third nanny in less than two years. I wanted to give her a chance. God tells us not to judge, and though I thought she was a controlling woman, I gave her time to get to know the twins and to ease up on them. I wanted her to love the girls, but—"

"Seeing the truth isn't judging. I'm sure your instinct told you the twins were unhappy."

"Yes, but so was I, and sometimes I couldn't sort out the difference. All kids hate being disciplined. I figured. . ." He brushed away his words. "Never mind that. When I talked with her as she was leaving, she became vicious. Her anger said things about you that I don't even want to think about. I finally spoke to Juanita. She would know if there were any truth in what Mrs. Drake said, and—"

"What things? What did she say?" Her nerves chafed with the waiting.

"That you were plotting for me to fall in love so you could get to my money and a green card."

The words knifed through her. She shook her head, unable to form the idea in her mind. The reality sank deeper and embedded into her brain. "Money? Green card? I told you I had a green card."

"I know," he said with a look that made her ache for him. "I knew you had a green card, but—"

Tears blurred her eyes and rolled down her cheeks. Why deny it? Some Americans—gringos, as her fellow workers called them—would think something this awful about her. She knew she didn't even fit into his world as a nanny.

"Please, Felisa," he said, rising and crouching beside her, his arms slipping around her shoulders and drawing her to him. "Please. I didn't believe it, but it made me question. She'd said you told her this. My heart said no, but my head said. . ."

His words faded away, and all she could hear was the beating of her heart and his deep breathing. His scent encircled her, a fresh, earthy aroma like lemons in a spring rain. She felt the stubble of his jaw against her forehead and his fingers caressing her arms. Ashamed and amazed, she lifted her head, not wanting to pull away but knowing she must.

"I'm sorry for crying. I—"

He looked into her face and wiped the tears from her cheeks with his finger. "I didn't mean to hurt you. I'm so sorry. All the things I've said to you—how you've changed our lives and made us happy again—all of those things I meant from the bottom of my heart. My daughters adore you. I ado—" He halted. "I can never express how I feel about your effect on this house. As I said, you made it a home again."

Sadness washed over her. Chad's wife had died, and he'd raised two little girls alone. She would have to raise Nate alone. Her son filled her thoughts—his sweet face and tiny limbs, but raising him alone seemed different. She'd sensed that Chad had loved his wife far more than she'd loved her husband. His sorrow had to be as deep as an abyss. Without thinking, she touched his face, her fingers tracing his unshaven face. His firm jaw jerked beneath her hand, his eyes searched hers.

"You don't have to apologize," she said. "I understand. We all have fears that scare us like a snake hiding in the grass, its tail giving us warning, but we can't believe what we hear."

He pressed his hand against hers, flooding her with warmth. The pressure deepened the scratch of his whiskers, reminding her that life could be a mixture of pleasure and pain. Her heart wanted to love him, but her wisdom told her to beware.

Felisa drew in a ragged breath, a shiver coursing through her body.

Chad released her hand, his eyes saying more than her reasoning could accept. He rose and looked into the distance. She followed his gaze to the purple haze of the mountains, the blue green of the thick growth of trees clinging to their sides, standing tall and straight as if God were holding them with a wire.

She tried to stand, but her legs trembled erratically. What had happened? What had been the meaning of the intimate moment they'd shared? Hearing a soft cry from her room, she grasped her courage and rose. "Nate," she said, her voice almost a whisper.

His tender smile filled her. "Can I come in? I've missed him."

She nodded, aware that she, too, had had her bad thoughts about him. She needed to confess her fear that he wanted to steal her son. Sadness bounded through her as she admitted to herself what she'd thought.

Inside, Felisa lifted Nate from his crib. He quieted as she kissed his warm cheek. "Hold him while I get a clean diaper," she said, handing him to Chad.

Chad opened his arms and cuddled her son to his chest, while she dug into a drawer for Nate's clean clothes. When she returned, Chad placed Nate on the bed. "May I?"

She eyed him. "You want to change his diaper?"

"Why not?"

"It's dirty."

"That's okay."

She sat on the edge of the bed, watching as Chad removed the diaper, cleaned the baby, powdered him, and attached the new diaper. He reached for the blue one-piece body suit and drew it onto Nate's legs, fitted his arms into the sleeves, and snapped it closed. "There you go, big man," he said, kissing the top of her son's head. "You're as good-looking as your mother."

He cradled Nate in his arms, giving him a slow bounce as his gaze met hers. "Was his father a handsome man?"

His question addled her. "Yes."

"You don't sound convinced," he said, seeing too deeply into her emotions.

"He had a handsome face, but his soul wasn't handsome at all." She felt sad saying the truth.

His expression darkened. "Why did you marry him?"

"Stupidity." She shook her head. "I was young and inexperienced. He was handsome and promised many things. It sounded better than the crowded conditions of my family, and. . .I knew it would be a relief to my parents. One less person underfoot, one less mouth to feed. You understand."

"So you married to make life easier for your family?"

She drew up her shoulders. "I was sixteen. I'm not sure I thought of it that way. I felt a burden to my parents. I wanted to go to school, but they wanted me to work. I thought of it as an escape."

He gave her a nod and studied her. "I'm sorry. Life hasn't been easy for you."

"But it's made me strong."

A telling look stole across his face. "Yes, you are strong."

He placed his hand on her shoulder and drew her closer as her pulse tripped along her limbs and thundered in her temples. She saw his lips twitch, and he leaned closer, their gazes locked, words unspoken.

A breeze must have set the wind chimes to swaying, because Felisa heard a soft tinkle. The distraction caused her to turn. Then footsteps sounded outside, and the girls' voices fluttered into the room. The girls, not a breeze, had touched the chimes, she realized as they arrived outside the door.

She'd been holding her breath, sensing something wonderful had nearly happened, but she released the pent-up stream of air.

Chad gave her an uneasy look and stepped back.

"What are you doing?" Joy asked, pressing her nose against the screen.

"Changing Nate's diaper," Chad said.

Faith's eyes widened. "Did you change it?"

"I did." He handed the baby to Felisa.

"It's almost dinnertime," Joy said.

Faith used her hands as blinders as she peered inside. "Juanita said come in five minutes."

Chad shot her a questioning look, and Felisa gave him a nod.

"I'd better get inside." He pushed against the screen and vanished with Faith and Joy chattering beside him, their voices fading with the distance.

Felisa sat on the edge of the bed, her throat tight with frustration. She was falling in love. She couldn't stop herself, and she would be so hurt. She nestled Nate against her, feeling the need to go somewhere. She needed to talk to someone who would listen and understand. She missed Maria, her coworker in the field. They used to talk about their troubles. She wondered if Maria even knew she and the baby were okay. Had anyone told her?

Tomorrow was Sunday. She would visit Maria. She could find her easily. She lived with her sister and brother in one of the low-income housing units. Maybe she would take Maria to lunch. That would be a treat for her friend, and the woman could see Nate. Yes. That's what she had to do.

She assumed Maria would be happy for her, but the more she thought about it the more the idea unsettled her. What if Maria gave her a hundred reasons why she should get out of the Garrison household? Would she listen? Felisa couldn't answer her own question.

Chapter 9

Felisa pulled onto the street and studied the houses. They all looked alike, and she hoped she could find Maria. Chad had seemed disappointed she drove her own car to church; but she explained her desire to visit Maria, and he understood. The twins had wanted to go with her, but that would have ended her purpose. She couldn't talk openly with Maria with the girls listening.

She'd enjoyed the service again today, but the more she listened and watched, the more questions arose. How could these worshippers be so joyful when God punished sinners? Why did they smile and raise their arms to heaven when she fell on her knees with downcast eyes for fear of God's anger? She related more to Chad's God than the God she'd known in Mexico, and it troubled her.

The familiar car outside the small house triggered Felisa's confidence. It belonged to Maria's brother. She would have called first if they had a phone. Felisa knew she would be disappointed if Maria wasn't home. She parked in front and climbed from the car.

She paused, looking toward the house and wondering if she should bother to unhook Nate from the carrier. But before she could move, the door flew open, and she heard Maria's voice.

"Felisa!" Her friend charged out the door, her arms open wide. "¡Hola!"

"¡Hola!" Felisa embraced her friend then pulled her toward the rear car door. "Come. Look," she said in Spanish, gesturing toward Nate.

"Your baby!" Maria cried in Spanish, clapping her hands then giving Felisa another hug. "Is it a girl or boy?"

"*Hijo*," Felisa said, letting her know she'd had a boy.

Felisa unlatched Nate from the car seat, still speaking in Spanish. "His name is Nataniel. I call him Nate."

"It's a beautiful name," Maria said, "and he's a beautiful boy. Does he look like Miguel?"

She gave a small shrug. "Chad says he looks like me."

Maria's eyes widened. "Chad?"

Felisa cringed, wishing she'd not called him by his first name. "Did you wonder where I've been?"

"I worried about you." She stood back and looked at her from head to toe. "But you look wonderful. Better than wonderful."

"I'm working for Mr. Garrison as a nanny."

"A nanny," Maria said, her face reflecting her surprise.

Felisa told her the story of her invitation to the Garrison home and how she'd worked as a housekeeper until the nanny left. She avoided telling Maria the reason for Mrs. Drake's leaving. Sharing the personal information wasn't her right.

"I'm happy for you, Felisa," Maria said, but Felisa heard envy in her voice and almost felt sorry she'd come to visit. She hadn't meant to make her friend jealous.

"I wish you could have this kind of gift from God," she said, deciding she'd said enough.

"I'm sure life is easier now without working the fields," Maria said, understanding what gift she meant.

Felisa only nodded and turned her attention to Nate. She'd come to ask Maria's opinion, but now the look in her friend's eyes made her have second thoughts.

"May I hold him?" Maria asked.

"Yes. Yes." Felisa bounced him lightly as she placed Nate into her friend's arms. "He's such a good baby."

Maria smiled. "I'm glad."

Felisa stood beside her, uncomfortable she'd come to see her. Her questions lodged in her throat, and she knew she couldn't ask them now. She would have to find the answers herself—between her and God—because she had no one else.

"Do you live nearby?"

"Nearby? No. I live in—" She faltered. "I live further out. I have a room."

"Good," Maria said. "I worried about you in your car. Will you come back to the fields?"

Felisa swallowed her discomfort. "One day, when Mr. Garrison finds a new nanny. The job is only temporary."

"That's too bad," Maria said, "but I'll look forward to seeing you in the fields again."

Felisa looked toward the sun, calculating the time. "I suppose I should be going. I just wanted to let you know Nate and I are doing fine."

Maria handed back Nate, then bit the edge of her lip. "I'm sorry not to invite you in. It's so crowded in—"

Felisa held up her hand. "No. That's okay, Maria. I understand. I only planned to stop for a minute." She buckled Nate back into his seat, then turned to Maria. "I'll see you one day again. I'm not sure when."

Maria opened her arms, and Felisa went into them, sharing an embrace. She stepped back and slid into her car. "*Hasta la vista*, Maria."

"*Adios.*"

She shifted into gear and pulled away, tears flooding her eyes. She'd meant well, but she'd blundered. Maria could never understand how she'd given her heart to a man so unreachable. *Father, I know my heart will break, and all I ask is that I do Your will.*

~

Chad sat at the umbrella table, playing kids' dominos with Faith and Joy. The tinkle of the wind chimes had set him in a melancholy state. Though he'd apologized and assumed Felisa had forgiven him, he still sensed her reticence. Maybe it would take time. He had to be patient.

"It's your turn, Daddy," Faith said, giving him a questioning look.

"Sorry," he said, placing his two pink dots against another two on the table. The dominos snaked across the round table in a nonsensical trail, about as ludicrous as his thoughts. Since Felisa had pulled away from church in her old clunker, he'd had a sense of loss. He feared she would leave him as she'd suggested—once he found a replacement nanny.

He watched Faith take her turn, and his mind drifted as Joy pondered her next move. Truly Chad had no intention of looking for another nanny. He wanted Felisa. He wanted her for a nanny and a housekeeper and. . . His chest constricted, and perspiration beaded above his lip. He wanted Felisa as his wife.

"Impossible." His voice startled him, and he shifted his focus to see both girls frowning at him.

"It's not impossible," Joy said. "I matched three blue dots with three blue dots. See?"

He gave them a feeble grin. "I was just thinking." About love. About a complete family. About—

Both girls giggled, and he studied his tiles, finding a match for his green dot.

Chad needed someone to talk with. Men didn't bare their souls, but he had the urge to talk about his feelings for Felisa to someone and thought of his best friend, Dallas Jones. Dallas was a Christian and might understand. But every time Chad had tried to contact Dallas, he'd lost courage, fearing Dallas would call him crazy or list the reasons why a relationship was hopeless, even impossible. Chad wanted hope and kept putting his trust in God's hands alone. Still, hearing a friend's supportive comments would give him assurance.

A car approached on the gravel drive, and he felt his hand twitch as he organized the tiles on the tray. He forced himself not to turn around.

"It's Felisa!" Joy shouted, glee filling her voice. She jumped from her chair and skipped across the patio toward the garage.

"Are we ending the game?" Chad asked, welcoming the break.

"No," Faith said, "we're not done yet."

But he felt done. Finished. Wiped out. He could hear Joy's chatter behind her and Felisa's voice greeting them. Felisa's heels tapped along the tiles as she approached.

"Having fun?" she asked, carrying Nate in the carrier.

"Yes!" both twins said at the same time.

"Sure thing," he said, giving her a look to show this wasn't his favorite Sunday afternoon activity.

"Wanna play?" Joy asked, patting the arm of the fourth chair.

She shook her head. "I'm a little late to get in now. Anyway I have to feed Nate."

Chad studied her, seeing the sun highlighting her dark hair, her cheeks tanned and rosy, and her summer dress as flowery as a florist's window. When he raised his head, his gaze captured hers. She smiled a warm smile that melted his heart.

"Hasta la vista," she said, waving and sending him a grin.

"Hasta la vista," he murmured. He watched her walk across the patio, listening to the wind chimes give a faint *ting*. He glanced nearby and saw the colorful butterfly flutter with the breeze. He drew in a deep breath, thinking that right now seemed heaven on earth.

Joy's whining voice caught his attention. "Daddy."

"Sorry," he said again and lowered his head to study his tiles.

To his relief the game finally ended, even if too many minutes later. He sent the girls off to find some puzzles, then leaned back in the chair, his gaze drifting toward Felisa's doorway. Though she had access through the house, he noticed she rarely used that door—only when it was raining—and she always entered the main part of the house from the portico. He wondered why.

He closed his eyes, listening to the soft chiming sounds and the rustle of a twig or leaf skittering across the patio. When he heard Felisa's door close, he lifted his eyelid a millimeter and saw her heading his way. She'd changed her clothes to capri pants and a coral knit top that made him think of a sunset.

"Where's Nate?" he asked, straightening in the chair.

"Sleeping." She sat in the chair Faith had abandoned. "The game's over?"

"Thankfully." He grinned. "You spend every day doing this, and I'm moaning over an hour of dominos."

"You have better things to do with your time. I don't. That's my job."

"But you love it, Felisa. I see it on your face. You were meant to be a mother."

She tilted her head, a tender look filling her face. "However God can use me. That's what I do."

"And you do it so well."

"Thank you." She settled deeper into the chair and leaned her head back for a moment. "I visited with Maria today." Her voice sounded bittersweet. "I'd planned to take her to lunch, but I—I decided against it." She opened her eyes and shifted upward. "It's unbelievable how a few weeks can make such a difference."

"Difference? How?"

"She was happy to see me, but when I told her I was a nanny I saw her change. I'm sorry I said anything."

"She was envious?"

She gave a slight shrug. "I don't know if it was that. She seemed to just back away as if she couldn't handle my news." She ran her hand down her hair, then twirled a ringlet with her finger. "Working the fields is a hard life. Being a nanny probably sounds like a picnic."

He studied her face, not knowing how to respond. He could imagine what Maria had said when Felisa told her who she was working for.

"I told her I'd be back soon, but I think she didn't believe me."

"You tried to be her friend, Felisa. She'll probably think it over and wish she'd been friendlier."

"I understand. I might have felt the same way if I had been in her place."

"You're a compassionate woman. You always put the best light on everything."

She shook her head. "No. I really don't. I—" She faltered and didn't finish.

He longed to pursue the topic but sensed she'd backed away from him for a reason. Felisa had probably been thinking of Mrs. Drake. He wouldn't blame her for having negative feelings about the woman. "Did you enjoy church today?"

"Very much." Her expression went from a frown to a fleeting smile and stopped with another scowl. "Can I ask you a question?"

He leaned forward. "Sure."

"You'll probably think I'm silly."

"I'd never think you were silly."

"You might," she said, "when you hear this question. Is your God and the one I've worshipped all my life the same God?"

He drew his head back, startled by her words.

"See," she said.

"You surprised me, that's all." He pondered her query.

"It may sound like a strange question, but in my church in Mexico we revere the Lord. He commands us to follow His will and punishes us when we sin. We pray on our knees for forgiveness. I've seen people walk to the church on their knees to beg the Lord to—"

"Felisa."

She looked at him wide eyed. "Did I say something wrong?"

"No," he said, now understanding her worries. "We believe in the same God. It's not God who is different. It's tradition. God allows us to express our praise and thanksgiving in different ways. In your church, you come to God in reverence and quiet. We come to the Lord with joy because we know He has already forgiven our sins by giving us Jesus, who died on the cross for us." He looked at her quizzical expression. "You believe in Jesus."

"Yes."

"And the Holy Spirit."

"I do. It's just different. I like your church. I leave feeling happy rather than ashamed I am such a sinner."

"We're all sinners. Every one of us. But our sins are wiped clean by Jesus' blood shed for us. So we can rejoice. We can clap our hands and—"

"Raise them to heaven," she said, extending her hands upward in praise.

"That's right." He chuckled at her huge smile.

"I like that feeling. I think God wants us to smile when we thank Him."

"Have you read the Bible?"

"Bible?" Her eyes shifted as if in thought. "I've heard scripture read in church. The padre explained it to us."

He held up his finger. "Wait one minute." Chad darted into the house and found a study Bible, then hurried back. "Here. Read the Bible for yourself. Sometimes it's confusing, but most of it is clear. And if you have questions, we can talk about it."

She took the scriptures in her hand and ran her fingers over the cover. "My mother had a Bible. She kept records of births and deaths of the family. The Bible was like our family history."

He nodded. "Bibles have been used always to record family trees, but they're also meant to be read."

"Thank you. I'd like to read it."

"Start with the New Testament. It will be easier, and you'll read the story of Jesus, and then you'll understand why we are so joyful in church."

She placed the book against her chest and hugged it. "Good. I want to understand."

He wanted her to understand, too. Having her know the Lord meant everything to him. His heart yearned to love her as a wife, but he wanted her to love Jesus more than she loved him.

Felisa had touched him like no other woman had since Janie. He wanted to know Felisa's dreams and longings, her plans for the future, and, most of all, whether she had feelings for him. Sometimes he caught her watching him, her face filled with such tenderness it wrenched his heart. Other times she looked at him with wary eyes. He knew they were worlds apart in society's eyes, but in his she'd become the air he breathed, offering him a sense of wholeness.

Chapter 10

The summer sun hung low on the horizon, and the day's heat had permeated the house even with air conditioning. Felisa stood in the doorway watching the girls finish their bath—their light brown hair now dark from shampooing and their soft cheeks rosy with the warm water.

"Ready?" she asked, knowing they wouldn't be, but it was time for bed.

"It's still daytime," Faith said, her usual whine making Felisa grin.

"I know," she said, encouraging Faith to smile back at her, "but it's always daylight when you go to bed. It'll be dark soon. It's eight thirty."

Faith raised her shoulders in a deep breath. "Okay." She dragged the okay out longer than a yardstick.

Nate's whimper came through the intercom, and Felisa paused, wanting to run to her son but knowing she didn't want to leave the four-year-old girls alone in the tub. As she listened, the cry faded, and she turned her attention back to the girls. Joy hadn't complained tonight, and she looked a little pale. That concerned Felisa. She grabbed two towels, and as the girls stood, she wrapped a towel around each. They stepped from the tub with her help, and she toweled them down, then handed each one her pajamas.

"You don't feel well, Joy?"

She gave a little shrug.

Felisa guided them into the bedroom, tucked them in, then headed for the door.

"What about our bedtime story?" Faith asked.

"I'll be right back," she said, hurrying to the bathroom for the thermometer.

When she returned she slipped it under Joy's tongue and grasped their Bible storybook, then sat on the end of Joy's bed. She waited a minute, then read the thermometer. "You have a fever. Before you go to sleep I'll give you some medicine." She patted the child's flushed cheek and opened the book.

"Today the story is about Samuel and Eli. Have you heard that story?"

"I think so," Faith said, curling on her side and pressing her hands beneath her cheeks.

"What do you remember about Eli?"

"He was old," Joy said.

"That's right. Let's listen to the story." She began to read how God called Samuel. "And Samuel hurried to Eli saying, 'Here I am; you called me.' Every time Eli sent him back to bed until the older man realized it was God who'd

80

called. So Eli said to Samuel, 'The next time you hear the voice calling you say, "Here I am, Lord. I am Your servant."' So Samuel did what God told him to do, and he heard God's message."

The story's truth struck her; she'd learned so much from the children's Bible stories. She finished the story, gave Joy the medication, and snapped off the light. As she headed through the house to the patio, anxious to check on Nate, her mind sifted through her thoughts. How many times had God spoken to her and she hadn't recognized His voice? She'd prayed for guidance, but she'd missed what the Lord was telling her and had no idea how to hear Him.

Felisa grabbed a soft drink from the refrigerator and stepped into the portico. The sun's colors had touched the mountaintops, and a splash of coral and lavender mingled with the heavenly blue in an amazing display. As she stepped from beneath the portico to the patio, she halted. Chad had pulled the umbrella chair close to the fountain and was holding Nate on his knees and patting his back. The picture touched her.

"Sorry," she said, striding his way. "I was giving the girls their bath. I heard him, but—"

"It's no problem," Chad said. "You know I love to hold Nate." He motioned to the table. "Bring another chair over and sit with me. It's a pretty sunset."

"As always," she said, so aware of the gorgeous evening skies. She did as he said and returned with the chair. "Joy has a fever."

He frowned. "Serious?"

"No, it's only a hundred. It's probably a summer cold. I gave her some medication. I'm sure she'll be fine in the morning."

"You care so much about the girls. It means a lot to me."

"They mean a lot to me," she said, wanting to add that he meant a great deal to her, too. She looked toward Nate. "Do you want me to do that?"

"Not on your life." He gave her a tender smile.

She stretched her legs in front of her and tilted her head back, breathing in a fresh breeze from the mountains as they cooled in the setting sun. Out of the corner of her eye, she watched Chad making gentle circles on Nate's back. The baby looked contented.

"I fed him a short time ago, so he shouldn't be hungry," she said.

"He wants attention. We all need that sometimes."

His words sounded melancholy, and her pulse tripped. Everyone needed to be loved and caressed. She'd been without that kind of relationship since she'd married Miguel. His love had become rough and his drunken words, vile.

Silence settled over them until Chad turned toward her. "Do you understand what I'm saying?"

She nodded. "The world's a lonely place when we don't have someone special to share it with."

His gaze captured hers. "I've found someone, Felisa."

Her stomach twisted, and she felt startled by her dismay and confusion. When had he found the time to meet someone? "You mean. . ." She couldn't find the words.

"I mean I've found someone who makes me want to live again, who's opened my eyes to what I've been missing."

Her hand trembled, and she couldn't look at him. "I'm so happy for you, Cha—" She had started to call him Chad, but the familiarity didn't seem right now.

Chad shifted his hand and rested it against hers, which had been clutching the chair arm. "I don't think you understand me."

"I do," she said. "You've found a lady friend who—"

He held up his hand to stop her, his eyes so amazingly tender, she thought she might melt.

"I've found you, Felisa."

Her lungs felt as if they had collapsed. She fought for air, gasped, then breathed again. "Me?" She forced herself to look at him, to see if he were laughing or teasing or—

"This is no joke. I know what others might think, and I've fought the attraction myself until I'm sick with trying. I can't fight my feelings any longer. I won't."

Dazed, she could only shake her head. He'd spoken aloud the dream she'd been ashamed to admit. She loved his girls, and he gave her delight with his smile and warmth. Yet she knew it was impossible. He'd just said the same. Others would scorn their friendship, let alone feelings stronger than that.

"Do you have feelings for me, Felisa? Any at all?"

His question dropped into her head and unsettled her. "I—I—"

"Please." He lifted her hand from the chair arm and held it in his. "I sensed that you—"

His voice sounded as if it failed him, and Felisa could not find the words to answer. What would God have her say? Should she answer with her heart or her reason?

"May He give you the desire of your heart." The scripture verse came out of nowhere and filled her mind. Wishful thinking? She faltered mid-thought. Samuel had heard God's voice and didn't recognize it. Had this verse come from the Lord?

Felisa lifted her gaze to Chad's. His jaw ticked with tension, and she raised her hand and pressed her palm against his cheek. "You're asking the impossible."

"That's not what I asked you. Do you have any feelings for me? That's what I want to know."

She pulled away her gaze and sensed his jaw tightening. "Yes," she whispered.

His free hand touched her cheek; his tender caress rippled down her back and warmed her heart. "Thank you. I know it's soon, and it's not easy."

"I love the girls, Chad. I think you are a wonderful father and a gentle man. I admire you from the depths of my heart. I've dreamed of this moment, but I fear it will only open us to so much hurt."

"Not if God is on our side, Felisa. I've prayed that the Lord would guide my words and actions. I would never do anything to purposely hurt you."

"I know that. I would never think that—" She stumbled over the phrase, remembering her earlier suspicion. She lowered her hand from his face. "One time I did question your motives for helping me. I was frightened, but I know better now."

"My motives?" His eyes looked concerned, and he lowered his hand and grasped hers.

"I didn't know what you wanted of me, and then I feared you wanted to take Nate from me."

His face grew ashen. "I would never have done that. I would never have thought to do that."

"I realize that now, now that I know you, but before, I looked for motives." She felt starved for oxygen. She gulped for air, then forced herself to calm down. "I'd never been treated so well. Never. You can understand why I would wonder about your reasons for being so kind."

"I do understand," he said, a frown settling on his face.

But Felisa studied his expression. "You probably don't. You haven't lived a life like mine, not that you haven't had your own sorrows, but life isn't easy for migrant workers. We're resented and distrusted by many people. Our lives are difficult and insecure, but it's usually the best we can do."

"You're right. I doubt if I can even imagine how it is."

The sun had settled behind the mountains, and a hazy glow tipped the distant peaks. Shadows lowered around them and took the edge from the day. The world seemed more peaceful and private. Felisa wondered in this quiet moment if she could ask the question that had haunted her for so long.

"I know you're a kind man. You're good to your workers. You've been more than kind to me, and I know you love Nate, and I just wondered—"

She saw him turn toward her, a heavy burden in his eyes.

A prayer rose inside her, a prayer for God's help to find the right words. "From the beginning, you've been attached to Nate." The words blurted from her. "You've been. . .interested in him, and that's not like most men. I want to know why."

Chad's shoulders slumped as if he'd been run down by a tractor in a lettuce field. His eyes darkened, and he raised his hand and rubbed the nape of his neck. She heard him sigh as he shook his head. "I had a son. He died."

Felisa's chest knotted, then coiled its way to her throat. "Died?" She felt breathless. "I didn't know you had a son."

"How would you?" He looked into the dusky sky for a moment, his hands unmoving in his lap. "It's difficult to talk about." His eyes glazed, and he looked beyond her as if remembering. "That was the saddest day of my life."

Felisa struggled to find her voice. "Chad, I'm so sorry. So horribly sorry." She swallowed back her tears. "What happened?"

"The umbilical cord became compressed during delivery, and before they could take him, he was gone."

Felisa lost the battle. Tears sprang into her eyes as she imagined the grief Chad and his wife had felt. "How horrible for you and your wife. I can't imagine bearing that kind of pain." She wondered if his wife gave up living from a broken heart. He'd never said why she died.

His head drooped, and he didn't speak for a moment. "Horrible for *me*," he said finally.

"For you?"

His gaze captured hers. "My wife died that day before she knew about our son."

⁓

My wife died that day. Chad hadn't heard those words spoken in nearly two years. The double grief seemed more than he could bear, not only for himself but also for his two little toddlers who needed a mother's love. If not for the Lord, Chad would have given up on life. But his faith had sustained him, probably the same as Felisa's faith had sustained her.

He lifted his gaze and, in the shadowed light, saw tears in Felisa's eyes.

He grasped her hand and cupped his fingers around it. "I've learned to accept it. I know there's a purpose for everything under heaven, but the memory is still raw. Sad days like that one seem to live in the memory without fading."

She nodded and brushed the tears from her eyes. "Miguel didn't know about Nate."

"But he would have been overjoyed."

Her gaze darkened. "I wasn't sure how he'd take it."

Chad's tension heightened, and he questioned, "How he'd take it?" He couldn't imagine a man not overjoyed to be a father.

"We depended on both our wages. A baby would only complicate matters in his eyes."

"But you wanted Nate." He saw a flicker of anxiety in her face.

"If I'm honest, no. I didn't want to bring a child into the ugly world I lived in. Moving from place to place is hard enough for adults. For kids, it's horrible. It's bad for their education and for them to feel safe, especially—"

Chad tried to control the frown that slipped to his face. "But I—"

"You look surprised. Upset." Her face filled with sadness. "When I learned I was expecting a baby, the amazing thought of giving birth to another human being, the gift that God had given me, made me think differently. I looked forward to the day when I would feel life, a tiny speck growing inside me. Despite my worries, having a baby seemed astounding to me."

"I can't imagine not being excited. Having a child is such a blessing. I have a successful business and a nice home, but Joy and Faith, in spite of their bad days, make my life seem purposeful."

"They're beautiful girls, and expecting the third must have given you and your wife happiness. I would have felt the same in your shoes, but you weren't married to someone like Miguel. You would see the situation differently."

"You said you weren't happy."

She lowered her head and seemed to stare at her woven fingers tensed in her lap. "He was a drunk. Every night he left for the bar and spent the little money we had. I hid my pay so we had food and sometimes a place to sleep, but he often forced me to give it to him. He would—"

"Forced you?" Chad's hands had knotted to fists. "What do you mean? Did he hurt you?"

"Sometimes when he was drunk." She shook her head as if the motion would chase away the memories. "I don't want to talk about it."

Chad rose and drew her into his arms. He felt her slender body, trembling against his, her head pressed against his shoulder. He could smell the scent of sandalwood and citrus wrapping around them. His chest tightened, wanting to protect her from hurt, wanting to cushion her against rumors, wanting to warm her with his love and respect. Yet he couldn't until she understood the depth of his feelings, until she trusted him.

She drew back and looked into his eyes. "I've never told anyone about Miguel. No one."

He caressed her. "Then it's time you did. It eats you up inside if you don't."

"And it's caused me not to trust. Miguel said he loved me, but he didn't."

"He did," Chad said, "but the drink became his greatest lover instead of you. He was ashamed and abused you because it was his love for you that caused him to feel guilt. Alcohol can turn good people into monsters."

"I know," she whispered into his chest.

He tilted her chin upward. "Let's go somewhere tomorrow night. Just the two of us. I'll see if Juanita can stay on. She sits for me when I have evening meetings."

Seconds ticked past before she answered. "Are you sure?"

"I'm positive. Let's drive into Monterey or Carmel for dinner, some nice place where—"

"Chad." Her voice was as soft as the flutter of a butterfly's wings.

His heart gave a tug. "What is it?" He gazed into her concerned face.

"We can't go anyplace too nice. I don't have the right clothing for—"

"I'll tell you what. Let's pick up a quiet dinner somewhere instead, and then we'll go shopping for a few things. I owe you a bonus for taking care of the girls so much while Mrs. Drake was still here. That wasn't your job, but you did it anyway. What do you say?"

"You don't owe me for that. I love spending time with the girls. I watched them change from two mean-spirited children to two little girls who love to play."

He brushed his hand down her thick, dark hair. "You let me decide about that. I can ask Juanita or even Gloria to watch the children, and we'll go to the Barnyard. You'll find some nice things there."

"The barnyard? But—"

Her face flickered with confusion. He wanted to laugh, but he held back. He could only imagine what she'd pictured in her mind. "It's a good place to shop. Trust me on this."

She gave a slight nod, and he could only grin, thinking of tomorrow.

Chapter 11

All day Monday Felisa's nerves seem frayed. A date with Chad seemed far beyond any reality she could have imagined. She'd dreamed of it, but never in a million years had she thought it might come true. She'd relaxed about leaving the twins with Gloria when Joy had awakened feeling better, not perfect, but with a normal temperature.

She struggled between exhilaration and edginess. He'd offered to take her shopping, and she felt it inappropriate for him to buy her clothes. Since coming to live in the Garrison household, she'd been able to save a little money for the future, and tonight, if Chad seemed determined for her to buy herself something, she would insist on paying for the items.

Standing in front of her closet, Felisa surveyed what she owned—denim jeans, a couple of pairs of pants, a few blouses and knit tops, three skirts, two of which she'd worn to church—nothing fancy enough for a dinner at a nice restaurant. She didn't fit in that world anyway. Who was she kidding? The thought gripped her stomach and sent her heart on an elevator ride. She sank to the edge of the bed and lowered her face into her hands. What was she doing?

Lord, I'm so afraid I'm making a mistake. I'm frightened I'll be hurt, that my heart will be hurt. I'm putting this job in jeopardy, and that means going back to the fields. Why is this happening? Why?

Tears blurred her eyes as she looked toward her closet, amazed she'd accepted Chad's dinner offer. She'd allowed her heart to step on her reason. She couldn't afford to make a mistake. If she managed to get through tonight, that would be the end of her going out to dinner with her employer. What would people think? What did Juanita think? Felisa had been pleased the new housekeeper had agreed to babysit. But she longed to talk with Juanita, with someone who understood her position, who understood the problems she could face.

Felisa brushed the tears from her eyes. She forced herself from the mattress edge, strode back to the closet, and pulled out the skirt with brightly colored flowers on a blue background. She'd never worn it since she'd arrived at Chad's. Felisa studied her tops. She had a blue knit top nearly the same color. She held them together in the mirror. Not bad.

Felisa tossed the skirt and top onto the bed and opened her dresser drawer, searching for a wide woven leather belt that she hoped would match her sandals. She found it and tossed it onto the bed beside the skirt. She had a pendant—not gold—but it looked gold and the same metal hoop earrings. Maybe she could survive tonight.

She dressed with haste and headed down the inside hallway to the main part of the house. She could hear the girls in the spacious family room, and when she entered, Juanita looked up from changing Nate's diaper and gave her a tense smile. Felisa suspected Juanita had reservations about the date.

"I want to kiss Nate good night," Felisa said, crossing the room to Juanita. "Thank you for changing his diaper before you go home. You're making the job easier for Gloria." She hoped to see Juanita smile, but she didn't.

"You're welcome. I hope you have a nice evening." She stood to leave.

When Felisa entered the family room, Gloria grinned, and the twins abandoned their puzzles to greet her. She'd noticed both girls eyeing her skirt when she came through the doorway.

"That's pretty," Joy said, touching the fabric.

"You look nice," Faith added, giving her a questioning look.

Joy leaned against her, her lips nearly forming a pout.

Concern popped into Felicia's thoughts. "Do you feel sick again?"

She shook her head. "No, but why can't we go with you?"

"It'll be late when we get home," Felisa said, grasping for the first logical answer she could think of.

"Can we go next time?" Faith asked.

Felisa knelt beside them and wrapped her arms around their waists. "It's up to your daddy, but next time we can check with him. Okay?"

They nodded but lingered beside her while Gloria tried to draw them back to the puzzles.

Felisa heard Chad's brisk footsteps coming down the hall and watched both girls run to him with their arms open for a hug when he came into the room.

"Felisa said we could come with you next time," Faith said.

"That's not quite right," Felisa said, correcting them. "I said it's up to your daddy."

"Listen, sugar cakes," he said, bunching them both in his arms. "I promise. The next outing, you can come, too." He shifted his attention to Felisa and gave her an admiring look. "Ready?"

She nodded, fiddling with the shoulder strap of her bag to hide her nervousness.

He stretched his arm toward her. "We won't be too late, Gloria. Thanks for sitting with the girls and Nate."

"You're welcome, Mr. Garrison. Anytime."

He gave Gloria the wonderful smile that made Felisa melt when he smiled at her, then grasped Felisa's arm as he steered her toward the door.

"You look lovely," he said, once they were outside. "I've never seen that outfit."

"I hope it's not too colorful."

"Not at all. You look beautiful, Felisa."

Her pulse raced as he opened the passenger door, and she settled inside. She placed her handbag on her lap and folded her hands, afraid to move or talk for fear she'd wake up. Then reality set in, and she wanted to wake up, afraid of what might happen to ruin her relationship with Chad.

Her mind tangling with unstable emotions, Felisa struggled to make even meaningless conversation. She looked out the passenger window, listening to the soft music that drifted from the radio. "Tell me about the barnyard. Is it something like a flea market?"

He glanced her way, a grin growing on his face, then burst into laughter. "You mean *the* Barnyard."

The barnyard. Isn't that what she'd said? She eyed him, wondering what he thought she'd said. "You told me we could go shopping at a barnyard, and I—"

He released the steering wheel with one hand and gave her arm a caress. "The Barnyard is a village of fine shops, galleries, and restaurants. It's made up of buildings called stables. Besides wonderful clothing, they have the gardens. It's really nice this time of year with so many flowers in bloom."

She could hardly speak because of her embarrassment. She'd pictured a real barnyard, not a shopping area—fine shops, he'd said—with flower gardens, art galleries, and places to eat. She didn't fit into a mall like that.

Silence settled over them, and she watched the scenery change as they took the Monterey Highway past the airport to Highway 1. Chad turned south, and Felisa remembered traveling this way to go to Carmel.

"You're quiet," he said, turning to look at her. "Are you okay?"

"I'm fine." She couldn't look at him.

"Are you upset because I laughed about the Barnyard? It's an easy mistake. It does sound like a flea market."

She heard an apologetic tone in his voice, and Felisa wished she hadn't let the situation upset her. "I'm naive about a lot of things. Fancy malls aren't the places I shop."

"I know that. Please forgive me for laughing."

She finally looked at him. His strong jawline tensed with his distress. "You're forgiven, but it's my problem. I feel silly that I made the mistake."

"You shouldn't. Let's forget it and have a good time."

She glanced at her flowered skirt, realizing she probably looked too casual or gaudy for the other shoppers. "Am I dressed okay? I don't want to embarrass you."

He released a sigh. "How could you embarrass me? You look gorgeous. You're a beautiful woman, Felisa, and if people look at you, it's not because you don't look appropriate. It's because they are envious."

She didn't believe a word of it, but his comment made her feel better. She brushed her hand over the cotton skirt. She liked cotton. She didn't need fancy clothes and furs. She wouldn't feel like herself in anything too fine.

They settled into an amiable silence while Felisa watched the landscape race by. When they passed Ocean Avenue, she knew they'd go around the downtown area of Carmel. She straightened in the seat, curious as to this barnyard place he'd told her about.

Chad made a turn away from the ocean, and soon he guided the sedan into a large parking area. "Here we are," he said, helping her from the car. "You can already see why I like this." He gestured toward the buildings ahead of her.

Felisa took in the rustic stable-style buildings with wide pine siding, stained in warm brownish hues, rising around her. As they followed the path, the stone walkway led them past lush gardens of poppies, snapdragons, cosmos, shasta daisies, lilies, and roses that trailed along the rocky slopes from the three levels. Felisa admired the vibrant trumpet vine and bougainvillea. The beauty took her breath away. "It's unbelievable, Chad."

He glided his arm around her back and gave her a squeeze. "So are you."

She sent him a grin, unable to respond with words. His fresh woodsy scent wrapped around her, and though his comment had addled her, she felt more secure and admired than she had in many years.

"Let's walk through the area so you can see it," he said, "and then we'll have dinner. Sound okay?"

"Sounds wonderful," Felisa said, unable to take her eyes from the unique setting.

Chad kept his arm around her as they wandered through the winding paths, gazing at shops that displayed breathtaking apparel, bath soaps and lotions, and gorgeous artwork. She wanted to press her nose against the windows and drink in the wonder. Chad guided her past a gurgling manmade brook, then through an open-air patio with an outdoor fireplace. She didn't know which way to look.

When she noticed him eyeing her, she grinned. "I don't know what to say. I've never seen anything like this before."

"It's time you did," he said, letting his arm drop from her shoulders so he could grasp her hand. "Hungry?"

She felt a hollow in her stomach and admitted she was.

"Then let's go back down to the first level. We'll eat there and shop later."

Felisa agreed, but the idea of shopping here disturbed her. She didn't have enough money to pay for the clothing in these wonderful shops. She could only imagine the price tags that hung on the lovely blouses and skirts, the dresses and shoes she saw in the store windows.

As they returned to the lower level, she walked with her hand in Chad's, his strong fingers engulfing her smaller hand. Feeling overwhelmed, she clung to him.

He steered her toward the Big Sur Barn, then to Bahama Billy's. She gazed at the small panes of the white-trimmed windows, looking like pictures she'd seen in magazines, and trellises covered with red vining bougainvillea. Stepping inside, Felisa felt as if she'd sailed away to another country. A buffet near the entrance was studded with Jamaican art pieces, including the bust of a man with tight braids covered by a colorful cap. The pale green walls and ceiling were decorated with murals of palm fronds, and palm trees stood at intervals in large pots, bringing the outdoors inside.

The hostess led them to a table, and above her on the wall, Felisa eyed a colorful piece of art. She chuckled when she noticed many of the paintings were in wavy frames that looked as if she were viewing them through a rippling stream. The rounded-back chairs had cushioned seats in a muted print beside red-topped tables with real flowers and dark green china. She clenched her jaw, afraid she was gaping.

The waitress waited until they were seated, then handed them each a menu. When she'd taken their drink orders, she walked away to give them time to study the menu.

Felisa opened the colorful folder and scanned the many Jamaican-style choices: jerk chicken, mango crab bisque, coconut prawns, Kahlúa pork, barbequed ribs, and steaks. But her focus kept slipping to the price of each meal, and the cost unsettled her.

Chad sat across from her, looking over the choices.

When she felt his gaze on her, she shrugged. "I can't decide. Everything sounds so good."

"Most everything is. Wait until you taste their calypso cornbread. It's *ciabatta* bread sliced and served with hot corn kernels, garlic butter, and cheese with serrano chilies. Nothing else like it."

Her mind spun with the choices and the cost. She could never afford to eat in a nice restaurant. Never.

‿

Chad gazed at Felisa's serious face as she perused the menu. He guessed this was a special treat for her. Today was an amazing event for him, too. "You're having a good time?"

She lifted her gaze slowly, a sweet smile curving her lovely lips to reveal even white teeth. One of her well-formed brows tilted in a beguiling arch. "I don't know which way to look. Everything is so wonderful. I suppose it's boring to you."

He rested his fingers over hers and pressed her small hand in his, amazed at the mixture of emotions that coiled through him—joy, surprise, tenderness. He leaned closer to her ear. "I've been here many times, but this is the first time I've seen the place through new eyes, and I'm enjoying it so much more."

She tilted her head and gazed at him with her dark brown eyes. "What do you see that I don't?"

"I see you."

She shook her head, her thick hair bouncing against her shoulders. "You're being silly."

"I'm being truthful." The delight of having her beside him bounded in his chest. "You make me forget my cares. You make me happy."

She squeezed his hand. "Happiness is within yourself. I can't give it to you."

Her wisdom astounded him, but he knew she'd learned that from her difficult life. "You help me find it, Felisa. You've given me the map."

He lifted her hand to his lips and pressed her soft skin.

Felisa's gaze followed his movement, and he feared he'd upset her; but when he looked he saw her cheeks had flushed a lovely pink.

As he lowered his hand, the waitress returned with their iced tea and lemon and was ready to take their order. "What would you like, Felisa?"

She gazed at the menu, and then at him. "It's all so—"

He held up his hand to stop her. It was expensive, but she was worth every penny. "Order whatever you'd like."

Finally she looked at the waitress. "Is the meat loaf good?"

Chad shook his head. She'd chosen the least expensive dinner on the menu.

"It's our specialty," the waitress said. "The loaf is wrapped in bacon and served smoky and crusty. It's everyone's favorite, and it comes with mashed potatoes and broccolini."

"I'll take that," she said.

"Give her a Bahama Billy salad with that. Make that two. One for me."

The woman jotted down the order. He added the blackened mahimahi with wasabi potatoes and their calypso cornbread.

He sipped his drink, watching Felisa's gaze dart from one table to the next. She watched patrons enter, and when she dropped her focus to her print skirt and plain top, he suspected she was worried about her appearance. "You look lovely, Felisa."

She flushed again, as if embarrassed she'd been caught in the act. "I can't afford items like these women. I have no use for such nice clothes anyway."

But she did, and he would tell her later. "We'll visit some shops after dinner. Donlé has everyday wear, and Mary's Boutique has nice dresses."

"But I can't—"

"You deserve a bonus. Please give me the pleasure of buying a couple of things for you."

She sank back in her chair, studying him as if looking for his motive again. He'd already told her how much he cared for her, but she obviously couldn't comprehend the depth of his feelings. Neither could he.

He let the conversation drift to the children and their preschool classes in the fall, the floral pathways they'd just wandered, the weather, and Gloria's love of the girls. Felisa was pleased with that, but something seemed to trouble her when he mentioned Juanita. He wanted to probe, but he decided to let it drop, hoping it was nothing serious. He also avoided the topic of shopping or of his feelings. This wasn't the place to delve into those issues that brought him great pleasure yet deep concern.

The food arrived, and the conversation turned to comments about the meal. They sank into their own silence; yet his gaze continued to settle on Felisa's lovely face, the delight he saw in her eyes and her haunting smile.

After they'd lingered over coffee and he'd paid the bill, he glanced at his watch and realized they should begin shopping before the time ran out. He'd never been more content than to sit beside Felisa after dinner and talk about nothing of consequence.

As they stepped outside, Chad felt a hand on his shoulder, and he spun around, surprised to see a familiar face. "Brook. How've you been?"

"Great, and you look well," he said, eyeing Felisa. "Very well, in fact."

Chad didn't like his ogling. "Felisa, this is Brook Garner. He owns a farm near Monterey. We sit on an agricultural committee together."

"Hello," she said, backing away as if uncomfortable.

Chad longed to put a protective arm around her, but with Brook's leer he stopped himself.

"Brook, this is Felisa Carrillo. She's the twins' nanny and—"

"Nanny." A taunting grin settled on his face. "My, my."

Chad saw Felisa shrink backward, moving away toward the path, and he felt helpless.

"You've got a good thing going with the sweet little nanny," Brook said. "You can send her to my house anytime."

Chad grasped his arm. "She deserves more respect than that, Brook."

"She's Mexican, Chad. What do you expect me to think?"

"Think this." He stood up to the man, nose to nose. "Hispanic, American, African-American, Chinese—I don't care. Everyone deserves respect unless you have the facts to know otherwise. If I hear one snide comment about her, I'll—"

"Chad, I was pulling your leg." Brook took a step backward. "You can date who you want to, but you can't expect everyone to have the same view you do." He gave a head toss toward Felisa. "Those people work in my fields."

"And they work in mine, where they receive a decent wage and respect. You should do the same." Chad shook his head. "You claim to be a Christian man. I've heard you. Tonight you'd better sit down with the Good Book and read 1 Corinthians 4. Then talk to me."

He gave Brook's arm an amiable shake. "Sorry about this, but I can't stand back and allow you to insult someone I care about very much." He took a step toward Felisa. "I'll see you at the dinner party next week." He said good-bye and turned.

"Chad."

He heard a woman call and pivoted to see Brook's wife, carrying a designer shopping bag and waving to him.

"Hello, Colleen," he said, waving back. "I'll see you soon."

He clasped Felisa's arm and headed down the brick walkway toward Mary's Boutique.

❧

Felisa sat in her room with her new garments spread on the bed. She'd entered the stores with Chad, afraid to look at the price tags and feeling out of place there. She didn't think Chad understood.

She'd wanted to turn and run; but he tucked his arm around her waist or held her hand, and the sensation covered the scattered moments of discouragement she felt. She feared the saleswomen were judging her—maybe because of the clothes she wore or maybe from prejudice. Could it be her own feelings of being out of place? Unworthy?

Chad had guided her through the shops, showing her racks with skirts and lacy tops. She'd tried to read the tags, but he'd sometimes nudge her hand away, letting her know price didn't matter. Finally he'd encouraged her to buy a teal blue pantsuit with a scoop-neck knit top in a lighter blue print. She loved the three pieces, and they felt so smooth on her. When she stepped from the dressing rooms to the large mirror, his smile had lifted her spirit.

At another store he'd shown her a party dress in deep coral. She tried it on and admired the rich fabric that clung to her form then swirled to her calves. She'd never seen anything more lovely. Chad had risen to meet her when she'd stepped from behind the dressing room's louvered doors and told her she looked like royalty. She'd never been told anything like that before.

On the way to the car, he led her to a shoe store and insisted she buy a pair of dressy tan sandal pumps and a matching clutch bag to carry with the coral dress. The gifts had cost more than any bonus she deserved, but he insisted it gave him pleasure, and seeing the light in his eyes, she knew he meant it.

Pushing the memory aside, Felisa hung the garments in her closet, fingering the soft fabric and admiring the lovely lines. She placed the shoes and handbag on the closet shelf, wondering where she would ever wear anything that stylish.

Turning from the closet, Felisa grabbed one of the shopping bags and began shoving the wrappings into it. While she worked, her mind slipped back to the man Chad had met coming out of the restaurant—Brook, if she remembered correctly. She'd been uncomfortable when she noticed he and Chad were having words. She'd never seen Chad so upset, and she knew it was her presence that had caused the spark of anger. Chad had said nothing about it to her, which was his way, and she hadn't wanted to ruin the evening by asking. After depositing the tags and tissue into the single shopping bag, she set it by her wastebasket. She'd take it to the trash later.

Felisa sank to the edge of her bed and rubbed her temples. Her rampant thoughts hammered in her head, and she tossed herself back against the pillow, wondering what God had in store for her. The sermons at the new church had given her hope and deepened her trust. She knew the Lord was her strength and shield, her rock and hiding place, but when she tried to put it into practice, she failed.

Nate gave a cry, and Felisa pulled herself up to a sitting position, then rose and strode to the crib. She lifted him in her arms and rocked him as she headed toward the bed. Nate had grown so much since his birth. At nearly two months old he'd become a little person, his bright eyes gazing at her and his tiny hands clasping her finger. He seemed to know her voice, and he kicked his feet when he heard the twins. They were so tender with him that it made her nearly weep with happiness.

She recalled her arrival at this wonderful home. She'd been frightened and confused, fearing the worst, but Chad had proven his word, and she'd touched his life by helping his two little bookend girls to be more lovable. All they needed was affection, attention, and assurance. She'd given those things to them, and so had Chad. He'd learned from her example and now spent more time with the twins. He doted on them to be exact, and they loved every minute of his time with them.

Felisa grinned, knowing the girls weren't perfect. They still had their bad moments—Faith's whining and stomping, Joy's quiet anger and narrowed eyes sending her a laser of contempt—but most of the time they were sweet and innocent.

Nate wiggled his arms, and she felt his diaper. He needed a change, and she drew him closer, kissing his cheek and cuddling him against her. She'd grown to love Chad's way with him. He loved her son, too, and the memory filled her with sadness when she thought of the day Chad had revealed that he'd lost his wife and son.

Since her faith had strengthened, Felisa had learned that when Christians left this world they walked into the arms of Jesus. But when Chad's wife and son had gone to heaven, it had left his arms horribly empty and with such a burden to bear.

Life. She felt so ignorant, so lacking when she thought of God's infinite ways. How could she, a mere mortal, ever understand God's plan? Chad's pastor had explained that people might not understand now but would when they met God face-to-face. She would have to wait for that day.

Chapter 12

With the girls occupied with a cartoon movie on the television, Felisa wandered toward the kitchen, her heart in her throat. As she neared the room, she could hear Juanita working, her knife smacking against the wood cutting board.

"Hola," she said, resting her elbows on the kitchen counter. "What are you making?"

"Apple pie."

She studied the woman who'd become her friend. A new reserve seemed to barricade their normally friendly relationship, and Felisa feared she knew why. She waited until Juanita stopped wielding the knife and had dropped the sliced apples into a readied piecrust. After she'd sprinkled the sugar and cinnamon onto the apples, Juanita lowered the top crust, crimped the edges, and made hasty slits in the top. She carried the pie to the oven, opened the door, and slid it inside.

When she turned around she faced Felisa. "You want to talk?"

"Yes," she said, her voice coming out a whisper.

Juanita motioned to a kitchen chair, and Felisa accepted her offer by sitting. When Juanita joined her she carried two glasses of iced tea and handed one across the table to Felisa. "I'm all ears."

Though her words were sharp, Felisa heard concern in her voice. "You know what I want to talk about."

"I do."

"Then what can I say? I–I'm—" Moisture blurred Felisa's eyes as she looked at the one woman she'd counted on. She lowered her face in her hands and let the tears flow.

Juanita didn't move while Felisa let her worry and fears flood from her being. Then the older woman rose, and the warmth of her hand spread across Felisa's back while the tenderness comforted her.

"What were you thinking, Felisa?" Juanita asked.

She wiped her eyes with her fists, then raised her head. "I wasn't. A person can't think with her heart."

"I know," she said. With a gentle caress, she straightened her back and looked in Felisa's eyes. "I saw it coming and not just from one direction. What could I do to warn either of you?"

Felisa lowered her head and shook it. "Nothing." She knew that love happened. It was like a corralled wild horse with a mind of its own and a driving will to be freed.

"Mr. Garrison has been lonely since his wife died. He'd turned inward and even lost track of his little girls. They were a mess. You know that."

Felisa nodded.

"Then you came along, bringing a little son and a heart full of love. You lavished the girls with your affection, and you pried open their father's heart."

"But I didn't mean to. I knew it was an impossible situation. I'm Hispanic. Worse. I'm a migrant worker who—"

Juanita stopped her with her hand on hers. "You're a beautiful woman who fell into a bad lot. You didn't want the life you found yourself in."

"No, I didn't. I hated it, but I figured it was all I had. I managed." She knew her definition of *managed* was a bad one.

"You survived," Juanita said as if hearing her thoughts. "You deserve better. Everyone does." She backed away and settled in her chair.

Felicia drew in a deep breath for courage. "Then why are you angry at me? You're the one person I counted on to listen when I needed someone."

"I'm not angry. I'm concerned. I know you've had a hard life, and I know the one you're heading for will be difficult, as well. But—" She pushed the tumbler with her finger, leaving a trail of condensation on the table, her gaze distant as if she had more to say.

Felisa waited.

"But people can change." She lifted her gaze, and her lips moved into a faint smile. "You're a charming woman, as well as beautiful. They'll learn to love you, and they won't care where you came from. You're a bright woman. Very capable. Just don't let anyone hammer you down."

Felisa leaned her head back, releasing a ragged sigh. "I've kept this bottled inside me for so long, not believing where my heart was leading and so afraid of being hurt. Then Chad let me know how he felt. I distrusted him for so long. I feared he wanted Nate, that this was all a trick to take my son, and when that fear passed I still wanted to know his motivation."

"Motivation?" Juanita gave her a full grin. "God's Word. He lives it. I admire him."

"I realize that now. He bought me some new clothes. Did you know?"

Juanita shook her head.

"I wanted to pay him back, but I didn't have the money. He insisted he owed me for giving the girls so much attention while Mrs. Drake was still here. I know it was just an excuse, because he knows I don't have much."

"Don't question the reasons or his generosity. I'm shocked to hear myself say this, but love him, Felisa. He's a good man, and you're a good woman. I've watched you with the girls and Nate. You're a great mother and a hard worker, you appreciate kindness, and you believe in the Lord. That's a nice bunch of qualities to add to being lovely and charming."

She rose, walked to Felisa's side, and gave her a hug. "Be happy. Block your ears from the comments and close your eyes to the looks. They'll go away with time and prayer."

"Thank you," Felisa said, forcing the air around the lump in her throat. "Thanks so much."

⌇

Chad opened the car door, and the girls scurried out, anxious to get inside. He'd promised them they could go on the next outing, and Felisa had mentioned the Monterey Bay Aquarium. She'd never been there, and he knew the girls were the perfect age to enjoy the hands-on adventures. Nate wasn't old enough to enjoy the day, but Chad hadn't wanted to leave him behind, so they'd brought him, stroller and all. He'd grown to love the boy as his own. The words filled his heart. He loved the child's mother, too, more than he could put into words.

"Hurry, Daddy!" Faith called, rushing toward the entrance.

"Hold on," he said, getting out his wallet to pay for the tickets.

The exuberant bunch bounded through the doors and bounced beside him at the ticket booth.

"If you hurry, you can see the shark feeding at the Kelp Forest," the woman said.

"Hurry, Daddy!" Faith yelled again, tugging at him.

"Hold on, Faith." He grinned at the woman. "Which way?"

"Just to the left," she said, motioning in that direction. "It starts at eleven thirty."

He paid for the tickets, and the girls scampered in front of him, veered left, then stopped to gape at the three-story-high tank. Chad grinned, noticing they were a little apprehensive when they saw the huge sea creatures—leopard sharks, stingrays, black rockfish, and wolf eels—gliding past the massive window and weaving through the fronds of kelp.

"Let's get closer," he said, encouraging the girls forward.

"They need their daddy to protect them," Felisa said.

"I guess." He gave her a wink and lifted Nate from the stroller, and they maneuvered their way into the group of people surrounding the three-story window.

In moments the stream of light from above the tank was broken by a diver, who plunged into the fray and was surrounded by large schools of fish. When he opened his bag of food, they swarmed around him. A huge shark headed for the diver, and Chad held his breath until the diver fed the fish and it soared away. He chuckled at himself. Obviously the diver would be safe, but watching the scene made him question his certainty.

Chad glided his arm around Felisa's back while the narrator explained the Kelp Forest, the kinds of fish in the tank, and what they ate. The girls were glued to the window, their eyes as wide as lettuce heads. Occasionally they looked toward them with broad smiles, then focused again on the tank. Nate cooed in his arms, and Chad felt Felisa nestle closer to him. He gazed down, admiring her well-defined lips that looked as soft as velvet. He longed to kiss her, but he hadn't done so yet. She needed time to trust his love and to accept what he hoped to offer her.

"Do you like this?" he asked, leaning close to her ear.

Her grin answered his question. "I feel like a little kid. I'm so excited."

"I love being here with you and the girls. Everything seems so much more purposeful now. I did things with the girls before, but I felt alone and it made me sad. Now it's different."

She only nodded, though he'd hoped she might have said more. He knew she loved being with him. He could see it in her demeanor, but he also knew she struggled with the situation. His mind slipped back to Brook Garner. The man's rudeness and disdain made Chad feel sick. Even before Felisa entered his life, he'd tried to be kind to those who worked his fields. He felt guilty when he knew some didn't have proper living conditions, but he did what he could to make life better for them.

Felisa's gaze had settled on him, and he turned to look at her, managing a smile.

"You're thinking," she said.

Her eyes searched his, showing her concern beneath her calm exterior. "Just some work issues," he said, hoping to cover his unpleasant memories. He tilted his head toward the girls. "Do you think we can pry them away from the tank?"

She chuckled. "I doubt it."

Before he moved forward to get their attention, the narration stopped, and people began to drift away. He returned Nate to the stroller, then called the twins and steered them across the skywalk to the Drifters' Galley and the Outer Bank. The journey took longer than he wanted, since they had to pass through the aquarium gift shop.

Chad clamped his hand on each girl's shoulder. "We'll stop back later. Okay? Let's go see the biggest fish tank in the whole world."

Joy's eyes widened. "Bigger than the one we just saw?"

He nodded, relieved he had her attention.

Faith looked dubious. "How big is it?"

"Do you know how much milk is in a gallon?"

"The big jugs?" Faith asked, holding her hands apart to demonstrate.

"That's it. Well, this tank holds more than a million gallons of water. A million is one with lots of zeros. This long." He demonstrated with his hands.

"I want to see it," she said, accepting his hand.

At the next display, bluefin tuna powered past the windows, sea turtles meandered by, and massive hammerhead sharks circled inches away from the thick Plexiglas of the Kelp Forest.

"Look, Daddy," Joy said, pointing to a huge school of carrot-colored jellyfish drifting past. Next she spotted comb jellies that pulsed with colored bands of light as they glided by.

He let the girls watch for a while, one hand on the stroller and his other hand wrapped around Felisa's, his mind reeling with the sense of family he hadn't felt since Janie died. Finally he dragged them away to the second floor and located the touching pools. Even Felisa knelt beside the tanks to handle the rays and starfish of all sizes and colors.

Chad's heart raced, feeling happiness that had eluded him for so long. The same sense of family, of belonging together, washed over him. He knelt beside Felisa, drawing in her flowery scent, and rested his hand on her shoulder, his fingers playing with her tight curls. He longed to run his fingers through her hair and capture her lips beneath his.

He rose, afraid of the feelings that stirred in him. He needed to give her time. Yet he'd waited so long even to think about loving again, and now that he'd found the one, he didn't want to lose her.

⚶

Outside, the salty breeze carried a faint hint of fish. Felisa couldn't help but smile at the girls and herself as they explored the sea life at the aquarium. She'd become one of the children, delving into the water to capture a ray and walking along the lines of water troughs dotted with colorful live starfish.

"That was fun, wasn't it?" she said to the girls as they bounced beside her, carrying stuffed animals from the gift shop. Faith had wanted a plush octopus, and Joy had chosen a toy jellyfish. Felisa loved the little creatures and had almost asked for one for herself. Nate was too young to use as an excuse. She feared the button eyes on the animals could be dangerous, but she'd purchased a knit shirt for him decorated with brightly colored fish.

"Let's walk down Cannery Row to the restaurant. We can have an early dinner." Chad pointed ahead to the red arch and row of old cannery buildings. "There's a Mexican restaurant there, or we could eat at Bubba Gumps."

"Bubba Gumps!" the girls called out.

"Run Forrest Run!" Joy sang out.

Chad looked at her, and she nodded. "Sounds good to me. I can get Mexican anytime." She chuckled at her little joke, and so did Chad.

Felisa pushed the stroller, and he tucked his arm around her waist as the girls skipped on ahead. Soon a large pink sign greeted them, emblazoned with Bubba Gumps. They left the sidewalk and headed through the parking lot to the weathered-looking grayish blue building with ornate embellishment at the top. Inside, Felisa didn't know which way to look. The movie *Forrest Gump* played on screens all over the restaurant, Forrest's bench sat near the door, and memorabilia adorned the nooks.

"We're between lunch and dinner, so the place isn't packed," Chad said.

"Usually we have to wait."

The hostess greeted them, then led them to a table along a window that captured a panoramic view of Monterey Bay. The girls wanted to be closest to the window, so they shuffled around, allowing Chad to sit nearer Felisa. She liked the arrangement.

"What's that?" Felisa asked, pointing to a bucket with two signs that looked like license plates.

Chad chuckled. "If you want the waitress, you flip it to STOP FORREST STOP. If you don't need service, you put up the RUN FORREST RUN sign." He flipped the sign to STOP FORREST STOP, and in a moment, a waiter came to take their soft drink order.

The novelty made Felisa smile, adding another bit of happiness to her day. She eyed the menu with so many choices. She'd learned to stop worrying about prices. Chad had given her a sweet lecture that she should order what she wanted. She spotted the baby back ribs, and her stomach growled. The girls wanted the Bucket of Trash, a pail filled with all kinds of seafood, probably enough for everyone.

"Let's just order a variety and share," Chad said.

"I love that idea," she said, wanting to try so many things.

When the waiter arrived with their drinks, they placed the order, and the girls asked if they could look out the other large window nearby.

"Don't be gone long," Chad said. "And don't go any farther than right there." He pointed to the open area where they wouldn't be in anyone's way and he could watch them.

The girls agreed and hurried off, leaving Felisa and Chad alone, except for Nate, for the first time that day.

"Thanks for the wonderful trip. You know I've never been to the aquarium. I've never been anyplace really, so this is as much fun for me as it is for the girls."

He scooted closer and wove his fingers through hers. "It's more fun for me, too. I love watching your face glow with excitement. You're so beautiful—inside and out."

"Thank you. The inside is most important to me. You know that."

"I do, and that's why I love you so much."

Love you so much. The words sailed across the space and floated into her thoughts. Did he really love her? She knew he cared. He'd told her she meant so much to him, but love? She managed to smile, afraid he'd think something was wrong.

Chad lifted her hand and kissed her fingers. His lips felt soft and warm, and her chest tightened at his gentle touch. Years ago, when Miguel came near her she cringed, fearing he would backhand her or worse. With Chad, his touch had always been a sweet caress, one that left her feeling safe and cherished.

He shifted to check on the twins, then turned back to her. "I've been wanting to talk with you about something, and I hope you'll say yes."

Her pulse tripped along her arms. "Talk about what?"

"Felisa, you look upset, and I haven't even asked you yet."

"I'm sorry. I'm afraid of hearing bad news."

His eyes filled with tenderness, and the look made her catch her breath.

"I'd like you to go with me to a dinner party." He held up his hand to keep her from responding. "You can think about it, but I'd like you to go with me."

"A dinner party? With your friends?"

"People from the agricultural society. Business people. It's a summer party they throw each year. Dinner, music, conversation."

She saw the urgency in his face, but the impossibility rose above her like a tidal wave. "Chad, I don't fit in with those people. You know how most of them feel about us, and I'm sure the word has spread about who I am. We work in their fields. They don't want to have us during a dinner party."

"Felisa, it's time you forget about the word *us* when you're talking about the fields. *Us* is you and me. That's the only *us* I want to hear. If people get to know you, they won't care anything about that. They'll find you as delightful as I do."

"But—" She grasped for reasons. She needed an excuse. No. No. She loved Chad, but this could never work. "Chad, I—"

"We have to do this sometime, Felisa. I'm not letting you go that easily. You're precious to me. I care about you more than I can say." He flung his arms open in his fervor and nearly collided with a waitress passing by. He gave her a look of apology. "I want people to get to know you. I know it's not easy, but we can't stay hidden from the world."

"It's your world, Chad. Not mine."

He turned and captured both of her arms, forcing her to look at him.

Panic filled her for a moment until she realized his grasp was firm, not bruising.

"It's our world," Chad said. "Our world. I don't want to hear *your world* or *my world*. It's ours."

He looked desperate, and she felt tears sting her eyes. She loved him, and all he'd asked was for her to accompany him to a party. One party. One party for him. "What do they wear?"

Hope filled his eyes, and when he looked down at his hands, he released her arms. "I'm sorry. I hope I didn't hurt you. I didn't mean—"

She gazed into his concerned eyes. "No, you didn't hurt me. You'd never hurt me."

"I know, but—" He waved his hand as if erasing what he'd begun to say, then turned to watch the girls for a moment before turning back. "The men wear suits, and the women wear party dresses."

"Like the one you bought me in Carmel?"

A teasing smile filled his face. "Just like that one."

"And that's why you wanted me to buy it?"

"I had it in mind. I hoped you'd go with me."

How could she say no? She glided her hand over his, her mind filling with his gentle ways, his loving concern for her and Nate. "I'll go with you, Chad. I'd love to go with you."

His mouth curved into a smile.

"I'm not sure about the love-to-go line, but I don't want to go without you, and I know you'll be the most beautiful woman there."

The most beautiful woman there. No man had ever said that to her. The lovely words touched her heart.

Chapter 13

Felisa looked in the mirror a final time before heading into the main part of the house. The silky dress shimmered in the early evening sunlight, the ripple of coral hues making her think of a glorious sunset. Chad had wonderful taste. She loved the way it wrapped around her and swirled at her calves. She gazed at the dressy tan sandals and clasped the clutch bag in her hand. She prayed the night would pass without incident. If she ever wanted to have the kind of love she dreamed of with Chad, she needed to get past this step. She needed to be accepted in his world.

The thought seemed so impossible.

Her legs trembled as she moved toward the hallway door. She shifted back and took another look at herself in the mirror. She'd tamed her hair, and tonight it fell in soft waves around her shoulders. Lacking jewelry, she'd worn the same imitation gold hoops and necklace she'd worn before. She hoped no one noticed it was costume jewelry.

She pulled in a breath and headed down the hallway, hearing the twins talk with the babysitter, a teenager who'd proven herself very competent. Felisa trusted her to watch Nate, also. When she stepped into the family room, the twins hurried to meet her, sliding their hands along the silky fabric of her dress.

"You look like a princess," Joy said, her voice expressing awe.

Faith only looked at her, speechless.

She saw the sitter eyeing her with an approving look.

"She looks like a queen."

Felisa twirled in the direction of Chad's voice and smiled while her heart danced in her chest. "Thank you," she said, smiling at the girls first and then Chad.

He had his hand behind his back, and she watched him as he strode toward her. When he reached her side, he revealed the package he'd hidden.

Felisa's pulse skipped when she saw the black velvet jewelry box. She couldn't move but stood in front of him looking at the box, then searching his face.

"Don't you want to open it?" Faith asked.

Chad gave Faith a crooked grin, then gazed at Felisa. "Do, please." He edged it closer to her and waited.

When she raised her hands to grasp the box, they were trembling, and she struggled to calm herself and hide her disquiet. "What is it?"

"Open it," he said.

The dialogue had captured the babysitter's interest, and she rose, too, to gape at the gift.

Felisa lifted the lid on the box and gasped. "They're beautiful. So perfect." She gazed at the necklace made of beads trimmed in gold with matching drop earrings. The colors amazed her—rust, muted reds, soft yellow, dark browns, and mottled earth tones. "What is this?"

"Minerals and quartz. Jasper, chalcedony, serpentine."

"Wow!" the teenager said, moving closer. "That's awesome."

"But it's too—"

"I thought it would look lovely with your dress."

"It does. It's beautiful."

"Put it on," Joy said, tiptoing to look into the box.

"Let me help." Chad took the box from her and released the necklace.

Felisa lifted her hair, unlatched the gold-toned necklace she'd worn, then felt the cool stones fall against her neckline as Chad's warm fingers latched the clasp. His fingers brushed across her nape; then he captured her shoulder and turned her to face him.

"It's beautiful, Felisa. Look in the mirror." He swung his arm toward the wide mirror in the back foyer.

She moved to the hallway mirror in a decorative frame and gazed at her neck in the glass. The vibrant earth-tone colors glinted against her tanned skin, and the coral in her gown was reflected in the various-shaped stones. She'd never seen anything as unique. "I love it. Thank you."

When she turned toward him, he dangled the matching earrings from his fingers. "I'll let you put these on," he said, striding forward to brush back her hair.

She removed her hoop earrings and felt his touch against her cheek as she attached the jewelry to her pierced earlobes. She turned again to the glass to see the effect. She longed to kiss him for the wonderful gift. Saying thank you didn't seem enough.

"You look lovely," he said, his eyes twinkling.

"Thank you," she said again, dropping her other jewelry into the velvet box and setting it on the lamp table.

He bent to kiss the children. "Ready?" he asked, holding his hand toward her.

She kissed the girls and Nate, then clasped Chad's hand and followed him outside.

A soft evening breeze rustled the smooth fabric against her legs. Her heels tapped along the tiles, and the stones around her neck shifted against her skin like a caress. Chad looked handsome in his dark suit and black tie with a tiny stripe of coral. She suspected he'd selected it to match her dress, and the sweet thought pleased her.

She heard his car keys jingle from his pocket, and his hand touched her arm as he opened the passenger door. She slid inside, making sure the skirt of her dress was safe, and then he closed the door. She breathed in the leathery scent of the sedan, mingled with her subtle perfume.

Chad slipped into the driver's seat and closed the door. He guided the key into the ignition, then turned to her. "You look wonderful, Felisa. If anyone looks at you curiously, remember it's as likely envy as anything. I'm proud to have you as my date tonight."

"I'll try," she said, knowing she'd prayed about it since he'd asked her to go.

He turned the key, and the car hummed.

Evening shadows hung on the mountains, and as they drove, dusk fell over the landscape. Felisa filled her mind with good things—her lovely dress, the perfect jewelry, the man at her side whom she'd begun to love. What would the night hold for her? The Lord had never promised to protect her from all of life's sorrows and hurts. Yet He'd promised to be at her side in times of trouble. That was her prayer.

"Where is the party?" Her voice broke the silence.

"Salinas. The rotunda of the Steinbeck Center. It's named after the writer John Steinbeck, who set many of his books in this area. The center is a great place for special events."

She'd heard of John Steinbeck, but as with most places Chad spoke of, she'd never been to the museum. She didn't bother to mention it. She realized by now Chad knew she had experienced so little in her lifetime.

&

Chad nosed the car down Main Street in Old Town Salinas and parked in the Steinbeck Center parking area. He climbed out and assisted Felisa from the car with his heart racing. She looked unbelievable; yet tension knotted his shoulders. He knew he'd stepped out of the boundaries of what society expected, but they didn't know the woman as he did. He'd wanted so often to talk with Dallas. They'd always been the best of friends, but he'd been afraid. What if Dallas advised him to forget Felisa? What if. . . ? He shook his head. Tonight he would put the problem in the Lord's hands. He tilted his head toward the glittering dark blue sky and sent up a silent prayer. *Lord, I put my trust in You.*

He slipped his arm around Felisa's back and guided her into the rotunda. Music greeted them as they entered, and he looked at the guest list and saw the number of his table. When he spotted it, Chad noticed that Brook and Colleen Garner were seated there, too. He cringed with the memory of their last meeting.

He guided Felisa to her chair and felt all eyes on him. "Hello, everyone. I'd like you to meet Felisa Carrillo."

She gave a silent nod and settled into the chair he held for her. "Felisa, you met Brook at the Barnyard after dinner, but I don't think you met Colleen."

Colleen gave a slight arch to her brow and said hello.

Chad finished the introductions, then pulled out his own chair and sat. The conversation seemed strained, but Chad wondered if it was his own tension and not the others'. He wanted to protect Felisa from rude comments, and he hoped no one made any.

The waiter arrived, and he gave their orders, then leaned back, listening to the conversation and inserting comments of his own; but he kept one hand encircling Felisa's. Once in a while he gave it a squeeze, hoping to assure her.

Chad heard his name and pivoted to see his friend Dallas approaching the table. Chad's pulse skipped. Then his spirit soared when he saw the grin on Dallas's face as he eyed Felisa.

He gave Chad a sly look as they shook hands, then turned to Felisa and extended his arm. "I'm Chad's good friend, Dallas Jones."

"This is Felisa Carrillo," Chad said, sorry he hadn't spoken with Dallas sooner.

"Nice to meet you, Felisa." He gave Chad a wink. "At least I thought we were good friends, but he's been noticeably absent. Where have you been?"

Chad winced at his friend's reminder that he had been preoccupied. "Working too hard, I guess. We need to get together. I'll give you a call. How about lunch?"

"Lunch sounds good. Call me tomorrow." Dallas gave him a knowing look, but beneath it, Chad spotted a smile.

"I will. Scout's honor."

"I hope to see you again, Felisa." He grasped Chad's arm and gave it a friendly shake. "Talk with you soon." He bent closer to Chad's ear. "I can't wait to hear how this happened, Romeo."

The waiter cut in, and Chad could only grin at Dallas before he left. But Chad had a good feeling and realized not everyone would condemn him for falling in love with this wonderful woman.

The waiter placed their sparkling water with a twist of lemon beside their plates and moved on with drinks for the others.

Colleen sipped from her fluted glass, and when she put it down she turned her gaze to Chad and then focused on Felisa. "The dress is a lovely color."

"Thank you," Felisa said, her eyes seeking Chad.

"She looks like one of our gorgeous sunsets," Chad said.

"I'm surprised we've never met before," Colleen continued. "How did you and Chad meet?"

He felt Felisa's fingers twitch, and he sensed her panic.

"She is the girls' nanny," Chad said. "They adore her."

"Nanny?" More than one voice responded.

"Yes." He shifted his gaze to Felisa and gave her a smile, hoping that ended the comments.

"But I thought you had an older woman caring for the girls. She wasn't—"

"Mrs. Drake left my employ awhile ago. The girls weren't doing well with her, and I think she was frustrated. Felisa has a way with the twins."

"I bet she has," Brook said. He gave Chad a pleasant nod, but his innuendo couldn't be ignored.

Chad swallowed his irritation and, not wanting to make an issue out of Brook's insinuation, lifted his glass and took a lengthy drink of water. As he did, the music softened, and a sound came from the microphone. To Chad's relief the talk lulled when the president of the association gave his welcome. When he finished, the conversation began again with no other comments.

Felisa seemed to relax, and Chad heard her talking about the twins to the woman next to her. He pushed aside his worries. Other members of the association stopped by to greet them, and he introduced Felisa to pleasant smiles and a few arched brows; but nothing was said, and he thanked the Lord.

The meal passed without incident, and Chad took a deep breath. Things had gone well so far. He'd noticed two of the women at the table responding to Felisa with smiles, and he hadn't missed a couple of the men admiring her. He gave them credit for excellent taste.

Before dessert, Felisa leaned close to his ear and whispered, "I'd like to use the restroom. Which way is it?"

He pointed the way, then rose to pull out her chair. Her dress glimmered when she walked away, carrying her clutch bag. The necklace and earrings he'd given her set off the deep color of her skin and the hues of her gown. She mesmerized him. He tried to hide his grin when he sat down again.

"She's a beautiful woman," Jim Brody said in his ear. "Is she Mexican?"

He gave the man a direct look. "Yes."

The man squirmed in his chair. "Does that bother you? You have Mexicans working in your fields."

Chad noticed the discomfort of the others at the table. "Felisa doesn't work there."

"I know, but—"

Chad held up his hand and scanned the table. "Let's get this out in the open. Felisa's family is from Guadalajara. I hired her as a housekeeper, and before I knew it the twins had fallen in love with her."

"And what about the twins' father?" Colleen gave him a teasing wink.

"That came later," he said, managing a smile. "Since you're all so curious, let me just give you the facts. When Mrs. Drake left, it made sense to ask Felisa to take over the nanny position."

Jim's wife, Della, leaned forward. "She said she has an infant. A boy."

Chad's chest tightened with the pride of a father. "Yes, Felisa's husband died before he knew about the baby. Life has been difficult for her. She needed work, and it all fit together. He's a beautiful little boy."

"A little muchacho, huh?" Brook said as he rose. He rounded the table and squeezed Chad's arm as he leaned down and whispered, "Any of the features look like yours?"

Chad's hands rolled into fists, but he controlled his frustration. "Not one bit. Sorry to disappoint you, Brook."

The man released Chad's arm and vanished behind him. The others watched him leave with uneasy gazes and then returned their focus on Chad.

"What should we make of this?" Jim asked, flashing two arched brows.

"It looks serious to me," Colleen said, a conspiring look settling on her face. "I think we're witnessing a little romance."

Chad only grinned and didn't respond. The conversation drifted to other topics, and he was pleased they hadn't asked questions while Felisa was present. His feelings and the situation were out in the open now, and most everyone seemed to understand except Brook. Chad scanned the room, looking for him, but he was nowhere in sight.

He felt edgy, wondering if Felisa had gotten lost. The feeling was foolish, he knew. Women often took a long time freshening up, and he realized Felisa was nervous as well. He turned and watched the doorway. If she didn't return shortly, he would go looking for her.

⁂

Felisa washed her hands and opened her bag. She located her lipstick and glided it across her mouth, then blotted it on a tissue. She continued to admire the necklace and earrings Chad had given her. She'd never received such a lovely gift. Then, having second thoughts, she recalled the gown she wore and the pants and jacket. Those were gifts, too, despite Chad's insistence they were part of a bonus.

Chad felt sorry for her. She could try to pretend it wasn't so, but she knew better. At times she felt sorry for herself, but when she did she pushed it far back in her mind and covered it with God's blessings. Chad's sympathy didn't undermine his feelings. He cared about her, too. She accepted that from the look in his eyes, his tender caresses, and his loving words. She couldn't ask for a better gift.

She dropped the lipstick into her handbag and pulled out her comb, caught a few straggly edges, and pushed them back into place. She replaced the comb, then stood back again. *Thank You, Lord. Thank You for tonight and for the past months. You know I love him, and it's in Your hands.*

The restroom door opened as a woman entered. They smiled at each other, and Felisa drew up her shoulders and caught the door before it closed. As soon as her foot hit the hallway, she saw Brook standing close to the men's room door. Fear skittered up her back. He appeared to be waiting for someone, and she prayed it wasn't her.

She gave him a faint smile as she tried to pass, but his hand clamped on her arm and pulled her back.

"What do you want?" she asked, feeling her heart pounding in her chest.

"Talk," he said.

"Talk? About what?"

109

"You. . .and me."

She shook her head. What did he mean? Thoughts swirled through her mind. "I'm not interested in changing jobs, Mr.—" She'd forgotten his last name.

He grinned and pulled her against his chest. "I'm not offering you a job, but maybe you'd like a few more pretty little trinkets like these."

He dragged his finger across her necklace, leaving her flesh prickling with fear.

"What do you say?" he asked.

"Please let me go."

She heard the desperation in her voice, but he only laughed.

"Chad Garrison will toss you to the hounds when he's through with you. Don't you know that?"

She cringed at his insinuation. "Chad is a good Christian man. He's kind. Please don't suggest that—"

"Look here, pretty lady. I can be kind, too."

She jerked away from him, but he lashed out for her again. She dodged his hand and raced down the hallway. She couldn't go back inside. She had to get away.

Felisa turned from the reception area and out the front door. Fear tore through her, and she looked over her shoulder to see if he might be following her. Her heels clattered on the concrete sidewalk, and she headed down Main Street, wondering what she would do now. Chad would be worried, but she couldn't go back.

At the cross street, Felisa paused, gasping for breath. She wanted to go home. She opened her handbag and looked inside. She had a few dollars in her purse. Should she take a taxi or try to call Juanita? She didn't know what to do.

⁂

Chad's neck ached from twisting toward the door. "Excuse me," he said. "I think Felisa may have gotten lost." He rose and headed toward the outside lobby.

As he stepped through the door he ran into Brook, his face twisted into a scowl, his skin flushed. Brook appeared upset, and his earlier comments about Felisa struck Chad's mind while a warning light triggered in his head.

"Where's Felisa?"

Brook shrugged and tried to pass him.

"Where's Felisa? What have you done?"

"Nothing, man. What's up with you?"

"You said something to her." He imagined the confrontation. "What did you say to her?"

"Neither of you can take a joke."

Chad grasped Brook's arm. "Where is she? What did you do?"

"It was a joke. I offered her a job at my house."

Chad pushed Brook against the wall. "It's time you learned how to treat people with respect, Brook. Would you like someone to make snide comments to your wife? I know Felisa is Hispanic. No one knows that better than I, and you know why? Because she's afraid of people's prejudice. I'm tired of it. Everyone deserves respect. Even you, though it's hard to give it to you when you disrespect others. Felisa's a beautiful woman, inside and out. I've never come on to her. Not even kissed her, though I'm dying to."

Brook drew back, his face filled with disbelief. "Are you serious? You haven't kissed her?"

"That's right."

"Why not?"

Chad's stomach churned. "You disgust me. Because I respect her." He looked at him nose to nose. "Where did she go?"

"I don't know. She left."

"Left?"

"Outside. She ran outside."

Chad's hand dropped from Brook's arm, and he spun around, then raced out the door. What did she plan to do? Where would she go? He halted the questions. She wanted to get away. He hurried to the car, then faltered, his chest aching. She wasn't there. He'd wasted time. He raced back to Main Street and down the sidewalk. "Felisa!" His voice tore through the darkness. He squinted into the dimly lit night. "Felisa!"

Beneath a streetlamp, he saw a flicker of color. His heart hammered as he darted toward it. "Felisa!"

The color stopped and turned toward him. He opened his arms, and Felisa rushed into them.

"It's okay," he said, pressing her head against his shoulder. "You're okay now. I'm so sorry. I'm so sorry."

Her sobs were muffled against his suit jacket. He had never seen her cry this hard before and didn't try to stop her. "I love you, Felisa." The words rolled from his lips like sweet music. Tonight he wanted the whole world to know.

She raised her head, the sound of her sobs diminishing. "I love you, too," she said. "I don't care what people think. I love you."

He drew her into his arms and kissed the salty tears from her cheeks. Her eyes glinted in the light of the streetlamp, and he knew she was speaking with her heart. Later he would tell her that most everyone had teased him about his feelings for her. Eventually everyone would love her just as he did.

Chad captured her lovely face in his hands. He kissed her forehead and the tip of her nose, and when she tilted her mouth upward, he took it as acceptance. He lowered his mouth to hers, tasting of tears, sweet lipstick, and love. *Thank You, Lord. Thank You for this amazing woman.*

Chapter 14

Ten Months Later

Felisa stood with her arms wrapped around her sister. "Estella, I can't believe it's happening," she said in Spanish.

"I am so happy for you." Her sister gave her a big hug and backed away, tears brimming her eyes. "I don't want to wrinkle your dress."

Felisa shook her head. "The dress isn't as important as you are. I'm so happy you could come here to be my matron of honor."

"I could never have come if Chad hadn't bought my ticket. I'm grateful to him. He's a good man, Felisa. I'm so happy for you."

"Thank you, dearest sister." She brushed tears from her eyes. "I wish Mamá and Papá could be here."

"They would never come so far, but they send their love."

Felisa drew in a lengthy breath. "Will you help me with the mantilla?" She lifted the lacy Spanish veil and handed it to her sister.

Estella fixed it to her hair with combs and arranged it around her shoulders. "You look so beautiful, Felisa."

"Today I feel beautiful." She touched the lovely lace mantilla her mother had sent and lifted her bouquet attached to a delicate fan. She couldn't thank Chad enough for encouraging her to add her Mexican traditions to the wedding. "Is it time?"

"Let me check," Estella said, heading for the door. "You can't see the groom until you come down the aisle." She opened the door a narrow width and slipped out.

Felisa leaned against the wall, reliving the past ten months since Chad had said the most beautiful words in the world—"I love you"—and she'd said them back. She'd opened her heart and let the truth find freedom.

When she'd told Chad the whole story of Brook's sexual harassment, Chad had been furious, but they'd prayed before he confronted Brook about his horrible behavior. When it was over, she and Chad had agreed to put it behind them and pray for Brook instead.

Felisa was so grateful to Juanita, who'd become a good friend, almost like another mother. Today she would sit near the front of the church with Nate, her sweet son who'd grown into such an amazing, smart one-year-old. Once in a while Nate chattered a sound she liked to think was *mama*, but he'd begun to say *dada*, mimicking the girls calling Chad daddy. Not one ounce of envy had entered her thoughts, and she was thrilled for Chad that he'd gained his little son after so much sorrow.

A soft knock sounded on the door, and she clamped her hand over the knob. "Who is it?"

"It's me," her sister said.

"Come in." She scooted out of the way of the door, and Estella ducked inside. "It's time. The girls are so excited. They want to come in and kiss you."

"Let them in," she said, overjoyed at the thought that she would be their mother after today.

Estella opened the door a few inches, and the girls hurried inside, giggling, their pink lace dresses billowing around their knees.

"You both look so pretty," Felisa said, bending down to give them each a hug and a kiss.

"Can we call you Mommy now?" Joy asked.

"I would love that," she said, giving the child's hand a squeeze.

"We love you, Mommy," Faith said.

"I love both of you with all my heart." She forced back the tears. "Now we'd better get out there so I can be your official mommy."

They giggled and hurried out the door with Estella behind them. As Felisa stepped into the hallway and closed the door, her chest filled with joy when she heard the mariachis begin. The wonderful sound of the trumpet, drums, and guitar made her feel at home. The men stood in front at the side, their blue shirts and colorful vests contrasting with the cascades of white roses. She looked ahead of her at the carpet strewn with rose petals, and as she gazed down the aisle she saw Chad and his best man, Dallas Jones, enter from the side.

She watched her sister, then the girls, move down the aisle sprinkling petals, and as the music swelled she took her first step, her eyes only on Chad, whose face glowed with more love than she had ever known.

~

Chad focused on the aisle, grinning at his beautiful daughters so excited to have a new mother, and then at Juanita holding Nate, who wriggled in her arms to get down. Hearing the boy say *Dada* had captured his heart a hundredfold. Though he wasn't the child's biological father, he would be his father in every other way.

His gaze shifted back to the aisle, and when Felisa stepped onto the carpet of flower petals, his heart swelled until he thought it would burst. The mariachi music filled the room and seemed so right. He'd been grateful to learn the other Mexican wedding traditions so he could please Felisa and let the world know he loved this woman no matter where she was born. God had orchestrated their meeting. He'd sensed it the day he met her.

Felisa seemed to float down the aisle in her cream-colored dress with only a single ruffle at the bottom. Her mantilla was held in place by an ornate comb, and she carried a fan adorned with white roses. She'd become his flower, a woman who'd also encouraged him to bloom into the man he was supposed to be.

She reached him, and he took her hands in his for the prayer. Then the pastor brought out thirteen gold coins and spoke. "These coins represent the twelve apostles and Christ. They symbolize Chad's unquestioning trust and confidence in Felisa. When Chad places the coins in Felisa's hands, it is a pledge that all of his goods are placed in her care and safekeeping. Felisa, when you accept these coins, it means you take them with trust and confidence. You accept them unconditionally with total devotion and discretion."

The pastor handed Chad the coins in his cupped hand, and he spilled them into Felisa's. He handed Chad a wooden box, and Felisa put the coins into it and passed it to her sister.

The pastor began, "Chad, do you promise to. . ."

The wonderful words of the marriage ceremony filled Chad's mind and heart as he and Felisa each said, "I do." After the vows, Dallas and Estella bound them together with a cord entwined with orange blossoms.

"This floral lasso is a symbol of fertility and happiness. This loop symbolizes the love that binds you together as you share equally in the responsibility of marriage for the rest of your lives. You are bound together with the Lord as we read in Ecclesiastes 4:12: 'A cord of three strands is not quickly broken.'"

Felisa leaned close to Chad's ear. "God has given us His unfailing love, and forever we will put our trust in Him."

"Forever," he promised her.

Estella and Dallas removed the floral lasso, and the pastor's serious face broke into a smile. "You will now kiss your bride."

Chad gazed at Felisa with misted eyes, his heart singing praise to God. He drew her into his arms, his lips against hers, warm and gentle as a summer breeze. "I love you," he whispered.

"Te amo," she answered.

Her eyes glistened with tears as she stooped to take the twins into her embrace. Chad hurried forward for Nate, the son he'd always wanted and the little boy he loved as his own. When he returned to them with Nate in his arms, he felt total completeness. "My family," he whispered, his eyes blurred with his love. "Thank You, Lord."

Garlic & Roses

Dedication

To Bob, who makes everything fall into place when things seem to be falling apart. A husband who brings me bouquets just because he loves me.

Chapter 1

"Will that be all?" Juliana Maretti asked from behind the checkout counter, her eye on the clock. She smiled at the couple gazing around the store, their mouths agape. The camera around the gentleman's neck validated her guess that they were tourists.

"What about those braided garlic bunches?" The woman pointed to the display. "How long will they last?"

"Months. Just let them hang in a dry place. Don't refrigerate them."

The woman studied the display for a moment then turned back to Juli. "We'll take one of those." She motioned to her husband, who headed for the display and brought a braid back to the counter.

She took it from him and held it in the air, tilting her head like a woman deciding which dress to purchase.

Juli managed not to tap her fingernails against the counter. She had paperwork to do and some orders to check before she could leave.

"Maybe we should buy two," the woman said, turning to her husband. "Do you think Mama would like one? She uses a lot of garlic in her cooking." She turned from her husband back to Juli. "She's Italian."

"So am I." Juli nodded then glanced at her watch again, wondering how much longer before she could get on with her work. That was the problem of managing a store. When an ailing clerk left, the manager took over until a replacement arrived. "Italians like their garlic, but then, so do many people." She motioned in a wide span toward the products filling the store. "We sell many garlic products—useful items and gourmet foods. I'm sure your mother will enjoy a practical gift like the braid."

The woman gestured toward the display, and her husband stepped across the aisle to grab another one while Juli totaled the sale. She bagged the produce, made change, and thanked them as they stepped away.

Some days seemed to drag on endlessly. Juli wondered what it would be like to love a job so much that the time flew. If she had a dream, that would be it. She eyed her watch again and released a sigh. Two hours to go and she still had her own work to do, and today she needed to leave early. She turned toward the door. Donna had promised to come in as soon as she could. So where was she?

Customers ambled through her father's store. The Garlic Garden brought in many customers each day, especially in the summer when tourists visited Gilroy.

"Juliana."

Juli turned toward the voice and eyed the woman's face, which looked uncomfortably familiar. "Can I help you?" She scrutinized the features, realizing she should know her.

"You don't remember me?"

The woman moved closer, and beneath the makeup and salon-induced blond hair, Juli recognized her, a girl from her graduating class. "Melanie."

"How could you forget?"

The barb in her voice dug deep. Juli ignored the question. "How are you?"

"Great." Her gaze did a slow scan of her father's store. "I see you're the same."

Another dig. "I'm glad you're doing well. What brings you here?"

"A sorority friend from out of town. She wanted to see the infamous garlic kingdom." Her lilting laugh had a biting edge as she waved across the room to an attractive young woman browsing through the garlic sauces.

Sorority friend. Juli not only had no sorority sister, but she had never gone to college. Instead she'd stayed home to manage her father's store, and her brother had earned his degree. Her father's old-world attitude butted against Juli's, but she believed in honoring her father and mother. The memory knifed her once again, leaving a reopened wound. "Nice of you to show her the town."

Juli peered at the growing line at the checkout. She looked over her shoulder. "Sandra, would you give Donna another call, please?" She eyed Melanie and motioned toward the customers. "Sorry. I need to wait on these people."

Melanie arched her eyebrow and shifted away.

Juli waited on the next customer while battling her desire to check on Melanie and her friend. Melanie had brought back bad memories of her senior year when she and Juli were both running for Gilroy High Garlic Queen. The incident pried out memories that hurt, and Juli struggled to push them from her mind.

"Thank you," she said, handing the customer his change.

The man smiled and moved off while she waited on another. When she'd finished, Melanie's overly friendly voice penetrated her thoughts. "Roxy, this is Juliana, the one I told you about."

Roxy eyed Juli and snickered. "You mean the garlic and roses bouquet?"

Melanie sent her a look as if warning her not to say any more, but the damage had been done. Juli knew the bouquet had been a mean prank played on her long ago, and she suspected Melanie had been behind the incident even though she came through it unscathed.

Juli managed to grin. "Yes. Garlic and roses. It was unique." Juli tried to keep her voice lighthearted. "Will this be it?"

"That's it." Roxy dug into her handbag while Juli rang up the items.

She ran the credit card and returned it to the woman along with her purchases. "I hope you enjoy your visit."

"It's been fun, but I don't know how you can live with this smell."

"Ask Melanie. She's apparently still in the area. It grows on you." Juli watched a flash of anger in Melanie's eyes and wanted to chalk up one notch for herself, but she knew it was wrong to hurt people. As the two women walked away, Juli looked heavenward, asking God to forgive her dig to Melanie. She knew better than to let the old situation get under her skin again.

Back in high school she and Melanie had been nominated for Gilroy High Garlic Queen in their senior year. Besides being queen of the senior events, the honor included participating in the garlic festival at the end of July. Melanie's competition with Juli had been fierce, and Juli never understood why. Melanie was pretty and very popular with okay grades. Though Juli had good grades, she wasn't popular. In fact, the popular kids considered her a nerd. While Melanie's father had a lucrative business, Juli's father's business had just become so, and the businesses were different. Juli had struggled with the question of how she'd even been nominated until she thought she'd finally learned the answer.

She let her thoughts dwindle and concentrated on the customers, and after Donna arrived, Juli focused on her paperwork and checked the orders. When the hour hand finally moved to four, Juli gave final instructions to her replacement manager, said good-bye to her coworkers, and scooted out the door. The drive to Seaside near Monterey would take her awhile in the heavy traffic, and she liked to arrive at the soup kitchen on time even if it was only a volunteer job.

❧

Juli found a parking spot behind the building and dug into her shoulder bag for a scrunchie. She pulled the soft fabric-covered elastic from the bottom of her bag and tied her hair into a ponytail. After locking the car, she hurried into the back door of the soup kitchen, knowing she had arrived late.

A mixture of smells met her at the door: tomatoes, beef, and the familiar scent of garlic. She eyed a large pot of beef and tomatoes stewing on the burner, elbow macaroni bubbling on another burner—goulash, she noted—and bowls of peaches lined up on trays.

"Sorry," Juli said, waving to a couple of volunteers she knew. "You know the traffic."

She darted past them to the storage area, stuffed her purse inside, and tied on the standard bib apron then checked the task chart. Her assignment: cookies. On the way to her station, Juli grabbed a pair of the plastic gloves sitting everywhere in boxes. One thing the soup kitchen demanded was cleanliness. She pulled out a carton of chocolate chip cookies and tugged on the stubborn lid.

"Juli."

She looked up as Bill Montego stepped to her side.

He tilted his head toward the dining room. "We have a big crowd waiting outside. It looks like we'll have a passel of people tonight. The doors open in twenty minutes."

"I'm on it," she said, pulling the carton closer, determined to pry open the lid without help.

Bill beckoned to someone behind her. "This is Alan, a new volunteer. Could you show him the ropes?"

"Sure thing." She glanced over her shoulder and looked into the most beautiful dusky lilac blue eyes she'd ever seen.

"I hope you don't mind," Alan said. "What can I do to help?" He motioned to the carton she'd been trying to open.

"Glad you've decided to join us. We can always use help." She stopped attacking the lid. "I'm Juli Maretti." She nodded toward the gloves lying beside her. "You need to be sterilized." She grinned and pointed to the glove box. "You can get yours over there."

He followed her directions and strode to the box of gloves. When he turned back, he waved them in the air, his warm smile sparkling. "I'm Alan Louden, by the way. If you're my boss, we need to be properly introduced."

She loved his lightheartedness. Realizing she was fighting an unending battle, she slid the carton in front of him. "Maybe you can do this."

He pried the lid open in the blink of an eye then slipped his hands into plastic gloves. Together they began unpacking the cookies and setting them onto trays.

In the monotony of the task, she wanted to talk, but she felt tongue-tied as she so often did when it came to socializing with men her age. Her dating experience had been basically nil.

Alan grasped a handful of cookies and paused. "How long have you been volunteering here?"

His voice broke through the silence and surprised her. "A year or more," she said, wishing she didn't feel so jumpy when she looked into his gorgeous eyes and friendly smile.

He removed the filled tray and replaced it with an empty one. "Are you from Seaside?"

She hated to say she was from Gilroy. It was the same old line—"You live in the garlic capital of the world" or some such comment. She couldn't bear any more Gilroy jokes. "A friend of mine lives in Monterey and dragged me here to be her moral support. Then she quit coming, but I was hooked."

"Good for you." His smile radiated to her heart. "Too many people take their good fortune for granted."

She liked the sound of his voice—a rich baritone with a hint of good humor. Most of all she liked what he'd just said. "You're right. People grumble about so many things when they have so much. Spending a few days in a soup kitchen would be a lesson in being thankful."

He patted her arm. "I like you," he said. "You're smart." He lifted the same hand with a chuckle. "But I'm not." He peeled off the plastic glove and reached into the box for a fresh one.

She chuckled at his blunder. "I think most of the volunteers here agree with you. They're giving from the heart."

He gave her a concurring nod and dug back into the carton for more cookies.

By the time they'd filled the trays, Bill flagged them into the dining room to help serve. As Juli dished out food, she thought about Bill's asking her to train Alan. He could have asked so many others, but he'd asked her, and it pleased Juli. She liked volunteering, and she liked Alan. Juli's work at the soup kitchen was fulfilling, and the time flew by, the way she wished her real job did.

Pulling her mind free, Juli concentrated on serving those in line. The next woman holding out her tray was one of Juli's favorites, and she sent the woman a smile. "How are you?"

The older woman shrugged with sad eyes. "Not so good today."

Juli noticed how worn and tired she looked and made a mental note to speak with her later. She made it a point to talk with those who appeared to need someone to listen.

Alan shifted beside her. "You seem to know a lot of these people."

Juli nodded. "They come back week after week. Sometimes it's hard to remember they may be down and out, but they're people just like you and me." She turned to face him and saw the seriousness in his eyes. "There but for the grace of God go I. I think of that phrase every time I work here. God's been good to my family, but it's due to His grace and nothing more."

Alan's expression darkened.

She searched his eyes for a moment, wondering if maybe he didn't believe in the Lord. Being a Christian wasn't a prerequisite for volunteering, but many of the volunteers were believers.

With the question niggling her, she focused on the line, trying to smile and talk with the homeless men and women she'd seen there so often, but despite her efforts her mind tangled with thoughts about Alan. When he wasn't on her mind, she thought back to her edgy meeting with Melanie earlier in the day. Why had Melanie found it necessary to mention the garlic and rose bouquet? That had been so hurtful, and yet what did it matter now? At the time she'd thought she had been the brunt of a class joke when the school voted her the Gilroy High Garlic Queen. The honor always went to the most beautiful and most popular. Melanie was popular and should have won hands down.

But after the event she'd learned the truth. She'd won mainly because of the underclassmen. They were apparently tired of Melanie's belittling comments. But still, something else had happened. Juli could only guess that when Melanie suspected she wouldn't win, she'd had her friends vote for Juli, too, to ensure she became the garlic queen so they could make a joke out of the situation. Juli recalled this had happened another time before she entered high school. Teenagers could be terribly mean at times.

"You just put goulash on top of her salad." Alan's voice jolted her.

Juli looked at the woman's plate and released a sigh. "Sorry." She reached out and took the dish, returned to the food stations, and refilled the woman's choices, adding a little extra to make up for her absentmindedness.

When she returned the plate, the woman eyed the portion and gave her a broad, missing-tooth smile. "Thank you," she said.

Juli grinned back. "You're welcome."

From her expression Juli guessed the woman hoped she would make the same mistake next week.

Alan leaned closer. "That was a kind thing you did. She'll remember that always."

"The goulash on her salad?"

His eyes looked unexpectedly serious. "You know what I mean."

Though she wondered about his comment, she grasped the ladle and doled out the goulash, forcing her mind to stick to her work.

&

As the crowd wandered back outside, Alan invited those left to have seconds, but he couldn't keep Juli from his mind. He'd been watching her stop to speak with some of the diners. He could tell she wasn't patronizing. She really listened to them, even patting their hands and giving a few hugs. He hadn't recalled ever seeing that kind of personal attention given at soup kitchens, and Juli's action touched him. When the people left, they seemed to be holding their heads higher and walking with a lighter step. Alan wanted to listen to what she said and learn from her example.

After leaving the serving counter, Juli had untied her ponytail, and now her dark curly hair hung in long kinks a little below her shoulders. He loved the wispy ends that seemed to have a mind of their own. He wondered if Juli had the same kind of stubborn independence. Her deep brown eyes flashed as she talked, and her warm smile tugged at his heart.

Alan glanced at his watch. Weariness had settled over him. He'd worked a twelve-hour day at the hospital, and standing on his feet the past three hours had added stress to his already aching back. Since the hall held only a few last-minute diners, he knew he could leave, but lifting his shoulders for a second breath, he devised a plan. Instead of slipping away, he rolled out the trash can to help clear the tables and wipe them down.

While cleaning tables, Alan studied Juli as she gave a tender pat to another homeless man who rose to leave. Alan waited until the man had stepped away before he pulled the trash can closer to her and stopped. "You amaze me."

Her eyes widened. "Really?"

"You do."

The wide-eyed look changed to a curious frown. "Why?"

Alan gestured toward the last people walking through the door. "You're so. . .so relaxed with these people even though so many are scraggy-looking. You seem to send them away with something special."

"Food for the stomach and food for the soul. I send them away with hope."

"Hope?" The word sank into his thoughts. These people needed so many things, and hope was definitely one of them. "That's a good thing."

"Especially for the people who have so little. Have you ever listened to their stories?"

He'd known only one story—his own. "No."

"Next time talk to them and listen. Anyone with compassion, and I think you have it, will want to do whatever they can to lift their spirits."

Guilt gnawed at Alan's usually well-fed stomach. Though he'd often been able to show he had compassion for the sick, he hadn't extended it here today and had the same problem at the hospital. "I will."

She joined him in tossing paper plates and napkins into the trash. "These people aren't all druggies and drunks. Some of them have other problems—serious family situations and no place to turn."

Alan nodded, knowing the truth in her statement. Juli had captured his interest. Whether it was her spirit, her faith that seemed so evident, or the good humor he'd seen, he wasn't sure, but he wanted to know her better.

He left her filling the trash can and went into the kitchen for a bucket of water and a cloth to wipe down the tables. Other workers were packing leftovers and cleaning the kitchen while some were pushing large brooms along the floor. People pitched in, he noticed. Nothing was too lowly for any of them. Good hearts, he thought.

Alan wiped down the final table, scanned the room, and dropped the cloth into the bucket then headed to the kitchen storage closet. When he disposed of the equipment, he turned and saw Juli draping her purse over her shoulder. "Looks like we're finished," he said.

"We had a big crowd tonight. Usually we're done sooner." She took a few steps then stopped. "By the way, it was nice meeting you."

Alan felt his stomach rumble as he searched her eyes. "Do you have time for coffee? I noticed a diner up the road."

She looked at her watch then lifted her tired eyes to his. "I'd love to, but it's getting late, and I have a long drive home."

He felt deflated. "I understand. Maybe another time." He stuck out his hand. "Thanks for showing me around tonight. I appreciate it."

"You're welcome," she said, grasping his hand in an amiable shake.

Her hand felt small in his, and the warmth rolled up his arm. He wished she had agreed to stop for coffee. His disappointment multiplied that she hadn't said maybe next time. Despite his letdown, he wouldn't give up. Trying to get to know someone here would be difficult. They had little time to talk about important things.

"I'll walk you out." He pulled the apron over his head and hung it on a hook.

"Thanks."

She moved into step with him, and he pushed open the door to the pleasant spring air.

Juli pointed. "I'm parked over there."

He walked beside her, wanting to talk but not knowing what to say.

When she stopped beside a small sedan, he finally found his voice. "I hope I'll see you next week."

"You'll be back?"

He heard the quiet beep when she hit the remote. "I want to spread a little of that hope you're so good at sharing."

"That's great," she said, opening the car door. She paused a moment then turned toward him. "By the way, Saturday is 'Dining Out, Helping Out' day. Some of the volunteers meet at Crazy Horse Restaurant to support the Monterey Food Bank. The restaurant's in the Park Hotel."

"I know the place."

Her eyes brightened. "Good, and 10 percent of the profits go to help the hungry, in case you didn't know."

"I know about the charity. A number of restaurants in the area donate some of their proceeds."

She nodded. "I've been to Big Joe's in Salinas. It's closer to me, but since this is central for the volunteers, we usually meet in Monterey." She sent him an amazing smile. "I'll be there about six. Come, and we can talk then. If not, I'll see you next Wednesday."

"I'll check my calendar." Her smile warmed him, and he hoped he could see her Saturday. He watched her settle into the car and start the engine before he dragged himself away, hungry and tired but feeling uplifted.

❧

Juli tried to keep up with the conversation at the Crazy Horse Restaurant. She'd been certain Alan would show up. Wondering why he hadn't come, she only half-listened to the conversation, trying to laugh at the right times and respond when it was appropriate.

The waiting rattled her. It seemed too much like her youth when she waited for someone to ask her to the sophomore party or the junior dinner. When she'd about given up waiting to be asked, someone—usually someone who'd been refused by numerous others—finally appeared with an invitation. By then she wanted to say no, but she'd always been taught not to "cut off her nose to spite her face," so she accepted the date.

She had some friends but no real boyfriends—just pals. She knew why. She'd never been allowed to wear jeans and the revealing tops the girls wore. Her dad insisted she wear loose-fitting clothing and sturdy shoes. She felt as if she'd come over from Italy in steerage rather than being a modern-day teen. He thought he was following God's Word and reminded her of 1 Peter 3:3: "Whose adorning let it not be that outward adorning of plaiting the hair, and of wearing of gold, or of putting on of apparel." He stressed modesty, but she felt so out of place in school. That was seven years ago, though. *Let it go, Juli.*

"What's happening?"

Juli turned and looked into a pair of brown eyes. "Nothing much." She'd seen the new volunteer before, but his name escaped her.

"Your watch seems better company than we are."

She clasped her palm over her watch and slipped her hands to her lap. "Sorry. I have a long drive home." She cringed hearing her comment. It was the truth, but it had nothing to do with her checking the time.

He gave her a little nudge. "Waiting for someone?"

She realized he was flirting with her, and she tried to smile. "A friend mentioned stopping by. We didn't set real plans."

"Good," he said, sliding his chair closer. "Did anyone ever tell you that you have a great smile?"

Here he goes. She shrugged, trying to find a good way to respond. "My dentist."

His expectant look opened to laughter. "That's a great one. I'll have to remember that."

She pulled her hands from beneath the table, taking another moment to glance at her watch.

He leaned in. "I've noticed you on Wednesdays. I love your hair and your smile, but you're quiet. You seem all business. You sort of give people the cold shoulder."

You seem all business. The cold shoulder. A light went on in Juli's head. Had she chased away young men with her quiet, businesslike way? Maybe she seemed aloof. She knew that could be a defense mechanism to avoid rejection. The possibility startled her. "The soup kitchen is serious business. I try to focus on the people who need help. It's what I feel is important."

His hand moved closer to hers, and he brushed the back of it with his finger. "I'm not criticizing. Focusing on people is a worthy purpose."

She looked at him, wondering if he was being sincere or just flirting.

"I choose to focus on you, Juli." He gave her a wink.

That answered her question. She felt uncomfortable with the man and even more not knowing his name. "Sorry, but I don't know your name."

He brushed his finger against her arm. "I know yours."

"I know mine, too." She grinned, surprised the comment gave her a chuckle. "But I don't know yours."

"Dill. Short for Dillon."

She extended her hand. "Dill it is. I like to know the volunteers."

"I'd like to know you." He took her hand and didn't let go.

Trying to ease her fingers from his, an uneasy sensation rolled over her. She turned in time to see Alan with his back to the dining room heading toward the exit. Before she could move, he'd disappeared.

"Excuse me a minute," she said, jerking her hand from Dill's and bolting toward the exit.

When she stepped outside, she looked both ways, but Alan had vanished. She closed her eyes, trying to fathom if he had seen Dill holding her hand. If so, what had he thought?

Chapter 2

Alan removed his scrubs and pulled on his jeans then tugged his polo shirt over his head. The day had been difficult following a bad car accident on Fremont Boulevard, and he was glad to leave the stress behind him. His thoughts stressed him, too. He kept picturing Juli holding some guy's hand at the restaurant.

Before the restaurant incident, Juli had filled his thoughts in a wonderful way. Now he felt confused. He looked forward to seeing her again so he could make sense out of the hand-holding circumstances. He'd hoped this time she would stop afterward for coffee. He'd thought about her relationship with the homeless, the way she seemed to befriend them, and he wished he could be a little mouse, listening to what she said to them. It had definitely made a difference. Though he spent his career working in the emergency room, he'd faced the sad fact that he didn't have the knack of comforting people in that situation, either. He worked to save lives but forgot about the whole person sometimes.

Alan dropped his scrubs into a duffel bag and swung through the doorway, whacking the bag against something solid.

"Whoa!" Tom Denny staggered back then arched his brows. "Where are you headed in such a hurry?"

Embarrassed at his preoccupation, Alan found his voice. "I volunteer at a soup kitchen on Wednesdays. Want to come along?" Though he'd asked the question, he counted on Tom's saying no.

"Since when do they take care of medical needs at a soup kitchen?"

Alan chuckled. "This isn't medical. It's soup."

Tom curled up his nose. "You ladle soup?"

"Last week I ladled goulash." The picture of Juli dumping goulash on the woman's salad made him grin.

Tom's frown deepened. "Why?"

The question caught Alan in the chest. He'd kept his personal life to himself, and he planned to continue keeping it private. "It's a good thing to do. Our focus at the hospital is good health, but without nourishment people can't have good health. The two go hand in hand." An uneasy truth skittered up his back. Juli had become another motivation.

Tom shrugged. "I suppose you're right."

"As always, Nurse Denny"— he gave Tom a grin—"you should know that for certain. Food and health were taught in Medicine 101."

127

He chuckled and shook his head. "You got me, Alan."

Alan gave Tom's arm a shake. "Now you know why I volunteer." He took a step away before Tom spoke again.

Tom crinkled his nose. "I suppose the volunteers are a bunch of old folks."

"Old? Not really. I've met some nice people of all ages."

"All ages?" Tom searched Alan's eyes a moment before continuing.

The question singed Alan's patience. "I don't ask to see their drivers' licenses."

Tom chuckled. "If there's a young crowd, maybe I'll go with you next week. I'd like to meet some new people. Where is the place?"

Though he was pleased Tom wanted to volunteer, the motivation irked him. Alan harnessed his irritation. "In Seaside."

"I'll think about it." Tom opened his locker.

"I need to get moving. I'll see you tomorrow." Alan turned away, and this time he kept going, wanting to kick himself for inviting Tom and feeling guilty that he wanted to discourage him from volunteering. The charity always needed help, but Tom was a charmer. He worried Tom might come on to the women—Juli in particular.

A sigh sneaked from him. He'd wanted Juli all for himself, and Tom was another good-looking bachelor like that dude at the restaurant. Tom had his choice of a number of lovely young nurses at the hospital, and he'd dated many of them. Alan, on the other hand, didn't have Tom's gift of gab, but more than that he wasn't comfortable with Tom's flitting from one woman to the next. If Alan was looking for a relationship, he would want one with some real depth that might lead to a commitment. Tom's values and his didn't mesh.

If Tom really wanted to volunteer, another problem centered in Alan's mind. He'd been quiet about his career at the charity, and he feared Tom might let everyone know. The last thing Alan wanted was a fuss about his being a physician. He wanted to participate by affecting lives in a different way, a way that meant too much to him. The need was great, and more hands made the work easier. His mother had often said something like that to him when he was a kid.

His mother. Every time he thought of her, he ached inside. Talk about a difficult life—his mother had been a prime example. Widowed with five small children and no work skills, she'd done everything to keep the family together, and Alan would always be grateful. Though he remembered the bad times, the rough edges were smoothed by what he had learned about survival and about the Lord.

Juli had mentioned God, and he wondered if it had been just a phrase—"there but for the grace of God go I"—or if it really reflected her relationship with the Lord.

He shook his head. *Stop guessing.* He felt like a kid who'd experienced his first heart flutter over a girl. He'd looked forward to seeing Juli again, but after seeing her with the other man on Saturday, confusion put him on edge.

What would he do when he saw her tonight. . .if he saw her tonight? Act normal, that's all he could do, and if she didn't mention the restaurant, neither would he. It would be easier.

Juli stirred the pasta, her attention more on the door than the noodles. Alan had said he'd be there again this week, and she'd expected him to follow through. Then something had happened at the restaurant. She could only guess he'd seen her with Dill and made an assumption. She felt awful. Dill was a flirt with no serious purpose in mind. And something about Alan made her feel comfortable, as if she'd known him for years. Maybe it was the kindness in his eyes. His eyes. She could picture the twinkle behind the dusky lilac blue that reminded her of rain clouds with a glimmer of sun shining through.

After she'd pulled away the week before, she wished she'd accepted Alan's invitation for coffee. They would have gotten to know each other better, and he wouldn't have reached the wrong conclusion at the restaurant. It had been late, but so what? Once again she knew why she'd hesitated. He would ask her more about herself, and she hated to talk about her life. Garlic. Why hadn't she outgrown that problem? Her father had been a garlic farmer since she'd been born. Just before she entered high school, he'd bought the building for a store, and now it was well known. Her father's hard work had grown into a lucrative business and given her many advantages. She should be proud rather than uncomfortable, and he'd changed, too, through the years. He'd softened.

But the taunts in high school still rang in her ears. Garlic Breath. Garlic Bud. Garlic Clove. Garlic Head. She'd heard them all from Melanie's friends. They all lived in Gilroy. If they disliked garlic so much, why didn't their families move away? Her shoulders tightened with the memories.

"Hi."

Juli jumped, and a few macaroni noodles flew from the spoon.

"Sorry," she said, amazed at how fast Alan had ducked from being splattered with the pasta elbows.

He bent down and picked up the mess from the floor. "I didn't realize you had a weapon in your hand."

She managed a grin while her cheeks burned with embarrassment. "Next time it might be more than buckshot."

"Noodle shot, you mean." He strode to the trash can and dropped the pasta inside then eyed the stove. "Same as last week? Is it goulash every Wednesday?"

"Macaroni and cheese tonight." She motioned with her free hand to the large pans of melting cheese.

"I love that stuff. Maybe I'll go outside and get in line."

Playing, she arched her brow. "I'd recommend you get to work."

"What's my job?"

"I think that's your station." She pointed to the salad area. "They're short-handed." She'd peeked at the task chart to see where he would be.

He turned and eyed the salad station. "Is there a place to double check?"

"The task chart is on the wall near the door." With his eyes he followed the direction in which she pointed then turned and walked across the kitchen to check the list.

After seeing him leave the restaurant on Saturday, Juli couldn't believe how natural and friendly he seemed. Had she been mistaken? Maybe the person she saw leaving wasn't Alan at all but someone who looked like him.

Alan returned, looking amused. "You were right."

She felt compelled to be truthful. "I checked earlier."

"Thanks. It's nice to know you care." He scanned the kitchen then gave her a questioning look.

She guessed he was looking for Dill and decided to ask. "What happened on Saturday?"

Alan looked uneasy. "Saturday. I—I—"

"Was it you I saw leaving? I ran outside, but you'd vanished. All I could think was it was someone who looked just like you." She could see the answer in his eyes.

"It was me. I'm sorry. I just—"

She knew the answer, but she wanted to hear it from him. "Did you see me with that guy?"

He lowered his head. "Yes. I didn't feel comfortable, and I didn't want to interrupt."

"Interrupt what? He was coming on to me." Her pulse galloped. "I was waiting for you to save me."

His eyebrows lifted. "Save you? Really?"

Heat rose up her neck. "Really."

Alan drew closer and touched her arm. "Juli, I'm so sorry. You were holding hands, and I thought I'd misunderstood your invitation. I assumed you'd met someone, and. . . My showing up with an idea of spending time with you would have been uncomfortable for you and me."

"I really don't date, Alan, and I'm not usually the type men come on to."

"What do you mean? Why wouldn't they?"

She thought about those dateless nights she'd endured and released a ragged sigh. "You don't know me very well."

"I don't, but I'd like to." His hand rested on her arm. "If you don't mind."

She felt heat rising to her face. "I don't mind. I'd like to get to know you, too." His hand slipped from her arm, and a smile lit his face.

"Now that we have that cleared up," Juli said, "I'd better get moving before Bill tosses me out on my ear for holding you up."

Alan eyed his workstation. "I'll see you later."

He walked to a glove box, grabbed a pair, then strode to the salad station while Juli wished she could forget her macaroni job and chop lettuce instead.

When the pasta had simmered long enough, Juli drained it and poured the contents into the cheesy sauce. In moments voices drifted from the dining room, and she saw Alan carry one of the large salad bowls to the serving area. She grasped a chafing pan and followed.

As she came through the door, Alan was standing with Angie, preparing to serve the entrée. With her heart sinking, she set the pasta container in front of them then stood behind the salad bowl. She'd gotten her wish to serve the salad, but not the way she'd planned. She clasped the serving spoons and prepared to add the salad mixture to the diners' plates.

The line began, and she sent out smiles and greetings, noting those who seemed to be most heavily burdened. Talking with them was her favorite part of the job, and lately she'd begun thinking about that. During high school she knew she wanted to help people in some way, but now social work had settled in her heart, and she sensed God had put it there. She should have insisted on getting a college degree instead of going right into the family business, but she'd felt she should follow God's commandment to honor her father, who asked her to work in the store and give her mother a rest.

She drew her focus back to the dining hall. Tonight seemed quieter with fewer people in attendance, and she figured they must have found their meals somewhere else. No matter; Juli always thanked God that they fed everyone who came through the door. They never ran out of food. Just like the Lord's unending blessings, she thought.

While Alan chatted with Angie, Juli dragged her flagging spirit from behind the serving counter and headed into the table area as she always did. She moved along the rows of chairs, speaking to people, until an elderly woman called to her as she neared.

She'd never noticed the woman before. She stopped and slipped into an empty chair. "How are you tonight?"

The woman shook her head, her weathered hands clutching the paper napkin. "I miss my home."

Juli wrapped her hand around the woman's, brushing her wrinkled skin. "What happened?"

"The apartment building was torn down. They called it urban renewal." Tears rimmed the woman's eyes. "I'm too old to work. I have nothing."

Sorrow knotted in Juli's chest. "No family to help you? Children?"

"One's dead, and one can't help—she's struggling herself. Living with a friend."

Juli's throat ached, trying to contain her emotion.

The woman brushed a tear from her eye. "I've seen you talking to the others. You always seem to make people smile."

Her words touched Juli, but today she had no practical answer to solve the woman's problem. She did, however, have a deeper message for the weary woman. "I wish I could help you find a place to stay, but I'll pray about it for you. I hope you know you do have a home for eternity if you love the Lord."

The woman's gaze lifted toward Juli. "That's what keeps me going. I often think of Job. He had real troubles."

Real troubles, yes, but this woman's were huge, too. Awareness struck her. Her own concern about garlic and Gilroy had no effect on anything important. The woman's reflection had given Juli far more direction than she could offer the homeless woman.

"Job said the Lord gives and the Lord takes away," the woman said. "Job was so right, but he ends that verse with even more powerful words. 'May the name of the Lord be praised.' So that's what I do."

Juli squeezed her hand. "You're a true believer, and God loves you."

The woman managed a weak smile and pressed her other frail hand on Juli's. "You're a kind woman. I see why so many like you. Take care of yourself, and thank you for listening to an old lady's mumbling."

"You're not mumbling, and you're very welcome." A smile filled Juli's heart. She was amazed that this woman with so much against her still had concern for others.

The woman kept Juli's hand pressed between hers. "My name's Rosie."

"Nice to meet you, Rosie. I'm Juli."

When she looked up, Alan stood nearby, listening. She gave the woman another pat and rose, her legs tingling from crouching too long. She moved in Alan's direction, wondering why he'd been eavesdropping.

Alan met her halfway. "I should apologize for listening, but I'm curious how you reach these people. Whatever you say puts smiles on their faces."

"I'm just talking with them." She nodded to one of the regulars seated a table over. "I'll come with you if you're uncomfortable."

He looked at the man then back at Juli. "Is this a challenge?"

She tilted her head in a playful pose. "You can call it anything you want."

He chuckled and moved ahead while she stood back and watched.

As he neared, Alan's face charged with concern when he heard the man's ragged cough. "That sounds bad, sir."

The scruffy man looked up in surprise. "Sir?" He appeared to question the title. He pressed his hand against his chest. "You talkin' to me?"

"I am. Are you taking anything for that cough?"

The man pulled out a grayish, soiled handkerchief and blew his nose. "Don't have nothin' to take, but I'll be fine."

"You'll be fine if you get some care. Do you have a place to sleep tonight?"

His shoulder twitched. "I do all right."

Juli knew he probably slept on the street somewhere, but Alan seemed to know it, too. He gave her a doubtful look. She wanted to step in and offer help, but she couldn't do that to Alan on his first try.

Alan squatted beside the man. "Maybe we can find a place for you tonight." He gave Juli a questioning look.

She beckoned him toward her and kept her voice low. "I called awhile ago for a woman, but they had no room for her. I can try again. They might have a spot in the men's section."

Alan's face lit with hope, and he nodded.

"I'll see what I can do." She squeezed his shoulder and stepped away. Her spirit lifted when the director gave the go-ahead. "But this is it," he said. "That's our last spot."

Forming a telephone with her hand, Juli gave a nod as she returned to Alan with the good news.

"Great," he said, rising from his haunches as he spoke to the man. "My friend here called, and they're holding a bed for you right down the street. Tell them the soup kitchen sent you, and they'll know who you are."

"Thank you," he said, extending a grubby hand to Alan.

Alan shook the man's hand without hesitation.

His loving response to the man touched Juli. She moved away, admiring Alan from the distance.

When the ailing man rose, Alan walked him to the door, pointing down the block, and then turned, his gaze searching the room until he spotted her. He strode to her beside the serving counter. "Looks like everything's pretty well cleaned up tonight." He motioned to the cleared tables.

"A smaller crowd makes it easier," she said, leading the way into the kitchen. She removed her apron, grabbed her handbag from the storage area, and slid it on her shoulder. "I'm glad you came back."

"Me, too."

He seemed to search her face. She didn't know what to say, and then it struck her. "You did a nice job, by the way. He really needed your help."

"He has a bronchial cough. It could lead to pneumonia, or he could have walking pneumonia. His coloring is bad."

Juli deliberated if she should tease him for giving out medical advice. She decided against it, not wanting to discourage him. Alan was a great addition to the volunteers. She hoped he would invite her for coffee tonight. He fell into step with her, but Juli sensed someone following behind them. She turned and saw Angie looking at Alan.

"Are you leaving?"

Juli frowned, waiting to learn if Alan had made plans with her.

A confused expression flew onto Alan's face. "Leaving? Yes."

Juli sensed Alan wasn't comfortable with Angie's attention, or was it her own wishful thinking?

Angie glanced at Juli then back to Alan. "I wanted to—"

While she hesitated, Juli's heart dipped into a dark hole before popping out again. She grasped her courage, knowing now might be her only chance. "I'll take you up on that coffee invitation, Alan."

Alan's confusion shifted to a smile. "Great."

Juli couldn't believe she'd had the nerve to ask him out for coffee.

Alan turned to the other woman. "Could we talk next week?"

"Next week? Okay." Her look sailed toward Juli like a poison dart before she turned to leave.

"Ready?" Alan asked.

Juli released a pent-up breath. "I sure am."

"Good night," she said to the young woman as she felt Alan's hand clasp her arm.

Juli wanted to sink through the floor. She'd never in her life asked a man to go anywhere, and now that she had, she felt great empathy for Alan because she'd refused his invitation last week. What would she have done if tonight he'd said no?

Chapter 3

Juli slid into the booth at the diner. Though not in the best area of town, the place appeared clean, and the food smelled good. Her stomach gave a soft growl, and she pressed her hand against it to hold back another grumble.

Alan scooted into the booth, shifted the menu toward her, and leaned back. "Thanks for saving me."

"Saving you?" She probed her memory. "You mean making the phone call? No problem. We do that once in a while when the person is bad off."

His expression melted to a smile. "Thanks for that, too. I meant Angie."

"Angie?" Heat crept up her neck. "Oh."

He looked disconcerted and played with the paper napkin. "She's nice, but I could sense she wanted my attention, and I wasn't interested."

Juli flinched, thinking maybe her invitation had sounded too eager. "I thought you looked uncomfortable."

"To be honest, I really wanted to ask you to stop for coffee. I hesitated because I was afraid I'd come on too strong last week."

"Too strong," she repeated, almost cutting off his sentence. "No. I was really tired." She wanted to tell him how sorry she was that she'd said no. "I hope my invitation didn't seem as desperate as Angie."

"Not at all. I'm glad you said something." He eyed his watch. "Would you like anything besides coffee? I don't want to keep you since you have a long ride, but I'm hungry."

"Thanks. I would," she said, feeling her shoulders relax and reaching for the menu.

They studied the selections and placed their orders, but when the waitress walked away, Juli felt tongue-tied again.

Alan leaned closer. "May I ask you a question?"

A serious look had settled on his face, and she nodded.

"This is really personal."

Really personal. She looked in his eyes and saw curiosity. "Sure."

"You said you don't date, and I. . .I can't believe your phone isn't ringing off the hook." He looked down at the table. "Is that a religious belief?"

She couldn't control the amazement that sputtered into a chuckle. "Religious? No. Do you think I'm a nun or something?"

He shrugged. "I've never known any woman as attractive as you are who doesn't date."

She drew back and took a lengthy breath. "It's a long story, Alan. I was tall and skinny. I was raised rather strictly, and I've never been one to wear tight clothes or a lot of makeup. I never appealed to most high school boys, and now..." Now what? "...I have this awful hooked nose that—"

"Hooked nose." He shook his head. "You have a beautiful nose. It's classic. Like a Roman goddess."

"Me? I think you'd better have your eyes checked."

He reached across the table and brushed her cheek. "Maybe you should. Take a long, good look in the mirror sometime. You might have been a gangly teenager once, but today you're really a lovely woman, Juli." His eyes widened. "And don't get me wrong. This isn't a come-on. I think of us as new friends. I'm just being honest."

She felt heat rising to her cheeks again and lowered her gaze to the table. "Thank you."

"You're welcome."

The silence grew again while Juli pondered what Alan had said. Lovely? Roman goddess? The words were alien to her.

"How long have you been a Christian?" Alan's question broke the silence.

Relieved, air whooshed from Juli's lungs. She had wanted to ask him the same question but wasn't sure she wanted to hear his answer. "My folks are Christians, and I grew up knowing Jesus. It was natural, but as an adult I've studied the Word and am convinced Jesus is the Way."

"I thought you were a believer."

She studied his face. From his response she felt afraid to ask. She gave him a moment to say something, and when he didn't, she drew in a lengthy breath. "What about you?"

"Am I a Christian?"

She nodded.

"Absolutely." He grinned. "I figured you knew."

She'd hoped with all her heart. "Next Wednesday there's a special service and speaker at Lighthouse Church a block down from the soup kitchen. Sometimes we go there. Would you like to go? They provide the meals on Tuesday nights."

"To which? The Tuesday soup kitchen or worship?"

She looked at his face and realized he was teasing. She waved away his question. "I supposed that was a little ambiguous. I meant worship." She gave him a playful look.

"Just teasing, but I'd love to if it's not too late when we finish. I need my beauty sleep."

His voice sounded good-natured but tentative. Still, she readily accepted his willingness to go.

In a few minutes her soup and his burger arrived. They were quiet as they bowed their heads and said their own blessings. When Juli took her first bite, she realized how hungry she'd been. The soup tasted homemade and delicious, and Alan looked contented with his burger.

He lifted his head and sniffed. "They're cooking with garlic."

Her chest tightened. "Is that bad?"

"I avoid eating too much of it. It makes me a little nauseated. I probably have an allergy. It's nothing serious."

She winced. "That's too bad. Have you had allergy tests?"

"No. It's never been a serious problem. I just avoid food with garlic."

Juli managed to give him an accepting look, but inside she wanted to scream. She'd finally met someone she felt drawn to, someone she really admired, and now he had a repulsion to garlic. She earned her living knee deep in garlic.

Silence fell between them as they ate. Her thoughts sifted through what she'd just heard.

"Why so quiet?" he asked, breaking the hush.

"My mother taught me not to talk while I eat."

He chuckled. "So true, but I don't always follow my mom's advice."

She grinned and motioned to the bowl. "Besides, I love potato and corn chowder. This is really good."

He'd already finished his burger. He wiped his mouth with the paper napkin and pushed away the empty plate. "How about some pie?"

"I couldn't eat a whole piece, but thanks."

He pulled the small dessert menu from behind the napkin holder. "Let's share."

She agreed, and they chose a pie from the menu. Then Alan flagged the waitress and ordered. When the woman left, he rested his elbow on the table. "Tell me about yourself. I'd love to know everything."

Her pulse skipped while she tried to sort through her life story. "I live up Highway 101 with my parents." She saw a flicker on his face. "I suppose that seems odd for a woman to still live at home, but they have in-law quarters separate from the house, like a guest room, I suppose, and it's convenient. It's close to work."

"What do you do for a living?"

Her muscles tensed. "I work in my dad's store."

"Your father owns a business." He gave an agreeable nod. "What kind of store?"

Juli swallowed. "Produce."

He chuckled. "What else in this 'salad bowl' community?"

"For sure. We're surrounded by every kind of produce farm—lettuce, celery, cauliflower, broccoli, spinach, and even avocados."

He scrunched up his nose. "And don't forget garlic."

She hoped to lead him away from the present course of conversation. "What about you? What do you do?"

"I work at the Community Hospital of the Monterey Peninsula."

"Doing what?"

"Nursing people back to health."

Nursing. "That's a worthy career."

"Worthy but difficult sometimes."

"I heard about the pileup on Highway 1 this morning."

"It was bad. We were running all day. I'm exhausted." He faltered as if he had second thoughts. "But talking with you keeps me awake." His eyes sparkled, and he reached across the table and rested his hand on hers. "You're the sunshine in my day."

"Change a couple of words and you could sing it." While he grinned, she could feel her face growing warm. She hated blushing like a schoolgirl and tried to get a grip on her emotions. "Thanks for the compliment."

He looked more deeply into her eyes. "I would have taken you for a nurse or a social worker. You're so good with the people at the soup kitchen. You surprised me when you said you work in your father's store."

Social worker. His perception validated her thought of a career change.

"I'm sorry. I wasn't putting down your work, but the way you treat those people is a gift."

Juli realized her expression said too much. "I didn't know what I wanted to do before I decided to stick with the family business. My dad needed me in the store." Her dad's deciding she would stay with the family business wasn't the full story, but she didn't want to get into that with Alan. "It gave my mom a break, but now the store is doing well. We have a number of employees, so I manage the business."

"So you're the manager."

She nodded. "But when I was younger, I always loved helping people. I volunteered to visit the elderly homebound in my church when I was a teen, and it was like having all kinds of grandparents. If anything, I'd thought about being in a career that helped people."

"Is your degree in business administration, then?"

Her degree? "My brother majored in business administration."

He looked at her as if waiting for more information.

"I didn't go to college."

"You didn't?"

The look on his face caused a knot in her stomach. "I know you must have attended college, but my job didn't require it. My mom trained me to manage the store."

"Not everyone needs a college education."

She heard an apology in his voice. "I didn't take offense at what you said." She waited for him to continue, but he didn't. "Where did you go to school?"

"University of California in San Francisco."

A twinge of regret settled in her chest. He'd gone to one of the best schools possible. She wanted to show she was impressed without sounding envious. "That's a great school."

Alan only nodded.

He seemed so closemouthed about his work, and her stomach knotted when she suspected he felt sorry for her. She wanted him to know it was okay that she didn't have a degree. She didn't want his pity.

"What department do you work in?" She managed to send him a light-hearted grin.

"I work in the ER." He looked uncomfortable.

Juli faltered, realizing the more she probed about his career, the more he would probe about hers. She didn't want to lie, but right now she wasn't ready to tell him about her situation. She might never be ready.

A questioning look grew on Alan's face. "I love my work, but keep in mind, Juli, that it's never too late to start a new career. You'd be a wonderful counselor or social worker. You have the heart for it."

"Thanks." She read sincerity in his eyes. "It's hard to find the time, though."

"God gives each of us talent, but it's in His time, not ours. I love that verse in Ecclesiastes—I think that's it, anyway. 'He has made everything beautiful in its time.' We do things on the Lord's schedule and not our own."

"A long time ago I gave up thoughts of changing my career. At twenty-five I'd find it too hard to go back to school."

He placed his hand on hers again. "Not if it's God's will."

She loved the feeling of his hand on hers, and she felt ashamed she'd given the Lord so little credit. "You're right. To tell you the truth, I don't have a lot of patience."

"Sure you do. Don't give up on your dreams. Maybe someday what you long for will come true."

Looking into his eyes, she realized it could.

గా

Juli heard a noise outside and opened the door. She waved to her friend Megan as she climbed the staircase to her apartment. "It's been too long," she said, opening her arms.

Megan hurried into her embrace, and Juli gave her a firm hug then motioned her inside.

"I'm so glad you called. I've been thinking of you." Juli headed across the room and halted at the kitchen door, waiting to offer her friend a soda.

Megan plopped onto the love seat. "I hope they were good thoughts."

"Naturally. Someone at the soup kitchen asked me when I started working there, and I told him about your inviting me and then pooping out."

Megan sat straighter, her eyes glinting. "Did you say *him*?"

Juli held up her hand like a traffic cop. "A guy I helped train on his first night."

"Hmm. Sounds interesting."

Juli propped her hand on her hip. "Don't start anything. I just met him."

Megan grinned. "But there's always hope."

"Only in your mind." She shook her finger at her as if Megan were a naughty schoolgirl then motioned toward the kitchen, wanting to change the subject. She liked Alan, but hoping too hard could only bring a letdown. "How about a soda?"

"That's good for me."

Juli stepped into her kitchen and pulled two drinks from the refrigerator. She emptied chips into a bowl and carried them and the sodas into the living room. After setting the bowl and a drink in front of Megan, Juli settled into an easy chair.

The conversation drifted to mutual friends, work, and high school memories. When the conversation centered on school, Juli recalled Melanie's visit. "Guess who came into the store a couple of weeks ago."

"George Clooney."

She waved her comment away. "Don't I wish? No. Someone we knew in high school."

Megan searched her face. "Don't tell me. Melanie Ives."

"How did you guess?"

"The look on your face." Megan twisted her face into a silly expression.

Juli couldn't help but chuckle. "I know it's been seven years, and I should be over it, but Melanie had to mention the bouquet." She made pretentious motions with her hands, mimicking Melanie. "And she did it in front of her sorority sister who was slumming at the garlic market." Her uncontrolled envy startled her, and she asked God's forgiveness.

"Juli. It's not like you to sound so catty."

"I know. It just got under my skin. I'm sorry."

Megan waved away the topic. "Let's talk about something interesting." She scooted forward on the sofa. "Tell me about him."

"Him?"

"Don't be coy. This guy you met at the soup kitchen."

Juli's nerves pinged with Megan's questions, and she knew Megan wouldn't give up. On edge, Juli reached for her soda, bumped her hand against it, and caught it before it fell from the table. "I don't know the man that well. He's nice, and I trained him. That's it."

"Sounds interesting. Maybe I'll show up next week so I can see this guy. Do you still go on Wednesday?"

"Wednesday. Right." Juli's heart sank. Megan was so pretty with her long blond hair and blue eyes.

Megan wriggled back against the sofa. "I'll have to see if I can make it. I should have continued volunteering. It's good to do things for others."

"I agree." But not now. Megan was so attractive. Concern prickled up Juli's back. Did Alan mean something to her? Juli had insinuated the opposite; yet saying aloud that she cared about him might raise her hopes too high. She decided to let well enough alone and hope Megan would forget by next Wednesday.

⁂

"Wait up!"

Alan looked over his shoulder and stopped as Tom caught up with him.

"Where're you headed?"

The question left Alan no choice but to tell the truth. "The soup kitchen." He felt his brow wrinkle. "You're not really interested in going, are you?"

Tom shrugged. "How long are you there?"

"That's hard to say. A big crowd takes more time to feed. Last week we were finished by eight thirty or maybe nine."

Digging his hands into his pockets, Tom appeared to ponder the information. "Can I go for an hour or so? You know, just to check it out."

The comment irked Alan. He guessed what really interested Tom. "An hour's work is better than nothing," he said, admitting he had to think of the needy people and not his own concern about Tom.

Tom nodded. "I'll follow you."

Alan motioned toward the staff parking. "I'll wait for you by the exit." He hurried ahead, hoping Juli wouldn't be beguiled by Tom's flirtatiousness.

He grumbled to himself as he waited by the exit gate. When he saw Tom's car behind him, he inserted his identification card and waited as the exit arm lifted; then he rolled onto the side street. Tom pulled from the exit and followed Alan as he continued to Highway 1, driving slow enough for Tom to stay in his view. Once in Seaside, Alan guided him to a parking spot behind the soup kitchen.

Inside, the scent of hot dogs struck him when they came through the door. Bill greeted them and after the introduction led Tom away for training. Angie nabbed Alan before he could check his station.

She gave him a smile. "Remember me?"

"I do," Alan said, trying to slip away to follow Bill and Tom.

She caught his arm. "I could use some help opening these cans."

Alan eyed the large containers of fruit cocktail and gave a huff. He hoped Angie hadn't heard it; he forced himself to remember he had volunteered to do charity work and not chase Juli.

"I'd better check my station, Angie."

"You're here. I already checked."

"Are you sure?"

She nodded.

He drew up his shoulders and grasped one of the large cans, trying to halt his exasperation. While he detached the lids, Angie dished the fruit into bowls, and Alan realized it could be a long project. With Angie's concentration on filling the dishes, Alan glanced over his shoulder and spotted Tom. This time he didn't care who heard his huff. Bill had asked Juli to show Tom around, and Alan saw the satisfied expression on his coworker's face.

An idea formed. He'd make sure to work in the food line beside Juli. At least they could talk without Tom hanging around. Feeling better about the situation, Alan cranked the can opener and finished the job in record time.

"There you go," he said, sliding the last can closer to her. Before she could ask him to help dish up the fruit, he made his way across the room to Juli and Tom. "I can help with the lettuce," he said, grabbing a head. But before he could wield the knife, Bill came past.

"They need help over there," Bill said, shifting Alan's attention to another area. "That's your station."

"My station?" Alan looked at Angie, realizing she'd tricked him. When he tried to catch Juli's attention, she was laughing at something Tom had apparently told her. Alan normally loved her laugh, but not when it was with Tom.

Disappointed in his overzealous feelings for a woman he barely knew, Alan turned away and strode to the butcher-block table.

"Here you go," the worker said, sliding him a knife and tapping his blade on a bag of onions. "Everyone likes these with hot dogs."

Onions. Alan's stomach knotted. Juli and Tom were tearing lettuce into small pieces, and he had to chop onions. He pulled out a large one, removed the skin, and attacked it with vengeance.

"Careful," the man said. "You'll be bleeding all over the butcher block."

Feeling as if he'd been sliced and diced beneath the man's questioning gaze, Alan shrank in humiliation and mumbled that he'd be more careful.

The juice from the onion smarted his eyes, and tears welled on his lower lashes then rolled down his cheeks. He brushed them away with his arm and noticed Juli watching him. She sent him a hello wave by wiggling her fingers, and he tried to grin back and forget the onions.

When voices sounded from the dining room, the workers headed to the serving area. As Alan scraped the last of the diced onions from the butcher block, he felt a hand on his arm.

"They gave you the rotten job."

Juli's voice glided to his ears, and he looked into her blurred face.

She lifted her fingers and brushed the tears from his cheeks. "It wasn't that bad, was it?"

A grin settled on his mouth. "No. I loved every minute of it."

She laughed, and this time he loved the sound because she was with him.

"We'd better get out there," he said, grasping the onion container.

She walked beside him to the doorway, her arm brushing against his, and to his delight Bill flagged him to the hot dog station and Juli to the buns. Together finally, he thought, even though it was the hottest job on a warm day. When he looked around, he found that Tom had vanished.

While Juli stood beside him with the open bun, he slipped the hot dog inside and listened to her friendly conversation with the homeless. He looked into the crowd, seeing a few bow their heads. But most eagerly ate the food that had to last many of them twenty-four hours or more.

Pushing aside his grumbling, Alan felt blessed. His own stomach was full, and the nicest woman in the room stood beside him. When he noticed Juli motioning, he looked down and saw an empty bun and a woman and young boy waiting on the other side of the counter. *There but for the grace of God go I.* The sentence filled his head, words that had such strong meaning for him.

Sorry he'd held up the line with his musing, Alan dropped a hot dog into the roll and gave Juli a wink. "Give the young man an extra one. He's a growing boy."

He remembered someone had done that for him once so long ago.

Chapter 4

Juli beckoned to Alan. "We'll be late if we don't get moving," she called.

He lifted the bucket into the air. "What about cleaning up?"

She loved the way he'd come on the scene and seemed to give the job his all, from onions to the cleanup detail. He never complained. "Bill lets people go early to make the service on time. Others are willing to clean up."

He held up one finger and pointed to the storage room then came bounding toward her and linked his arm in hers. "Let's go."

He pulled her toward the front door, but she stopped him. "Everyone's waiting in the back."

His smile faded. "Everyone?"

She realized he hadn't understood her invitation. "I mentioned sometimes others like to go along. I thought you knew."

Alan's mouth tugged into a half smile, and Juli sensed he'd struggled to put it there.

"I guess I didn't hear that part. It's not a problem." He released her arm and strode toward the back door of the kitchen.

But it was a problem, and she knew it. What could she do? Others liked to attend the service, and she'd always been happy they wanted to hear God's Word. Thoughts tossed in her head as Juli decided not to say anything more. She hoped Alan would understand and enjoy the praise service with the rest of them.

The others joined them as they came outside, and they headed down the alley to the sidewalk then made their way to the church. Music streamed through the open door, and as they stepped inside, the spirit of the worship filled her. Among those who had come were some of the homeless who found strength in the Lord.

The group slid into chairs, most sitting together. Before she could slip in beside Alan, a new volunteer she hadn't met had shifted between them, and she had no way to correct the situation without making the newcomer feel unwelcome. She leaned around the man and smiled, but Alan didn't smile back. Instead he shrugged and looked toward the platform.

Juli managed to keep her eyes forward and ignore him. When she'd invited him to attend worship, she'd never said it was a date. She would have liked that, but a number of people attended the special services together, and it had become a tradition. They gathered by the back door and walked over together.

With Alan's silence, Juli's thoughts drifted. She recalled Megan had said she'd be at the soup kitchen tonight, but she hadn't shown up. The music began, and voices lifted in praise, but tonight her voice seemed constricted. She gave in and glanced Alan's way, but he only looked toward the praise group singing.

Juli lowered her head. Her purpose here was to worship and not stare at Alan. She felt ashamed of her preoccupation and sent up a prayer asking for God's help, but as she prayed, an uncomfortable weight pressed against her stomach. The heat of the room and the stench of those who didn't have the luxury of a shower filled her nostrils then churned inside her. Unable to sit any longer, she explained to the person sitting beside her that she had to leave. She looked at Alan then decided to let it go.

While the crowd stood, clapping their hands to the rhythm of the music, Juli slid past the worshipers to the end of the row and hurried outside. She drew in a deep breath of warm fresh air and wondered why she felt so ill. She looked down the dimly lit street toward the soup kitchen then lifted her shoulders and strode toward her car. She would explain everything to Alan the next time she saw him.

Each dark doorway sent a trickle of fear along her limbs. Anyone could be hidden against the inset of the shop doors, the homeless or someone out for no good. Juli had always walked back from worship to her car with the others, and she hadn't thought about being in a crime area. She moved closer to the street and increased her pace.

The farther Juli walked away from the church, the more edgy she became. She gripped her shoulder bag to her side and increased her speed. As she approached the corner with one more block to go, a hand jutted out from a shadowy store entrance. A sharp pressure jammed against her shoulder as the strap of her purse dug into her skin. Fear clenched her throat. She tried to pull away but suddenly tripped over something—was it the thief's leg?—and fell to the ground. Her handbag was yanked from her arm, and she heard heavy steps running off.

"Stop!" An angry voice cut through the night.

She heard footsteps again, this time coming closer, then Alan's breathless words. "Are you okay?"

"Yes, but he grabbed my bag."

Alan dashed off in pursuit of the purse snatcher.

Tears rolled from her eyes, and nausea rose to her throat. She swallowed the acrid bile and sat a moment to gain control while her mind went over all the things she'd have to replace. A new driver's license, her cell phone, her house key, credit cards—so many things she'd have to cancel and—

She pushed herself upward, her hands stinging from skidding across the concrete sidewalk. Brushing away the dirt, she felt the burning sensation increase; she saw the skin peeled back but no serious damage. She looked up and noticed a police car heading her way. It rolled to a stop at the curb, and the officer leaned out of the window.

"Are you okay, miss?"

She nodded. "I'm fine. Just frightened." To her surprise, Alan stepped from the other side of the vehicle. Knowing he was there helped her feel more secure.

"Can you give me a description?" The officer had left his car and was standing beside her.

"I didn't see him. He jumped out of there." She pointed to the shadowy door entrance.

"That's always the way. Come down to the station if you want to make a report."

"I'm fine. Thanks."

He got back into his car, nodded to her, and drove off.

Alan drew closer. "Are you sure the guy didn't hurt you?" He put his arm around her.

Tears blurred her eyes, and she released the torrent.

Alan nestled her against his shoulder.

"I'm sorry," she whispered when she'd gained control. "I didn't mean to cry."

He stepped back. "You're sorry? Juli, you could have been injured or killed. Thugs will do anything for money."

"I was so stupid to leave the church, but—"

He pressed his finger to her lips. "But nothing." He lifted her hands and saw her skinned palms. "You need to get some antiseptic on these hands."

"I'm fine. . .except for my shoulder bag."

His expression changed to a silly grin. "Here."

He was clasping her bag in his other hand.

Her eyes opened wide. "Wow! I guess you're my superhero. How did you get it?"

"When the kid darted around the corner, the cop pulled up, and he dropped your purse and ran. The officer made a call then drove me back here."

Grateful, she smiled and patted his arm. "You saved me from having to replace everything in it."

"You can thank the cop. He saw me chasing the guy and figured out what had happened. I'm sure that's what scared the guy away."

"Praise God for that." She hugged her bag to her chest. "How can I thank you?"

"Now that's an interesting question." He linked his arm with hers and took a step toward the car then stopped. "But first tell me why you left the church."

She lowered her head, realizing the scare had replaced her sick feeling. Juli told him about the heat and her nausea. "I wasn't thinking about the walk back to the car."

"No more of that. Never walk alone. Promise me."

Her pulse skipped at the concern in his voice. "I promise. It was thoughtless."

"That's right. It was."

His grin unsettled her. "Don't be so enthusiastic."

"The only thing I'm enthusiastic about is taking you up on that offer."

She faltered and turned to him. "What offer?"

"You asked what you can do to thank me."

In the dim light she could still see the twinkle in his eye. "And what would that be?"

"Seeing me sometime outside the soup kitchen."

"I'm seeing you right now."

"Seeing as in a date."

"You want me to go out on a date with you?" Her heart thundered.

"It would make me very happy. Plus it would pay off your indebtedness."

"I'm known for always paying my bills."

He slipped his arm around her shoulder and gave her a quick hug. "That's what I hoped."

Her laugh joined his. Somehow Alan usually managed to say the right thing, and tonight it was the most right thing she'd heard in a long time.

﹏

Alan ripped off his protective gloves, moved to the next patient, pulled on a fresh pair of gloves, and stepped beside the nurse. He eyed the monitors then studied the deep gash in the patient's chest. "Maintain compression." The wound lay too close to the heart for his expertise. "Call surgical. Stat."

Another major car pileup. His mind spun with the horror one speeding driver could cause. He tore off his gloves and tossed them in the receptacle then brushed the perspiration from his eyes and glanced at the clock. His heart sank. His date with Juli.

As the patient with the chest wound was being wheeled to surgery, Alan drew in a lengthy breath, thinking of the stressful day. The man had been the last injury brought in from the accident, and Alan knew he could leave.

He took the hall toward the locker room then veered away and strode to the cafeteria. He'd been without food for hours.

Why had he been so negligent? Juli had suggested meeting him in Monterey. She insisted, and he hadn't even asked for her telephone number. Hours had passed since they were to meet. He could picture her waiting fifteen minutes, a half hour, an hour, then leaving. She'd be long gone and angrier than a cornered bear, and he wouldn't blame her.

Alan headed for the sandwich bar, selected a tuna-filled pita wrap, and paid for it and a coffee at the cashier. He spotted a table looking into the courtyard and sank into a chair. Though he was hungry, his appetite had waned at the realization he'd missed his first date with Juli. What would she think of him? If she heard about the accident, she may have guessed. If not, he was history.

A hand pressed against his shoulder, and he jumped.

"What's up with you?" Tom pulled out a chair and sat down.

"Another accident today."

"I know. We had a full house in the surgical unit."

Tom eyed him, and Alan waited for his next question.

"What's really troubling you? You've handled a truckload of accident cases. That's nothing new."

Alan sank deeper into the chair, not wanting to tell Tom, whose mouth was often bigger than the Pacific. "I had a date tonight."

Tom shrugged. "She'll understand. Getting involved with a physician makes it part of the deal."

Guilt rolled up Alan's back. "She doesn't know I'm a physician."

"You're kidding." His eyes widened like two blue moons.

Alan shook his head. "I have my reasons."

"Who is she? She can't be from here."

Alan gave up. "Juli. From the soup kitchen. But listen—I want you to keep your mouth shut if you're going back there." He gave Tom a probing look. "When you were there last time, you didn't make the big announcement I was a physician, did you?"

"I didn't say anything about you. Why would I? I figured they knew, and I talked about me."

"They don't know, and I want to keep it that way. It's not why I'm there, and it's important to me that it's not broadcast around."

A crooked grin grew on Tom's face. "So the good Christian boy has told a lie."

"No, I haven't."

Tom's smile slid to a questioning look. "How did you avoid that?"

"Juli asked what I did, and I said I worked at the hospital in the ER and nursed people back to health. That's all the truth."

"She thinks you're a nurse, then, I suppose. Why the secret? You should be proud you're a physician, pal."

How could he answer this question without going into his background and his motivation? "I don't have to be a physician to volunteer at the soup kitchen. I want to be me and not a doctor. Can you understand?"

Tom frowned. "I guess not."

Alan didn't understand himself either, but it was important to him. "Can you keep your mouth shut? Please don't say anything to anyone. Let me do that when I'm ready."

Tom shook his head. "Whatever you say, pal."

Alan took a bite of his sandwich, wishing the subject hadn't come up. Maybe he was being foolish about this, but for once in his life he wanted to be Alan Louden, volunteer at a soup kitchen. He didn't want to be anyone special, and he certainly couldn't practice medicine at a soup kitchen.

He lifted his gaze and saw Tom staring at him. "What?"

"I'm trying to figure you out. That's not easy."

"Sorry."

"Then tell me about Juli. I didn't know you had a thing for her, although I don't blame you."

"I don't have a *thing* for her. She's a nice woman, and things fell in place for me to ask her for a date."

"What kind of things?"

Alan gave up again. Tom was worse than a nosy neighbor, so he told him about the purse-snatching incident.

"You're a hero in her eyes." He rose and slapped Alan on the back. "Good thinking."

"I didn't plan it."

Tom squeezed his shoulder. "I know. Maybe it was providence." He waved. "I'm not off duty yet, so I'd better get back."

Alan watched him vanish around the tray return and let his word sink in. *Providence.* To Alan that meant God. Was meeting Juli God's doing? For the first time since he'd left the ER, his shoulders relaxed. If this were God's doing, then he had nothing to worry about.

৵

Juli parked her car in the Del Monte Shopping Center outside Elli's Great American Restaurant. She'd agreed to meet Megan for dinner and then shopping, but her heart wasn't in it. The mall was crowded, and she'd stood much of the day at the Garlic Garden pitching in to help with the busy store again and watching her paperwork pile up.

"I can't fool myself," she mumbled, sliding from her car and heading for the restaurant. She knew her non-date with Alan had set her on edge. She hadn't expected him to stand her up. He seemed too real and thoughtful. It took her back to high school days when she'd longed for a date, and then when one finally happened, she'd been stood up. So many disappointments.

Juli reviewed over and over what she and Alan had agreed on. She was to meet him in Monterey Joe's parking lot at six. Alan worked in Monterey, and it saved her from admitting she lived in Gilroy. Another totally useless worry. She had to give that problem to the Lord.

Juli had even hoped she'd set her watch wrong—anything but to be stood up. The time had been accurate. That night she'd waited until after 6:45, every minute torture.

"Hey, girlfriend!"

Juli turned toward Megan's voice and saw her coming through the parking lot, waving.

She waved back and headed for Elli's.

Megan greeted her outside the entrance and flopped her arm over her shoulder. "You look tired. Up late?"

"No," Juli said, wanting to stay away from the subject but knowing that wouldn't be possible.

"No?" Megan opened the door and motioned her inside. "Something's wrong?"

Juli let the hostess distract them as she guided them to a table and handed them each a menu. Juli flipped it open and studied the fare, hoping that time would move their conversation to a new topic. "I think I'll get something fattening like the All-American Burger." She closed the menu. "And their fresh-cut fries."

"Hmm. That's not like you. You're always watching calories." She tossed her menu on the table. "What happened?"

"Nothing." She could say that honestly.

Megan didn't appear to be dissuaded "What *didn't* happen, then?"

"Come on, Megan. If I wanted to talk about it, I would." She folded her arms across her chest. "I thought this was a fun evening for us. Shopping and dinner. Grill the burger, not me."

Megan grasped the menu again and flipped it open. She didn't say a word, and Juli's chest ached that she'd spoken so harshly to her friend.

Juli waited a moment then spoke. "Megan."

Her friend's eyes remained focused on the menu.

"Listen. I'm sorry. Please forgive me."

Megan didn't move for a second; then her head inched upward over the menu, and she looked into Juli's eyes. "I didn't mean to grill you. I'm your friend, and I care what happens to you."

"I know you do." A waitress stopped at their table, and Juli faltered. "Let's order, and then I'll tell you."

When the waitress had gone, Juli told her about Alan and the purse snatcher.

"Why did you go out on that street alone at night? You know better than that."

"I wasn't thinking."

"Juli, you treat the homeless with such compassion, but not everyone out there in the world is as kind as you are. You have to be careful."

"I know. I wasn't feeling well, and—" She thought back to that night. "I'd upset Alan unintentionally, and I think that just got to me."

"Upset him?"

She explained the misunderstanding then continued. "But I felt better when he ran after the guy who took my bag. He brought it back, and the whole situation led to a date. I'm so startled he stood me up."

"He stood you up? Didn't he at least call to explain what happened?"

The question sank into her thoughts like an anchor. "I never gave him my phone number. He never asked, and I didn't think about it. Not too bright of me."

"Or him," Megan said.

The waitress appeared with their drinks, and the conversation halted until she left.

Juli grasped the iced tea and took a long, cool drink.

Megan moved her glass to the side of her plate. "You said Alan works at the hospital in the ER. Did you know about the horrible pileup yesterday? He might have gotten held up at work."

"What accident? You mean the one on Highway 1?"

"No, that was a week or so ago. This was a different one. A speeder lost control, and a number of cars were involved. I think it was on Highway 68."

The possibility washed over her. Had Alan been held up at work? An accident should have entered her mind. She'd seen enough ER TV shows with all the doctors and nurses scurrying around after a highway tragedy. She knew his work would come first.

"You've made an assumption and judged Alan without knowing what really happened."

God's Word flew into her thoughts. *"Do not judge, and you will not be judged. Do not condemn, and you will not be condemned. Forgive, and you will be forgiven."* Juli lowered her head. "I'm too inexperienced with these emotions, Megan. It's been too long since I've even given one look at a man, and now I'm so afraid."

"Afraid?"

"Of being hurt, I guess. I really like Alan. He's intelligent and funny, but I see something in his eyes. A kind of compassion or deep hurt. Something. I don't know him well enough yet to understand, but I know it's there."

"Then give the relationship time."

"I suppose I'm rushing things, but it's just a feeling—"

"Maybe it's the Lord talking to you. You need to listen."

Juli's fingers uncoiled from the glass. "I wish this weren't so important to me. I feel like a kid instead of an adult."

Megan slipped her hand over Juli's. "When the heart is involved, we're kids again. Talk to the Lord. Let Him guide your heart, Juli. You just met this guy, but if it's part of the Lord's plan, then don't worry."

A ragged breath escaped. "Thanks, Megan. I needed to hear that." She thought for a moment then moved to a new topic. "I thought you were coming to the soup kitchen last week."

"I meant to, but things happened."

"Alan brought a friend with him."

"Really." Megan grinned. "Are you playing matchmaker?"

"Maybe. I'll see you next week. Right?"

Chapter 5

Alan wiped perspiration from his palms as he opened the soup kitchen door. He didn't know what to expect from Juli, but he couldn't blame her. Any man who asked a woman for a date and then didn't write down her telephone number was a jerk. He was one with a capital *J*.

He scanned the workers while he moved through the kitchen, and his heart sank. He headed for the doorway to the dining room and glanced inside, hoping, but Juli wasn't there either. He checked the list and moved to his station, another hot job at the oven. Eyeing the recipe on the corn muffin bag, he watched the door with his peripheral vision. He felt his shoulders slump.

Forcing them to rise, he reviewed why he was here. His first purpose was to serve the needy. *There but for the grace of God go I.* He let the words wash over him, remembering the struggles from his youth and thanking the Lord for so many blessings he'd received. A scholarship to college made his life different. His mother couldn't have afforded tuition, and even though he worked, he wouldn't have had enough. Every extra penny went to help his mother.

When Alan looked at the faces of the homeless, he saw his own. He wondered if he'd ever adjust to being in a different financial position now. As a physician, he'd earned so much more than he'd ever dreamed. Though he still helped his family, he had a small condo, and that was more than anyone needed, unless—

A prickle of awareness moved along his neck, and he turned. Juli stood inside the doorway, the shoulder bag he'd recaptured hanging over her arm. Alan stood motionless, not knowing the best approach. Juli shifted, and her gaze met his. He pressed his hand to his chest and mouthed, "Sorry."

She gave a brief nod, stopped to talk with Bill, then headed his way.

Alan set down the bag of cornmeal mix and walked toward her, a muscle ticking in his jaw. "Juli, I'm so—"

"Was it the pileup?"

Relief flooded him. "Yes, and I didn't have your telephone number. When I got out of there, I tried to look you up, but I didn't find your name in the book, and I had no idea where you lived, except north of Monterey."

"My friend Megan told me about it. I'd hoped that was the reason."

"I felt like a heel. I can't imagine what you thought of me."

Juli's eyes darkened, and he wondered what she was thinking. If the look reflected what she thought of him, he didn't want to know.

"Let's forget it," she said. "I understand."

"But I don't want to forget the date. Can we try again? This Saturday I'm off." She hesitated.

To reassure her, he added, "I want your telephone number this time."

Finally she grinned. "Same plans as last time?"

Bill's voice cut into their conversation. "Let's get busy. Time's fleeting."

Alan touched her shoulder. "Let's talk about it later."

She nodded and moved away, and he went back to the corn muffin mix. As he worked, his frustration rose. He saw Juli busy near the stove, and with her was the guy from the restaurant. He gave her a playful poke. He didn't like what he saw. Apparently neither did Juli. She gave the guy a look he'd never seen her give before, and from her body language, he suspected Juli had told him to keep his hands to himself. Alan's spirits lifted, and the next time he looked, the guy had moved to another station.

Happy, Alan turned on the huge oven, and with the utensils gathered in front of him, he measured the mix, added the eggs and liquid, then followed the directions and spooned the goop into the muffin pans. Although many of the greatest chefs were men, Alan had somehow missed the talent of getting the mix into the muffin cups. He pulled off a paper towel, wet it, and tried to wipe away the excess.

A snicker sounded behind him, and he saw Juli with a wide grin on her face. "You're no Wolfgang Puck, are you?"

"Isn't he a character in Shakespeare's *Midsummer*—"

This time she laughed. "He's a chef, but you're partly right. Puck is a character in a Shakespeare play. I read it in high school."

He'd read it in college, and once again it irked him that Juli hadn't had a chance to reach her dream. He could picture her trying to help her family as he had done, and he felt proud. Though he never wanted to talk about his past, he and Juli apparently had that in common.

He slid the muffin tins into the oven and started another batch, his eye on the clock. The muffins needed to be ready in a half hour, but the time meant more to him than that. He'd have a chance to talk with her. When the next batch was ready, he pulled the other tins out of the oven to cool.

While transferring the muffins to the serving tray, Alan noticed Juli greeting an attractive blond. The friend she'd mentioned, he guessed, and now Alan wondered if the other woman would stand in their way of talking privately later.

Feeling like a novice at dating, Alan struggled with his emotions. He'd never felt this way about a woman so quickly—at least not in his adult life. His teen years were filled with emotional ups and downs that never settled in one place. His finances held him back from dating anyone except those in his situation, and then a walk on a summer evening or an occasional discount movie had been the highlight of his dating.

Noise rose from the dining room as those waiting outside crowded into the building. He carried the large trays to the serving counter. Juli and her friend were side by side with soup ladles, and the salad bowls stood between him and Juli, so he turned his attention to the line of hungry people, smiled, and served the muffins and butter.

Time seemed to drag, but finally the crowd thinned. Juli had wandered among the crowd as always, this time with her friend at her side. Both women spoke with the needy men and women, but only Juli's face seemed to reflect the sincere concern and compassion that made her so appealing.

Alan helped pull the serving dishes into the kitchen then grasped the bucket filled with disinfectant and water. He picked up a large cloth and headed back into the dining room to perform his usual task. When Juli finally noticed him, he nodded but let her make the first move. Tonight he felt uncomfortable, both with the bungled date and with two sets of eyes looking at him as he worked.

"Alan."

Juli's voice reached him, and he turned.

"This is Megan. She's the one who told me about the accident last Saturday."

"Thanks," he said, reaching out to shake her hand, but he stopped himself and wiped his hand on a towel to dry off the soapy water.

"Nice to meet you, Alan." She gave him a grin. "You owe me one for the save."

It took him a moment to realize she meant his missed date. "I knew I was in hot water."

She chuckled. "Boiling water."

"Hush," Juli said, bumping her hip into Megan's. She reached into her pocket and handed him a piece of paper. "This is for you."

He glanced at the note and slipped it into his pocket. "Thanks." He studied Megan, wondering if she understood their conversation. "Are you leaving?"

Juli nodded. "Megan and I are stopping somewhere to chat."

He tried to keep from showing his disappointment. "Have fun."

Juli took a step backward then halted. "By the way, where's your friend?"

"Tom?"

She nodded.

"He had to get home tonight. The family was celebrating his nephew's birthday. He turned four today, and he loves Tom."

"I just wondered." She motioned toward the note she'd given him. "Call me."

She waved and moved off, leaving Alan to figure out why she'd asked about Tom.

⌒

Juli relived her telephone call from Alan as she slipped into a new dress she'd picked up at Ross's during her outing with Megan on Saturday. It was a coral and white halter sundress with a sweeping skirt that looked not too casual and not too dressy. She hoped it fit the occasion. She slipped on natural-colored strappy sandals, added a clutch bag, then eyed herself in the mirror. She cringed when she saw her hair curling into frizz, a casualty of the humidity.

Alan insisted he pick her up at home, and she insisted not. Until she knew where things were going, she didn't want her parents' questioning looks. Though she had her own apartment, living so close meant they were able to watch her comings and goings. It made her feel like a child. Alan said he would go along with her request this once and instead suggested they meet by the aquarium on Cannery Row in Monterey. She loved the old part of town that had been brought to life in John Steinbeck's novels.

The traffic moved well until she hit Seaside. Maybe if she was late, she'd make Alan worry this time. "Sorry, Lord," she said, disliking her "get even" feelings. She'd lived too long wishing she could have gotten even for hurtful things of the past. That wasn't the way of a Christian.

When she turned toward Cannery Row, the traffic bogged even worse, and after finding a parking spot, Juli tried to shake off her stress. She grabbed her clutch bag and sweater, locked her car, and hurried toward the aquarium.

Nearing the building, she spotted Alan leaning against a signpost. He waved when he spotted her. She waved back, feeling as if her feet were flying beneath her.

"No mishaps this time," she said when she reached him.

He studied her a moment before he spoke. "You look amazing. Like a spring garden."

"Thanks." She gazed at his periwinkle-hued polo shirt and noticed it was nearly the color of his eyes. She wanted to tell him he looked amazing, too, but she felt it would be forward.

They stood a moment in anxious silence until he grasped her elbow and pointed. "We're heading that way for dinner." His smile was as warm as the June sun.

She nodded and walked beside him, more comfortable this time in their silence. When Alan stopped, he motioned to a doorway. "I thought we'd try the Blue Moon Bistro. I've never been there, but I've heard good things."

"It looks expensive."

"You're worth it, and it makes up for last week. I still feel bad about that."

"You don't owe me anything, Alan. I really understand. You were needed on your job. You had no choice."

"Thanks."

She sent him a reassuring smile as he led her inside, her steps bouncing with anticipation. Inside the dining room she hesitated, viewing the lovely surroundings. Every table overlooked Monterey Bay with a decor of soft blues and greens that reminded her of the sea.

They were led to a table along the windows and given menus. Her eyes focused first on the view, the late afternoon sun dotting the seafoam green water. Seagulls soared against a deepening blue sky. She pulled her gaze from the view to the menu, and when she opened it, the prices jumped from the page.

"Do you like steak?" Alan's voice cut through her thoughts.

Her attention skipped to the entrées, and she held her breath. "Could we share?"

"Share?" A frown replaced his smile.

"Like the pie. I thought—"

"Do you like steak?"

She nodded.

"Good. Do you mind if I order?"

She shook her head, embarrassed that she'd suggested sharing, but she wanted to save his money. She had no idea how much income a nurse made, but steaks at this price couldn't be everyday fare.

When the waitress appeared, Alan placed their order then turned to her. "What would you like to drink?"

"Water's fine."

"Iced tea?" His eyes studied hers.

She nodded.

The waitress left, and Juli turned again to the sunlight dancing on the ripples of the bay. "It's gorgeous, Alan. Thank you so much."

"You're welcome. I have another surprise when we leave. I hope you don't mind." His lips curved into a smile.

"You like surprises."

He nodded. "Good ones."

"Me, too, but not bad ones. I've had too many of those." She wished she hadn't been so open.

He didn't ask, and the tension in her shoulders subsided. She studied his profile as he looked at the bay. The sun had begun to lower toward the horizon, and she could imagine the magnificent sunset that would follow.

"Tell me about yourself." The words sailed from her mouth without her control.

Alan's smile tightened, and she sensed he didn't like to talk about himself. She could understand that, because she didn't either, so why had she opened the door to sharing personal information?

He shrugged. "Nothing much to tell. Mom lives near Marina. I have four siblings and—"

"Five kids in your family?"

He nodded. "Two brothers, one's deceased, and three sisters. Two live on the East Coast. I'm the youngest. My dad died so long ago I don't remember him."

"I'm sorry. That must have been tough on your mom." She couldn't imagine being without her dad, even though he'd put many demands on her. She knew in her heart that he simply wanted her to follow God's Word.

"It was, but let's not talk about that now." He reached over and rested his hand on hers. "We're here to have a good time."

The waitress arrived and ended the serious moment, and they focused on their dinners, with further conversation only about the delicious food and ambience of the restaurant. The tender steak was excellent, served with a wild mushroom sauce and garlic mashed potatoes. She noticed Alan had replaced his with red potatoes.

"You're quiet," Alan said, setting his iced tea glass on the table.

"Enjoying the food and the view."

"I'm glad." He pushed aside his plate. "We should leave room for dessert. Did you notice the menu? Warm chocolate lava cake. That has to be enticing."

She grinned, thinking it wasn't nearly as enticing as he was. "I couldn't eat a morsel."

"Really. How about tiramisu?"

The look on his face made her laugh. "That's hard to resist, but no. I'm filled to the brim."

"Me, too," he said. "You fill me to the brim."

Feeling a flush, she thanked him and looked again at the golden speckles glinting on the water and thought of how the Lord blessed her every day. Like Alan, He offered surprises beyond measure, and meeting Alan had been one of those wonderful unexpected gifts. *Thank You, Lord,* she thought.

Comfort wrapped around Juli as she sat in quiet conversation with Alan. Nothing profound was said, but he talked again about her compassion with the homeless and how much he enjoyed her company. Bolstered by their open conversation, she admitted she loved being with him. "Did you know your shirt matches the color of your eyes?"

His mouth curved into a smile. "I just slipped it over my head. I'm not even sure what color my eyes are."

"Periwinkle. A beautiful shade of dusky lilac blue, like periwinkle."

"And yours are creamy milk chocolate."

His hand slipped over hers for a moment before he checked his watch. "I hate to leave, but I think we'd better get going."

Juli rose, curious to learn the surprise he'd planned. But while they were heading back on Highway 1, she was surprised in a different way.

"Do you like Tom?" Alan's voice jarred the quiet.

"Tom?" She felt her forehead crinkle with a frown. "I don't really know him."

"You asked about him, and I wondered."

She thought back to that day and remembered Megan had been there. Was Alan jealous? Butterfly wings tripped through her chest. "Tom seemed nice, and I'd told Megan he might be there."

His strained expression softened to a grin. "Ah, so you're matchmaking."

"Not really, but"—the truth struck her—"possibly."

He removed his hand from the steering wheel and brushed her arm. "That's kind of cute. Tom should be there next week. I'll tell him he was missed."

"Not by me, please."

"Guaranteed. I'll tell him about Megan."

He focused on the traffic, and Juli wondered how he could be so unaware she was attracted to him. She found Alan amazing. Funny and handsome. Kind and thoughtful. Everything she'd dreamed.

When they veered onto Highway 68, Juli caught on to the surprise as they inched down the road beside the Monterey County Fairgrounds. A billboard announced, MONTEREY BAY BLUES FESTIVAL.

She chuckled, and Alan glanced her way.

"That's sort of a giveaway," he said, motioning toward the sign. "I hope you like blues."

"I do, and I've never been to this festival."

"Then you're in for a treat."

He guided the car through the gate and found parking, and they headed into the fairgrounds, looking at the venue choices. Three stages had crowd-pleasing blues, and they settled at a bandstand, listening to the slow tempo of the melancholy music.

Alan slipped his arm across the back of her seat, and his fingers brushed her bare shoulder. The warmth radiated down her arm with a sensation too wonderful to put into words. She felt part of something special, and though she'd known Alan for only a short time, a sense of wholeness filled her. He was a believer, a man who understood God's love as she did.

With the sun beneath the horizon, Juli wrapped her sweater around her shoulders, and Alan snuggled closer, his arm lowering to add more warmth. The sky darkened, and she looked into the starry night toward a slender crescent moon. The music washed over her as Alan held her close.

"The sky's amazing," Alan whispered in her ear.

She felt a tickle against her skin. "I know. It's as lovely as the music."

"I'm looking at something even lovelier."

She lowered her gaze.

"I'm talking about you, Juli."

In the dark she could hide her blush. She couldn't remember being told she was lovely by anyone, except maybe her mother. "Thanks, but—"

"No buts. Please accept the compliment."

She could only nod and cling to the compliment as if it were a treasure. "This has been a great evening."

"I'm glad you took another chance on—"

She pressed her finger against his lips to silence him, and he kissed it. She drew her hand away, feeling the tingle of his touch. "We'll forget that first date. Let's pretend this is our first."

"I like that idea." He drew her closer. "We'll do this again, and soon."

She sent him a smile as big as the one in her heart. "I'd love to."

"But this time it'll be different. I don't like your driving alone at night. I'll pick you up."

"No. Please. I don't mind—"

This time his finger covered her lips. "Let me be a gentleman. I want to pick you up. We can do something in your area."

Like smell the garlic. Her spirit slumped. One day he'd have to visit her home and family. *Lord, help me get over this weirdness.*

"What's close to you?"

She drew up her shoulders. "Lots of places. Prunedale. Salinas. Let's talk details later."

His quizzical expression troubled her.

He tilted her chin upward. "But we've agreed it's a date, right?"

It's a date. She nodded, realizing she needed to get a grip on her hang-up. She had to learn to ignore the garlic jokes. She'd always been grateful she had dark hair because she felt so sorry for blonds, like Megan, who had to endure all the blond jokes. Megan didn't let them bother her. She laughed with the crowd while Juli felt bad for her. So why couldn't she be like Megan and laugh about garlic?

∽

On Tuesday Alan headed across the hospital staff parking lot to his car. He'd come in early, and the day had weighed on him. Late afternoon sunlight spread through his tired body, and his stomach growled, reminding him he hadn't eaten in hours and that like Mother Hubbard's, his cupboard was bare. He needed to stop for some groceries.

Heat radiated from his car when he opened the door, and he climbed in and turned on the air then waited a moment for it to kick in. When the steering wheel felt cooler, he drove a short distance to the farmers' market held every Tuesday in Old Monterey. Alvarado Street was blocked from traffic so the vendors could sell their wares.

He parked near the conference center and headed along the main thoroughfare, eyeing the boutiques, book shops, and unique home furnishing stores until he reached the market, with the outdoor stands filled with produce and food specialties.

At the first stand he tossed a couple of lettuce heads into a bag; then he moved to another stand for broccoli, cauliflower, and a bundle of fresh spinach. As he selected his purchases, Juli entered his thoughts. He sensed she was holding back. Something troubled her about him or about herself. As much fun as they had together and as much as he cared about her, Juli's hesitation concerned him. Her "too many bad surprises" comment wouldn't leave his mind, and one day, if they were ever going to move ahead in their relationship, he would need to know what bothered her.

Forcing the worry from his mind, he focused on his shopping. He picked up a package of mushrooms, his favorite for salads and steak, and when he turned the corner, he could see a sign ahead for avocados. As he headed that way, he spotted a large sign, GARLIC GARDEN, and a woman who looked like Juli. He held back, watching until he knew for certain it was Juli. *Garlic Garden.* She'd said her father had a produce store. Garlic was produce, but she hadn't been specific.

Everything fell into place. His dislike of garlic—an allergy, he'd called it. This was her family's livelihood, and she'd been too embarrassed to tell him. Though her discomfort might seem silly to some, he knew how he felt about his career as a physician. He'd made a big deal to Tom about hiding it at the soup kitchen. He and Juli were both victims of their pasts, and they'd let the past affect their present, but not their future, he prayed. If he spoke to Juli here, catching her in the situation she'd tried to hide, he could embarrass her or worse. It wasn't worth the chance. He cared too much. He would let Juli tell him in her own good time. But if this was what bothered her so much, they needed to get it out in the open. He needed to be honest with her, too.

Foolish hang-ups.

So many things fell into place. Alan guessed Juli lived in Gilroy, garlic capital of the world. Was that why she'd been so hesitant to have him pick her up? Her father's owning a garlic store couldn't be all of it. The problem had to be deeper than that, and his curiosity rose. How many years had Juli allowed her past to hold her back from being the delightful person she was? She rarely dated, she'd said. She didn't recognize her attractiveness. She seemed so dedicated to giving that she didn't know how to receive.

Alan took a different route for the avocados, his mind spinning with questions. Perhaps her family was poor. That made sense. She was uncomfortable about his knowing that. She must have figured he had a good job at the hospital. How much money did a garlic store bring in? This whole thing couldn't stem from her father's garlic store.

Or could it?

Chapter 6

Alan stood near the soup kitchen door and waited for Tom to catch up with him.

"I know I'm supposed to keep my mouth closed about the physician stuff," Tom said, rolling his eyes. "I still don't get you, pal."

"Trust me until I tell Juli myself. Please."

They passed through the doorway into the heat of the kitchen. Alan saw Juli and headed her way.

"Where's—"

Juli lifted her index finger toward the back door. Alan turned and saw Megan's blond hair and smiling face as she waved.

Tom nudged his shoulder. "Is that Juli's friend?"

"Sure is," Alan whispered.

"Wow!"

"Hi," Megan said, walking toward them, her gaze settling on Tom. "You're Tom." She extended her hand.

Tom grasped it. "And you're Megan. It's nice to meet you."

Juli took a step backward. "We'd better get to work before Bill squawks."

The foursome divided and found their workstations. Alan made a quick move to the cans of peaches. Today with the heat he could avoid the stoves and definitely the onions. He began opening lids, his mind sailing back to his great date with Juli the previous Saturday. Everything had gone well, except his discomfort when she'd asked about his family. He suspected she came from a poorer family, too, so it should be easy for him. Still, it wasn't. It was a time he wished he could forget, except it had instilled in him the values and character that made him the man he was today. When he felt confident Juli really cared about him, he'd tell her about his childhood poverty. He wanted no pity while dating.

When Alan got into the swing of filling dishes with peach slices, he scanned the kitchen and noticed Tom and Megan working together at a counter chopping vegetables. He could smell the aroma of chicken stock rising from the large soup kettles. When he looked Juli's way, she was watching him. He needed to dig deeper and see what made this wonderful woman tick.

The evening flew, and plans settled into his mind with the Fourth of July only two days away. When the food had been doled out, he watched Juli visiting with the homeless. Sometimes she knelt beside them, while other times she sat in an empty chair at the person's side. Alan listened and could hear the hope she offered them with her words of faith. When he noticed her take a young woman's hands, he moved closer.

"May I pray with you?" Juli asked.

The woman nodded, and Alan felt drawn to her side.

"Lord, bless Anne's efforts to reconcile with her family. Open their hearts to her needs and provide the light of forgiveness to touch them all. Jesus, You promise to be at our sides. Let Your light shine for Anne and her family. In Your name we pray. Amen."

"Amen," Alan added.

Juli raised her head in surprise. "Where did you come from?"

"I saw you praying and believe the more prayers, the better."

The young woman gave Alan a faint smile; then her eyes narrowed. "Haven't I seen you somewhere before?"

Her words triggered a memory. He felt nailed to the floor.

Recognition lit her face. "In emergency at the hospital. I had a knife wound and—"

Alan recollected too well. "I remember. How are you?"

"Fine, thanks to you. I only have a small scar between my ribs."

"You were blessed to have it nick the bone and not go any deeper."

Her expression said it all. "I know it could have gone into my heart."

Alan heard Juli's intake of breath.

"Praise the Lord," Juli said, reaching out to touch the girl's shoulder.

"Thanks so much," Anne said, knotting her hands in her lap. "To both of you. I wouldn't have survived without medical care, this food, or prayers. I've messed up my life, but I'm trying to make it better. Now if my family will give me a chance."

"Be confident, Anne. God is good, and He hears our prayers. I'll continue to pray that your family opens their hearts."

Tears welled in the young girl's eyes. "Thank you." She rose and looked as if she wanted to hug Juli, but she hesitated.

Juli stepped closer and embraced her without faltering. Her compassion and concern wrapped the girl in a healing balm, and Alan could only reiterate the prayer already sent up. *Lord, bless this girl. She needs Your help.*

Anne said good-bye and headed toward the door while Alan stood with Juli, his admiration increasing for Juli's ability to love and care about people. She truly followed God's instruction to live a life that emulated Jesus.

Before he could say anything, Megan headed their way with Tom close behind.

"We're going out for a bite to eat," Megan said. "Would you two like to join us?"

Alan looked at Juli but saw a no in her expression.

"I have a long day tomorrow, and I'm really tired tonight," Juli said. "I'd love to, but I should head home."

"What about Friday?" Alan asked, jumping into the conversation. "It's the Fourth. Would you like to go to the Monterey fireworks?"

A grin broke out on Tom's face. "I'd planned to ask Megan at the restaurant. What about it?"

"Sounds like fun." Megan turned to face Juli. "What do you think?"

Juli hesitated, and Alan felt his neck prickle.

"Well, I—"

"Idea," Megan burst in. "How about meeting at my place? Juli could spend the night with me. That'll save Alan the long ride to Gil—"

"What do you say?" Alan rested his hand on her shoulder.

"Say yes, Juli," Tom said. "Alan really likes you."

"That'll work," she said, a slight flush on her cheeks.

"Then it's a yes all the way around." Tom slipped his arm into Megan's. "See you on Friday." He and Megan turned away and headed out the door.

Alan stood beside Juli, wanting to press his hand against her rosy cheeks, but he knew she would be even more embarrassed. "Sorry for Tom's exuberance. I think he's doing a little matchmaking, too."

"I think so," she said, her flush fading. "Thanks so much for your prayers for Anne. She has such needs."

Alan knew more about Anne than he wanted to share. He nodded. "Let's hope God intervenes."

"She said a knife? How was she hurt?"

"An attempted robbery, sort of."

Juli's expression changed to a frown. "Robbery? But she doesn't have anything."

"A man owed her money for her services and didn't want to pay."

Juli lowered her gaze, and he sensed she understood. "Well, she's on the right road now. She told me how she'd been going to the church down the block. She realizes her sins, and she's asked God for forgiveness."

"Sometimes it takes us awhile to give up our foolish ways and let God take over. We drag a lot of baggage around with us."

"I know. It's time to put it in the Dumpster."

Alan realized Juli was referring to the baggage they'd talked about the other day. She needed to let it go.

And he needed to do the same.

⁂

Juli looked out the window toward the road, waiting for Alan and Tom. Megan had given him directions to her apartment, and she hoped they had been clear. She grinned at her worrying.

"I guess I'm ready." Megan's voice cut into the silence.

Juli pivoted away from the window. "You look great," she said, admiring Megan's red, white, and blue knit top over walking shorts. Even her sandals were the colors of the American flag. Juli looked down at her coral capri pants with a navy and coral striped top and felt very unpatriotic. She should have thought of the holiday when she selected her outfit.

"You look good in—" Megan's attention flew to the window. "Here they are." She headed for the door.

Juli picked up her navy sweater and shoulder bag. "What about a sweater for tonight? It could be cold on the beach."

Megan released a giddy laugh. "I've got love to keep me warm."

Love? Juli tried to control her raised eyebrows. Megan hardly knew Tom. Megan flagged her through the doorway, and as Juli stepped outside, Alan opened the driver's door and met her. "You look wonderful."

She peered down at her outfit then at Megan's. "I forgot to look festive."

Alan slipped his arm around her back as he walked her to the car. "You look more than festive." He opened the passenger door.

She pondered his words as she slid into the seat. Behind her she saw Tom slide over while Alan held open the door for Megan. Megan gave Alan a smile as she joined Tom in the back. Alan closed her door then settled behind the wheel.

Juli noted that Tom hadn't moved to help Megan into the car. Alan had. His gentlemanly ways grew more wonderful each time she saw him.

He slipped his hand over hers. "You okay?"

"I'm fine." She managed a smile.

"Good. Buckle up, everyone. We're on our way."

She attached her seat belt as Alan backed down the driveway and pulled onto the highway. As he drove, Juli noticed most of the vehicles seemed to be headed toward the bay. The Fourth of July meant the beaches and parks would be filled. Alan maneuvered his way through the holiday traffic as the scenery became filled with celebration. Large flags flew from buildings, and children waved miniature ones as they bounded beside their parents. As they approached Fisherman's Wharf, the traffic came to a halt.

"It's good we came early," Alan said. "I thought we'd buy food on the wharf then sit on San Carlos Beach for the fireworks."

No reply came from the backseat.

"Or we could go to Colton Hall," he added. "They have food there, plus music."

Juli glanced over her shoulder, waiting to hear what Tom and Megan preferred to do, but then spun forward after seeing them in a deep kiss that embarrassed her. Megan barely knew Tom, and that kind of familiarity seemed terribly inappropriate.

"The wharf sounds fun," she said, managing to control her uneasiness. "We'll want to find a place on the beach early anyway."

He slipped his hand over hers. "Right. We want a good spot for the fireworks."

She rolled her hand upward beneath his, wove her fingers through his, and gave them a squeeze.

Alan's face lit with a smile that brightened his eyes, and Juli smiled back, sensing the same light in her eyes.

A horn tooted behind them, and the traffic began to move. "Finally," Alan said as he released her hand and gripped the steering wheel.

Juli watched him concentrate on the traffic, relishing the memory of his fingers on hers.

"Look at this traffic," Tom said.

Juli assumed they'd finally come up for air. The image of them set her on edge. She hoped they'd manage to harness their affection at the wharf.

When they arrived, Alan parked, and Juli stepped out into the warm bay breeze. The unique scent filled her senses—bay water, fish, and warm sand. As they neared the wharf, new aromas of food drifted on the air.

Megan and Tom walked ahead, talking with their faces close, their hands clasped together. Juli liked hand-holding and wished Alan was holding hers. He walked beside her, his arm brushing against hers, his fingers only inches away. Juli knew she and Alan weren't in love, but she'd felt a strong interest that had grown into attraction, and she'd thought it was reciprocated. A picture rose in her mind—Tom and Megan kissing in the backseat. Alan had never asked to kiss her, never tried. Men and women sometimes had platonic friendships. She hoped Alan's feelings had grown deeper than that.

They passed the weathered FISHERMAN'S WHARF sign and wove their way through the crowd toward the pink building sporting a bright blue lighthouse. They passed Harbour House and shops selling silver, pearls, T-shirts, and artwork. Tangy aromas drifted from the restaurants—seafood, steak, Mexican spices. Tom headed for the Casa Carmelkorn shop, but Alan whistled and cupped his hands over his mouth to form a megaphone. "Let's eat dinner first."

Tom sauntered back with Megan's hand woven in his. "I'm ready." He turned to Megan. "I'll pick up some caramel corn to take to the beach."

Megan nestled against his shoulder as they discussed their restaurant options—Crabby Jim's, Captain's Gig Restaurant with its covered porch for outdoor eating, and Cabo's Wild Mexican Seafood. They walked to the end of the wharf and back, eyeing the possibilities, and eventually agreed on Café Fina. They returned to the butter-colored clapboard building and went inside. The air conditioning felt great to Juli, and she was pleased to see the broad windows offered a sweeping view of the harbor.

Juli listened to the conversation, the romantic tones of Tom and Megan and Alan's witty comments. She perused the menu, especially the wood grill fare of chicken and veal dishes. She noticed the New York steak and wondered if that would be Alan's choice. When Megan mentioned that Café Fina's pasta was homemade, Juli settled on Italian sausage with fettuccini.

"Sounds good," Alan said, "but I'll take the Pasta Fina. It has baby bay shrimp, Roma tomatoes, and onions covered in clam butter sauce."

The waitress wrote down their orders, and Juli turned to the window and watched the sun lowering in the sky. Its golden hues spread across the bay like deep yellow oil on water floating along the top, creating a vibrant splash of color.

"You're quiet," Alan said, leaning closer. He glanced at the other two, and Juli followed his direction. Seeing they were preoccupied, Alan leaned closer. "Are you upset with me about something?"

Her pulse tripped. "No. Not at all. I'm just distracted, I guess."

Alan tilted his head toward Tom and Megan. "You're surprised about—"

He didn't continue, but she knew what he meant.

She gave a faint shrug. "A little."

He nodded as if understanding.

She felt his fingers brush against her lower arm, a touch so gentle it sent a tingle to her heart. She felt her pulse give a jig, and it left her confounded. She longed to know how Alan really felt about her. Did he think of her as a friend, a girlfriend, a date, a what?

Letting the question slide, Juli managed to be chattier. She and Alan talked about the soup kitchen, past Fourth of July experiences, and the ambience of the restaurant, anything to help her avoid watching Tom and Megan. Occasionally one of them added a comment, but the conversation tended to be hers and Alan's until finally the food arrived.

They quieted and concentrated on their meals. They skipped dessert and ordered coffee, letting time pass as the sunlight turned to dusk and the lights came up on the wharf. The crowd thickened, and they discussed the need to find a spot on the beach. Alan motioned for the bill. When they stepped outside, he and Tom agreed to run back to the car for blankets while Megan went for the caramel corn and Juli headed for Carousel Candies to pick up some sweets.

Inside the store she made her purchase—and faced the truth. She really liked Alan, and if they were going to get anywhere, she had to stop her worries. She had to do something to get rid of her ridiculous attitude about Gilroy and garlic. She needed to give her concerns to the Lord and let Him guide her. Juli knew she had to take a leap of faith, to step outside her comfort zone, but she sensed that was what the Lord would have her do.

When they reached the crowded beach, they found a spot and spread their blankets close to the water. With the lack of sun and a breeze from the bay, a chill had settled over the sand. Megan and Tom stretched out on their blanket, arms wrapped around each other, while Alan and Juli sat Indian-style. She reached for her sweater tied to the strap of her shoulder bag, and Alan helped her slip it on then stretched out his legs and patted the blanket between his knees. "Come over here. We might as well stay warm."

She looked at his face in the dim light. "Are you sure?"

"Am I sure? I insist."

His voice rang with good humor.

"Want a piece of candy first?" She pulled a small package from her shoulder bag.

He shook his head. "You're sweet enough for me."

The look in his eyes sent her heart on a wild ride. She scooted across the blanket and settled down with her back against his torso. Alan wrapped his arms around her and rested his chin on her shoulder. "Now isn't that much better?"

Better. It was wonderful to be so close yet show good taste. "It's much, much better, but are you comfortable?"

"I'm very comfortable. Isn't that like you to be concerned about people?"

His words settled over her. "Is it bad to be so concerned?"

"Juli, it's what the Lord expects. How can you ask? It's what makes me care about you so much."

She stopped herself from asking him to define "care about you." She decided to enjoy his words and leave the situation in God's hands.

Music from the wharf drifted down to the beach, and they sat without talking and watched people wander along the bay searching for a place to sit. She loved the feel of Alan's arms embracing her and keeping her warm. It reminded her of the Bible verse in Ecclesiastes that began, "Two are better than one," and went on to say, "But how can one keep warm alone?" The beautiful words that defined a loving relationship hung in her mind. *Two are better than one.*

Tom and Megan were lip-locked again. Juli averted her gaze, and Alan gave her a firm squeeze.

"I know that bothers you," he whispered in her ear. "It bothers me, too."

Juli turned, her mouth close to his. "They don't know each other that well."

"I know."

She saw something in his eyes, and butterfly wings revisited her heart until she nearly lost her breath. "They just met," she was finally able to say.

She saw his lips move, and she felt them brush the end of her nose. The sweetness of his kiss washed over her. She loved that so much more than tempting herself to sin. Too much passion too soon wasn't what the Lord expected, and it wasn't what she expected.

Alan's gaze sought hers, and she smiled to let him know she loved his kiss. She felt his shoulders relax, and she turned again to face the water, nestling inside the circle of his arms. Tonight she knew why he'd never tried to kiss her. Alan respected her, and he'd waited for her permission to move forward. She needed to decide what she wanted, and if she wanted Alan, she needed to be honest with him. So many things piled up in her mind.

A hiss and a bang charged the sky, and a burst of color shot through the night, with red, white, and blue fairy dust floating downward to the water.

"That surprised you," Alan said, nuzzling his chin against her shoulder.

Another burst lit the darkness like a golden chrysanthemum followed by tiny pinwheels spiraling through the air. The crowd responded with applause and cheers.

Juli watched one display after another, each more beautiful than the last, bursts in the shape of hearts and stars, fountains of brilliant color, but she realized the glorious glow held nothing to the light in her heart. The Lord had sent her a man who respected her and cared about her, a gift greater than any fireworks display on earth.

Chapter 7

Juli's voice rose in song as the words to one of her favorite praise hymns flashed on the screen, "Lord, We Lift Your Name on High." The words and tune rang in her heart. Her father's deep bass voice rumbled beside her, while her mother's softer tone blended with the others nearby. Juli lifted her hand, grateful to belong to an active congregation and to have Christian parents.

The thought skittered down her back. They were great parents, but they knew how to pull her strings, and lately she felt tied by their expectations. The problem had really been her dad. He seemed bound to old traditions, and though she loved him deeply, sometimes she resented his expectations. Alan had drawn out her earlier desire to help people, to be a counselor or social worker. While she honored God by following her father's wishes, her own desires had fallen by the wayside.

A few years ago her father had wanted a family member in the store, so she took over, releasing her mother from the day-to-day work there, but now the store had prospered. They had trusted employees. Why did he still need her there every day? The question charged through her like a volt of energy. She'd never really thought of it that way before.

Lord, is that what You want for me? The question niggled her. She knew that if God had a new course for her to follow, she would sense it. The Spirit would guide her. She believed something would happen to make her know for sure that she was following God's will.

The congregation sat, and Juli followed, opening her Bible to the verse the pastor had stated, Romans 12:6. As he began to speak, Juli held her breath.

" 'We have different gifts, according to the grace given us,' " he read from scripture.

Different gifts. Juli closed her eyes, knowing God had given her a gift. Alan had spoken of her gifts often, and so had others. Juli's pulse skipped as she listened.

" 'If it is serving, let him serve; if it is teaching, let him teach; if it is encouraging, let him encourage; if it is contributing to the needs of others, let him give generously.' "

God's Word settled into her mind. Serving. Encouraging. Contributing to the needs of others. Wasn't that what she wanted to do with her life? The pastor's words wrapped around her senses as she slipped into her own thoughts. What had her life become? Keeping books, writing up orders, doing inventory, waiting on customers who bought garlic braids, garlic mustard, garlic pasta sauce, garlic salsa, and garlic bread. Pickled and roasted garlic. Garlic in jars, cans, shakers, and fresh. Garlic peelers, presses, and slicers. Is that what the Lord expected of her when her heart yearned to serve others?

"Listen to God's words," the pastor said.

Juli's thoughts faded.

" 'Honor one another above yourselves. Never be lacking in zeal, but keep your spiritual fervor, serving the Lord.' Each of us can walk our own path, but we are challenged to use the gifts given to us by the Holy Spirit by honoring others above ourselves."

Tears welled in Juli's eyes. *Lord, is that what You want for me?* God had answered her question in an amazing way, and she couldn't wait to talk with Alan. He seemed to understand. He'd encouraged her, and before she spoke to her parents, she wanted to digest what she'd heard today.

The sermon had ended, and they stood as prayers rose for the needs of others. Juli managed to quiet her excitement and concentrate on the petitions. The music began, and voices lifted in praise as high as Juli's heart had raised at her amazing awareness. God wanted His children to use their gifts, and she was sure hers didn't involve managing a garlic store.

Now all she had to do was convince her parents.

⌇

"Why so quiet?"

Her mother's voice edged into Juli's thoughts. She shifted on the family room sofa and saw her mother's face filled with questions. "I was thinking about the sermon."

Her mother smiled. "I thought maybe you had a problem."

Juli grinned but didn't respond; if she said she didn't, it would have been a lie. She set her feet firmly on the floor and leaned forward. "What are your gifts, Mom?"

"My gifts?"

"Gifts of the Spirit. From the sermon."

Her mother waved her hand in the air as if she were brushing away cobwebs. "The Bible says we're given gifts according to God's grace. Who's to say some of those gifts aren't being a mother and a wife? I believe those are my gifts."

Juli shook her head. "That's not an easy job, Mom. If you break it down into parts, you've been a teacher, nurturer, nursemaid to Jim and me, and business partner to Dad."

"I'm no such thing. Your father is the businessman."

"Don't wave away your gifts as if they're not important." She looked at the carpet, trying to pose the right question. "Did you ever want something more? Something deeper?"

Her mother tilted her head upward as if looking for the answer on the ceiling. "I had childhood dreams but nothing that meant anything."

"Really? What kind of dreams?"

"Children want to be nurses and firemen, the typical things, you know." Juli chuckled. "So you wanted to be a fireman?"

Her mother laughed. "No, I wanted to be a nurse."

"A nurse." Juli realized her mother's dream and hers had similar purposes—to help others become well. "What happened?"

"What happened?" She shook her head. "Marriage, Jim and you. That's what happened."

Her mother's words kicked at Juli's heart. "So you gave up a dream because you got married and had kids. Did you ever resent us, Mom?" Looking into her mother's startled eyes, Juli wished she could have retracted the question.

"How can you ask me that? You and Jim mean everything to me. I wouldn't have given you up for a hundred nurses' uniforms. In fact, they don't even wear regular nurses' uniforms anymore. They wear little smocks. Not even a hat."

Her response made Juli chuckle again. "Then definitely it wasn't worth it," Juli said, making light of her question.

Sinking back into the easy chair, her mother released a sigh. "To be honest, sometimes I wonder how it would have been to have my own career and come home, knowing I'd helped someone regain their health. But then I'd think of you and your brother, and I realized this was where God wanted me to be. I've raised two wonderful children I've always been proud of. That's a parent's real dream."

"Children I've always been proud of." The words fell like a weight on Juli's shoulders. Would her mother be proud if she decided to strike out on her own after living at home and working in the family business? She couldn't look into her mother's eyes for fear her quandary glowed like a neon sign on her forehead.

She slapped her hands against her knees and rose. "I'd better get home. Tell Daddy I said good-bye. The last I saw him, he was taking a nap in the living room recliner."

"That's his gift," her mother said with a twinkle in her eyes.

Juli laughed and headed toward the doorway. "Thanks for Sunday dinner, Mom. It was great as usual." She waved over her head and didn't look back.

When she stepped onto the veranda and took the stairs to her own apartment, Juli's head spun with their conversation. Every Sunday she had dinner with her parents. Every Monday she went to work in the store. Her life had seemed like a broken record for so long until Alan had entered it, and now she didn't want to hear the same repetitive tune. She wanted to hear the rest of the symphony.

She headed into her bedroom and stretched out on the bed, watching the sunlight dance on the ceiling. She'd come to realize her pulse also did a jig when she spent time with Alan. Since Friday, images of the evening filled her. The fireworks erupting overhead like colorful flowers provided an amazing backdrop to the blossoming emotion of being with Alan. She remembered the solidness of his chest supporting her as they watched the brilliant display, his chin nestling against her shoulder. The sweet memory rolled over her like silk. She could still recall his lips brushing against her nose in that tender kiss. He meant so much to her, and she feared for her heart, despite her longing to feel confident and trust Alan.

She pressed her palms against her temple, trying to hold back the uneasy feelings that stomped over her confidence and caused her to question herself. If she could learn to believe in herself, she would be more fulfilled. This meant she had to stop doubting what Jesus said and what He could do. He came into the world to give believers an abundant life. Abundant life meant ample, full, a fulfilled life, didn't it?

In the distance Juli heard her telephone ring. With Alan still on her mind, she hurried to answer it, but she covered her disappointment when she heard a different voice on the line.

"Hi, Megan."

Megan went on and on about her Saturday night date with Tom, and though Juli had enjoyed the wonderful Friday night with Alan, she felt envious. Alan hadn't called her or asked her out for Saturday evening.

"I'm glad you had so much fun," Juli said, keeping her voice as bright as she could.

"I think I'm falling in love, Juli."

Love? Juli felt the air leave her lungs. "Megan, you said that on Friday. Please be careful. You've only known Tom a short time. Love is something that has to grow. Love and passion aren't the same."

"What does that mean?"

Juli bit her lip, realizing she'd opened up a touchy subject. "Passion is arousing desire in the body, but love is a deep emotion that moves the heart and soul."

"This is more than passion. He does move my heart."

Juli cringed at the upset tone of Megan's voice. "I'm sor—"

"Just because we kiss a little doesn't mean we don't talk and have a good time."

Kiss a little. Juli bit her tongue to avoid saying her thoughts. "Those long kisses can lead to—"

"Long kisses. What were you doing, watching us?"

Juli's back stiffened. "Megan, I turned around to ask you a question, and you were. . . I don't know. I turned away to give you privacy, but what I saw didn't look like a little kiss to me."

"From what I can see, you and Alan don't do anything."

Her comment smacked Juli, but she figured it was Megan's defensiveness. The word *respect* bounded to her tongue, but she swallowed it. "I believe in taking things slow, and so does Alan."

"You two seem to be at a dead stop, in my opinion."

The line went silent until Megan's soft sob came over the wire.

"Megan, are you okay? I'm really sorry. I know I should be happy for you, but—"

"It's not you." Her voice broke with another sob. "It's me, Juli."

"You? What do you mean?"

"I'm rushing things, I know. I talk to you about God, and then I forget what I should do. I know I need to be careful. Tom told me he's been footloose for a long time, and you've just reminded me of that. Do you think he's trying to use me?"

"I hope not, Megan, but you're aware of that. Remember that passion is the body's physical reaction. Love comes from the heart."

Juli heard only silence.

"Megan?"

"I'm here. I know. I really like him, and I want things to work out."

"Pray about it. You told me to listen to the Lord awhile ago. You do the same. You can't go wrong." She heard Megan chuckle.

"I guess I should heed my own advice."

"Can we forget this happened? I didn't want to hurt you."

"I know. You're being a good friend, and I'm sorry for what I said. I didn't mean it."

When the call ended, Megan's words hung in Juli's thoughts. She'd heard judges tell the jury to disregard testimony, but Juli figured once they'd heard it, they'd heard it. She and Megan had both said things that had hurt the other, but they'd ended the conversation with advice that made sense.

Juli sank onto her living room sofa, thinking about Megan and Tom and then Alan. The call had made her appreciate Alan even more. He respected her, and that was a tremendous gift. She prayed Megan would listen to the Lord, and Juli knew she should, too.

Before she could think any more, the telephone rang, and this time she knew it was Alan.

❦

When Alan heard Juli's voice, he realized something was wrong. "You sound upset. What's up?"

She hesitated and then told him what had transpired.

"I feel the same way, Juli," Alan said, hoping to reassure her they were on the same page. "Tom isn't a guy to last long with a woman, and I'm afraid Megan trusts him and what he's saying, and—" He stopped himself, realizing he should keep this to himself. How could he judge Tom? "Let's see what happens. Maybe one day Tom will change." He heard Juli's intake of breath.

"I think she understands now. At least I hope so. And you know what she told me?"

"What?"

"Tom admitted to her that he liked to play the field."

"Really? That's a good sign. Tom doesn't usually admit that to himself."

"We can pray that Tom cares enough to change and Megan uses wisdom. I have to leave it to the Lord."

Listening to Juli's voice as she worried about her friend touched him. Juli had captivated him with her concern for others, but he worried that she over-looked her own needs. He wished he could draw out all the hidden things in her heart. Then maybe he could open up more about his own. They needed to have time alone when they weren't surrounded by other people.

A smile lingered in his heart. "I wish I hadn't needed to work the past two days. Twelve-hour shifts can be so long. I miss you."

"I miss you, too. I wish we had time to talk. Alone, I mean. Wednesday is always too difficult."

Alan drew back, pleased to hear what he'd just thought. "How about tomorrow? I'm off. Let's do something different."

"Like parasailing?"

He heard laughter in her voice. "Sure, why not?"

"I'm even nervous on a ladder. That's why not."

He chuckled with her. "Do you have a bicycle?"

"A bicycle? I have an ancient one. I haven't been on it in years."

"Then it's time to dust it off and have some fun. What do you say?"

"Biking?" She paused. "Okay, but I hope I can still remember how to keep my balance."

He grinned. "Maybe we should rent a bicycle built for two."

"I wouldn't put you through that. Where do you want to go?"

"I don't care. Up your way. I'll pick you up, and we can—"

"How about the old Fort Ord bicycle trails? That's nearly halfway for both of us, and we'll have a beautiful view of the bay."

His shoulders drooped. "You want to meet again, Juli. That's so frust—"

"I'll take the day off, and we can get started earlier. I'll save you all the time of driving here, and I'd love to go to Marina Dunes Beach. It's beautiful and quiet."

He gave up. She'd been holding her secret back for too long, but so had he, and it all seemed so foolish. "We can sit on the beach and talk there. I'll bring a blanket."

After they'd made plans and he'd hung up, Alan lowered his head, facing his own quandary. He should have been up front with Juli from the beginning about his work. He'd never told her he was a physician to prevent a slip-up at the soup kitchen, but now he'd dragged it on so long it would be shocking to her, and she'd be disappointed in him that he hadn't been open with her. She hadn't either, but that didn't excuse him.

He buried his face in his hands, realizing he always expected the worst to happen. For so many years he'd prayed for things to be better in his life, and they seemed to get worse. When blessings came, he waited for them to fade away again, just as they had in the past. Juli had become one of those blessings, and he feared losing her. He longed to develop a healthy relationship with her, and that meant they both had to be open and trusting. *Lord, help me trust Juli and trust You. You promise good things for those who wait and those who put their confidence in You. You know my needs, and I pray for Your guidance.*

⁓

The warm breeze fluttered through Juli's hair, and perspiration beaded along her forehead. Her old bicycle hadn't been that bad once she cleaned it up, and even though it wasn't a mountain bike like Alan's, they managed to stay together as they soared along the bike trails on the old Fort Ord land. Horses, hiking, and biking had returned this discarded army base to a valuable piece of land that offered enjoyment to many.

She pumped harder as Alan moved farther ahead. "Going to a fire?" she called. The wind carried her voice behind her, but she knew Alan heard because he glanced over his shoulder and sent her a teasing smile. He slowed then grinned when she reached him.

"We're not too far from the pedestrian access to the beach. I got carried away."

Juli knew he was holding back for her. "I know the way. I'll meet you there."

He didn't refuse. His long, muscular legs gained momentum, and she watched him shoot ahead then vanish down an incline. She slowed, catching her breath and admiring the wonderful view. The amazing silvery blue water rolled in white foam to pale sand, colors so muted they looked surreal in the summer sun. Above a baby blue sky spread a misty haze that lay over the foothills in the distance. The scene was breathtaking and inspiring, and her enthusiasm rose. Today she wanted to open her heart and share her dreams with Alan.

When the beach access came into sight, she veered downward toward the lake and climbed from the bike. The nearly empty beach seemed to be a splendor hidden from the world. The miles of sand and surf offered them solitude. Alan had spread a blanket at the foot of a sand dune, and her feet sank into the crystals as she made her way to his side.

He pointed to the sky, where a hang glider drifted above, his sail adding a splash of color to the pastel surroundings. "It's gorgeous," she said, sinking to the blanket.

Alan unzipped a backpack. "I brought a treat."

He pulled out two cans of soda and a cylinder of potato chips.

Juli popped open the soda tab and took a long drink then reached for a small stack of chips from the container. She nibbled on them, took another drink, then leaned back on one elbow and admired Alan's summer glow.

"You look so healthy."

"I've been trying to jog a little every day. Working long hours inside a hospital isn't good for a tan."

Neither was working at the Garlic Garden. "This is a good day, Alan. We're so rarely alone, and I've been doing a lot of thinking. I could really bounce some thoughts off someone."

"Bounce away."

He joined her on the blanket, his legs extended, leaning on one hip and propped on his elbow.

Juli adjusted herself and sat up with her legs crossed in front of her. "I know this is nothing new, but it is to me in a way. We talked before about my interest in social work and my lack of college."

"I hope I didn't cause you to feel that not having a college degree made you inferior."

"No. It wasn't that at all. I've looked into my own heart and realize I've pushed away my dream for fear of upsetting my parents, but yesterday in church some things struck me, and now I'm so confused."

"What happened yesterday?" He pulled his knees upward and scooted to a seated position beside her.

"God's Word." Juli shared the message she'd heard and the verses that had caused her new thoughts. "The verses about how God gives each of us different gifts. The one that really hit me was 'If it is contributing to the needs of others, let him give generously.'"

"You do give generously. Every time I see you with people at the soup kitchen, I admire you. Even though I work with people dealing with health issues, I'm too consumed with getting them better and not even thinking about their emotional needs. I need to work on that."

"But God's given me that gift, and couldn't I use it better in a field like social work or counseling? That's why I'm confused. Am I just falling back on an empty dream that should stay where it is?"

"I told you the other day you should use your talents to the fullest. Certainly you could be of greater service working with people dealing with problems."

Juli nodded, feeling emotion lump in her throat. "I want to do what God wants me to do. That's all I can say. Starting college at my age seems—"

"Your age?" Alan chuckled. "Juli, you're twenty-five."

"I'll be twenty-six in September, and I couldn't go full-time. I need money to live on, so it would take forever."

"You work for your dad. Maybe you could work full-time in the summer and fall when the produce is harvested and then work part-time in the spring and winter so you can go to school full-time. That would speed up schooling."

"That's what I need to hear. Practical ways to approach the problem. That's a great idea. I wouldn't have to dump everything on my dad all at once. I don't want to upset them."

176

Alan slid his arm around her shoulder. "I can't image your parents not supporting something you want so badly."

Her pulse gave a kick. Alan didn't know her parents. They were good people, but the focus had always been on being a good Christian and on the garlic business. She'd fallen into their needs so easily. "You'll have to meet them to understand."

Alan frowned.

"You don't want to meet them?"

"No, it's not that. I'd love to meet them, but I guess I don't understand your relationship with them."

"That's the paradox. I love them, but I feel bound to them." Her eyes blurred again. "I sound like a teenager trying to break loose from the proverbial apron strings. That's really what my problem is. I've never cut the ties and struck out on my own. I don't even know that I could."

Alan rose and reached toward her. She placed her hand in his as he helped her stand, and he drew her into his arms. She rested her head against his chest and savored his support. Alan gave her courage to take steps forward, and she knew God had blessed her with this friendship.

"You can do anything you want, Juli," Alan whispered in her ear. "With God all things are possible. You know that."

"I do," she murmured against his T-shirt. "I just need to remember it."

He drew her closer, and she stood beside him feeling the wind ruffle her hair and hearing the sound of the surf. She'd let so many things hold her back, and today she knew it was time to step forward and make her life different.

She drew her head back to look into his face. "Would you really like to meet my parents?"

"Absolutely."

"I'll invite you to dinner. You can see where I live, and we'll go down later and meet them."

"I couldn't be happier."

"You're kidding, right?"

He grinned. "I thought you lived in a tent and didn't want me to know."

She chuckled. "Sorry to disappoint you. I really live in a nice apartment in"—she needed to be trusting and honest—"in Gilroy."

"Gilroy." He let out a laugh. "You mean the gar—"

"The garlic capital of the world." The situation struck her as funny, and she laughed. Laughing about it felt so much better than the irritation that rankled her so often. She lifted her eyes to the clear blue heavens and sent up a grateful thank-You.

Chapter 8

Wait up."

Alan halted and turned in Tom's direction. He waved then waited for him to catch up.

Tom strode to his side and grinned. "You have a bounce to your step. What's up?"

"I'm off tomorrow."

"Not me. I have to work. I hate working the full weekend. Sunday's supposed to be a day of rest." He gave Alan a grin, as if wanting him to know he knew what God said in the Bible. "Any plans for the weekend?"

"Juli invited me to her house for dinner. I've never been there."

"You're kidding."

"No. She takes her time, and I don't mind that."

Tom winked. "I hope not too much time."

Alan didn't like the sound of his comment. "Just right for me. She's perfect."

"So is Megan. I'm seeing her again tonight. She's quite a woman."

"I've noticed." The words flew from his mouth before he could stop them.

Tom faltered. "What does that mean?"

Alan tensed, wondering how much to say, but he felt compelled. "You two seem to have dived right into a pretty heavy relationship."

Tom chuckled. "Jealous?"

Alan shook his head. "Not at all. My dating style is different."

"Different?" Tom stopped. "In what way?"

"I like to know a woman before I get carried away, and even then I want to respect her."

Tom drew up his shoulders. "Listen. I respect Megan, and I was honest with her, and I really do care about her a lot. Anyway, she knows what she's doing."

Alan wondered if Megan really did know. "I mean respect in a biblical sense." He placed his hand on Tom's arm. "I've heard you mention the Bible. Are you a believer?"

Tom's eyes widened. "I believe. . .I believe in God, but I'm not a churchgoer if that's what you mean. I know Jesus died for my sins, but—"

Alan waited, hoping he'd continue. "But what, Tom?"

"I don't know. If I sin a little, then I'm forgiven. Right?"

"You'd better start reading that Bible instead of talking about it. You need

178

to be sorry for your sins and repent."

Tom looked away, his head drooping.

"I don't want to judge you, Tom, and I think what you do is between you and God, but I also think it can lead to trouble."

"Trouble? You mean you're afraid she'll get preg—"

"I'm talking about friendship." Alan struggled to keep the shock from his face. "To me, an intimate relationship means commitment. I can't make a commitment until I know someone's heart and soul."

Tom kicked a stone with the toe of his shoe. "I'm not stupid, Alan. I'm not going to get either one of us in trouble."

"You're missing the point, but it's your life. Yours and Megan's. I think too much of Juli to use her."

"Use her?"

"I haven't even kissed Juli on the mouth, Tom. Not that I don't want to, but I'm giving it time. I want her to know that when I do, it means something."

Tom held up his hand like a traffic cop. "Stop right there. I'm not looking for marriage. I'm looking for a good time."

Alan shook his head. "That's my point. What about Megan? Maybe she expects more."

"I suppose you'll open your big mouth to Juli about this."

"It's your business. You lead your life the way you want. I just wanted you to know Juli and I were both uncomfortable last Friday with you two carrying on in the backseat. I'd like you to respect Juli at least."

"Sorry." He gave another stone a quick kick, and it skidded across the pavement. "I'll make sure we drive separate cars next time."

At least Tom would keep his hands on the steering wheel, Alan hoped. "I don't want to argue with you over this. I'm just letting you know I've thought it over, and I wanted to let you know how I feel."

"Consider it done," Tom said, stuffing his hands into his pockets. "See you Monday."

Alan watched him stride away and knew he'd caused stress between them, but he cared about Juli, and he knew she'd been ill at ease the week before. So had he. All he could do was hope that what he said might give Tom something to think about.

⁓

Juli stared into her refrigerator, eyeing the pork chops. Not only had she invited Alan to her house, but she'd also invited him for dinner. What was she thinking? She usually had Sunday dinner with her parents, and once she told them she was having company, her mother was all over her for details. She thought by the time she'd reached her midtwenties they would see her as an adult, but she had been totally mistaken. Her father still called her his little girl.

She released a stream of breath and pulled the chops from the refrigerator.

She planned to bake them in the oven. The oven heat came to mind. Today was too beautiful to turn it on. She'd barbeque, but that meant going into the yard, and her parents would be out there in a flash, probing Alan with questions. All she'd planned to do was drop by for a minute and introduce him to her parents.

For the hundredth time Juli realized she needed to move to her own apartment. She sank into a kitchen chair, knowing the convenience of living close to her work, but—

But what? If she had her own place, she wouldn't feel so hemmed in. What did Alan think of her still living at home, even if it was separate from her parents' part of the house? She could only imagine.

"Why did I invite him?" The words sounded in her ears and surprised her. She glanced at the clock, knowing she needed to start cooking. He'd be here soon.

Juli rose and opened the cabinet. She would make pork chops in mushroom soup. They were always tender and formed wonderful gravy. Alan would be impressed. After searching for a few fruitless moments, she realized she'd used her last can of soup. Drawing up her shoulders, she opened the door to the outside walkway, followed the stairs to the first floor, and stepped into the foyer.

"Mom?"

The scent of home-baked bread filled the air along with the sweet aroma of something else.

Her mother's distant voice greeted her. "I'm in the kitchen."

She followed the lengthy foyer past the staircase, through the family room, and into the kitchen, where her mother stood beside the oven.

"Mom, it's too hot to bake."

"We have air conditioning." She turned to greet Juli. "You know your father and his homemade bread, and I couldn't resist trying this new cake recipe."

"It smells wonderful." Seeing her mother's eager look, she knew the cake was probably her favorite.

"It's poppy seed cake with lemon zest. Your favorite."

She grasped her courage. "Remember, Mom—I told you I'm having company for dinner today."

"I know, but maybe you could bring your friend here for dessert." She gave Juli a broad smile.

Juli's stomach did a slow dive. "We'll come down after dinner for a minute."

Her mother faced her, waving an oven mitt that looked like a pig puppet. "What are you serving?"

The coincidence nearly made her laugh. "Pork chops, but I need to borrow a can of mushroom soup."

"Pork chops and mushroom soup? On Sunday?" She waved her pig puppet-encased hand again.

"It'll be good. The chops are so tender."

"Is Megan coming over?"

"No."

Her mother stood in front of her, waiting.

Juli looked at the pattern of the tile floor and exhaled. "It's a person I met at the soup kitchen."

Her mother's eyes widened. "It's not—"

"Mom, it's not one of the homeless, although that would be a very kind and Christian thing to do. Doesn't Jesus tell us to—"

"I'm sorry, Juli." She pulled off the oven mitt. "I know that some of the people have problems and—"

"It's one of the volunteers."

"Well, that's easy. Invite her to eat with us. That makes perfect sense."

Juli's heartbeat kicked up a notch. "Him."

"We always like to meet your fri—" Her mother's gaze focused on her. "Him?"

Juli put her hands on her hips. "Don't sound so shocked."

Her mother began to laugh. "Juli, you so rarely date that I am shocked, but pleasantly so. Your father and I have been worried you'll end up not finding a husband. You know the Lord said—"

"I know what the Lord said. It's not good that man should be alone." She tried to make her voice lighthearted. "But the Bible doesn't say anything about women."

"Juliana. Don't you make jokes about—"

"Mom, I'm sure God knows I'm joking. Don't you think He has a sense of humor?"

"Well . . . ," her mother sputtered. "No matter, I'm sure your father would like to meet your friend. Please invite him to dinner. I'm making pasta, and we have the homemade bread and the cake." She gestured to the oven. "Please."

Juli swallowed, anticipating her mother's response to her next question. "Are you using garlic?"

"Garlic? I always use garlic in pasta."

"Alan has an aversion to garlic. It's best we—"

"You won't even know it's there. I'll only put in a drop. How's that?"

Juli held up her hand to stop her mother's pleading. "I'll ask him, Mom, but if he seems uneasy, I'll cook as planned. I'm sorry, but I wasn't thinking about it being Sunday when I invited him."

Her mother's gaze dropped. "Okay. I can't ask any more of you."

She could, but Juli hoped she wouldn't. "Do you have a can of cream of mushroom soup I can borrow?" She eyed her mother's face. "Just in case."

Her mother opened the small kitchen pantry, pulled out a can, and handed it to Juli. "Here."

"Thanks, Mom." She leaned closer and kissed her cheek then stepped back. "Where's Dad?"

"He was reading the Sunday paper in the living room, but I'll guess if you check, he'll be sleeping."

Juli took a step backward. "I won't bother him, then." She inched closer to the door. "I'll call you after Alan gets here. Okay?"

"Okay." Her voice didn't convince Juli that it really was okay, but her mom was apparently trying to be agreeable.

Easing past the living room, Juli peeked inside and saw her dad tipped back in the recliner, an open newspaper ready to fall to the floor, his eyeglasses skewed to one side from the tilt of his head. She grinned and slipped outside.

As she darted up the stairs, the image of her mother's face hung in her memory. She didn't want the day to be stressful, but she'd told Alan she would introduce him, and she would. Juli wondered how Alan would react to her parents and then wondered what they would think of him.

Inside, she faced her refrigerator then tossed her hands in the air and sat on a kitchen chair. If Alan didn't want to eat with her parents, she would get creative. She wasn't sure what that meant, but that's what she would have to do.

$\sim$

Alan turned onto Wildrose Court, amazed at the homes. With Juli's reticence to let him pick her up, he'd suspected Juli's parents were hardworking people without a lot of finances, but the surrounding area gave him another perspective. Expensive two-story estates sprawled among rolling hills, pastel-painted stuccos and dark-stained homes with windows that opened to a grand view of the green fields in the valley.

When he spotted Juli's address, he put on the brake and sat a moment, wanting to turn around and leave just as he'd done at the restaurant. He could never be in Juli's league. Her family had to be wealthy with a Spanish-style villa with its tile roof and beige stucco. He studied the arched veranda and the wide outside staircase leading to the second floor. Juli's apartment, he guessed.

He couldn't run away. Instead he tried to face the truth. Juli hadn't missed going to college because of funds. She'd followed her father's wishes and worked in his store. Store? Garlic Garden had to be a massive business. Knowing he couldn't sit there all night, Alan grasped his good sense and pulled into the driveway.

When he turned off the motor and stepped out of the car, Juli's voice greeted him. "I'm up here," she said, waving from the second level. He took the steps to the top, facing her bright smile, but behind it he saw worry.

"Come in," she said, motioning him through the door.

He stopped his mouth from gaping when he entered. Decorated in Southwest style, the room burst into sunset colors taken from a large painting hanging above the arched fireplace. "This is awesome, Juli. I can see why you don't want to move."

"But I must. I realize that more and more."

Her tentative comment caused him to ask, "Why?"

"I told you on Monday. I need to stand on my own and get out from under my parents' guidance. I'm twenty-five. Don't you think it's time?"

How could he answer that question? He bit the corner of his lip, wishing she hadn't asked. "I think it depends on the person. I couldn't answer for you."

She nodded. "I know, and it's my answer to the situation. Thanks so much for listening to me at the beach. It was so helpful. I felt you understood."

"I do. As much as a person can who doesn't know the whole situation."

"Today you will." Her face brightened. "Let's enjoy the day. Would you like to look around?"

He did, and he didn't. "Show me the way," he said, noticing the lavishness of the decor. The more he saw, the more ashamed he was of his small condo. He'd cut corners, even with his good salary, to help his mother.

She led him into her kitchen, where he noticed she hadn't begun to prepare dinner; then he glanced through the doorway of the other rooms, admiring a private balcony where she could read or sun herself. "It's a wonderful place, Juli. I'm sure it will be difficult to leave."

"It will in some ways."

He watched her expression change and wondered what was coming next.

"By the way, my mom insisted I invite you to dinner in their house. I tried to say no, but my mom is very persuasive."

His chest tightened. "You mean have dinner with your parents?"

"If you don't mind. It would make my mom happy."

Juli had mentioned meeting her parents but not eating dinner with them. He'd already been startled by their wealth, and now he'd have to make conversation. Then he was bowled over by another issue. He'd never told Juli he was a physician. It didn't seem right telling her in front of her parents.

"Mom promised she would go light on the garlic, but if that's a problem, we won't go."

He started to say it would be a problem, but he saw the look on her face and realized what he had to do. "Will it make you happy?"

"When Mom's happy, I am."

Her comment gave Alan great insight. She hadn't learned to say no. He knew Juli's faith was strong, and he wondered if the commandment about honoring parents had kept her tied to them so tightly. Maybe she thought following their every wish was honoring them, but *honor* had a deeper meaning to him. "I'll be careful with the garlic. It'll be fine."

"Thanks. I wanted you to meet them anyway."

Her face filled with relief while he managed to cover his hesitation. Juli telephoned her mother, and she said they would come then hung up and returned to his side. "They're ready with hors d'oeuvres."

Alan hoped he was.

He followed Juli down the staircase and along the veranda to the front door. Inside, the opulent space almost knocked him over. A grand foyer with a large open staircase greeted him when they entered. A tile floor led in a multitude of directions. Alan noticed a dining room to his right with the table set for four places. To his left he glimpsed a sizable living room, and ahead he could see a massive fireplace and assumed it was the family room.

Juli guided him in that direction, and the scent of herbs and beef met him as they neared the kitchen.

"Mom." Juli halted in the doorway. "This is Alan Louden." She turned to Alan. "My mother, Grace Maretti."

"Mrs. Maretti, your home is beautiful," Alan said, extending his hand.

She wiped her hands on a towel and greeted him. "We're so happy you're joining us." She motioned toward the large window facing the backyard. "Your dad's outside with the appetizers, Juli. You know how pleased he is with the patio. I'll give a call when dinner's on the table."

One down, Alan thought as he followed Juli into the backyard, again overwhelmed by the view and the size of the house grounds.

Juli's father rose from his chair and crossed the flagstone with long strides. "Alan, how nice to meet you."

"Same here, Mr. Maretti," he said, noticing a spread of fresh vegetables and chips with bowls of dip nearby.

"Would you care for some lemonade?" He gestured to the large pitcher. "Or Grace has some iced tea inside if you prefer."

"Lemonade is fine," he said, following Juli to the table for a glass. He put a few vegetables on the plate but skipped the dip, fearing it contained garlic.

Once he was settled, he addressed Juli's father. "Juli tells me you have a produce shop."

He sensed Juli's discomfort, and now he wished he'd told her he'd seen her at the farmers' market in Monterey.

"We focus on garlic along with gourmet products and a gift shop. Would you believe last year we had over 140,000 visitors?"

Alan drew back, not able to imagine that many people wanting to purchase garlic. "That's amazing."

"We own a large garlic farm, as well." His face filled with pride.

Confusion settled over Alan as he wondered what troubled Juli about her father's business. He owned a huge farm and an amazing store and had gained wealth from garlic. Alan bit into a celery stick.

Juli gave him a furtive look then turned away.

"I'm impressed," Alan said, hoping to waylay some of Juli's concerns. "Juli didn't let me know how extensive your business is."

"My little girl's modest."

Juli gave an exasperated huff. "Dad, I'm not a little girl anymore."

Her father just grinned. "To me you always will be."

She gave Alan a desperate look. "I know," she mumbled.

Alan saw the tension in her face. He was certain her parents were good people, but they had a firm grip on Juli. Until she let herself do what her heart desired, she would never be free.

"Our son helps run the business. He's got the business sense—went to college and all that."

"I've heard," Alan said. "Juli mentioned she didn't attend school so she could help you in the store."

"I did all of this without college myself. God gave me good old common sense, and I inherited some land from my father then added a few hundred acres later. Amazing what a person can do with the Lord's help." He sent a loving smile to Juli. "She's a great manager. We'd be lost without her at the store."

Alan watched the comment knife through the air and stab Juli in the heart. "You'd manage. She's trained everyone well, I'm sure."

"Dinner." Juli's mother's voice cut through his comment, saving them from further discussion. Alan sensed Juli was uneasy about what had just happened, and he hoped he hadn't added to her stress.

When they gathered around the dining room table, Juli's father offered a blessing, and the food was passed. The salad came first, followed by a pasta dish with a green sauce that made Alan pause. Had this been the pasta that had made him ill?

Mrs. Maretti must have noticed his questioning look. "I hope you like pesto. It's made with olive oil, basil, and pine nuts, mainly."

She hadn't mentioned the garlic, but he thought he caught a faint scent of it. "I'm not sure I've had it," he said, spooning a little on his plate. Next came a bowl of mixed vegetables and large hunks of homemade bread. He took a forkful of the pasta and enjoyed the delicious flavor. If it had garlic, it wasn't overpowering. Alan was thankful for that. While they ate, Juli's father talked about garlic. Alan learned about types of garlic, including California early and California late, the most common. Mr. Maretti detailed the planting and growing of garlic and explained how to break the bulbs into cloves. Alan had become an authority over a twenty-minute meal.

Mr. Maretti used his fork to make a gesture. "Did you know garlic is a bulb of the lily family?"

"No. Really?"

"It's also related to the chive and onion, but now that doesn't surprise you. Some garlic is flowering and edible."

Alan began to panic. He didn't know if it was too much information or if he was becoming ill. He felt a tingling sensation along his limbs, and he began to itch.

Mr. Maretti's voice faded in and out. "Did Juli tell you she was the Gilroy High Garlic Queen the year she graduated? It was—"

"Dad. Please." Juli's voice split the air. "That's enough about garlic."

She looked at Alan, and her eyes widened.

Alan gasped for breath.

"Are you okay?"

Juli bounded from her chair and darted to him. "Alan, you're sick." She turned to her father. "He can't breathe. Please call 911."

Chapter 9

J uli paced in the emergency waiting room while her father sat in a chair reading a magazine, but she witnessed tension in his face. At the house the EMT gave Alan a shot of epinephrine before taking him to the ambulance. Garlic. It had to be. Before she and her father left, her mother had been distraught, promising she'd put very little garlic in the pesto sauce.

"I added oil, pine nuts, basil, and just a pinch of garlic," she'd said.

Juli's frustration had reached its peak. "Our whole lives revolve around the rotten stuff."

"Juliana!" she'd snapped. "It's garlic that gave you this good life. I don't want to hear you talk like that."

"I'm sorry, Mom. It's just that—" How could she have explained that she'd allowed garlic to cause her so much unhappiness?

Pushing away her thoughts, Juli drew in a lengthy breath and plopped back into the chair beside her father.

He lifted his head from the magazine. "Alan will be fine, Juli. I've never heard of anyone dying from garlic." He patted her hand and gave her a gentle-hearted smile.

She pressed her hand against his. "I know."

She hung her head and closed her eyes. Juli wanted someone to blame for her troubles, but she had to face the truth. She had caused most of her own undoing. She'd blamed her mother for the sauce even though she'd made an effort to adjust the ingredients. She'd blamed garlic for all the problems in her life, and now that she looked back, she'd probably caused her own lack of friendships, just as Dill had said. When her confidence flagged, she'd apparently become all business, in some way putting up a wall to avoid being hurt. How many people had she rejected because of the barricade she'd set up for herself?

College had been the same story. She'd wanted to go so badly but blamed her parents for not encouraging her. She'd put her dreams on hold for them, but was it really a fear of failure? *Lord, am I missing opportunities because of fear? If so, I haven't trusted You. Help me to see clearly.*

"Is someone waiting for Alan Louden?"

Juli spun around. "Yes." She rushed to the waiting room doorway and stepped into the hall with the doctor.

"Mr. Louden had dinner with you tonight."

"Yes. At my parents' house."

"He said he ate pasta. Could you give me more details?"

She explained about the meal, including the pasta dish. "Alan told me he had a problem with garlic."

"His reaction isn't from garlic."

"Not garlic?"

"That causes some stomach problems, and garlic dust can cause asthma symptoms, but Mr. Louden's problem was anaphylaxis."

"Anaphylaxis?"

"It's a severe and potentially fatal allergic reaction."

Juli felt breathless as her pulse accelerated. "Fatal?"

He nodded. "I'm afraid so. If he hadn't gotten here when he did, there would have been no guarantee. But don't worry—he's doing fine. He's been treated with corticosteroids, and he'll be able to go home, but he needs to carry an EpiPen with him. Certain nuts can cause this kind of allergic reaction, not garlic."

"Alan ate pesto sauce. It has pine nuts."

"Pine nuts. Now I understand. I'll talk with him about that."

Her shock gave way to relief. "Thank you, Doctor."

"You can see him in a few minutes. I'll send a nurse down."

"We'll be here. Thank you."

He walked away, and Juli stood there reeling with the news. Fatal. And more likely pine nuts than garlic. She turned and stepped back inside the waiting room.

"It's not the garlic," she told her dad. She sat beside him, and her tears broke through as she explained the news to her father. He wrapped his arm around her shoulder and let her weep against his chest. When she gained control, she sat up and wiped her eyes. "Sorry, Dad, but it was such a shock to hear the doctor say *fatal*."

"You don't have to apologize. I'm shocked, too." He patted her hand. "You really like this fellow, don't you?"

She saw something new in her father's eyes, tenderness she'd never noticed before. Swallowing her emotions, she nodded. "I do, but I don't want to rush anything, and I don't want to get hurt."

"Put it in the Lord's hands, honey. Listen to God in your heart, and you'll do okay."

She leaned her head against his shoulder. "Thanks, Daddy."

Juli sat there, resting against her father's chest and feeling safe and loved. Sadness washed over her as she thought how often she'd felt angry with him for his control when she'd been as much to blame for not expressing her desires and dreams to her parents.

"Juli Maretti."

The nurse's voice startled her. She pulled away from her dad and rose. "I'll be back in a few minutes," she said, hurrying toward the nurse.

"Don't rush," her dad said. "I'll call your mom. I know she's sitting by the phone."

The nurse's shoes scuffed along the corridor as Juli followed. The woman punched a button, and the emergency room doors opened. Juli stayed close behind her. White curtains divided the room into spaces, and they passed three before the woman stopped and pulled back the drape.

Juli stepped inside, and when she saw Alan, tears pooled in her eyes. "How are you feeling?" she asked, trying to control the quake in her voice.

"Much better now. I'm so sorry for this, and I'm totally embarrassed. Your parents must think I'm an oddball."

"No, they don't. They're concerned. Daddy's in the waiting room, calling Mom. I know she's worried." She rested her hand on his arm. "The doctor said you can go home."

"Good. I have medication, and I'll be fine now, but it came on so quickly I couldn't talk. I felt as if my throat had closed, and I couldn't breathe. I've never experienced that before."

She sat on the edge of the chair beside his bed. "And don't do it again, okay?"

Alan grinned. "I'll vote for that." His eyes searched hers. "It wasn't garlic, you know."

Her chest tightened at his smile. "I heard. He suspects pine nuts were the culprit." She brushed a strand of hair from his forehead.

"I've eaten nuts all my life. I assumed the problem was garlic. Not fair to judge without having all the facts."

"We do that all the time, don't we?"

He nodded as if understanding she meant far more than judging food.

The curtain shifted, and the doctor she'd met stepped into the cubicle. "You look much better. How are you feeling now?"

"Almost like new."

"You'll need to make an appointment with an allergist and go through the testing, but my guess is pine nuts. They come from a family that's different from most nuts, so often people don't realize they have an allergic reaction until times like this. It's good your girlfriend was on her toes."

Juli opened her mouth then closed it when Alan gave her a wink.

He tore a sheet from his prescription pad. "Here's the name of an allergist in Monterey you can call, unless you have someone else in mind."

Alan glanced at the paper and grinned. "I know him. He works with me at Community Hospital."

"I'll send him your records."

"Thanks."

The doctor slipped the prescription pad into his pocket. "I suppose you'd like to get out of here."

Alan smiled. "I can't wait."

The doctor grinned at Juli. "I think I can leave you in the hands of this lovely young woman if you'd like to go."

Juli felt the same old heat rise on her neck. *Lovely young woman.* One day she hoped she could accept a compliment without blushing.

◌

Alan leaned against the chaise lounge on Juli's balcony and licked the fork. "This cake was delicious." He set the plate on a table beside him. "We should have stayed down with your mom and dad. They're probably disappointed."

"They understand. They're both happy you're okay."

Alan brushed strands of hair from his forehead. "I'm mortified that I scared them like that. I'll make an appointment with the allergist tomorrow, but until I learn differently, I know not to eat pine nuts."

"You'll have to be careful and check ingredients on any food that might have them."

"I will." His gaze drifted to the hilly landscape beyond the house. The sun had sunk below the mountain, and now the expanse of green trees had darkened to blue and the landscape lay in shadows. The sky had colored like an artist's palette of Southwest colors—orange, coral, and deep purple, reminding him of Juli's living room.

He watched Juli gazing at the sky. "The view is gorgeous. You'll miss that if you move away."

Her shoulders lifted in a sigh. "I know, but I'll never be who I want to be if I don't. You've met my parents, and you can see they are strong people."

"But strong in a good way. They've stuck together and made a wonderful life for you. I admire that."

She nodded. "I know, and that's why it makes leaving difficult. I'm not sure they'll understand."

A question niggled his thoughts, and this seemed as good a time as any to ask. "Juli, why are you so uptight about your father's business? It's more than wanting to be a social worker."

Her head shot up as if she'd been stung by a bee. "What do you mean?"

"You told me your father sold produce. You said he had a store. You never told me he had garlic farms and a huge shop that made him a wealthy man. I was bowled over when I pulled up to the house today. I almost wanted to leave."

"Leave? Why?"

"I'm not wealthy, for one thing."

"Neither am I, Alan. My parents are."

"But mine never were. I grew up in a whole different world from yours, Juli. I'm rattled by the assumption I made, thinking you were trying to hide your poverty from me, a poverty I knew so well as a kid. I'm hurt that—"

"I'm sorry, but poverty or wealth makes no difference to me. I like you for

190

who you are and not for how much money you have."

He straightened his back. "I'm happy to hear that, but along with everything else, you've been evasive. I pictured your family working in a little store that sold produce. Your life seemed on the same level as mine. You—"

"I'm going to move, Alan, and then I'll be really poor the way you want me."

He gave her a placating grin. "I don't want you poor, but I thought you were. Anyway, you'll never be poor. Your father—"

She drew back as if he'd slapped her. "I know it seems I've lived off my father, but I pay rent and work hard. I'm finally getting the gumption to make changes, and all I can do is hope the Lord will bless me."

Silence hung on the air except for the buzzing of cicadas filling the night sky.

"You're right." He leaned forward and folded his hands on his knees. "You're being positive, and I'm dragging along my old memories instead of accepting my blessings."

She didn't respond for a moment. "Me, too, Alan. We're all lugging the old baggage around." She tilted back her head and rubbed her neck then released a lengthy sigh. "Maybe I should try to explain what's bothered me for so long."

He swung his legs over the edge of the chaise lounge and motioned her to his side. She rose, and they sat together facing the foothills and the first stars of evening.

"I wasn't popular in high school. I had bookish friends. The popular kids called us nerds."

Disbelieving, he shifted his gaze to her dark curling hair and her lovely mouth that so often curved to a smile for him. "You're kidding."

"I wouldn't kid about something like that. When the popular kids gave parties, I wasn't invited. It hurt me."

"Did you ever think they were envious?"

Her hand flew to her chest. "Envious of me? Now you're kidding."

He grasped her shoulders and turned her to face him. "I can't believe you don't know how amazing you are. You're beautiful, Juli. Inside and out." His eyes swept over her frame, her slender body, the slope of her delicate shoulders, her graceful neck covered by the dark curling waves.

She didn't speak, and her eyes searched his as if she were waiting for his admission of a cruel joke.

Alan opened his heart. "I'm startled you really don't know this."

"My family never looked for outward beauty. We grew up to be grateful for God's goodness to us. My dad worked hard. He was a wonderful employer and had good workers who returned every harvest. I never judged people that way."

He slipped his arm around her shoulders. "But others do. People try to undercut things that are a threat to them."

"I've never been a threat. Many of those kids' families had money. Maybe it was my personality. I was quiet. I know you don't see that now, but I was. I didn't have a lot of confidence. I didn't dress the way they did. I was different, so how could I be a threat?"

"Your goodness is a threat because it makes you stand out. People can ignore those who aren't a threat, those who aren't in their way to success, but they plot a course to wipe out competition. You must have been an amazing threat to those people. Were they all as wealthy as your family?"

"Wealthy? You mean with money, right?"

He nodded, astounded at her philosophy, a wonderful one he had to admit, and it made him care about her even more.

"No. Many of them lived in smaller houses, but I never flaunted my home."

"You didn't have to. They saw it and your life as better than theirs, and they couldn't handle it."

She shook her head. "I can't believe that."

"You can't understand it. That's all." His mind shifted back to earlier in the evening. "Your dad started to tell me something about your being the Gilroy High Garlic Queen. What's that all about?"

"That was the worst."

"What do you mean 'the worst'? Wasn't that an honor?"

"Yes, it was a big honor because the Gilroy High Garlic Queen also participated in the garlic festival each year in July."

"Did they pick someone or—"

Her eyes widened. "No, it was a vote. The whole school voted."

"And you won." His mind spun with confusion. The whole school voted, and she won. He couldn't understand her problem.

"It turned out to be a plot to embarrass me."

"A plot? The whole school was in on a plot?"

She lowered her eyes, and he waited while she pondered what he'd asked. When she lifted her head, he saw confusion in her eyes. "That's what I thought when it happened."

"You assumed that those who taunted you controlled the vote."

"They were popular and usually did."

Alan tilted her chin upward to look in her eyes. "Apparently not this time. The underclassmen voted for the person they liked and thought was worthy of the title."

She nodded. "I learned the truth later. The underclassmen were tired of the snobbishness and decided to vote for me, but the others—the popular kids— decided to make sure I won."

"Why?"

"The king always presented the queen with a bouquet of roses, but that year it wasn't roses."

"Okay." He hung on her every word and waited.

"It was roses and garlic bulbs."

"Garlic bulbs." He chuckled. "You mean the things that look like onions?"

Her face filled with mortification.

"That's inventive. Why didn't you laugh?"

"How could I? I was horrified."

"Why? *They* gave you the flowers, dear Juli. If anyone was at fault, it was the person who gave you the flowers."

"He and a couple of others were suspended and missed the graduation ceremony, but meanwhile I could never let it go." Her eyes widened. "The other day a girl I knew in high school came into the store with a college sorority friend. Guess how she introduced me."

"The Gilroy High Garlic Queen?"

She closed her eyes and shook her head. "The one who received the garlic and rose bouquet."

Alan drew her into his arms. "I love it. What could be more perfect for a garlic queen than a rose and garlic bouquet?"

Her eyes widened as if discovering a truth. "You love it now that you know."

In a moment she began to laugh, and Alan drew her closer, enjoying every moment.

When they'd quieted, he brushed her cheek with his hand. "We've known each other for nearly a month."

"We have. It's been so nice, and thank you for the good laugh. I need to learn to do that more when it comes to things that really hurt."

"Laughter is the best medicine."

"Proverbs says a cheerful heart is good medicine."

"You see, even the Bible agrees." He felt his mouth next to hers. "Juli."

She lowered her gaze, and he felt her release a faint shudder. Without asking, he lowered his lips to hers. Her mouth felt soft and warm. When he drew back, her eyes stayed riveted to his mouth, and he lowered his lips again and kissed hers lightly.

They sat in the quiet of the evening with the cicadas' song as their music, but nothing filled his heart more than holding Juli in his arms.

Chapter 10

Juli closed her cell phone and slipped from her car then hit the remote. As she headed toward the soup kitchen, she noticed Alan's car already parked in the lot. Her heart skipped, and she grinned, recalling his caring ways. He'd opened so many doors for her and helped her admit what she longed for so often.

The stuffy kitchen pressed against her as she stopped at the list to check her station then headed toward the salad bar, grateful she didn't have to cook.

Alan waved, and she waved back then noticed Tom had come again. He looked at her with expectation.

"She's not feeling well," she mouthed.

Tom shrugged and came closer.

"Megan just called," she said. "She's feeling ill. It's the sunburn. She said you went to the beach."

"I told her to use lotion," he said, rolling his eyes. "I'll check on her later." He walked away and settled in beside Angie.

Seeing the two together gave Juli a start. Angie seemed to gravitate toward the unattached males, and Tom appeared to be enjoying the attention.

Alan stepped beside her and rested his hand on her shoulder. "What's up?" He tilted his head toward Tom.

"He asked about Megan. She's too sunburned to come."

"Too bad," he said, but he seemed to linger.

Finally she turned toward him. "Is something wrong?"

His face validated what she sensed, and she looked over his shoulder. "Tom?"

He nodded.

"I've warned Megan."

He drew in a breath. "Tom's looking for fun. If Megan's getting too serious, I think she'll scare him away."

As they spoke, Juli could see Tom using the same come-ons he used with Megan. He whispered in Angie's ear, and she touched her chin to her shoulder with a giggle then shooed him back to his job.

"We've done all we can," Juli said, wishing Megan had listened, but Tom's behavior upset her anyway.

"Talk later," Alan said and headed back to his station.

Juli pulled the packages of lettuce from the double refrigerator, removed

194

the cellophane, rinsed the leaves, and began to chop the greens. She wanted to throttle Tom then asked the Lord for forgiveness. She expected he would eventually break Megan's heart. Friendship was precious, and she again thanked the Lord for someone in her life like Alan.

Megan had become too involved with Tom. She'd said it to her face, and though Megan claimed to be a believer, she'd missed the mark with her behavior. Juli cringed. She'd done the same but in a different way. She'd lacked trust in both the Lord and Alan, but she was working on it and prayed she could truly place her confidence in God and rely on Alan.

Her gaze drifted back to Tom, and she turned away, disgusted at his behavior. While she worked on the salad, she noticed they were shorthanded tonight. As much as Tom upset her, his being there helped them get the food ready for the people waiting outside. She could credit him for that. She hurried to finish her job, and it wasn't long before Bill gave the signal he was opening the doors. Everyone moved as fast as they could to bring the food trays into the dining room. Alan stepped beside her with the rolls and butter, and he and Juli doled out the portions.

After serving, Juli took time to speak to those who looked lonely or needed a listening ear, and she noticed Alan kneeling beside a woman who'd been sitting with her head braced on her hand. The earnest look on his face touched her. She'd been pleased to see he'd become more confident in speaking to the people, and she witnessed real concern on his face.

When people began to leave, Juli looked at the wall clock. They could be out of there by nine o'clock if they hurried. Alan had said they would talk later, and she'd set her heart on it. As she neared him, she noticed him holding a younger man's hand, and she suspected he was taking his pulse. She thought of something her father had often said: "You can take the boy out of the country, but you can't take the country out of the boy." It reminded her of Alan. He could leave the hospital for the evening, but he seemed to bring his nursing skills with him. Maybe that's what loving a career meant.

She carried trays into the kitchen and pulled out the cloths and bucket, poured in the disinfectant, added water, and returned to the dining room to clean the tables. This time she saw Alan sitting beside an elderly woman, her hand in his. She paused a moment, struck by what she'd missed earlier. Alan's head was bowed, and her heart melted as she saw him in prayer with the woman.

The next time she looked, Alan was nowhere to be seen. She hurried into the kitchen and found Alan standing beside the commercial dishwasher, moving a receptacle of trays into the machine.

"How did you get stuck here?" she asked after putting away the bucket and cloths.

"I might as well help while I wait for you."

"Looks like I'm finished."

He pulled off the plastic gloves and wrapped his arm around her shoulder. "I have something I want to show you. Want to go for a ride?"

"A ride?"

"Just for a while. It's warm, and I thought we could zoom down to the beach and take a walk."

The thought of a cool breeze excited her, and though Juli disliked the ride home after dark, spending time with Alan made it worthwhile. "Okay. I can't pass up a beach walk."

They said good night to Bill while he packed the last of the supplies away; then they headed outside. Even there the fresh air felt wonderful. She settled into Alan's car, and he walked around to the driver's side and slid in.

"Here's an offer for you," she said, grasping the opportunity.

"That sounds interesting."

"Have you ever been to the Gilroy Garlic Festival? I know how much you love garlic."

He chuckled. "I think you have your facts wrong, but no, I've never had the pleasure. Tell me about it."

"It's a fund-raiser that supports charitable groups and service organizations in Gilroy. I'm expected to be there, but it's not just garlic products. They have music and crafts. Dad has a booth in the vendors' section and donates his profits to the cause. It's a nice event."

"And you were the queen of garlic."

She waved his comment away. "Forget that. I try to."

"Never forget, Juli. People chose you to be the queen. It was an honor, and it will be an honor for me to go with you."

"Thanks. I wanted you to see the good side of garlic."

"I know one good side. You."

She gave him a poke. "I suppose I should say thanks."

He slid the key into the ignition, but before pulling away, he leaned around his headrest into the backseat.

"Here," he said, handing her a pile of brochures.

Looking at the one on top sent Juli's heart on a wild ride. "Where did you get these?"

"I stopped by the university and picked them up for you."

She gazed at the brochures, touched by his thoughtfulness. "That was so sweet of you."

"Not as sweet as you are." He started the engine and headed out to the highway.

Juli grinned then opened the first pamphlet and studied the information. "What's this Collaborative Health and Human Services curriculum?"

"It looked like what you need for social work. It gives you all the essential skills and training needed in the health and social service area. A bachelor's degree in that prepares you for a master's program in public health or social work." He pointed to the information. "I read a couple of them. They explain a lot of things, and from what I can tell, you can work in a related field while getting your master's."

She chuckled. "You know lots more than I do about this."

"You'll know it, too, once you read the material. I'm excited for you."

"So am I." She ran her hand over the shiny pamphlets. Holding them in her hands made her decision seem more real than she imagined; yet it also added to her difficulty. "I have to talk with Mom and Dad. I know it's going to shock them."

"It'll grow on them, Juli. When you look over the pamphlets, you'll see that some of the classes are offered online, or part of the class is that way. It will help when you're still working at the store."

"Online. I hadn't thought about that possibility." She shuffled through the brochures, noting the information each covered as Alan slowed and pulled into the beach parking area.

He found a spot, turned off the engine, and opened the door. "I checked Gavilan and Harnell College on the Internet, but they don't seem to have a social work curriculum. I know they're closer to you than Monterey."

"You did all that for me?"

He winked at her, closed the door, and came around to the passenger side. He held the door while she climbed out, and when she rose, they stood nose to nose. "I'll climb a mountain for you, Juli."

His lips were so close to hers, and her heart skipped as she felt herself stretching to kiss him. Her lips touched his as he drew her closer in an embrace that made her giddy.

"I've never kissed anyone before," she said as she tilted back to look into his eyes.

He gave her a questioning look. "That can't be true. We kissed the other night. You haven't forgotten already?"

She looked into his moonlit eyes. "I'd never forget that. I mean I've never initiated a kiss before. I can't believe I did that."

"Believe it, and don't stop. I loved every second. You're amazing."

She gestured toward the brochures on the seat. "So are you."

He wove his fingers through hers as they ambled to the sand. They slipped off their shoes and walked barefoot toward the water. Juli stepped in first, the white foam rolling forward. She felt the wave recede, pulling the earth back into the bay from beneath her feet. Alan rolled up his pant legs and joined her. They laughed when a wave splashed higher than the others and dampened their clothes. Then, throwing caution aside, she ran along the surf with Alan as the wind blew through her hair and a cooler breeze swept across her arms.

When they tired of the run, they returned to the sand, their feet sinking into the crystals while Alan enfolded her shoulders with his arm.

She nestled against his side. "You always think of the most wonderful things to do."

He chuckled. "A walk on the beach is wonderful?"

"I've never had this kind of relationship."

He arched his eyebrow.

"Really."

He arched both eyebrows.

"Never. Honest. You're such a special friend."

"You're special, too, Juli, and never forget it."

Alan became quiet. He shifted his gaze ahead of him as if in thought. "You've been so blessed, Juli, and yet you're so down to earth. So humble."

"I'm who I am. It's my parents' money, not mine."

He turned and faced her. "But you had luxuries and benefits a lot of kids don't have." He closed his eyes, and when he opened them, they were filled with sadness. "Kids like me."

"Kids like you? You went to college. I didn't."

"But that was hard work and blessings. I told you my dad died and my mom raised all five of us, but it wasn't easy."

The serious look she saw concerned her. "What is it, Alan?"

He shook his head. "Remembering."

She moved closer and twined her fingers through his. "You can tell me."

"It's hard to talk about it, Juli. Really difficult."

"I told you about my teen years. That was hard for me to talk about."

"I know it was, and I'm glad you did, but this is different."

Juli's mind spun with possibilities. She wanted to know everything about him, but she wanted to respect his privacy. "Never mind," she said, seeing the distress on his face. "Some other time." She moved ahead of him.

He followed her back to the car, both of them in silence. Alan opened the passenger door, and she slipped in. He rounded the car and settled beside her. When the engine kicked in, Alan pulled from the parking lot onto the highway.

The situation had put a strain on their conversation, and Juli slumped against the seat while another problem dropped into her thoughts, a problem she'd meant to discuss with him. Tom and Angie.

Since she'd watched Tom with Angie, Juli wondered what she should say to Megan. Nothing would be best, but how could she witness Tom's behavior and not say anything? She needed to pray about it. Juli looked at Alan out of the corner of her eye. "What should we do about Tom and Angie?"

She'd pulled him from his thoughts, she guessed, because he gave her a blank look before he seemed to understand. He shook his head. "Best to stay out of it, I suppose."

"But it's so difficult. I should avoid spending time with Megan, I think, because that's the safest. I'm so afraid to say something yet afraid of not saying anything. When Megan starts mooning over Tom again, I don't know how I can keep quiet."

Alan kept his eyes focused on the traffic. "It's difficult, but I'm not sure either of us can do any good. We've both tried."

She nodded, recalling the edgy conversations she and Megan had already had and how little good they did. Megan would have to learn the hard way, but it saddened her.

"Tom was open with me about his attitude." He glanced her way. "Marriage isn't in his future. If Megan assumed it was, she'll have to deal with it. I know that sounds cruel, but your getting involved can destroy your friendship with her, and when things end between Megan and Tom, she'll need a friend."

His words spread over her like a balm. "You're right. She'll really need a good friend."

She looked out the passenger window into the night sky. "I'll have to keep quiet, but that's going to take a lot of effort."

They fell into silence again, and soon Alan pulled into the soup kitchen lot beside Juli's car. He turned toward her. "Juli, I'm sorry about tonight. I've been plagued by my past, and I've allowed it to affect who I am today."

"I'm fine now. I understand. I did the same thing with my hang-up about Gilroy and everything related to it."

He reached for her hand and wove his fingers between hers. "The reason the soup kitchen means so much to me is because that's where we ate many of our meals. Not this soup kitchen, but others."

A wave of sadness washed over her. "You did?"

"My mom struggled to feed us after my dad died. The little insurance he had barely buried him, and his illness had eaten up most of their savings. Mom did the best she could, but when we were desperate, she marched us into a soup kitchen. It was usually the only real meal we had that day."

Juli felt tears pool in her eyes. "Alan, you could have told me. I understand."

"You understand with sympathy and pity, but no one can understand unless they've lived in that situation. I dealt with it, but watching my mom's shame and seeing her deprecated is something I still can't bear."

His words were disconcerting. She had never known poverty, and he was right. She could never really understand. "I don't know what to say."

"Say anything but you're sorry. I don't want pity, Juli. I'm proud we got through the bad times. I'm thrilled I did well in school and got scholarships and government aid because of our poverty status. God's been good to us, and now I can help my mom."

Juli shifted and put her hand on his face. "You're a good person, Alan. I won't say I'm sorry. I'm grateful you've been blessed."

She leaned back and spotted the car clock. "It's really late. I need to get going."

Alan grasped her arm. "One more minute? While I'm talking, Juli, I might as well clear the air completely. I've wanted to tell you something else. It'll sound dumb, but I hope you understand why—"

A loud *thump* sounded as something hit the car window, causing both of them to jump.

Juli saw a man's face peering in the window. "Who is that?"

"A drunk." Alan shook his head. "He probably wants money. I'll give him a couple of bucks, but he looks in bad shape—so when I step out, I want you to open your door and get into your car. I don't want any trouble. He might be on drugs. Are you listening?"

"I can't leave you."

"Yes, you can. I want you to get in your car and lock the door then get out of here."

The man tugged on the door handle then pounded against the window again until Juli feared it would break.

She riveted herself to the seat. "I won't."

"You will."

The determination in his voice forced her to give in. Alan wouldn't move until she left, and she feared the man would break his window or get more violent.

"Be careful," she said, pushing her remote then flinging open the door and bounding into her car. Her fingers trembling, she slammed the door shut and slipped the key into the ignition. Outside, she heard the man cursing and Alan's softer voice mingling with his.

She backed up and pulled down the driveway, but instead of leaving, she watched through her side mirror until the man spotted her and started running toward her. She shifted into drive and tore out of the parking lot, praying Alan would be safe.

Chapter 11

Alan watched the man veer toward Juli's car. The man's stagger delayed his steps while Alan prayed she would get out of there fast. When she sped away, he jumped into his car and peeled out toward the parking lot exit with the man chasing him. The man's muddled thinking saved Alan. No reasoning would have delayed the thief from using the knife he'd pulled from his pocket to take Alan's wallet. He wasn't happy with the couple of bills he'd tried to give him.

Alan wanted to wring Juli's neck for not leaving immediately. He understood why. She was worried about his well-being, but her delay could have caused both of them problems. He wouldn't let that happen again. "Thank You, Lord," he said aloud, grateful for God's protection. He shook his head, trying to clear his thoughts.

Alan pulled out his cell phone and hit Juli's number. Instead of getting the usual voice mail, he listened as her phone rang. When he heard her voice, he relaxed. "I'm fine," he said. "Are you okay?"

"Scared, but fine. What happened?"

He told her about everything but the knife.

"I'm sorry I didn't leave as you told me, but I wanted to make sure you were okay."

"We're both fine now, but let's not do that again. We should have learned our lesson from the purse-snatching incident. I'm sorry—I wasn't thinking."

He heard her deep sigh. "And ruin the most excitement I've ever had in my life."

He chuckled but managed to remain firm. "I mean it, Juli."

"I know you do."

Her contrite voice touched him. "Call me when you get home. Please. I want to know you're safe."

"I will. Promise."

He closed the lid of his cell phone and slipped it into his shirt pocket. Weariness rolled over him, some due to the adrenaline rush he'd had from the addict who wanted his money and some due to frustration.

Tonight he'd planned to be open with Juli. He'd made such a secret out of his career, and now it had turned into a monster. Since he had opened the door to his difficult past, he thought the time seemed right to tell her about his work. He wanted to do it face-to-face and not over the phone. He didn't want to make a big deal out of it either. Driving to her house made the revelation too dramatic. He wanted it low key, but he had to work long hours this weekend, and seeing her soon seemed unlikely.

Alan wished Juli lived closer to Monterey. Gilroy was a lengthy drive to Monterey to see each other when they had conflicting work schedules, but even though that was the case, right now he wanted to advise her to stay in her apartment. Paying for school and cutting back on work meant less income. Living where she did made more sense

Conflicts. They seemed to be a part of life. Not everything went smoothly, especially when working on a solid relationship. Juli had made it clear that trust was important to her. Despite her own misgivings, she'd opened up about the things that troubled her, and she'd told him her dreams. He'd fallen short by not being open and honest with her. He'd never lied, but he'd left things unsaid.

Lacking openness and honesty seemed to be Tom's problem. He'd led Megan astray with his empty promises. The situation turned Alan's stomach. He believed respect was a major part of any relationship, especially a romantic relationship. Yet Tom had led Megan on, letting her think he had serious intentions when he had nothing but getting his way and then dropping her for a new opportunity.

Do not judge. The words washed over him. Maybe Tom had been open, and Megan had failed to heed his warning. Either way it was a rotten situation.

~

When the telephone rang, Juli dropped the brochure and headed for the phone. Her hello was greeted by sobs.

"What happened, Megan?" Juli didn't have to ask. She could guess Tom had dumped her for Angie. In a few weeks Tom would dump Angie for some other woman eager for love, but what they found in Tom wasn't love. It was empty desire and nothing more.

"Tom dumped me," Megan finally mumbled between her tears.

"Megan, I don't know what to say." Good riddance was one thing, but Megan's feelings were what mattered now. "When I introduced you to Tom, I had no idea who he was. I thought he was Alan's friend, and Alan is such a good Christian."

"It's not your fault. You warned me, and I didn't listen." A hiccup sob cut through her words.

"Forget that now. That's not important. Do you want me to come over?"

"You're not busy?"

"I'm just sitting here. I'll get ready and be there in an hour or so." Juli looked at her watch, calculating Saturday's traffic.

"What about Alan?" Megan's question gave away her sadness.

"He's working a long shift this weekend. Everyone at the hospital seems to be taking vacations."

"Could you"—another sob broke into her sentence—"could you come?"

"Right away. See you soon."

Juli placed the receiver in the cradle and hurried to her bedroom. She took out a pair of capri pants and a top, pulled a comb through her tangled hair, and ran gloss over her lips.

Before she drove away from the house, Juli took a chance and hit Alan's cell phone number. If he was busy, she knew he would ignore the call. When he answered, her heart soared. "I hate to bother you."

"What's wrong?"

The concern in his voice meant so much to her. "It's Megan. She called, and I'm heading over that way. She's so upset."

"I know. Tom told me this afternoon he ditched her. I wondered if she'd call you." His voice softened. "I should have warned you, but I didn't want to upset you."

"It's okay, but I honestly don't know what to say to her. I feel bad even though I know it was as much her fault as his."

"Be supportive and speak from your heart. That's all you can do."

"It seems like so little. They saw each other so often, too often, really, and—"

"I know. What can you say to someone whose trust has been shattered? I'm glad I'm not in your shoes."

"They're way too small for you," Juli said, struggling to be lighthearted. "I'd better go. It'll take me awhile to get there."

"Be careful driving home."

"Maybe I'll stay there overnight. Don't worry. I just wanted to hear your voice."

"I miss you, Juli. That's the bad thing about this job. The hours are crazy. You know I'll be sending up prayers for both of you."

"Thanks. That's what we need. I—I'll talk with you later." The words *I love you* had nearly slipped from her mouth. She closed her cell phone, wishing she could say those words aloud to Alan.

To her, those three words held a deep commitment. She felt certain she loved Alan, but making a lifetime commitment tied her in knots. They'd only met weeks ago, and how could she be sure this wasn't puppy love rather than the real thing? Megan's situation came to mind.

Still, confidence burned in her heart. Alan filled her image of a soul mate, a man who respected her, who wanted only the best for her and could trust her with the story of his difficult childhood, and a man she could trust. It had taken time for him to open up, but he had. She'd told him everything, and now that the doors were opening, each had shared their deepest hurts and worries. To Juli that was love.

Even more wonderful, he was a Christian, and she sensed that God had guided their steps to meet. She thought back to the day Bill had asked her to train Alan at the soup kitchen. They'd hit it off so well that day. They'd teased and yet talked about having a purpose in life to help others. It seemed perfect.

As Juli drove, she dug deep for any wisdom she might have tucked in the caverns of her mind. She searched in her heart for God's Word. Thinking of Megan feeling abandoned and used by someone who had such little feeling for her overwhelmed Juli. How could Megan be so blind?

Blind. What if she'd been in Megan's situation? What if Alan had been taking her for the same kind of ride? Would she have been wise enough to see the truth? The idea unsettled her. She clamped off the thought. Alan would never hurt her. Never.

The traffic thickened as Juli drew closer to Monterey. Instead of driving on the main tourist thoroughfare, she turned away from the bay toward the city, where traffic would be lighter. The closer she came to Megan's, the more uneasy she became. "Lord, give me words and wisdom." Her prayer rose, and she felt her shoulders lift.

When she reached Megan's building, she took time walking to her apartment. Every step that drew her closer made her feel less capable of being a source of help. Source of help? What made her think she would be Megan's source of help? A Bible verse entered her thoughts. *"My help comes from the LORD, the Maker of heaven and earth. He will not let your foot slip—he who watches over you will not slumber."* This was Megan's source of help. Juli recognized she was only the messenger.

Alan leaned back in the cafeteria chair, thinking about Juli. He couldn't wait to see her. The past week they'd talked on the phone, but that was it. She worked during the day, and he'd been working the long night shift then sleeping during the day, exhausted from overtime in the ER. He'd even missed Wednesday at the soup kitchen. Though the volunteer job meant work, too, he loved it there. Another week of nights, and then he'd be scheduled back to his regular shift and have some days off. He couldn't wait.

This weekend he finally had a day off, and he planned to catch some sleep tomorrow morning and then go to the garlic festival with Juli. The idea made him chuckle. Alan Louden and the garlic festival—but he was falling in love with Juli, and garlic was an important part of her life. What he wouldn't do for love.

"What's so funny?"

Alan turned to face Tom. "Nothing's funny."

"You had a stupid look on your face."

"I was thinking about Juli and the garlic festival."

Tom snorted. "With your aversion to garlic, this sounds like love to me."

Although Tom was kidding, Alan wasn't. "I think you're right. She means more to me than I can tell you."

"Really?" He tucked his hands into the pockets of his lab coat. "Sorry I can't say the same."

Alan didn't want to deal with his romantic liaisons. "You already told me you broke up with Megan."

"Not Megan." He grasped a chair, pulled it to the end of the table beside Alan, and sat.

"No?"

"Angie."

"What do you mean?" Alan braced himself and wondered what was coming next.

"I really had fun with Megan, and she cared about me."

Alan had to bite his tongue from saying what was on his heart. "She did. She trusted you."

"I know. Now I realize how much I care about her. It's a new experience for me, Alan." He lowered his head. "I messed up. You got me thinking about being a Christian and about what God expects. I messed up double. Megan and God."

Alan's eyebrows raised. He'd never seen Tom look so serious. "What made the difference now?"

"I've thought about you and Juli. Your relationship is so strong. I've thought about what you said about respect, and I realize I haven't respected women much at all. Not even Megan." He lifted his head, discomfort on his face. "And I want to be honest with you. I didn't get that intimate with Megan. I tried, but she held me off. What I insinuated was just locker room talk. I should have respected her more."

Tom's confession startled Alan. He drew in a lengthy breath. "What do you want to do, Tom?"

"I want to make it right with Megan. What would you do, Alan?"

"I can't imagine being in that situation, so I'm not a good person to ask, but first you need to make it right with God. You need to open your heart to Him and spend some time in prayer, asking for His direction."

Tom closed his eyes and nodded. "I know. I've followed in my dad's footsteps, I think. He ran around on my mom, and they finally got divorced. It wasn't fun, Alan. It's not an excuse, but I guess I thought men were supposed to be like that. That's why I never thought about marriage. I guess I didn't want to ruin my own kids' lives with divorce, so it seemed impossible. But now. . .it's different."

Alan had never known about Tom's past, and he prayed the Holy Spirit would give Tom a double dose of God's direction and assurance.

"I know you're not an expert, but I'd still like to hear what you have to say."

Alan thought a moment. "You know I move more slowly than you. First I want to like and respect the woman I'm dating." He held up his hand. "And don't think I don't feel passion. I'm human, but passion doesn't last forever. Love does, and once trust is destroyed, it's difficult to regain. I guess my advice is move slowly. Prove yourself."

"I realize there's no guarantee with Megan. I don't know if she'll take me back, but I could try."

Alan shifted closer and rested his hand on Tom's shoulder. "This is when I turn to God for help. You've probably not been on speaking terms with the Lord very often, but it's never too late. Our imperfections allow God to show His power. 'My power is made perfect in weakness.' That's what He tells us. Think about it."

Tom looked thoughtful. "Thanks. I know you could blow me off and tell me I made my bed and can lie in it now, but you didn't. That means a lot to me." He shook Alan's hand then stood and walked away.

Alan let out a lengthy breath, amazed at Tom's revelation. He'd never seen Tom regret his actions, at least not like this, and to hear him say he needed God was awesome. He'd bounced from one woman to another. Each romance lasted until a new face came along and caught Tom's attention. He'd never shown a sign of remorse, and from Alan's memory he'd never longed to return to an old girlfriend. Something had happened to Tom.

&

"Juli."

Her mother's voice floated down the hallway, and Juli came from the bedroom, adjusting the second outfit she'd tried on. "Hi," she said, surprised to see her mother. "I thought you'd left for the festival."

"Your dad's slow this morning, and he wanted to know where we should meet for dinner."

Juli held back a frown. "Meet for dinner? Alan's picking me up. . .and I'm not sure if we're eating at the festival. You know how he is about garlic."

Her mother widened her eyes. "I thought his allergy was pine nuts."

"Yes, but—" How could she explain that some people weren't crazy about garlic? "He should be here any minute. I'll ask him."

"Good. Your dad wants to get to know him better."

Juli grinned. Not just her dad—her mom wanted to know Alan, too. She heard it in her voice, and she knew why. They realized Alan had become important in her life. "I'll give you a call when he gets here."

Her mother's gaze lowered to the lamp table beside Juli's recliner, and Juli's stomach rose to her throat. She watched her mother reach for the brochures she'd been perusing.

"What's this?" Her mother turned the pamphlets over then turned them back. She flipped through the stack then lifted her head. "What's this about?"

Juli drew up her shoulders. "I'm thinking about taking some classes."

"But these are health and human service classes. What does that have to do with business?"

Juli's chest tightened. Today of all days wasn't a time she wanted to get into this. She'd been praying and searching her heart for the best way to explain her longing to her parents. "It has nothing to do with business, Mom."

Her mother tossed them on the table. "Then I don't understand."

"It's something I would like to do for me."

Her mother's face filled with a quizzical look.

"Like nursing. You said you'd thought about being a nurse."

Her mother shook her head as if Juli were dense. "But I didn't become a nurse, did I? I became your mother. Your dad counts on you in the store, Juli. What would he do without you?"

She drew in a lengthy breath. "Alan answered that the other day. I've trained people well, and we have trusted employees who've been with us, Mom. Dad would manage fine without me, but I'm not leaving the store tomorrow or next week." She released an exasperated sigh. "Please—I'm just looking at the brochures. Let's not get into this now. I'm not you. I don't have children to raise."

"But you will." She swung her hand toward the doorway. "Alan's been seeing you for some time now. He's a nice young man, and your dad and I have hopes. I realize he's not in the same financial situation we are, but he's young. Your father and I struggled at first, too, and look at us now."

" 'Store up for yourselves treasures in heaven. For where your treasure is, there your heart will be also.' " The scripture verse sailed from Juli's mouth before she could stop it.

Her mother's eyes widened, and Juli wanted to pull the verse back into her heart.

"My heart is with the Lord, Juliana. A person can be well off and still be a believer. I'm shocked at what you've insinuated."

Juli crossed to her mother's side and put her arms around her. "I wasn't insinuating anything. I was trying to make a point. For me, wealth isn't important, but being of service to others is. I've had the longing for years to help people, and lately I've thought about being a social worker, even a counselor. But I put it aside because I know how much Dad wants me at the store. You know how much I love volunteering at the soup kitchen, and I realize it's because that's what I want to do."

Her mother flung her arms upward. "If that's what you want, I can't stop you."

"I'm not going to abandon the store. I can go to school part-time."

"I suppose Alan gave you this idea."

Juli pulled away. "Alan has nothing to do with this, but he's listened, and he supports my idea. He's the one who told me classes are offered online so I could still work."

"At least he has a brain in his head."

Juli's arms went limp. "And I don't?" She wanted to ask why her brother had been encouraged to go to school and she hadn't been after she'd graduated, but that would only cause more dissension.

"I didn't mean that." Her mother sank into Juli's favorite chair. "It's just a shock, and you've never talked it over with us." She fingered the brochures then pushed them into a stack.

"I'd planned to discuss it with you and Dad once I decided what I'd like to do. I wanted to have a plan—find a way I could attend college and still work, at least part-time."

Her honesty had caused another notch in the argument. "Part-time?"

"Whatever. I'm still giving it thought." She crouched beside her mother. "Please don't run downstairs and start something with Dad today. Alan will be here any minute, and we're going to the festival. I promise I'll talk with him tomorrow if you think I should, but I really thought you'd both be more encouraging if I had solid plans in my mind."

Her mother drew in a lengthy breath and released a deep sigh. "I hate keeping things from your father."

"I know, Mom, but—"

The doorbell chimed, and Juli froze for a moment then closed her eyes and opened them again. "Please." She turned and headed to the door.

Alan's face glowed when his gaze met hers. "I've missed you so much."

She tried to give him a signal with a slight tilt of her head. "I've missed you, too." She opened the door wider, and when he stepped in, she saw the surprise on his face.

"Hello, Mrs. Maretti. It's good to see you again."

Her mother nodded and rose from the chair, looking as if she carried the weight of the world on her shoulders. "Thank you, Alan." She walked past him toward the door. "Call me when you decide where we should meet for dinner, Juliana." She hustled outside and shut the door.

Alan's befuddled look would have made Juli laugh if she were in a better mood.

"Juliana?"

Juli tried to push her doldrums aside. "That's my full name. Everyone calls me Juli unless they're upset."

"I guessed something was wrong."

Juli motioned toward the table. "She walked in and found those. I didn't know she was coming."

Alan eyed the brochures then looked back at her with a frown. "You mean you have to hide them from your family?"

"Unless I want a big commotion, like right now."

"You're not a child."

"Tell them, Alan." Tears blurred her eyes. "I love my parents to death. They're wonderful and so good to my brother, Jim, and me, but they get an idea in their heads—an idea they think is good for us—and they can't get it out. It's like a legacy, I guess. My dad created this huge business and expects us to love it as much as he does." The tears couldn't be contained, and she felt them flowing down her cheeks. "I hurt my mom's feelings today with scripture. Can you believe it?"

"With scripture?" He gave her a dubious look.

"I'm not kidding." She told him what had happened as he drew her into his arms and brushed away her tears.

"Sweet Juli," he said. "Once they think about it and understand, it will work out. If God wants to bless you with a new career, then He knows exactly how to do it."

"Trust in the Lord," she said, realizing how little she trusted even her heavenly Father. "Thanks. It's so easy to try to handle everything myself."

"That's just your way. Our way. I'm guilty, too." He took her hands in his, leaned back, and broke into song to the tune of "Oh, Susanna." "Oh, Juliana, oh, don't you cry for me, 'cause I come from—"

She pulled away and gave him a poke in the side. "Don't make fun."

"But it's so cute." He pulled her into his arms. "So what's happening now?"

"My parents want us to eat with them at the festival. I reminded her you don't eat—"

"Everyone eats garlic at the garlic festival. Anyway, how can we say no? You're already in hot water. Maybe my being around you will keep things calm."

"Would you do that for me?"

"I told you. I'd climb a mountain."

She threw her arms around his neck. "But that's probably lots easier than dealing with my dad."

⁓

Alan had never seen Christmas Hill Park before, but today it appeared to hold the population of Monterey. He'd had a difficult time finding a parking space, and they'd had to walk to the park since many of the roads were barricaded. He slipped his hand into Juli's as they headed inside.

"I can't believe this many people like garlic."

"Everyone likes a party."

He squeezed her hand. "True." He glanced at the throng, wondering if they might have lost her parents. He'd so longed to talk with her today and tell her he was a physician, but adding to her stress now didn't make good sense.

He'd begun to understand why she'd been so hesitant to change her career or even discuss it with her parents. They didn't understand that one person's treasure was someone else's junk. A poor analogy, he knew, but it worked for him.

"I told Mom we'd meet them by the Garlic Garden booth. Dad hangs around there a lot anyway, schmoozing."

He grinned. "Makes sense to meet there," he said, letting her pull him along. "In all the confusion I forgot to ask how things worked out with Megan."

"She's okay. We talked about a lot of things. She's confused, but I hope she's on the right track. I brought up God's expectations and His blessings. She really listened."

"I'm glad." He slipped his arm around her waist and held her close.

"But it gets more interesting. Megan called me this morning."

"What happened?"

"You'll never believe this."

He looked at her dubious expression. "Believe what?"

"Last night Tom sent her a huge bouquet of flowers—roses and orchids. She said she'd never seen such an arrangement, except at a funeral."

Alan chuckled at the description but not at the news. "He told me yesterday he'd made a mistake. I didn't know what to think. I've never heard Tom talk like that."

"Really?" She put on a playful pout. "And you didn't tell me."

He shrugged. "I didn't want to get your hopes up. I never know what to expect from Tom." He patted her hand. "What did Megan say?"

"She had mixed feelings, I think. She was flattered but doubtful it could make a difference. Trust is trust."

"It is," he said, his own messy situation coming to mind. Next week he was on overtime again, and he knew he had to broach the subject of his career. "It's odd how something that seems so unimportant can become so important."

"Trust? You think that's unimportant?"

"No. I didn't mean that. I meant sometimes—"

"I'm teasing." She smiled and pointed ahead. "The vendors are this way."

Alan decided to let the topic drop. This wasn't the time, and it was probably for the best. Maybe today if they found a quiet spot, they could talk. She spoke about trust often, and he had no doubt not telling her would also be a trust issue. He needed time to explain.

As they wended their way through the crowd, Alan spotted five young ladies with tiaras and long gowns—the garlic queen and her court, he assumed. "Look." He pointed through the mob. "That was you a few years ago." He actually felt proud.

"No, that's the real Miss Gilroy Garlic Festival Queen and the runners-up."

He drew back. "That's not the same queen you were back then."

"Right. I was the high school garlic queen. I participated during the crowning of the real Gilroy Garlic Festival Queen. I wasn't eighteen yet, and you have to be for this contest. Anyway, this one is based on an interview, talent, evening gown, and a speech—like a beauty contest. That's not me."

"What do you mean? You have tons of talent. I think you're gorgeous, and I've never seen you in an evening gown, but I'd love to."

"What about the speech?"

He wrapped his arm around her shoulders and drew her to his side. "You make me smile, Juli. I love. . .the way you can do that." He'd swallowed the word that seemed so logical.

As Juli maneuvered her way through the crowd, Alan followed. Stands had been erected displaying everything from wooden and metal crafts to handcrafted jewelry, leatherwork, and dried flowers, and ahead he saw braids of garlic. Finally they entered the food area with ice cream, strawberry desserts, garlic cookbooks, souvenirs, and root beer floats. When he spotted the sign announcing the Garlic Garden, Juli hesitated.

"There they are." She gave him a plaintive look. "I hope my mother didn't say anything about the brochures. I'll be able to tell, and I'll really be irked if she did."

Alan understood but wanted to avoid any confrontation, especially here. "Think positive. Just be yourself."

She gave him a feeble grin then charged off, waving as if nothing were wrong, and her father waved back, a smile lighting his face.

"There's my girl," he said then extended his hand toward Alan. "Good to see you again."

"Thank you, sir. I've looked forward to today." Not to eat garlic, he added to himself, but to see Juli.

"Alan, this is my brother, Jim." Juli motioned to the man standing inside the garlic booth.

"Jim," Alan said, extending his hand. "It's nice to meet you."

"Same here," he said with a crooked smile. "I hear you've been spending time with my little sister."

Juli shook her head. "You sound like Dad, except I'm his little girl."

Alan ignored the banter. "Yes, I've been enjoying your sister's company."

"I heard you met at a soup kitchen in Monterey."

"True. Juli trained me on my first night, and that was the beginning of a great friendship."

Jim chuckled. "Friendship?"

Juli shook her fist. "Stop teasing, Jim. Yes, friendship."

"No fighting, kids," her father said, chuckling. He turned to Alan and made a sweeping gesture toward the surroundings then back to his stand. "What do you think of the place?"

Alan eyed the braids of garlic, bins of garlic buds, and jars of something he assumed contained garlic. "Unbelievable." That was also true. He couldn't believe how many people flocked to the park to celebrate something he'd avoided for so long.

Mr. Maretti patted his belly and eyed his wife. "Ready to eat?"

"We're ready," Juli said, her expression still cautious.

Her father turned to Jim. "You're okay for a while?"

"Fine, Dad. Have fun. And, Alan, I'll set you straight later. You know, give you the lowdown on my sister."

"I can't wait," Alan said, giving him a thumbs-up as they stepped away, pleased to see the brother was a nice guy and Juli held no resentment that he could see.

They walked a short distance until Juli's father stopped and gestured toward the booths. "Who wants to get what?"

Alan noticed Juli studying her mother, who seemed very quiet. He hoped, for Juli's sake, her mom had kept the brochures to herself.

"Can we look around?" Alan whispered to Juli.

She shrugged. "Dad's hungry." She moved closer to her father. "Alan and I'll look around. He's never been here."

"Well, hurry back. The lines are long already."

Alan and Juli dashed through the stands as if they were taking a crash course in home economics while he tried to calculate which food he dared try. When he and Juli returned, each was sent to a different booth to purchase food for the group. Alan stood in the line for barbeque ribs and sandwiches, while Juli headed for the lemonade stand. Her mother had been assigned corn on the cob, and Mr. Maretti had suggested Thai food.

Music spilled from the amphitheater as they made their way to the picnic area, and when they spotted a family leaving a table, Alan rushed ahead to claim it. Their purchases were shifted and moved so everyone could reach them, and finally they bowed their heads as Juli's father asked the blessing.

Alan took a bite of his sandwich, followed by a few fries. Fearing the items were loaded with garlic, he waited a moment to see if he sensed any reaction, but perceiving nothing, he dug in.

Two passersby approached their table, and Mr. Maretti scooted from the bench, his voice booming his greeting. Juli's mother joined him, and grasping the moment alone, Alan slipped his hand in Juli's. "What do you think? It's going okay, don't you think?"

She nodded. "He doesn't know yet."

Alan pressed her hand. "I'm glad. It's hard to believe this caused such excitement."

"Told ya," she said, her voice playful yet disheartened.

Alan nibbled at a pork rib, hoping he and Juli could get away to spend time alone; but in another minute the friends said good-bye, and Juli's parents sat back down on the picnic bench.

Silence filled the air a moment, and Alan sensed tension.

"Do you want to tell your father about the brochures?"

Her mother's voice struck Alan like a dart coming from nowhere.

"What brochures?" Her dad's face filled with question. "A new idea for the store?"

Juli looked as if she wished she could shrink into the picnic bench. Her eyes snapped fire, and she sat with her mouth half open as if she could find no words.

Alan swung his leg over the bench, unwilling to stay and witness the private family discussion.

"Nothing for the business, Dad," Juli said, irritation in her voice. "Just some brochures I was looking at for me."

Her dad did a double take, looking at his wife and then at Juli again. "What kind of brochures?"

"College classes."

A heavy frown settled on his face. "Your brother handles all the business matters, Juli."

"I know, Dad."

"Then you don't really need classes, do you?"

Alan patted Juli's hand. "I'll take a walk."

Juli stiffened. "Mom, why did you do this today?"

"Do what? You said you'd planned to talk to us."

Juli's face sank with discouragement as she looked at Alan. "You don't have to go."

"It's best. I'll be back."

As he stood, he could hear Juli's volume rise. "Mom, Alan's here, and we were having a nice day. I don't understand your reasoning."

"I don't understand yours," was the last thing Alan heard Juli's mother say. He headed toward the music. He didn't want to abandon Juli, but he didn't want her to be mortified by his witnessing a family argument.

Chapter 12

Juli sensed movement behind her and felt Alan's hand touch her shoulder.

"How did it go?"

The confrontation flashed through her mind. "It could have been worse, I guess."

"Really?" He slid onto the bench. "What happened?"

"Daddy was angry at first, but I told him I'd waited to talk to them until I had a clear picture of how I could attend school and still be part of the business."

"For now."

His understanding covered her like a balm. "For now, but I didn't say that. I think it was understood. He appreciates my consideration, but naturally he's dubious about a new career."

"You expected that."

"I did, but I chuckled to myself because afterward he kept telling me how long it would take to get a degree. I think he figures I'll get discouraged and give up so it won't be a problem."

"And will you?"

"I don't think so. I really don't." She wove her fingers through his. "Now that it's in the open, it feels real to me, and I'm excited. I know it'll be difficult and stressful, but anything that's important makes it worthwhile."

He nodded as if he understood. "So where do you go from here?"

"I need to apply and see what happens. I was a good student. I think I'll be admitted with no problem."

"I agree." Alan drew closer, and his gaze searched hers. "Are we alone finally?"

Juli glanced at her watch. "Dad asked me if we were going to the amphitheater for the next show. It's swing music. He gets a kick out of the dancers. I hated to say no after the fiasco, so I told him we'd find them there. I think we'd better go." She saw disappointment in Alan's eyes.

He rose and offered his hand as she climbed from the picnic bench. He didn't say anything but slipped his arm around her waist. She nestled her head against his shoulder a moment, wanting to kiss him so badly, but the picnic area was filled with people, and she resisted the desire.

They headed toward the music event in silence, Juli thinking about the fracas and Alan apparently thinking about something else. She knew he was disappointed.

"I didn't mean to abandon you earlier," Alan said, his comment unexpected now that the subject had dropped. "I thought you'd be more comfortable, but after I walked away, I hoped you wouldn't think I didn't care or didn't want to support you."

"I understood. I would have been uncomfortable if I'd been in your shoes, too."

"They're too big for you."

She chuckled, remembering her earlier shoe comment. Her spirit lightened, knowing they'd make the best they could of the day. Any time with Alan seemed magical.

When her cell phone sang a tune in her shoulder bag, she stopped. "Who could that be?"

"If you'd answer it, you'd—"

She bumped him with her hip and finished his teasing comment. "I'd know." The phone struck her fingertips as she dug through her purse. She pulled it out and glanced at the caller. "It's Megan. I hope nothing's wrong." She flipped open the phone and answered.

"Tom sent me another huge bouquet of flowers with a note. He wants to see me. What should I do?"

Juli bit her lip then glanced at Alan and mouthed what Megan had said.

He shrugged. "It's up to her."

"Megan, listen to your heart and do what you think is best, but I want you to remember that going slow is better than racing into a problem."

"I know. My heart wants to see him, but I don't know if I can trust him anymore."

"Tell him that. Tell him you'll be on a slow track. If he's willing to wait, and I mean *wait*, then your question has been answered. Jesus told us to forgive if a person repents. Give him a chance to do that."

"Thanks, Juli. You're the best friend anyone could ask for. I should have listened to you weeks ago."

"That's the past. This is the future."

"I love you," Megan said.

"Love you, too." She flipped the phone closed and dropped it into her bag with the words *I love you* ringing in her head. She longed to say those words to Alan, but she wanted to take her own advice. *Take things slowly. Love doesn't run away. It grows and is nourished by patience and thoughtfulness.*

She slipped her arm around Alan's back and smiled at him. When he grinned back, her heart started to swing just like the music that filled the air from the amphitheater.

❧

The heat of the kitchen smothered Juli as she walked through the back doorway. Why on such a hot day were they frying meat? She passed the large pots filled with tomato sauce then spotted the fried hamburger. Spaghetti. She managed to smile at the people she passed, knowing her bad mood wasn't anyone's fault. The confrontation with her parents lingered in her mind, and today she knew Alan wouldn't be there either, and that always disappointed her. Next week he'd be back on his regular shift, and that gave her something to look forward to.

Bill strode toward her, and she recognized the need for a favor on his face. She eyed the sauce, and her heart sank. Not today.

"Hi," he said, giving her a bright smile. "Can you handle the sauce? We're shorthanded. You know how it is in the summer. I started browning the meat."

Juli eyed the simmering sauce, its steam misting the air, and nodded. Bill had always been kind, and today she couldn't refuse him the favor, no matter how stressed she felt. She turned down the flame under the burner, slid the huge pan to the back, and emptied a large block of ground beef into the new pot. Someone had diced onions, and as the meat sizzled, she added them to the mix.

Dill slipped behind her and rested his hand on her shoulder. "You got the hot job. Want to trade?"

Though she always suspected Dill had an ulterior motive, his offer seemed genuine. "No, it's okay. Bill asked me, and I can do it."

"I don't mind. Really."

She shook her head and brushed the perspiration from her forehead with her arm. "I love making spaghetti." Her tone had a facetious ring to it.

"I bet." He chuckled. "If Bill asks you to dole it out later, I'll take over then."

She agreed and concentrated on browning the ground beef.

As always, Alan filled her thoughts. She'd recognized his frustration on Saturday when they had no time alone, and between that and the upsetting talk with her parents, she didn't blame him for having a strange look on his face. She'd thought he wanted to tell her something or ask her a question, but he never did, so she'd decided it was her imagination.

Megan had called again on Sunday and said she was having dinner with Tom. Monday when she called, she told Juli he'd apologized and given her a gift, a gold necklace with a heart pendant.

"Will you wear it?" Juli had asked and was happy to hear Megan had thanked him but asked him to keep the gift until she knew what she wanted to do. Juli praised God for Megan's courage. The difference in her actions today compared to a week ago seemed a 180-degree turn. The most surprising news was that Tom accepted her offer and promised he would prove himself worthy.

The meat's sizzle drew Juli back to her work, and she lifted the heavy skillet, poured some of the grease off, then spooned the meat into the sauce. Her hand trembled from its weight, and she hurried to empty the pot before she dropped it. With a relieved sigh, she set it down.

She turned off the burner on the second pot and lifted it; but this time her arm couldn't keep the weight steady, and grease splashed from the pan to the floor. She looked around for help then spotted Dill and called to him. As he bounded toward her, she nodded toward the floor. "I spilled grease. Be careful!" she yelled so everyone could heed her warning.

"You want me to wipe it up?"

"First could you hold the pan while I empty the meat into the sauce? I did the first pot, but this one is too heavy."

He lifted the kettle, and she used the large spoon to scoop the meat into the other pot of sauce and give it a stir. "Thanks."

He lowered the pot to the counter. "Anything else?" He gave her a wink.

"No, I'm fine. Thanks." When he stepped away, she rolled her eyes, recognizing one of Dill's toying come-ons. As she moved to stir the meat into the sauce, Juli felt her foot slip on the greasy floor. She tried to catch herself, but the hot burner seemed her only choice. Instead she reached for the center island without success. She lost her balance, her ankle twisted, and she tumbled to the floor. Pain shot up her leg, and a groan escaped her. She heard a gasp from others. Before she could move, Bill reached her side.

Gritting her teeth, she pressed her hands against the floor to rise, but he knelt beside her, holding her in place.

"Don't get up," he said with such authority he sounded like her father.

"Why?" Although she kept her voice steady, her hand trembled as panic gripped her.

"I want to check your ankle. You might have broken it."

"I'm fine." She waved him away.

"Let me decide that."

"Should I call you Dr. Bill?" She tried to grin, but she knew her expression looked more like a grimace.

Bill didn't smile back. "Someone put ice in a plastic bag."

"I'm okay. Really." While she said the words, a sharp pain charged up her leg, and she couldn't hold back the moan that followed.

Bill rose, his hand spread over her as if holding back a lion. "I'm not sure if it's sprained or broken, but we're not taking any chances. I'll call 911."

"911? Please—that's ridiculous. I can walk, and I'm not going to the hospital in an ambulance."

Dill stepped forward. "Would you go to the hospital if we can get you into a car?"

Juli stopped fighting. Her ankle throbbed, and she felt miserable. She'd bumped her shoulder when she fell, and she was sure she would have a horrible bruise. "Okay. I give up."

Bill thought a moment and dug in his pockets for the keys. "Put her in my car right outside the door, and I'll be there in a minute. I'll get Randy to take over." He tossed Dill the keys and hurried away.

Dill helped her get up while another young man moved in, and together they made a seat with their arms and lifted Juli off the ground. She felt like a child on a swing, except for pain rolling from her foot up her leg.

Juli clung to their shoulders. Once she was settled in Bill's car with the ice bag tied around her ankle, she leaned against the headrest and tried to control the pain pulsing along her limb. *So dumb,* she thought as she recalled how she'd warned everyone else of the grease.

Bill slipped into the car and started the engine while Juli closed her eyes. "Would you mind taking me to Community Hospital in Monterey? Alan's working tonight, and—"

"It'll take a few minutes longer, but I can manage that."

She felt ridiculous asking, but she wanted to be with Alan, and she hoped she would see him there.

Bill pulled out of the parking lot and switched on the radio to a blues station. The music lilted her into a calm as she sent up a prayer that the Lord would bless her injury with an uncomplicated diagnosis like a simple sprain. Anything but a break.

Bill hummed along to an old tune, and she let her mind wander, thinking of the past couple of weeks and all that had happened. Tonight Megan and Tom hadn't been at the soup kitchen, and now they would be very shorthanded with her mess-up.

When Bill's voice jolted her, she wondered if she'd fallen asleep. He'd turned into the emergency entrance of the hospital and slowed to a stop near the door. In moments she was helped into a wheelchair and taken through the wide double doors, where she presented her insurance information and was wheeled to the side to wait.

As she felt her chair move and saw an aide behind her, Bill came through the door and signaled he'd wait in the lounge. Poor Bill, getting waylaid by her carelessness. She nodded to him, wishing she had someone else and thinking of Megan, who lived close by. If she could come and give her a ride back to her car, then Bill could return to the soup kitchen.

"Could I make one call?" she asked over her shoulder.

The aide shrugged, so she took that as a yes and opened her bag to find her cell phone. Megan answered. "Don't panic. I'm in emergency at Community Hospital right here in Monterey."

"Emergency?"

Before Megan lost it, Juli told her what had happened. "I'd like to send Bill back to the kitchen. They're really shorthanded, and I thought maybe you could drive me back to my car unless you're not feeling well."

"I'm fine. Just tired, but I'm not too tired to come. I'll hurry over."

Confident Megan would be there, Juli asked the aide to send someone to the waiting room and tell Bill she had a friend on the way so he could leave. She looked at the clock, longing to get into a room and learn what was wrong. Sitting there wasn't accomplishing anything but making her more nervous.

The aide returned and in a moment whisked her through the doors and settled her inside a curtained cubicle. He walked away without a word. She sat, waiting and glancing at her watch until finally a nurse entered with a million questions and took her vital signs. A male nurse joined her and helped Juli onto the table. They left and slid the curtain closed.

Juli wished she'd thought to ask for Alan or at least asked one of them to let him know she was there. Time dragged, and she wondered if Megan had arrived yet. Finally she heard sounds outside the curtain, the fabric slipped back, and Alan stepped inside. Juli watched his face shift from one expression to another until he seemed to accept that she was sitting there on the examination table.

"What happened to you?" His gaze shifted over her frame like a searchlight, apparently noticing the slight redness on her arm but ending up on her swollen ankle.

Seeing him in a lab coat sent her pulse on a jog. He looked so handsome and professional. "I slipped on grease. Really stupid. I'm sure it's nothing, but Bill insisted on bringing me here."

"Why here?" He frowned. "You'd have been closer if—"

The look wasn't what she'd expected. "I knew you were working. I asked him to come here."

"Let me take a look."

His concern was riddled with another expression she couldn't understand. "Maybe I made a mistake. I wanted to see you."

He pulled gloves from a box on the wall and tugged them on as he moved to her ankle.

When he touched it, she tried to control a moan but without success.

"Can you point your toe upward?"

She forced it up, trying to cover the stabbing ache. He had her move it right and left. The movement sent pulses throbbing through her foot.

"It hurts here?" he asked, probing the area.

She tried not to groan. "Maybe it's just a little sprain."

He raised his head. "It's not a little anything until we get some X-rays. It's probably a second-degree sprain, but you could have a fracture."

Even with the throbbing, she couldn't avoid being amused. "Who do you think you are? A doctor?"

When he lifted his head, he didn't smile, and her gaze moved to the ID tag on his lab coat. ALAN LOUDEN, MD, COMMUNITY HOSPITAL OF THE MONTEREY PENINSULA. She felt as if she'd been punched in the stomach and then dropped three floors in an elevator. MD? But she thought he was a nurse. A multitude of emotions washed over her. Confusion. Disappointment. Pride. Her focus adhered to the ID tag. "You're a doctor? You told me you were a nurse."

His face tensed as he gave her a brief nod without looking at her. "I didn't, Juli. I told you I nursed patients, and I do."

She searched his eyes, wanting more answers. "How many times have I asked you about your day? You just told me you were busy with a motorcycle accident or a child's broken arm or someone with a dog bite or someone with an allergic reaction. When I asked you where you went to school, you told me University of California at San Francisco. They have a huge nursing program there."

His head lowered. "They have a medical program, too, Juli. I'm sorry."

"Is Tom a doctor, too?"

His eyes shifted from her ankle to her face. "No, he's a nurse." He shook his head. "It's a long story, Juli, and I tried to tell you a few times, but something always got in the way."

"Got in the way? Of something this significant?" The word *trust* knifed through her. Why would he hide part of his life from her? How could she trust him now? What other secrets did he have?

"I'm sorry, Juli." He leaned over her. "Could we talk about this later? I want to arrange for X-rays, and we're really busy tonight."

Before she could respond, he slipped through the curtain and vanished.

Physician? Medical doctor? She had pictured him as a nurse but never a doctor. She shook her head, trying to imagine his reasons for not telling her. Had he felt sorry for her never going to college? Had their relationship been that shallow? She couldn't believe it.

She closed her eyes, willing herself not to make a rash decision. She needed to hear his explanation.

While her mind raced, the curtain parted again, and another aide arrived to take her for X-rays. Alan hadn't returned, and she felt confused beyond words. She'd gotten involved too fast. She'd given Megan advice about the same thing, but she hadn't heeded her own warning. As the aide wheeled her down the corridor, she had to fight back her tears.

Juli was shifted and jiggled while the technician took the X-rays, and then a different aide arrived to take her back. When she returned to emergency, he set her beside the wall in the corridor. She heard Alan's voice float from a cubicle, but Juli couldn't see him. Did she want to? Her heart told her yes, but her confusion told her no. When Alan found her in the hall, a nurse joined them, leaving Juli no time to ask questions other than inquiries about her ankle.

"The X-rays show no fracture, Juli, but sometimes it can take up to fourteen days to show a hairline fracture. We won't hold you here, but you need to stay off that foot and keep it elevated to help prevent any more swelling. Compression is important, so I'll have someone wrap it before you leave, and you'll need to use crutches. You can get instructions on using them at a medical supply store. Understand?"

He sounded so formal and professional that Juli felt as if she couldn't relate to him. Where was the Alan she'd come here to see, the one who would empathize with her pain and kiss it away? She wanted a signal to show he cared.

"Juli? Do you understand?"

She fought the tears welling in her eyes. "Yes, I understand."

"I want you to ice the area with a cold pack at least twice a day for about fifteen minutes, and I'll give you a prescription for pain medication. If it hasn't improved in two or three days, then we'll need to check for a hairline fracture." He pulled out a prescription pad, and as he jotted on it, another nurse appeared.

"Someone is here to pick you up," she said.

Alan glanced at her with curiosity.

"It's Megan." Juli turned to the nurse. "Thanks."

Alan tore off two sheets, and as he handed them to her, the two nurses walked away.

Juli glanced at the prescription sheets, unable to make sense out of the squiggle. Had she seen his penmanship before, she might have realized he was a physician from the illegible scrawl. "What are these for?"

"Pain medication, and the other is for the medical supply store for the crutches and some compression wraps."

Her gaze locked with his, and for one moment she saw a flicker of the Alan she'd grown to love.

"I'm sorry about this, Juli."

"It wasn't your fault. I slipped on the grease."

He touched her arm. "No, I mean about your learning I'm a doctor this way."

Her throat constricted, and her response tangled in a knot. She shook her head.

Behind Alan she saw an aide arriving with a wheelchair. Alan and the young man helped her into it and adjusted her feet on the footrest.

Alan's gaze probed hers. "I'll call you later."

Anger loosened her voice. "I thought it was 'Take an aspirin and call me in the morning.'"

His expression looked as if she'd slapped him.

Silence fell between them, and the aide unlocked the brake and pushed her down the corridor toward the emergency room exit. She prayed Megan was waiting for her alone. With her heart in her throat, she needed a friend who'd understand how much it hurt to lose trust in someone.

Chapter 13

Alan looked at the food choices in the cafeteria and walked past. Instead he grabbed a soda from the cooler, paid the cashier, and found a table in the back corner where he hoped he could be alone. He'd tried Juli's cell twice and her home phone once. She didn't answer, and he'd left messages in both places. Was she ignoring him or staying with her parents? Even if she was there, she had her cell phone. She never went anywhere without that.

He popped open the tab on the soda and took a long drink, then put his elbows on the table and lowered his face in his hands. The long shifts had worn him thin and thrown his system out of whack. Now to have this situation with Juli was almost more than he could handle.

Deciding to give her another try, Alan flipped open the cell and pressed the button with her number coded in. "Please answer," he said aloud as he slipped it to his ear and listened. Nothing but the telephone voice telling him to leave a message. He'd done that. He slapped the phone closed and slid it into his pocket.

Alan knew he'd made a mistake not telling Juli, but when he'd tried to rectify it before the last unbelievable situation, he'd failed. Something always happened. Interruptions. Bad timing. Lack of good sense. That was his problem from the beginning. He closed his eyes and talked to the Lord, asking Him how to solve the situation. *Trust in God.* The words rang clear in his head, and a verse he'd learned so long ago entered his thoughts. He suspected he didn't have the words exact, but it was close enough to remind him of God's promises. *"Trust in God all the time and open your hearts to Him, because God is our refuge."* Alan trusted God, and he trusted Juli. Now if only he could convince her to have confidence in him.

He opened his eyes and pulled the phone from his pocket. One more try couldn't hurt. He pushed the button. The computerized message sounded in his ears. "Your call has been forwarded to an automatic voice answering system." He closed the cell phone.

Giving up wasn't in Alan's vocabulary. Tomorrow he'd call, and the next day, and the next. Flowers worked for Tom. He'd buy Juli so many flowers she wouldn't know where to put them. He shook his head. Juli cared about him, he was certain, and if God had a part in their meeting and their lives, He would bless their relationship. Juli had to listen to his reasoning.

Juli waved good-bye to Megan from the top of her apartment staircase, leaning on crutches, while her mother hovered behind her.

"You need to get that leg up, Juli," her mother said, holding open the door. "I can't believe you did this. You knew the grease was there."

"I wasn't thinking, Mom." She hobbled into her apartment with more on her mind than her sprained ankle.

Her mother stood beside the recliner. "At least you called me last night. I would have been worried to death."

"It seemed wiser to stay with Megan than to call you and Daddy to drive down and pick me up. I couldn't ask Megan to drive me home and drive back so late at night. And I would have had these stairs to deal with in the dark."

Juli crumpled into the chair, dropped her crutches by her side, and leaned back. "It was a horrible night."

"I'm sure it was." Her mother pivoted then looked back at Juli. "You said you had a prescription."

"It's in my purse."

Without asking, her mother dug into her shoulder bag and pulled out the prescription bottle and eyed the label. "You're supposed to take one of these every four to six hours for pain."

"I know. I'll need one soon. My ankle's really bothering me."

Her mother set the shoulder bag on the arm of Juli's chair, and Juli moved it to the lamp table. When she looked up, her mother was staring at the bottle. "What's wrong?"

She held the bottle out to Juli and pointed at the label. "This is a coincidence."

"What?"

"A physician named Alan Louden was your ER doctor? Did you realize that?" She lowered the bottle, her eyes widening. "Alan works at Community Hospital of the Monterey Peninsula, doesn't he?"

Juli knew what was coming. She nodded.

"Do you mean to tell me Alan is a physician and you never told me?"

Juli faced her options—tell her mother she didn't know Alan was a doctor either or just agree she'd never told her mother. *Lord, what do I do now?* If her parents knew the truth, they would distrust Alan, and Juli needed time to understand.

"Are you okay?" Her mother stepped closer. "I asked you a question."

Her mind ached nearly as much as her ankle. "Mom, I really need that medicine now."

"I'm sorry," she said, looking confused for a moment. She set the container beside Juli and headed into the kitchen.

Tension knotted Juli's stomach. She didn't want to lie to her mother, but she didn't know how to get out of answering her question. She'd planned to tell her parents, but once again she hadn't had time to decide how. Before her mother returned, Juli's cell phone rang, and she dug into her bag, located it, and flipped it open. Alan's voice floated through the line.

"I'm home from work, Juli. I'm tired, but we need to talk. Can I come over?"

"I'm feeling rotten. I really need to get some rest, Alan. This whole thing has put me in a bad situation with my—"

Her mother strode into the room with the glass of water.

Juli stared at the phone. "My mom's giving me a pain pill."

"I'll hang on, and I understand. I'm sure they're wondering why I didn't say anything either, but I can explain."

"Just a minute." She placed the phone in her lap and opened her hand for the pill then grasped the glass. The pill slid down, and she finished the water before handing her mother the glass and picking up the phone. "Okay, I'm back."

"Can I come?"

Juli eyed her mother, not wanting to call Alan by name because it would remind her of her earlier question. "I need to take a nap. I'll talk with you later." She closed her phone and set it beside her on the lamp table. "Mom, I really need to sleep."

"Let me get you a pillow to put under your leg. Are you hungry?"

"No, Megan made breakfast. I'll eat later."

Her mother scurried from the room and returned with the pillow. She lifted Juli's leg and slid the pillow beneath her calf. "Are you comfortable?"

"It's fine. Thanks." She closed her eyes, hoping her mother would leave.

"I hate leaving you alone. What if you need something?"

"Mom, I have the crutches. I can get up if I must. Leave the door unlocked, and you can get in later, or call me in a couple of hours. I'll be fine."

Her mother leaned over and kissed her cheek as her palm rested on Juli's forehead.

"I don't have a fever."

Her mom pulled her hand away. "I was just checking." She paused then kissed Juli's cheek. "I love you."

"Love you, too, Mom."

Juli opened her eyes a crack and saw her mother creep across the room and exit. Juli's head dropped against the recliner, and she drew in a breath. Tiredness swept over her, but her mind didn't want to rest. Last night she'd talked to Megan until late, thinking about so many things. All Alan's wonderful qualities had filled her mind, but something else had struck her.

She recalled Alan's complimenting her on her bedside manner, as he sometimes called it. She thought he was joking with the terminology because he worked at the hospital. Now it angered her. He was a doctor. He had her teaching him how to talk with people when that was part of his job. Why had he played games with her like that? He'd kept his career a secret and then made her look foolish with his "teach me to be like you" talk. And she'd fallen for it.

No matter where her mind went, it always came back to one truth. She'd fallen in love with Alan, and she didn't want to let him go. Megan shared her experience with Tom. Although Megan and Tom had been separated only a few days, the absence had definitely made a difference in their relationship because they'd found the time to think about what was important. Should she tell Alan not to come when he called again?

⚬

Alan stood outside Juli's apartment, holding a bouquet of summer flowers. He'd thought through the reason he hadn't told her, and now his concern seemed as purposeless as a broom on a beach. His chest felt tight as he struggled to draw in air. After willing his hand to move, he pressed the doorbell and waited.

He pictured Juli trying to rise from her seat and maneuver across the room with her crutches. He should have called to tell her he was on his way. When he heard nothing, he faltered outside the door. Was she below with her parents or perhaps asleep? He tried the doorknob and opened it an inch. "Juli?"

Finally he heard her voice. "It's open."

He pushed the door wider and stepped inside. Juli sat in the recliner, her foot propped on a pillow and her eyes heavy with sleep. "I thought maybe you were with your parents."

She shook her head then opened her eyes. They shifted to the flowers. "I didn't know you were coming."

"You said we'd talk later. I realized you couldn't say much because your mother was here."

"I meant I'd talk with you on the phone."

Her comment punctured his balloon of hope. He felt the flowers droop in his arm. "I'm sorry. I misunderstood."

"You're here now." She straightened her back and let the recliner seat lower while keeping her foot elevated.

"These are for you," he said, holding the flowers toward her, feeling as if they were a pitiful token of his apology.

"They're beautiful. Could you find a vase and fill it with water?" She motioned toward the kitchen. "I think I have a couple in a lower cabinet next to the sink."

Alan carried the bouquet into the kitchen, uneasy that he'd shown up unwanted. His mind reeled with her attitude and his bungle. Two bungles, he admitted—not telling her he was a physician and showing up without calling. He crouched beside the cabinet and located a large vase in the back. He rose and filled it with water then pulled off the floral wrapping and dropped the flowers into the vase. He knew there was some kind of art to arranging flowers, but he'd never had to do it before. He drew back then stepped closer and moved a few blossoms from one side to the other, trying to balance height and color.

As he lifted the vase, he noticed the packet of plant food inside the wrapping. He read on the label that it was meant to help the flowers last and sprinkled the food into the water. He wished he had something to sprinkle on his relationship with Juli—if it were only that simple.

He stood in the doorway with the arrangement, feeling as if he should set them on a table and leave, but that would be unproductive. He'd come for a purpose, and he hoped the Lord would open the door to heal the hurt he'd caused. Juli held her purse in her lap, and he noticed she'd combed her hair and put on lipstick while he was in the kitchen. Her action gave him hope.

"You can set the vase right there," Juli said, pointing to a table beside the doorway.

Alan noticed they looked nice there when he walked away. "I guess I should have called, but when you said we'd talk—"

"It's okay." She motioned to the sofa. "Have a seat."

He wanted to put his arm around her and kiss her, but he saw she wanted distance between them. Still, his doctor persona caused him to move toward her. "Do you mind if I look at your ankle first?"

She looked down then lifted her head. "You're the doctor."

Her barb dug deep, but he went to her anyway, unwrapped her foot, and studied her ankle. "Have you been putting cold compresses on it?"

"Not this morning yet. I was tired when I got home. I stayed with Megan last night, and she brought me home this morning. We stopped on the way for the prescription and to get the crutches. They were out of cold packs."

"Do you mind if I make a compress for you?"

She gestured toward the kitchen without answering.

With her direction he located plastic bags, doubled them, then filled them with ice and carried them back. "How about a hand towel or something to put around it?"

"You'll find them in the bathroom."

He located a towel, came back, and applied the cold pack before he sat on the sofa. "How are you doing with the crutches?"

"It's not easy. Did you count the stairs to get up here?"

"I thought about that." He had so much to talk about, but she seemed too far away, as if a wall had dropped between them. "I know you don't want me here, Juli, but I want to tell you I'm more sorry than you can ever imagine. I know the Lord forgives, and I hope you can, too. . .in time."

She closed her eyes a moment without saying a word.

"I could give you a million reasons why I wasn't open about what I do at the hospital, but it boils down to my past. I was at the soup kitchen because I felt drawn to help others who are in the same situation my family was in a few years ago. I didn't want to be there as a physician or spend my time diagnosing everyone's illnesses rather than what I went there to do. I wanted to serve people in a different way—as a plain guy who volunteered." ·

"But you could have told me."

"When we first met, I didn't know how I would come to feel about you, so I was evasive. I never lied. When Tom came to the soup kitchen, I feared he'd say something, so I pledged him to secrecy. That's how important it was to me. I didn't want to be the kindly physician. I wanted to do this as me, the little boy who stood in a soup kitchen line one time when a person gave me a double portion in the same way I asked you to give that child an extra portion one day. Remember?"

Remembrance filled her face.

"After a while I realized I'd messed up. You began talking about trust, especially with Megan and Tom's situation, and I knew you would consider this a trust issue, and I suppose it was. It's not that I don't trust you implicitly, but the more people who know I'm a physician, the easier it is to slip."

"I should have known. You used your doctoring skills when you talked with the people. You saw them always with their health in mind."

"While you looked at them with their souls in mind."

Her forehead wrinkled as she weighed what he'd said. "I suppose that's right, but I'm so hurt that you spent so much time complimenting me on my 'bedside' manner. Bedside manner? That's what doctors have. Why didn't I realize you were patronizing me?"

Alan couldn't remain seated. He stood then knelt beside her chair. "I wasn't patronizing you. I found your ability for compassion and concern amazing. I'm a good doctor, Juli, but what I lack are bedside manners. I don't look at the person's fears and needs beyond their health. You do. I wanted to learn from you."

She studied his face for a long time, recalling how cold he'd seemed at the hospital. Could this be what he meant? "I need to think about this, Alan."

His fingers itched to weave with hers, to touch her in a loving way, but he held back to respect her wishes. "So where do we go from here?"

"I need to think. I'll have to explain this to my parents. My mother saw your name on the pill container. She won't let her curiosity die until she knows why I never told her you were a doctor."

"And that'll put me on the wrong list." He looked at her face. "If I'm not there already."

She drew in a ragged breath. "Maybe you had a reason you thought was a good one, but it's upset me. I really need time to work this through, and yes, it has to do with trust. I'm not feeling well, and I'm out of patience. . .spelled with a *ce*. Give me some time. Okay?"

Patience spelled with a ce. He wanted to hug her for her lighthearted comment, so much like the good times.

"I'll respect your wishes because I respect you." He rose and pulled his car keys from his pocket. "How long?"

For a moment she looked as if she didn't understand. "Give me a couple of weeks."

A couple of weeks. Impaled to the spot, he let his gaze wash over her a moment. "I not only respect you, Juli. I love you." He turned away, fearing he'd lost the love of his life. He headed to his car filled with regret and emptiness.

Chapter 14

I *not only respect you. I love you."* The words had echoed in Juli's thoughts every day since Alan had walked out the door. She missed him with all her heart.

When she'd finally checked her cell phone, she'd noticed how many times Alan had called the night she'd stayed with Megan. He'd left a message on her home telephone, as well. She'd tossed his reasoning around in her mind, looking at it one way and then another, often accepting what he said then negating it. The issue had grown from the proverbial molehill to a mountain.

Alan had sent her another bouquet, and she wondered if he'd learned that from Tom. Again her trust wavered while she made two steps forward and one back. She'd been more depressed than she could have imagined. She'd talked often with Megan, who had told her Alan was a mess at work.

Yet Alan had kept his promise. He hadn't called in twelve days, but she wished he would. Until the day he walked out, he'd never said he loved her, although her senses told her he did. One thing she knew for sure—she loved him with all her heart. So why had she let this drag on so long?

Because, to Juli, a relationship that seemed to be leading to marriage was to be taken seriously and with thought. She sensed God had led her to Alan, but she wanted to know it was true and not just her own desire. Megan and Tom's relationship had progressed, and it gave her hope. Tom had begun attending church, Megan told her, and they had agreed to go slowly. From what she could tell, they were following the agreement no matter how much human nature tried to take control. Juli guessed they would be engaged before the end of the year.

While recuperating, she'd filled out her application for the university. Her father admitted the store had been surviving well without her being in it every day. She could still do inventory, ordering, scheduling, and overseeing. Computers were amazing.

Juli eased herself from the recliner, but overcome for a moment with dizziness, she grabbed a crutch and steadied herself then made her way into the kitchen. She had graduated from having her mother bring up food to preparing some things on her own. Doing things for herself felt good. When she opened the refrigerator, she felt the room rock. The refrigerator door swung back then slammed shut, hitting her and throwing her off balance. She toppled to the floor. They were having an earthquake, she realized as she struggled to right herself.

Before she'd pulled herself up, her mother's voice sailed from the living room. "Are you okay, Juli?"

"I'm fine, Mom."

Her mother appeared in the kitchen doorway. "It's an aftershock."

"I know. Can you help me up? The refrigerator door whacked me."

On her feet again, Juli made her way back to the living room, where her mother turned on the TV. "How close is it?"

"An earthquake hit Morgan Hill."

"That's only ten miles from Gilroy."

"Hush," her mother said, waving at her.

Juli balanced on her crutch, feeling a rumble that knocked a picture cock-eyed on the wall. She made her way to the chair, sat down, and listened to the newscaster.

"The last earthquake measured 4.5 on the Richter scale," he said.

"Let's watch the program downstairs, Mom."

Her mother rose and clicked off the TV. "I want to call your dad and see if he's okay." She crossed the room to Juli's side. "Let me help you."

As Juli stood, another aftershock rattled through the building and sent the vase of flowers Alan had given her tumbling to the floor.

☞

Alan had been counting the days. Only two days to go and he could call Juli, and by then, he prayed, she would forgive him for his error and, most of all, trust him. On working days the time didn't drag as much as it did on his days off. He'd cleaned his apartment twice in the past days, trying to find things to do that would take his time.

How had he spent his time before Juli? He couldn't remember, but he knew his life had revolved around his work with an occasional date that always left him wishing he hadn't gone. Dates seemed to set up expectations, but that had never happened with Juli. They met and fell into step like two old friends who'd been apart but had come together again. They shared so many things. Even their opposites seemed compatible.

Alan sank into his favorite easy chair, stacked the morning paper in a jumble at his feet, and reached for the TV remote. He never watched TV during the day, but he couldn't stand the quiet any longer. He pushed the power button, and as the picture and voice came in, he stared at the screen. A 4.5 earthquake in Morgan Hill. He raised the volume.

"Aftershocks are being felt as far away as Gilroy with some damage being reported in some areas. Let's go live to Ron Brice in Watsonville."

Alan lowered the volume and grabbed his cell phone. He punched in Juli's apartment and heard the answering machine kick in. He hung up and tried her cell phone. The phone rang three times followed by the voice-mail message. "Where are you?" he yelled into the air. He waited a moment, knowing it still took Juli awhile to get to the phone, and tried the numbers again. Nothing. She didn't answer.

He snapped off the TV. He didn't care how many days he was supposed to wait. If she didn't answer, then he was going to her. He wouldn't take a chance. Alan dashed from his apartment, jumped into his car, and headed up Highway 1 through Castorville then took Highway 101 toward Gilroy. He switched on the radio and listened to the news accounts—one bridge was down and a few buildings damaged. He pushed the button for another station.

Traffic slowed going into Gilroy, and he took a cutoff to Juli's house, hoping he'd made the right decision. When he arrived, everything looked normal, but as he stepped from the car, he felt the rumble from an aftershock and waited for it to pass. He darted toward the staircase and rang Juli's bell. He tried the door and opened it, calling as he did. No sound.

He ran down the steps and headed for her parents' front door. Before he rang the bell, Mrs. Maretti pulled it open. "She's in the family room, Alan."

"I'm sorry, but I heard about the earthquake, and I—"

Her mother nodded silently and gestured down the hall.

"Thank you." He hurried past the open staircase and stepped through the family room archway.

Juli was seated in an easy chair, her leg propped on an ottoman, but her back was straining forward. He guessed she'd heard his voice. Now that he was here, he felt foolish. "I was worried," he said, his voice sounding hollow in his ears. "Are you okay?"

She shook her head no, and he faltered. "What is it?" He shifted to her side.

"I miss you," she said, tears brimming in her eyes.

He knelt beside her. "And I've missed you so much."

She opened her arms, and he fell into her embrace. Her tears dampened his cheek as he drew her as close as he could, whispering all the things he'd held in his heart for so long. Finally he pulled back and looked into her shining eyes. "Do you forgive me?"

"Do you forgive me?"

They needed no answer. He clasped her hands in his then wove his fingers through hers, something he'd longed to do since the day he'd walked away from her door feeling empty.

"I understand," she said, running her finger from his jaw to his lips.

He kissed her finger and held it there so he could kiss it once more. "Let's never let this happen again." He lowered his hand and brushed her cheek.

"Never," she agreed. "My devotional today really spoke to me."

"What did it say?"

" 'Let the morning bring me word of Your unfailing love, for I have put my trust in You.' I realized by trusting God I can also trust you with my whole heart, because He gave you to me in an amazing way. There we were at a soup kitchen, a place for giving to others, and that day the Lord gave me you."

"And today I promise you my unfailing love."

His lips met hers in the sweetest kiss she could ever remember, and when he drew back, she kissed him again. Kisses were meant for love, and so were they.

Epilogue

The following June

As Megan adjusted Juli's wedding veil, Juli stood in the bride's room and watched the beads wink in the sunlight streaming through the window. She loved the fitted bodice with more beadwork and the flow of the white dress around her feet. As a little girl, she'd longed to be a bride, and today her dream was coming true.

She turned toward the door, expecting her mother to appear any minute with their wedding bouquets and last-minute instructions. She knew it would be another time for tears, but now she wept tears of joy. She couldn't believe how amazingly her life had evolved; even her sprained ankle last July had given her dad proof the Garlic Garden could get along without her. She'd begun her classes in late August the previous year, and on her birthday she and Alan had become engaged. He'd given her a beautiful wristwatch as a birthday gift, and beneath the box's velvet lining he'd hidden the marquis diamond engagement ring that had now been mounted into a gold filigree ring jacket to form her wedding band.

Everything had flown by before her eyes, meeting Alan's wonderful mother then later his brother, who was to be their best man, and his sister. Juli couldn't wait to meet his other sisters when she and Alan honeymooned on the East Coast.

"You're absorbed in something."

Megan's voice jolted her back to the present, and she turned from the door to face her longtime friend. "I'm thinking how fast the time has flown since my engagement." She gazed at Megan's floor-length gown in summer green with a cummerbund waist of embroidered pastel flowers. The gown looked perfect with her blond hair and slender frame. "You look lovely, and it won't be long before your wedding."

"Soon, but today it's yours."

Her sweet smile touched Juli. "I'm happy for you and Tom. See what God can do when you give Him a chance."

Megan nodded. "And when you do it His way. Look what the Lord has done with Tom. He's become a Christian man with a new heart, Christian morals, and new goals."

They embraced, and as they parted, Juli recognized her mother's quiet rap on the door. She came into the room, her eyes moist with happiness. "Everything's so beautiful, and the church is packed."

Concern skittered up Juli's arms. "Didn't the flowers come yet?"

Her mother smiled. "Your dad is bringing them to you. He wants to be here."

Tear's blurred Juli's eyes as another soft tap on the door answered her question. When her mother opened it, her father walked in with Megan's bouquet resting on top of a floral box. Juli grasped the maid of honor's flowers and handed them to her.

Megan gazed at the blossoms then at the similar smaller design adorning her waist. "Perfect. This is beautiful."

Her father held the floral box and looked at Juli. "This isn't exactly what you ordered."

Her father had been trying to hide his grin, but his comment concerned her. "What do you mean?"

"Alan bought these flowers especially for you."

"Alan?" Juli lifted the box lid and let out a little cry. On top of the tissue she found a card written in Alan's peculiar scrawl. *Special flowers for a special lady. When all else fails we can laugh our cares away.* They had certainly done that, but the cryptic message added to her curiosity. She pushed back the tissue, and inside lay an arrangement of white roses with sprigs of long-stemmed scarpes, delicate white flowers on curling stems, and small lavender allium, both grown from garlic bulbs. Tears blurred her eyes. "He's amazing."

As she pulled the bouquet from the box, her father's chuckle greeted her. "It's a rose and garlic bouquet."

She held the arrangement against her beaded dress. "But this one I love."

"I thought you would." He stepped to her side and kissed her cheek. "We'd better get out there, little girl."

He grasped her arm, and today she loved hearing him call her his little girl. Sometimes she was. "Let's go, Daddy."

Her mother and Megan left first, and Juli held back as the others went down the aisle. When the "Trumpet Voluntary" began, she knew it was her cue, and she and her father moved into the archway and began the long walk down the aisle. Ahead of her she could see Alan, looking so handsome she could hardly contain herself. His blond hair appeared even blonder against his black tuxedo, and those dusky periwinkle eyes she loved followed her as she walked toward him.

At the front her father released her to Alan's care and settled beside her mother, and the pastor began, his words wrapping around her heart.

Alan squeezed her hand, and she heard him murmur, "You're too beautiful for words." Today she felt that way. As they spoke their vows, she saw the sun stream through the magnificent stained-glass windows and tint her dress with its hues. To her it was the Lord's way of sending His blessing as she stood beside the man God had given her to respect, love, honor, and trust always.

Butterfly Trees

Dedication

To my nieces Andrea Lemon and Jodi Fernandez, who lived on the Monterey Peninsula for years and gave me the opportunity to visit and enjoy this wonderful area. Love and blessings to you both.

Chapter 1

An exasperated sigh slipped from Alissa Greening's throat.

The clock's hour hand inched toward the seven as if it were the turtle in the infamous tortoise and hare race. Alissa longed to finish her workday and looked forward to relaxing for the evening, but once again she awaited the late arrival of one of her guests.

She shifted to the registration desk and eyed the registration list. Ross Cahill? Maybe it was Rose. She studied her sister's penmanship then leaned closer and squinted at the nearly illegible scrawl. Fern should have been a physician. Room for two? She shook her head, wishing she'd asked Fern before she'd left earlier in the day. One or two. It didn't really matter. Husband and wife or a single. Either way she had the room ready.

Alissa straightened the pamphlets on the desk, lined her pen parallel to the registration book, then bent beneath the counter to pull out a few more of the monarch butterfly brochures. This time of year, most everyone who registered as a guest at her bed-and-breakfast inn arrived in Pacific Grove to see the phenomenon of the butterflies' migration.

A sound from outside drew her attention toward the entrance. She waited, eyeing the doorway, but no one appeared. Her shoulders sagged, and she turned away, coming face-to-face with one of her guests.

"Do you have any more of those great cookies?" The man's belly lapped over his belt, giving evidence to his enjoyment of food.

"I liked the peanut butter with chocolate chips." He gave her an amiable grin.

"They're on the buffet," Alissa said, pointing to the doily-covered cherrywood sideboard she'd inherited from her mother—against her sister's wishes, she could add. Though she tossed off the guilty feelings, it bothered her that Fern had resented their mother's leaving Alissa her antiques.

The man waddled to the buffet, piled a few cookies onto a lace-patterned lavender paper plate, and grinned. "My wife will probably eat a few."

"Enjoy them," Alissa said, guessing the wife wouldn't have a chance. She motioned toward the two carafes on the sideboard. "There's tea and decaf coffee if you'd like."

"This is great," he said, lifting the plate in a good-bye salute.

Alissa closed her eyes, wishing she'd thought about cookies earlier. Tonight she'd have to bake another batch, or she'd run short tomorrow. As she turned toward her own quarters, a new sound caught her attention, and as she'd hoped, this time her late guest had arrived.

A well-built man who looked in his forties—about her age—strode through the doorway, pulling two pieces of luggage. His tanned face gave his well-defined features a rugged look.

She sent him a welcoming smile. "Mr. Cahill?"

He nodded without returning a smile. "Sorry we're late."

We're late. Then it was a Mr. and Mrs. At least that's what *we're* made her think. She'd noticed his good looks and apparently had ogled a married man. A sense of guilt slid over her. "It happens. I have your room ready."

A slight frown knitted his brows, but before he spoke, he glanced over his shoulder.

Alissa followed his gaze. Behind him a petite woman stepped through the doorway, her gray hair giving her an air of sophistication, and though Alissa had been taught not to judge others, she did just that when she spotted the woman. "Mrs. Cahill?"

"Yes," she said, a lovely smile filling her face. "Maggie Cahill, and it's all my fault we're late. Ross hates when I—"

She noticed Mr. Cahill roll his eyes, and her back stiffened. Obviously he didn't like waiting on anyone.

"Please, it's not a problem." Alissa gave her a comforting grin, having learned, whether she believed it or not, the customer was always right. "I have your room waiting for you."

She slipped behind the registration desk and turned the book toward the man, but she couldn't stop her gaze gliding from the younger man to the older woman. She realized society looked at things differently now, and May-December marriages were not that uncommon, except in this case the age difference seemed—

"I think there's been a mistake."

His baritone voice jerked Alissa to attention. "A mistake? You are Ross Cahill."

"Yes, but Mrs. Cahill is my mother. We'll need two rooms."

"Mother?" An airy sensation flittered past. "You'll need two rooms." She clamped her jaw closed to keep herself from sounding her frustration. Her sister, Fern, had goofed again. She needed her sister's help, but sometimes Alissa wondered if hiring someone else to fill the part-time position would improve her and Fern's strained relationship. Since Fern needed the money, replacing her would just be another blow. "Let me see." She flipped through the registration book. "I have. . . No, that won't work." She got a grip on herself. "Yes, I have a room that should be ready, but—"

"Is this a problem?"

Alissa's back straightened with the speed of a switchblade, and she looked into Mr. Cahill's concerned yet very attractive eyes. "Problem?" She tried to control her flush, realizing she had been babbling. "Not at all. I have two rooms, although they aren't together. Whoever took your reservation didn't indicate you needed two rooms." *Whoever.* She knew it was Fern. She could tell from her hen-scratched penmanship.

"They don't need to be together, dear," Maggie Cahill said, resting her arm on the counter. "I'm sure my son will enjoy the distance."

"Mother." Exasperation filled the man's voice.

Her soft chuckle left Alissa wondering. "Great. I have a lovely room on the first floor if that will work for you, and your room, Mr. Cahill, will be—"

"Ross," he said. "The second floor is fine for me."

She extended the key toward him. "We have no elevator."

"Stairs are fine." He took the key. "I'll help with my mother's lug—"

"Don't bother." Her back stiffened. Did he think she couldn't pull a piece of luggage? "That's my job."

Though his mouth sagged with her abruptness, he didn't argue and headed for the staircase. She watched his agile frame ascend the steps before she walked around the desk and grasped the handle of the woman's luggage. "Let me show you to your room."

"Thank you." Her warm smile contrasted with her son's cold departure.

Alissa pointed down the short hallway. "It's this way, the second room on the right, overlooking the ocean." She'd given Ross a room looking out over the back garden, and now that she'd met him she figured he wouldn't care. In fact, she sensed he'd rather be somewhere else.

Alissa pulled the luggage toward the hallway, beckoning Maggie to follow. "Painted Lady is your room."

"Painted Lady," Maggie repeated as she followed. "You name your rooms. What a lovely idea."

"It seemed fitting. I name them after butterflies." Alissa paused outside the door. "Here we are." She turned the key in the lock, and when she pushed back the door she heard an appreciative gasp.

"It's lovely." Maggie paused again just inside and gestured toward the Victorian furnishings. "Just beautiful. Such lovely shades of blue and white. In the daylight I imagine the view from these windows is glorious. Blue ocean and white waves. Blue sky and white clouds. Truly exceptional." She ambled toward a wingback chair. "Is this an antique?"

"It is." Alissa joined her. "Most of the furniture in this room is from the same era. I love it."

"So do I," she said with a genial smile. "You have a lovely home. The setting is magnificent, and I was drawn to the name—Butterfly Trees Inn. That's why I chose your bed-and-breakfast."

"Really? I'm pleased you chose us." She motioned toward the bay-view window. "We have an excellent location on Ocean View Boulevard. You can watch the seals loll on the rocks, and we're very near Asilomar State Beach for people who enjoy swimming in the summer."

"I do, but I came here for the monarch butterflies."

"They are beautiful. We have many tourists this time of year to see their migration. It's amazing." Alissa dropped her key on the table near the door. "Breakfast is from seven to nine unless you need something earlier. Please let me know."

"Earlier? No. Seven is fine. Thank you so much. I'm here to relax and get some fresh ocean air. My son isn't as excited, but I hope he will be once he's been here a few days. He works too hard. But, you know, mothers aren't supposed to interfere once their children are past eighteen. He's forty-five, but I can't stop myself from being concerned."

Forty-five. Only five years older than Alissa. The immediate calculation gave her an uneasy feeling. She'd never cared about the age of any of her other guests before. The woman's smile drew her back. "You sound like a great mom. I wish I still had mine."

Maggie patted her hand. "I don't feel that way when Ross bites my head off for making comments. Sometimes he's so quiet, and I know he's under stress. Then he just loses patience, though I'm sure he doesn't mean to. He's so like his father. He has work on his mind all the time."

Alissa didn't know what to say or if she should say anything at all. "He must be stressed."

"Yes, he is." She gave Alissa a smile. "You should have seen Ross and his father clash. They were too much alike when it came to business. Both self-assured and stubborn. My husband could fly off the handle, too, at work, but when he got home and put the work aside, he was the most loving and thoughtful man. I'm hoping this trip will distract Ross and help him relax. My husband had me to distract him. Ross has no one. He's too focused on his work."

"Being in business does that to people." Alissa took a step backward, thinking of her own short temper with Fern. "Have a good rest, and if you'd like some tea or cookies before bed, you'll find them on the buffet in the parlor where you entered. The sitting area is comfortable, and you'll find magazines and a few novels you're welcome to read. My guests leave them when they're finished, so I have a nice collection."

"Thank you, dear. I'm just fine."

Alissa backed away and closed the door softly, chuckling that she'd thought this lovely woman was Ross Cahill's wife. She couldn't imagine his wife having such a gentle personality and friendly smile, living with his abruptness or crabbiness, as his mother had mentioned. As soon as the thought filtered through her mind, she hung her head. *Do not judge, or you'll be judged.* The Bible warned of that.

As she stepped from the hallway, Alissa came to a halt. Ross Cahill sat on the parlor love seat reading a newspaper. She veered toward the desk, hoping to make her getaway. Although she found him attractive, she sensed his personality had the raspiness of a file. Anyway, she had cookies to bake and breakfast to get organized for tomorrow.

"You tucked my mother in?"

Hearing his voice, she spun around, managing to bite back a caustic remark. "I think she can tuck herself in." She added a smile to her clenched-teeth statement.

"I'm joking," he said, folding the paper and laying it aside. "I want to apologize for my grouchiness."

His apology caught her off guard. "That's no—" Yes, it was a problem, but she had to monitor her statement. "We all have bad days."

"It wasn't right to take it out on you. I know better, but sometimes parents can—how should I put it?—bring out the worst in their children. Although we both have to admit, I've long since passed the child stage."

She nodded. "By about twenty-seven years, I'd say, if we define a child from birth to eighteen."

His head drew back, and she could see the glazed look in his eyes. "My mother provided that information, right?"

Alissa grinned, enjoying the sight of his baffled expression changing to acceptance.

"What else did she tell you?"

She moved closer and settled on the edge of an easy chair. "I should plead the fifth or maybe client confidentiality."

"Never mind. I already know. I work too hard, and she worries about me. I didn't want to come here, but I felt obligated. She's a wonderful mother who sometimes drives me nuts."

"She forgot to tell me she's a wonderful mother. The rest is correct."

His eyes widened. "She told you she drives me crazy?"

Alissa laughed aloud at the look on his face. "Not in those words. It was more a subliminal message."

He didn't speak but seemed to study her before a grin grew on his face. "You're an observant woman."

"It's part of running a business. We have to anticipate our guests' needs. . . and thoughts."

"I'd better be careful then."

She felt heat rise up to her neck. "I'd better get busy. Breakfast comes early."

"You do your own cooking?"

"Most of the time. My sister works for me part-time, and during rush season she helps in the kitchen, but I enjoy preparing the meals and baking homemade cookies."

"Cookies?"

She gestured toward the buffet. "Peanut butter with chocolate chips or oatmeal with raisins." Alissa glanced toward the plate, hoping the other enthusiastic guest hadn't wiped the dish clean.

He rose and ambled toward her. "I think I'll say good night to Mom before she falls asleep."

He stood a full head taller than she, and the scent of his aftershave wrapped around her, a heady mixture of cedar and citrus, she suspected. Very manly. When she looked into his eyes, he was staring at her.

"That would be thoughtful, and on the way back, please, help yourself to some cookies." She swung her hand forward and clipped his arm. "I'm sorry." She hurried to her desk and put away the registration book. "You're welcome to coffee or tea, and I have brochures here if you'd like to see a list of activities and sights in the area, and I'd be happy to recommend places for dinner, and—"

"You're tired."

Tired? Alissa heard an amused tone in his voice. Yes, she was tired, but why would he say that? When she looked up, she spotted his crooked grin as he approached the check-in desk.

The answer came to her with his look. "Am I rattling on too much?"

He only chuckled.

Her nerves were showing, and she tried to calm herself for a moment. "I'm sorry. I don't think I properly introduced myself. I'm Alissa. Alissa Greening."

"You're probably tired, Alissa. You've been waiting for us to arrive. You can relax now." He gave her an unexpected grin and headed down the hallway.

Alissa heard his knock on the bedroom door, and she suspected he'd opened the door to say good night to his mother. Maybe he wasn't such a bad son after all. She'd certainly jumped to that conclusion.

Footsteps sounded, and when she looked, he'd ambled over to the buffet and stopped.

His shoulders rose, and he drew in a lengthy breath then shook his head. "I love my mom, but I hate being late. Traveling with her is always an adventure." He grasped a napkin and picked up a peanut butter cookie. "The only thing I like better than these are lemon bars." He took a bite and licked his lips.

The *adventure* comment had caught her interest, and so had the lemon bars. Alissa had a good recipe for those bars. . .if she had all the ingredients. She waited for him to go on, but instead he returned to the buffet and took another cookie. "Are you going to leave me hanging?"

He brushed the crumbs from his lips with the back of his hand. "Hanging?"

"The adventure."

"Oh." He chuckled. "First she called to say she'd gotten hung up at church."

"If you're hung up someplace, church is the best place to be."

He arched a brow. "Not in this case. She met with the pastor to tell him what important point she thought he'd missed during his last sermon."

Alissa sputtered a laugh. "You're kidding?"

"Wish I were."

She loved the sparkle in his eyes, azure eyes like a summer sky, and despite his complaints, she sensed he adored his mother. If not, the man was a great actor. "You said that was first. What was next?"

"We were on the road for twenty-five minutes when she demanded we return home. She'd forgotten her binoculars."

"Binoculars?" Her frown faded. "Never mind. I know. So she can get a closer look at the monarch butterflies."

He glanced at the cookie plate but didn't return for a second helping. "That's why she's here. . .to see butterflies. I could have bought her a big box of her own."

"But that's not the same. These are migrating butterflies that come here year after year. That's really amazing. And beautiful."

"I offered to stop at the nearest town where we could buy another pair, but she would have none of it. These are special ones for butterfly watching my dad gave her for her birthday, his last gift to her."

Alissa's chest constricted. "He died?"

Ross nodded. "He's been gone about three years. They were a team."

"I'm sure it's still hard for her."

He lowered his gaze. "I know. It's difficult for—"

"I still miss my mom, and it's been six years." She'd noticed his distress and had decided to end his pain. "Death is difficult for everyone."

He turned his back and headed toward the coffee carafe.

Alissa watched him pour the coffee into a mug, his head bent as if watching the black liquid proved his greatest challenge for the evening, but she read more beneath his slumped shoulders. Apparently his father's death had made a major impact on him, an unresolved impact.

She busied herself behind the desk, not wanting to invade his privacy, and finally Ross turned and ambled back toward her. "What kind of activities?"

Her brows tensed then knit as she pondered his question. Feeling the glossy paper beneath her fingers, she caught on and lifted a brochure. "You mean these?"

He nodded and stopped beside her. "If you're tired, please don't let me stop you, and if not, then join me." He motioned toward the comfortable furniture. "At least you can rest your feet while you tell me."

Though she had a multitude of things to do before bedtime, she selected a variety of brochures and followed him across the room. He chose the love seat, and she sat in a nearby chair, hoping to ease the astounding emotion that skittered through her when she stood too near him.

"I'm sure you know what's on Fisherman's Wharf on Cannery Row." She handed him a flier. "It's just up the road, and a major attraction is the aquarium, as well as all the shops and restaurants. The drive along Ocean View Boulevard in the daylight is wonderful. You can watch the seals play on the rocks, and there's Lovers' Point over on—"

Ross's hand rose, and she stopped.

"Alissa." He looked into her eyes. "I hope you don't mind my calling you Alissa."

"Not at all," she said, feeling the familiar heat slip toward her neck.

"I can't relax when you're on the edge of your chair. Can I make you some tea?" He stood and shifted past her. "Plain? Or with something?"

A guest waiting on her. She'd never heard of it. Alissa rose. "You don't have to—"

"You'll never rest tonight if you don't unwind. A cup of tea, decaf naturally, will help you relax."

He didn't listen to her but kept moving toward the urn of hot water. When he had grasped the cup and tea bag, he turned to face her. "Plain or—"

"Plain." She nodded, struggling to keep her mouth from gaping.

Busy filling the mug with hot water, Ross wouldn't see her place the brochures on the low table in front of the love seat. She adjusted a doily beneath a monarch butterfly sculpture and slid back in the chair. A hostess was supposed to offer relaxation to her guests, not the other way around. Her discomfort tightened the cords in her neck.

"Here you go." Ross extended the mug.

Alissa took it and held it between her cupped hands, feeling a tremor in her fingers. She felt like a guest in her own home.

"Now then, let's talk about the activities tomorrow. I'm just riling you, I'm afraid."

She managed a pleasant expression. "I'm fine. Really. Thanks for the tea." She gave a faint nod to the table. "You can take those to your room and look over them. If you have any questions, you can just ask. You know we have tremendous golf courses in the area. Pebble Beach and—"

"I don't golf much, but thanks." He shifted against the cushion.

"I don't either."

He tilted his head. "What do you do for relaxation?"

"Relaxation?" What did she do for relaxation? The question stymied her. Relaxation hadn't found a home in her vocabulary. . .actually, in her life.

Ross chuckled. "That's not a difficult question."

She lifted her gaze, drawn to his cloudless-sky eyes. "Apparently it is for me. I run this place, and that's a big job."

"I run a couple of large ranches, but I do find time for relaxation."

"What do you do?"

He looked at her a moment then burst into laughter. "Not much either, I guess, now that you put it that way."

A smile crept to her lips.

"Maybe it's time for both of us to change that." Ross lifted the coffee mug toward his lips. "What do you say?"

Alissa had no idea how to be any different from the way she was. "I'll have to think about that, I guess."

A curious look filled his eyes. "Don't think too long. The idea will just fly away like those butterflies."

Chapter 2

Squinting his eyes against the sunlight edging beneath the window shade, Ross lay in bed and listened to the quiet. He'd had a restless night. Against his will, his thoughts kept slipping to his conversation with Alissa. She seemed so sweet but very nervous, and he wondered why she'd appeared on edge. She had a great business right on the water, and she seemed gifted running it with her cookies, brochures, and amenities he couldn't even remember.

He'd only glanced at the brochures she'd given him, too tired and distracted to concentrate, but he had seen a few things he'd like to do, although doing them alone seemed less interesting than staying home where he should have been managing his ranch.

What do you do? The question tugged his mouth into a grin. He'd asked Alissa the question then had to face his own situation. He didn't do much at all besides work at the ranch. Attending a few social outings here and there, ones he had to attend as a businessman, certainly didn't count. His social life was zilch.

He studied the attractive room. A huge stone fireplace graced one wall, and nearby sat a rocking chair, its oak back etched with a design and a colorful patchwork coverlet draped over one arm. Across the room, an antique armoire towered toward the ceiling, and beside his four-poster bed stood a nightstand that had been a commode table many years ago, he suspected. Throughout, the rich oak wood made the room feel cozy and comfortable. Outside the door, he'd noticed a small oval plaque reading Emperor Room. He grinned. If he were the emperor, he hadn't noticed his royal throne, but he certainly felt like a king with the comfortable bed and even a vase of fresh flowers on the lamp table beside the window.

A door closed, and footsteps thumped past his doorway. Ross turned and glanced at the clock, surprised to see he'd slept until seven thirty. That was unheard of at his ranch. Workers appeared by seven to get into the orchards and fields before the harsh afternoon sun, although the temperature had certainly softened now that October had arrived. Ross slipped his feet over the edge of the bed and rested them on the carpet. He eyed the pleasant room as he stretched his arms out shoulder width with a yawn.

He stood and ambled to the window, lifted the shade, and looked outside. From the view, he realized he had to be at the back of the house. The front and sides would offer views of the ocean. Instead he looked into a courtyard flower garden with a gazebo beyond, and in the distance past the rooftops rose tree-covered foothills of the coastal mountain ranges. He lifted the window and drew in a breath of fresh air. Birdcalls volleyed into the air with their chirps and songs while the birds fluttered their wings in a birdbath or clung to perches of the bird feeders outside.

With their songs in his ears, Ross turned from the window and headed for the shower. The water beat against his back, loosening his tight muscles, and he drew in a lengthy breath of steam as tension washed down the drain. Back in his room, he selected his clothes: a blue-checked shirt with a navy sweater and jeans. He dressed, combed his stubborn hair that he tried to control with gel, then opened the bedroom door.

Before he could step into the hallway, fragrances greeted him—the scent of coffee mingled with the aroma of breakfast sausage. His stomach rumbled, and he recalled that he and his mother had stopped to grab only a bowl of soup on the way up. They were running too late to eat a full dinner, and he'd feared the door would be locked before they arrived at the inn. No room at the inn. The Christmassy thought jumped into his mind, which seemed unwarranted since Christmas was still two and a half months away.

He bounded down the steps, drawn by the tempting scents and the thought of seeing Alissa again. Through an archway, Ross saw the dining room table seated with strangers except for one—his mother, who seemed to be enjoying the company of the other guests. He stepped through the archway, noticing the antique buffet laden with breakfast. He said good morning and lifted a plate, eyeing the fare. Fresh fruit, a sausage casserole—he decided from the scent— muffins, and juice. He filled his plate, poured coffee from the decanter, and settled into a chair beside his mother.

A large man with a protruding belly rose and headed back to the buffet, telling everyone how delicious the casserole was, while a woman who seemed to be his wife encouraged him to leave food for the other guests.

Ross eyed his plate then bowed his head, silently asking the Lord to bless his food and day. When he lifted his gaze, he noticed a few pairs of eyes focused on him. To be polite, he introduced himself then lifted his fork and tasted the sausage dish. The blend of eggs, sausage, bread, and cheese met his hopes, and he had to agree with the rotund man that the casserole was excellent.

His mother lowered her coffee cup. "Did you sleep well?"

He hadn't slept well, not that the accommodations weren't wonderful, but he'd awakened numerous times, thinking of Alissa. He didn't want to go into that with his mother, so he just said, "The bed was very comfortable. And you?"

"Like a baby. I think the sound of the ocean lulled me to sleep."

"I have birds."

"Birds?"

"That's what I hear. My room looks out on the flower garden."

"Flower garden! I'll have to take a walk and see that."

Ross preferred to see the ocean, but he nodded, knowing his mother's love of flowers.

"I suppose the bouquet in my room came from her garden."

"Good possibility," Ross said, forcing his eyes to focus on his mother and not the kitchen door.

When the door finally swung back, he lifted his gaze and readied a smile, but it faded quickly.

"Good morning," the woman said. "You must be Mr. Cahill."

"Ross Cahill."

"I'm glad to meet you. I'm Fern. My sister owns the inn." She extended her hand, and Ross grasped it in his, biting his tongue so he wouldn't ask where her sister was. "If you need anything, just ask."

She shifted to the buffet. Then he watched her leave through the swinging door with an empty serving dish. Sounds came from inside the kitchen, and Ross wondered if the clanging was Alissa cleaning after the breakfast preparation.

The other guests chatted, discussing what they planned for the day and where they lived. His mother added a comment on occasion, but he had no interest in learning anything about the guests. What he wanted to know was Alissa's whereabouts. Four of the guests left, and another followed soon. The only other couple remaining was the overweight gentleman and his wife. The man rose again and returned to the table with a sweet roll.

Ross finished his breakfast and scooted back the chair. "I think I'll read the paper and enjoy my coffee in the parlor," he said. "When do you want to leave?"

"In a bit. I'll finish getting ready, and then I'd enjoy walking through the garden before we go."

"We can do that." He refilled his cup before giving a nod to the other couple and headed into the parlor where he had visited with Alissa the evening before. He sank into a chair cushion and located the newspaper, his gaze shifting from the paper on past the dining room to the kitchen door.

When the telephone rang, his hopes lifted as he focused on the swinging door, but Fern appeared and answered the call. Ross forced himself to look back at the news, feeling disappointed. The emotion didn't sit well with him. He was far too busy to be admiring a woman who lived more than a hundred miles from his ranch.

He paused, captured by the thought. He'd felt a connection to Alissa from the moment he saw her. Something in her eyes—maybe the same kind of loneliness he felt. Yet he hadn't allowed himself to get involved. His work took too much time. *So why—?* Ross drew in a breath. *Lord, is this Your doing? I know You guide our steps, but. . .* He grasped the mug and took a swig of coffee, knowing that what he felt made no sense. He didn't know the woman at all.

"Are you waiting for me?"

His mother's voice pierced his thoughts as she came from the dining room.

He dropped the newspaper. "If you're ready, I am."

"I want to read my devotions this morning before we leave, if that's okay."

"That's fine, Mom. I'll go up and make a few calls. How about an hour?"

"Perfect," she said, her smile so gentle that emotion caught in Ross's throat.

He watched her head toward her room, and he took the stairs, thinking that after his phone calls, he might catch a quick nap since he'd had such a restless night.

Inside his room, he checked in with his managers in Paso Robles and San Luis Obispo. He almost felt disappointed everything seemed status quo. No problems. He wasn't missed. Ross shook his head at the ridiculous thought. He should feel relief instead of disappointment.

He set his cell phone on the dresser then plumped the pillow on his bed and stretched out, trying to force his mind into quiet. His brain had other ideas, and after a while, he gave up. His thoughts were one floor down, so he might as well be down there, too.

When he returned to the parlor, quiet had settled over the inn. He heard no sounds from the dining room or kitchen. Most of the tourists were out sightseeing, he guessed. He'd be doing the same soon. He grasped a tourist magazine and flipped through the pages. When he'd settled on an article that had caught his interest, he heard footsteps and saw his mother.

"Are you ready now?"

"Are you?"

"As ready as I'll ever be." He saw the look in her eyes and wished he'd sounded more positive. He added a lighter tone to his voice. "Where are we headed today?"

"Let's visit the garden behind the inn, and then I'd like to head over to the Monarch Butterfly Sanctuary. It's not too far."

"This is your holiday, so I want to do what makes you happy."

She pursed her lips and faced him. "This is our vacation, Ross. I hoped you'd find some pleasure in our trip."

He cringed beneath his mother's words. Didn't honoring his mother mean to respect her and favor her in special ways? Why did he have to be so grudging with his time? He wouldn't have her forever. "What I mean is, I want you to enjoy yourself."

"Then we have the same goal. I want you to enjoy yourself, too." She brushed her hands together as if removing dust.

Her smile had a hint of "I put you in your place," but she always did that with love. After he'd become an adult, Ross realized his mother had to have been a strong woman to deal with his father. Ross and his dad butted heads often, especially as adults in the business. Yet, when he thought about it, at home his father seemed to drop his work at the door and focus on Ross's mother. His mom often said he and his father were too much alike. Maybe that was the problem.

Ross motioned her forward then followed her onto the gingerbread-style porch and down the front steps. The view of the ocean awed him: the rugged rocks and the sun glinting off the waves that dashed in a billow of white foam. The scene tugged pleasure from beneath his internal rock-hard determination to be miserable on this trip as he'd planned. Instead he felt the opposite.

"This is lovely," his mother said, drawing in a breath of air. She closed her eyes, and he could imagine she was remembering times when she and his father had come to Pacific Grove for vacations.

He moved ahead of her down the flagstone path that led to the back of the Victorian house. In the daylight, he noted its lemon yellow clapboard siding with white trim. Its many gables sloped in every direction, giving a mysterious aura of secret nooks and crannies. He chuckled to himself, thinking he'd read too many old classics in college.

His mother's footsteps scuffed behind him on the stone, and when he reached the garden, he paused and waited for her. When she saw the gazebo, she cried out with delight and headed for it. He studied the picturesque summerhouse with its circle of benches and low tables that looked like the setting for a ladies' tea party.

Passing beside colorful autumn blossoms he couldn't identify, except for bushing mum plants and some colorful asters, he mounted the three stairs behind his mother. The gazebo appeared in good condition, no paint chips and recently dusted and swept. The question arose again. Who did all the work? He hoped Alissa had plenty of help besides her sister, whose smile appeared much less good-natured than Alissa's.

"I love it here," his mother said. "Look at the view—the flowers and the foothills—and I can hear the ocean."

When his mother sat on the bench, Ross remained where he was, but when he realized she wasn't planning to move, he sat across from her and waited.

"Good morning."

Ross's neck jerked upward, hearing the feminine voice call from the distance, and his heart gave a lurch when he saw Alissa heading his way.

"Good morning," his mother called while he sat tongue-tied.

In the lamplight last evening, he hadn't noticed the color of her hair. This morning it looked like buttered toast, a blend of tan and gold, appearing so soft in the breeze. Ross liked the short, feathered waves rolling back from her forehead and curving in a soft curl below her ears. Last night Alissa had been amiable yet with an air of business about her. This morning she appeared more carefree and youthful. He'd taken her for his age, but now he guessed she might be younger.

He rose as she approached them with a warm smile on her face. "I wondered if you were away." He wished he'd held back those words. Obviously they meant he'd been looking for her.

"I was tired last night. So this morning, after I prepared breakfast, I had to bake cookies. I usually take care of that the night before." A slight flush colored her cheeks. "I didn't mean to say—"

Ross stopped her. "No need to apologize. I shouldn't have cornered you with all my questions."

"Questions?" His mother's voice lapped over his.

He turned to face her. "I was asking about activities. Alis—Mrs. Greening gave me—"

"Miss, but please call me Alissa."

Miss. Had she never married? He covered his surprise then had second thoughts. Or had her husband died? Perhaps that was the edginess he'd noticed. "Alissa gave us some brochures about activities in the area."

"You don't need brochures." His mother rose and stood beside him while Alissa remained on the grass below. "I've been here many times. I've enjoyed so many things."

"I'm glad," Alissa said, staying where she was. "What have you planned for today?"

"The sanctuary," his mother said before he could respond.

Alissa straightened. "But you don't want to miss the parade. I'm getting ready to go."

"Parade?" Another unison response.

"The second Saturday of October, the school district puts on its annual Butterfly Parade and Bazaar. It's wonderful to see. The children and teachers dress in costumes and parade through town. Have you passed the post office yet?"

"I don't think so," Maggie said, turning a questioning look toward Ross.

He shrugged. "I didn't notice."

"If you're on Lighthouse Avenue, you'll see it. They have a darling bronze statue called the Butterfly Kids. It's two children dressed in their butterfly costumes to commemorate the event."

His mother turned to Ross. "We'll want to see it, too, then."

Ross questioned her remark, but she gave him a hopeful look. He responded with a nod. His goal had been to please her, and the past day had aroused new thinking in his mind. He'd been uncertain that he would enjoy the vacation since his mind kept veering to his business, but now he had second thoughts.

Alissa's enthusiasm seemed on a roll. "After the parade, you'll find a bazaar at the school, and it's great for buying Christmas gifts."

"I'd love to go to the parade. When does it begin?"

"Soon."

"Wonderful. I can go to the sanctuary later." His mother gave him a cursory glance but responded without waiting for his reaction. "May we join you?"

Ross shifted his gaze from his mother to Alissa, trying to anticipate what would result. Though he didn't want to, he liked the idea, and a surprising sense of anticipation waved through him. Yet a parade and bazaar didn't seem like something a man should want to do.

Alissa's face brightened. "Certainly. I'd love for you to come along." She turned toward Ross. "Although I don't suppose you'd be interested."

If he behaved as he normally would at home, he would run from an offer to attend a children's butterfly parade or a bazaar as if his life depended on it. He managed to open his mouth, mustering a playful tenor of a man who really didn't want to go but would. "I suppose I could come along. I've never seen a butterfly parade." He cringed at his mother's questioning look.

"You're not doing this for me, I hope?"

She'd put him on the spot. Now how to respond? He garnered courage. "I'm on vacation, Mom. You told me you wanted me to enjoy myself."

Her look segued to a grin. "That's good."

"Okay," Alissa said, also with a question in her eyes as if she knew she was missing something between them but had to live with it. "Fern will take over the inn for me this afternoon. If you wait just a moment, I'll let her know I'm leaving, and we should probably be on our way soon. I'll meet you out front in"—she looked at her watch—"in fifteen minutes." She gave a little wave and bounded across the grass.

Ross watched her go, admiring her guacamole-colored slacks and matching top with a deeper green trim. But the color also reminded him that if he were at home he would be trying to accomplish a few household chores before he drove to his office in San Luis Obispo to catch up on the avocado business's paperwork. The out-of-his-domain feelings he'd experienced grew to an out-of-his-world sensation. He glanced heavenward and gave the Lord a plaintive look.

※

Alissa grasped her shoulder bag and pulled out her car keys. The excitement rippling through her made little sense. She'd guided people to interesting events before today. So what made the butterfly parade so different? The answer came as her mind filled with the image of Ross's azure eyes crinkled with smile lines—or maybe worry lines—a look that made her want to probe deeper.

Sinking to the edge of her bed, Alissa pictured Ross sitting in the gazebo in the shadows. His hands were folded, his elbows on his knees, his head bent almost like he was praying, but she guessed he was trying to keep his patience while waiting for his mother. Maggie appeared to be a sweet woman yet seemed to grate on Ross's nerves—as parents can—even though God's Word tells Christians to honor their parents. Alissa refocused on her purpose, slipped her feet into walking shoes, and rose. She opened the door to her quarters and headed to the sitting room.

Ross stood near the exit with Maggie nowhere in sight.

"Where's your mother?"

He shrugged. "She can make a simple task into a major project."

Alissa gestured to one of the comfortable chairs. "You'll be on your feet once we get there. You might as well relax."

He eyed the chair and shook his head, his keys jingling in his hand.

Alissa dangled her keys so he could see them. "I'll drive. I know where I'm going."

A scowl sprang to his face. "I really—"

Determined, Alissa pushed forward. "I'll drive so we don't waste time."

He blanched as a deeper frown knitted his brows, but as he slid his car keys back in his pocket, Alissa wanted to notch one up for herself. She could tell they were both strong willed, and she wondered how that might play out in his days at her inn.

A door closed in the hallway, and in a moment Maggie appeared in the doorway with a warm smile, a white-haired woman with a youthful air about her. "Are you both waiting for me?"

Ross made a guttural sound. "What do you think we're—"

"There's no problem. We were settling some matters before you arrived." Alissa gave him a don't-you-dare-say-anything look. "We'll take my car. It's a two-door, but I know where we're going."

"Your car? Really?" Maggie flashed a look at Ross, who only shrugged.

She motioned them outside then faced the next battle.

"Mother can sit in front," Ross said, trying to manipulate his long legs into the backseat of her car.

"I will not," Maggie said, squeezing past him. "You're too big, and I prefer being in the backseat." She slipped into the seat with no effort.

Ross settled into the passenger seat and closed the door with an emphatic *thud*. "I'm not used to this."

Though it was a mumble, she'd heard him. "I'm not trying to make you uncomfortable. I thought it would be easier for everyone." She tried to keep her voice hushed, but despite her effort, Maggie, with the hearing of a hawk, overheard her.

"Ross, stop complaining" sailed from the backseat.

Ross opened his mouth to respond then snapped it shut and chuckled. "I remember Mom complaining when I was the kid sitting in the backseat."

Alissa laughed, too, enjoying his contrite tone. "You'll cherish those memories one day."

"I suppose," he said, settling back and seeming to accept the reality that she was driving.

She found a parking space just off Forest Avenue near Pine Avenue then guided them back toward Lighthouse Avenue, where she hoped they might find seats in the reviewing stand. Ross walked between her and Maggie, and his cedar-and-citrus scent floated toward her on the late morning air.

"This must be a huge event," Ross said. "I can't believe the number of people."

"It's a welcome party for the monarchs. They've begun arriving already, but in another week they'll fill the trees."

"Another week?" He turned to his mother. "Why didn't we come next week?"

"This is a vacation. Your father and I always came for a couple of weeks. There's more to do than the butterflies, although that's my favorite."

His attempt to grin at her left a little to be desired, but Alissa gave him one point for trying.

A few seats remained in the reviewing stand, and Ross climbed first, taking his mother's hand to get her safely seated. When he offered his hand to Alissa, she wanted to evade his touch, knowing how her emotions were playing games with her, but she had little choice. She took it, feeling the pressure of his fingers on hers, his large palm swallowing hers like a protective covering. She sank onto the bench, Ross between her and Maggie, and they settled in.

The children's voices and the noise of the crowd rose, and soon schoolchildren of all ages came into view, costumed as butterflies and monitored by their teachers, who'd also dressed for the occasion. A crowd had joined the parade, heading toward Down Elementary School for the bazaar or perhaps for their vehicles.

When the parade had passed them, Alissa rose and Ross followed, putting his hand beneath her elbow as she stepped down then helping his mother to the ground. They joined in behind the parade walking down Fountain Avenue. Ross shifted closer as they walked, his arm brushing against hers. "Yesterday I asked you what you did for relaxation, and I guess this is one of those things?"

She grinned. "Community functions, church activities. I sing in one of the church's praise choirs, for example."

"What do you sing?"

"Praise songs."

He gave her shoulder a nudge with his. "I mean, what part? I'm sure you're not a bass."

She careened a step away from his playful poke. "Alto when they let me. When we're short sopranos, then I'm a soprano."

"Hmm. Versatile as well as talented."

"I'm not sure I'd say that." The sparkle in his eyes nearly undid her.

"Do you sing tomorrow?"

"Our young adult group does. Why? Are you interested in joining us for the service?"

"I think that could be arranged. Mom never misses a service unless she's ill, and she rarely has even a cold."

"You're very welcome to join me. Fern attends a later service so she fills in for me on Sunday morning." She pointed ahead. "You'll see the building. It's not far from the school."

Maggie leaned across Ross. "What are you two talking about?"

"Going to church," Ross said, giving his mother's cheek a pat.

"Good. I thought maybe you were complaining again."

Ross slipped his arm around his mother's shoulders. "Me? Your son? When do I complain?"

She snickered and wiggled away. "I'll let you demonstrate that for yourself."

Alissa enjoyed the bantering. Playful banter had never been part of her family. Fern's sense of humor was like her mom's, much more serious than Alissa's. Alissa was probably more like her dad, but he'd died in his early fifties, and now he was only a memory. Still, she could hear him laugh at a joke or a comedian on TV. Sometimes he laughed at himself. Her mom hadn't found him that funny, but Alissa recalled she had.

When they reached the school, Alissa led them around the building to the back where the outdoor bazaar was held.

Ross pointed to the banner strung up at the head of the bazaar tables— BUTTERFLY TOWN, U.S.A. "Is that really what it's called?"

Alissa nodded. "That's our nickname. It's sort of like Gilroy on Highway 101—'The Garlic Capital of the World.'" She turned to Maggie. "Have you ever been there?"

"No, but I've heard of it." Maggie continued to gaze at the colorful banner.

"You should take a ride up there sometime, especially if you enjoy garlic."

Maggie grasped Ross's arm. "Do you hear that? You should take me to Gilroy. Your father never did. I'd like that."

He winked at her. "Anything you say, Mom."

She gave him a playful swat and turned back to Alissa, motioning toward the booths. "Where should we begin?"

"We could split up and then meet if that's easier."

Ross chimed in. "Good idea. I can find a seat somewhere."

"Spoilsport," Alissa said, assuming he was being his usual devil's advocate. "Let's meet by this sign. We can't miss that."

They agreed on a time to meet, and Alissa headed off on her own, stopping to greet people she knew and eyeing items that would make nice gifts. She noted the time; still an hour to go. She continued perusing the booths until she spotted a couple of items for herself, but as she so often did, Alissa hesitated. Her needs were few, but sometimes doodads intrigued her, although her finances often helped her make wise decisions.

"You're empty-handed."

She spun around, hearing Ross's voice so close behind her and noticing his package-free arms. "What about you?"

"Men aren't supposed to buy things, are they?"

"Something nice for your mom, maybe. A remembrance of her trip with you. I'm guessing you don't do this often."

He shrugged. "Not if I can help it."

Alissa shook her head.

"I know," he said. "I can be a jerk. I do really want to please my mother, although I don't suppose I sound like it. She and my dad traveled so much, and they enjoyed each other's company. He was rather headstrong, and she didn't always get what she wanted, so on this trip, I let her pick the location."

"You mentioned your father's deceased."

He nodded. "It's been difficult for Mom."

"Both of my parents are gone. It's because of Mother I have the inn."

"Was the inn her house?"

"No, but she had a nice home and a little savings from Dad's insurance. She left Fern and me everything—except she stipulated the house was mine. She knew I wanted a bed-and-breakfast, and I suppose she thought I'd use it for that."

He looked confused. "But you said the inn wasn't your family home."

Her shoulders knotted as the memories came crashing back. "I sold my mother's house in the downtown area and bought this one with the help of a large loan."

"I suppose that took a lot of faith. Are you happy you did?"

"*I* am. It's been successful, and I keep paying the loan. One day it will be paid back, and the house will be mine."

He gave her a curious look, and she realized she'd said too much. Letting her guests know about her personal problems with Fern wasn't wise. Ross didn't question her, and Alissa didn't offer an explanation.

"Mind if I tag along?" he asked.

"Not at all." The answer flew from her mouth with ease. She'd begun to enjoy his company, and beneath his sometimes abrasive comments, she liked many other qualities she'd seen in him.

He walked beside her as she picked up a few items—a piece of stained glass, a new Christmas wreath for the front door, a hand-knit sweater for Fern in her favorite shades of mauve and blue. Then a metal sculpture caught her eye, and she paused.

Ross seemed intrigued, too, and he purchased a spinning sculpture for his mother to hang from a hook or a tree. "Mom loves her flower garden, so she'll like this."

"It's pretty, and look how it catches the sunlight and seems to change colors." She faltered when she eyed a plant adornment, a metal rod with a monarch butterfly at the top in burnished tones of copper and black.

"That's nice," Ross said, watching her admire the plant stick.

She studied the price tag and set it back. Though the cost wasn't prohibitive, it seemed a waste of money, especially since she'd just mentioned her big loan. With winter coming, the tourist business slowed, and wasting money on thingamabobs seemed foolish.

Ross frowned when she returned it to the display. "You don't like it?"

"I do, but I shouldn't spend the money."

He gazed at the butterfly stick for a moment and then stepped away to follow her.

Alissa headed for a display of stained glass with Ross quiet beside her. She wondered what he was thinking, but since it was none of her business, she turned her attention to prices of the glass items then moved on. When she eyed her watch, she faltered. "I can't believe it, but it's almost time to meet your mom. Are you ready?"

"You go ahead. I saw something back there I want to look at again. I'll meet you in a minute."

He turned away, and she headed for the area where they'd agreed to meet, more and more curious about this stranger who'd become a special person in her life in less than a day.

Chapter 3

With his eyes on the cross emblazoned in front of him, Ross listened to the Bible verse as God's Word sank into his heart. "And whatsoever ye do, do it heartily, as to the Lord, and not unto men; knowing that of the Lord ye shall receive the reward of the inheritance: for ye serve the Lord Christ." How many times had he heard Colossians 3:23–24? But today the message held a different meaning.

Do it heartily, as to the Lord. He'd thought about good deeds, kindness, and witnessing but never thought of his job, his work on the ranch, in that way. His father had not given his blessing to his decisions, and Ross realized his own pride and spirit of independence had stood between him and his father. Now it was too late to make amends. His father lived in heaven. Still, at times the longing to relent and beg his father's forgiveness smothered him.

He eyed Alissa sitting on the other side of his mother. She looked ahead without blinking, as if she had always worked for the Lord and could reap His reward without hesitation.

Ross lowered his head, studying the nubby-patterned carpet in earthen colors, colors that reminded him of the soil beneath his trees and vines. God watered them with rain, and his business had grown. So why would he even think the Lord didn't approve of his work? The answer rang in his head. *Because my earthly father disapproved, and I was to honor him.*

That was the core of his struggle. Which one to believe, his earthly father who had strong sentiments about what was right and wrong according to the Lord or God's Word that seemed so hard to understand because people tended to put their own spin on the meaning? How convenient to interpret God's Word to fit a person's needs and wants.

Ross rubbed his temple. Had he done that?

The congregation rose and startled him. He'd been too deep in thought to listen to the pastor's final message. Words to the next song flashed on the screen, and the band began to play while people's arms rose in praise as music and words blended into a joyful song to the Lord: "Glorify His Name." Ross sang along, wishing he were closer to Alissa to hear her singing voice. A comfortable feeling washed over him. He did glorify God's name in all he did. At least he hoped he did.

The next song flashed on the screen—"Seek Ye First"—as if the Lord wanted to put a pin in his balloon. The text filled his mind as if affirming his early thoughts. What had he been seeking when he went against his father's advice and bought the vineyard? Was it financial success? Yes and no, but the business seemed to have no relationship to God's Word in Ross's eyes. Why hadn't his father seen that?

In the softer sounds of the song, Alissa's voice drifted to his ears, and a Bible verse pounded in his head. *"Ask, and it shall be given you; seek, and ye shall find; knock, and it shall be opened unto you." Ask.* It seemed so simple yet so late to ask God now what He thought of decisions made and contracts signed too long ago.

Thoughts weighed on Ross's shoulders, and he closed his eyes, wishing the Lord would lift his burden. *Ask. Ask. Ask.* His eyes snapped open. He needed to seek the Lord and ask. It was as simple as that.

Outside in the sunlight, Ross shooed away his darker thoughts. Once again Alissa seemed as lustrous as the morning sun. Her dark blond hair glowed with that buttery beige color he'd noticed before. Today, though, not only her hair sparkled but also her eyes, with light and a dark blue color that made him think of violets. Beautiful eyes to go with her beautiful face.

"You're thoughtful," Alissa said, walking beside him to the car.

He'd insisted on driving today since he'd been on that route for the parade, and he jingled his keys in his hands, wanting to respond but not wanting to be specific. "I guess I am" was all he could think of.

"Did you enjoy the sermon?" she asked.

Enjoy wasn't the word.

"We all needed to hear that message, don't you think?" His mother's voice jutted between Alissa's question and his attempt to find an appropriate response.

He grinned at her. "That's why it's God's Word," Ross said, grateful for the direction she gave to the conversation.

They all chuckled, and Alissa's question, to his relief, went by the wayside.

He hit the remote, unlocking the car doors, and he helped his mother into the back where she'd wanted to sit again then closed the passenger door for Alissa. As they headed back to the inn, he dug deep to find conversation. "I noticed you've named your guest rooms."

Alissa glanced his way, a crooked grin stealing to her mouth. "They're butterflies."

He thought of the small marker outside his room. "Emperor?"

She nodded. "Yes, emperor is a butterfly, as are admiral, viceroy, monarch, mosaic, shasta, angelwing, and painted lady, your mom's room. Each room is named after a kind of butterfly."

"Thanks for letting me be the emperor. I've always wanted to oversee something huge."

"You do," his mother said.

Ross wished she hadn't been listening.

Alissa's eyes widened.

"She means my business," he said to explain.

"What is your business? You've never mentioned it."

"I have an avocado ranch near Santa Barbara in San Luis Obispo and another ranch in Paso Robles. That's where I live." He winced, waiting for his mother's next comment.

"Avocados. I love them," Alissa said. "They're great in salads, and guacamole is wonderful. Sometimes I put out chips and make it for my guests in the afternoon."

He thanked the Lord for the distraction. "Then you'll have to try my special recipe."

She tilted her head as if to see if he was joking.

"Really. It's great. I'll e-mail it to you when I get home."

Her eyes flickered as if she were still questioning him. "When you get home." She paused. "I'd like that."

Her voice had softened as if she were disappointed, and he wondered if she didn't want to wait that long. "I could call up and see if my housekeeper can find it."

She shook her head. "You don't have to do that." Her face brightened. "Speaking of avocados and guacamole, it's lunchtime. I should get back home and let you eat at one of the great restaurants on the wharf on Cannery Row."

Grasping the opportunity, he let his heart respond. "Would you care to join us?"

"I'd love to, but I need to get back. Fern has plans, and I can't be away much longer."

The hope he'd had fluttered away like dried leaves. "Maybe next time."

"Who knows?" she said, her eyebrows rising.

That wasn't what he wanted to hear. A rousing *yes* or *for sure* would have pleased him. Her *who knows* left him disappointed.

❧

Alissa waved as Ross and Maggie pulled away. An uncomfortable loneliness settled over her. She'd developed a feeling of attachment to Maggie. And Ross? He'd aroused sensations in her that she hadn't felt in years—heart palpitations, pulse skipping, flush rising—foolish and impossible feelings that kept growing.

Using the back door, Alissa slipped inside, expecting the scent of home-baked cookies. Instead she smelled nothing. She dropped her handbag on a kitchen chair and strolled into the parlor and registration area. As she passed the buffet, the scent of freshly brewed coffee wafted past her, and except for Fern on the telephone, the room was empty. She moved closer and peered over Fern's shoulder, watching her chicken scratches entering something in the reservation book.

"Two for October eighteenth," Fern said, making a notation in the book.

Alissa thought of the mess-up with Ross and his mother. "Is that two people or two rooms?"

Fern shot her a frown and dropped the pencil.

Alissa gave her an apologetic look and walked away.

"That's two rooms for the eighteenth," Fern repeated.

Alissa watched Fern's face as she scratched out something in the registration book. "One room. Two people. Good. May I have a credit card to hold the room?"

Alissa headed back to the kitchen, expecting an argument but not wanting one in the guest area. She glanced at the buffet, hoping to see the cookies on the platters along with the coffee. Her shoulders relaxed as she spotted two plates piled with cookies, but as she neared, tension flared. She slipped her fingers beneath the plastic wrap and lifted one. From the feel, she had her answer, and though she had no need to test, she did anyway and took a bite. She knew it. Glowering at Fern's profile, Alissa charged into the kitchen and tossed the store-bought cookie she'd tasted into the wastebasket.

She'd prided herself on nothing but homemade in her bed-and-breakfast. She'd never taken shortcuts, so why had Fern taken it upon herself to bring bought cookies into the inn? Before she could calm herself, the swinging door flew back and Fern stomped into the room.

"You are always questioning me, Alissa, and I'm tired of it."

Alissa raised her hand to calm her, but she noticed her own fingers trembled as she did. "I'm sorry, but I just told you about the misunderstanding with the Cahills' reservation. We have to make sure we understand clearly what the guest wants. Apparently you didn't, because I saw you scratching out the other information."

"If you're going to spy on me, then you need to find someone else to do this job."

Her heart bucking inside her chest, Alissa bit her lip a moment to regulate her tone. "Please, Fern, I don't want to argue. It's Sunday, and—"

"Oh, so no arguing on Sunday, but I suppose Monday through Saturday is fine."

"That's not what I meant." She opened the freezer door and pulled out a few cookies she'd frozen, thinking she'd save them for herself, but now she had no other choice today.

"What are you doing?" Fern swung her hand toward the two plastic containers Alissa had taken from the freezer.

"They're cookies."

"We have cookies. I filled the plates already."

Alissa pried the lid off the first container. Peanut butter. Ross liked those. "They're store-bought. I serve homemade."

Fern put her hand on her hip. "I didn't feel like messing around with baking this morning. As you just reminded me, it's Sunday, and I'm heading for the late service."

"We have aprons. That would protect you from the mess."

Fern flashed a fiery look at Alissa. "These aren't store-bought anyway. They're from a bakery."

"They're still store-bought." Alissa raised her hand again. "Let's stop this now. Please."

"Great." Fern did a dramatic curtsy, grabbed her handbag, and charged out the back door.

Alissa stood there a moment, tears blurring her vision, before she sank onto a kitchen chair and braced her head in her hands. Why did she get into these verbal attacks with Fern? She wanted to be a good sister, but Fern and she disagreed on so many things. *Lord, You know what I should do. Please give me wisdom and even a hint of what I can do to bring peace to our relationship.*

The prayer hung above her as a chill prickled down her back. Words from Ecclesiastes filled her thoughts. *"Better is the end of a thing than the beginning thereof: and the patient in spirit is better than the proud in spirit."* The verse sank into her mind, leaving her uncertain. The beginning of the verse gave her hope if that was God's purpose in sending her the verse. She sensed the Lord was telling her things would end better than they were now. That's what she wanted.

But what about the last part? *Patience is better than pride.* She'd tried to be patient with Fern. Was Fern's pride getting in her way? Fern had been envious of their mother's bequest. Alissa knew that from day one, but Fern had received a greater portion of the life insurance. She should have been happy, and what had she done with her money besides squander it away? And in such a foolish way at that.

With the questions still nudging her for understanding, Alissa pulled out two crystal platters and filled them with the frozen cookies. By the time any guests came back, she hoped the cookies would be thawed. She carried them into the guest area, replaced the store-bought ones with her homemade ones, and returned to the kitchen. She looked at the cookies and tossed them into the wastebasket. No store-bought cookies for her. She prided herself in homemade.

⌇

Ross watched his mother head down the hallway while he let his nose lead him toward the kitchen. The scent of something sweet and lemony filled the air. He glanced at the buffet but saw nothing lemon; then he spied a peanut butter cookie like the one he'd enjoyed the day he arrived. He lifted one and took a bite. As he did, the swinging door flew open, and Alissa strode through, a smudge of flour on her face.

"Something smells good," he said, longing to brush the flour from her cheek.

"I made lemon bars for tonight."

"I love those things."

"I know. You told me." Her expression looked as if she'd just caught herself from stepping into a rabbit hole, and a tinge of pink brightened her expression.

"So I did. Thank you."

She shook her head as if clearing away the cobwebs. "They're for all my guests."

"I know." He opened his mouth to add, *But you knew I love them.* Instead he let well enough alone. She'd already embarrassed herself by telling him as much as she did.

She moved toward the buffet and transferred the cookies from one of the two platters to the other then draped the plastic wrap over the top. "Did you have a nice lunch?"

"We did. We ate at Bubba Gump's. It's a fun place."

"It is. I always chuckle when I see the 'Run Forrest Run' flip cards."

He grinned. "Afterward we sat on the wharf awhile watching the waves roll in."

"Sounds relaxing." She lifted the empty plate.

"It was, and now I'd love a nap, but Mom has other plans."

Alissa laughed, the plate tucked against her slender waist. "And what is that?"

"She wants to go to the butterfly sanctuary. She's in changing from her church clothes, and I'm about to do the same. I can't see looking at trees in dress pants."

He loved her smile. She gave him a nod. "Jeans work better."

"And sneakers."

She grinned. "Well, you'd better get ready, or she'll beat you."

"You're right." He gave her a playful salute and charged up the stairs, feeling heady and confused. He bantered with his mother, but the lighthearted chitchat with Alissa had never been his style. A businessman talked business, usually with businessmen. What did he know about women anymore? That hobby—and he knew he called it that in self-defense—had been put on a shelf like model cars and video games.

He used the key and pushed open his bedroom door. The flowers still stood on the table, but beside them, he spotted a bowl of fruit—an apple, an orange, a banana, and a plum. *Nice touch.* Alissa had added so many nice amenities to her inn, including those wonderful home-baked goodies.

He slipped off his shoes and tossed himself onto the bed, closing his eyes a moment to sort out his thoughts. His ranches needed attention, he knew, but for the first time in his life, he didn't want to contact anyone to find out what new problems had arisen, if any. They had his cell phone number in case of an emergency. Since he'd bought the vineyard, his life had revolved around work. Running two different produce ranches kept him hopping. His father had told him that, among other things, but his wealth had grown as he thought it would.

Wealth. What good was it in the bank? He reinvested, but otherwise it was just piling up. No wife to leave it to, no children to benefit. He'd leave his money to his church perhaps, or. . . He pulled a pillow from beneath the bedspread and tossed it over his face. *Stop thinking about death and bequeathals.* It was too depressing.

His father filled his mind again, and Roger. . .his brother.

He tossed the pillow to the foot of the bed and raised himself on his elbows. Outside was a blue sky with promises of a bright day, a pleasant day, so why had he filled his mind with gloom and doom?

Ross rose and slipped off his dress pants, hung them over the rocking chair, and grasped his jeans from a chair, though he'd left them on the floor. He figured Alissa hadn't cleaned his room, but in case she ever did, he needed to be more careful. Neater for sure. He tugged off his shirt and grabbed a knit pullover from a dresser drawer where he'd tossed his folded clothes. Tucking his shirt into his pants, he did a balancing act while slipping on his shoes. A mirror reflected his image—hair messed and a hint of a five o'clock shadow. Before going down, he grabbed his shaving kit and headed into the bathroom.

⁓

Hearing someone in the other room, Alissa left her pan of lemon bars and stepped through the swinging door. Maggie stood beside the coffeepot as if considering whether she wanted a cup. "Would you like some tea instead?" She motioned inside the kitchen. "I have water on the stove."

"Thanks, but I suppose I don't need anything. We had a lovely lunch."

"Ross told me, and he said you're going over to the Monarch Butterfly Sanctuary now."

"We are." She gave a little nod, but her eyes looked past Alissa into the kitchen.

Alissa guessed at her thoughts. "Would you like to look around?" She motioned inside.

"I'd love to." Her steps quickened as she passed through the doorway and stopped. "This is so nice. Everything so clean and bright, and look at those." She pointed to the lemon bars. "Ross loves those things."

"Yes, I—yes, he told me earlier."

Her eyes softened when she looked at Alissa. "He's a good son. Ross. I'm proud of him."

"I'm sure you are. He's a successful businessman, and that would make any mother proud."

"You never had children?"

"I never married. Time ran away with itself. I dated a few nice gentlemen, but I never met anyone I'd consider a soul mate, and I never felt the Lord encouraging me to give my heart to any of them."

"God will bless that strong faith," Maggie said, resting her hand on Alissa's. "And don't give up. You never know when that special someone will appear in your life. One day you'll feel an immediate connection and. . ."

Though Alissa heard the rest of Maggie's comments in the periphery of her mind, she felt frozen to the floor. That exact feeling had washed over her the day she'd met Ross. He'd been irritating and cool, but when they'd talked later after his apology, she sensed a connection, a strange sensation that they'd known each other forever. The emotion seemed so foolish under the circumstances. She'd just learned his name, and she saw his eyes. How could anyone recognize a soul mate based on that little bit of information?

But she had.

"Ross is an only child?" Alissa asked, forcing herself to concentrate.

Maggie's face darkened. "No, he had a younger brother." She closed her eyes. "Roger."

"I'm sorry. Had he been ill?"

"Yes, but not in the way we think of illness."

Alissa felt herself frown, confused by Maggie's comment. "Was it a rare disease?" She shouldn't probe, but her desire to know more about the Cahills overshadowed good sense.

"It's very common. Roger died in a car accident. A drunk driver accident."

"That's so tragic."

"Our faith is strong, and we chose not to drink alcohol in our family."

"I understand. I've never indulged either. It's safer that way. Alcoholism sneaks up on people without their even realizing it."

Maggie's head lowered. "It does, and no matter what a family does, it doesn't help."

"Alcoholics need the Lord," Alissa said, hoping to soothe the woman's sorrow. "Did the driver die in the crash? So often they survive."

Maggie's head lifted, her eyes glazed. "Roger was the drunk driver. He killed a mother and her child." Maggie rested her cheek against her hand. "It's difficult to forgive him for that."

Air escaped Alissa's chest as if she'd been kicked in the stomach. Maggie's tone, so harsh and bitter, seemed out of place coming from this gentle woman. Alissa struggled for words of comfort. "But we must forgive."

She opened her arms, and Maggie melted into her embrace. They stood there until Alissa heard Ross's footsteps on the stairs. Was this the dark shadow she'd witnessed in his eyes when he didn't realize she was looking? Feeling guilt for someone else's sin seemed natural when it came to family. She thought of her relationship with Fern and faced the truth. She'd never felt guilt for her sister's envy. Maybe it was time to put herself in Fern's shoes.

"Thank you," Maggie said. "I don't talk about that often, and maybe I should." She stepped back and pushed open the swinging door.

Through it, Alissa saw Ross standing near the registration desk, his hands in his pockets, looking toward the outside door. Across the highway, the ocean sprawled before them, dashing against the rocks as if trying to shatter the hard stone. Life seemed that way. Waves of guilt, fear, and sadness lashed against life's stability, and only a rock could endure the usual corrosion that destroyed life's beauty.

Alissa knew she had her Rock, her Savior, but how often she found herself wallowing in the waves without clinging to the Rock for support. How long did it take God's children to trust in Him and believe His promises? *He is my Rock and Fortress*, she reminded herself.

Chapter 4

Fern, we have to talk." Alissa gripped the telephone receiver, managing to keep her voice under control.

"I think you said all you needed to say yesterday, Alissa. I'm looking for another job."

Alissa blinked back her surprise. She hadn't expected her sister to go this far; she needed to get the conflict under control, and now. "Please reconsider. I can't leave here, so could you come over? Let's talk and see how we can resolve this. You're my sister, and I love you. I'm sorry for hurting your feelings."

The line was silent, and Alissa held her breath for a moment.

"This wasn't the first time, you know. I can't seem to please you. You have your ways, and I'm different. I do my best, but apparently I'm not perfect."

"I'm not perfect either, Fern. I'm so far from it. I made a mistake, and I want to talk about it but not on the phone. Please stop by."

More silence.

"I'll come over later. I have an appointment this morning."

The telephone clicked and went dead. An appointment? Was her appointment regarding a job? Alissa recalled how many times she'd asked herself, even the Lord, if she should let her sister go and hire someone else. Now was her chance, so why did she feel so guilty?

With the receiver still pressed to her ear, Alissa was provoked by the sound of a dial tone and dropped the receiver onto the cradle. She turned and braced her arms against the kitchen island. Had this been her fault? Did she expect too much from Fern? Her thoughts flew back to months after their mother's death when they'd reached a peak of stress. She and Fern both dealt with her death in different ways. While Alissa turned inward, Fern took her inheritance and went on a spending spree. Worse than that, the image of a man Fern had met filled Alissa's mind. Anger prickled up her back. How could Fern have been so stupid? She forced the image from her mind, wanting to forget the disaster that had followed.

Awareness replaced the prickle along her back. Alissa knew she had harbored resentment and frustration with Fern during this time. She'd behaved like a teenager who'd been released from her curfew and given too much money to spend. Fern had done everything that went against her better judgment then came back hangdog, wanting forgiveness. Though it was hard, Alissa had granted it.

Or had she?

Forgiveness. The word roared in her ears like a Harley revving outside her door. She'd told Fern she'd forgiven her, but now she wondered if she had. Or had she just begun treating her as if she were a little slow-witted and needed to be pitied?

Fern had made one major mistake, but Alissa looked into her own past and asked herself if she'd been perfect. Never. Not if she were honest. Alissa had asked the Lord to forgive her sins, and she believed He had. Fern had believed her, too, but unlike God who was faithful and true, Alissa realized today she had failed her sister.

"Hello."

Ross's voice sailed through the kitchen door, followed by his tap. Every time she heard his voice, her heart did a jig and she had to steady herself. She pushed open the door. "Looking for those lemon bars?"

He grinned. "Now that you mention it."

She opened the door farther and motioned him inside.

When he stepped in, he paused and looked around. "So this is where you do all your cooking magic. You make the best of everything."

"I think that's stretching it a little, but thank you."

He rested his hand on her shoulder. "Nice place you have here. It even smells good."

So did he, she thought. The warmth of his palm radiated down her arm, and heat rose to her cheeks. She knew she was blushing again, so she moved past him toward the refrigerator where she'd placed a tray of lemon bars. She pulled it out and turned back the wrapper. "Would you like one?"

His hand shot forward almost before she'd finished asking. "How could I refuse? These are my favorite."

I know clung to her lips, but she held back the admission. She didn't want to cause herself any more embarrassment as she had with his mother. "How was your day?"

He lowered the lemon bar. "Mother had a wonderful time."

Alissa placed the tray on the kitchen island and picked up a bar for herself. "That's not what I asked." She took a bite, enjoying the sweet-sour tang that pinched her cheeks.

He shook his head as if upset with himself. "It was okay. We took a drive north and then back to the sanctuary again. Today we did see monarchs, but not as many as Mom hoped. At least it was more than yesterday afternoon. I suppose the trees will be filled with them soon enough."

"Next week it will be glorious. Did you bring a camera from home?"

"I think Mom brought one."

"Be sure to take photos. I've known people who've had them enlarged and framed and used them in their homes as artwork. It's a magnificent sight."

His gaze searched hers for a moment as her discomfort built.

"I'm sure it is," he said, his voice sounding throaty.

His heady aftershave enveloped her, and she wanted to turn from the searching look in his eyes. "I should buy one of those photos and hang it in the parlor." Her voice sounded foreign and far away.

He didn't say anything.

"Photos can make. . ." Alissa caught herself rambling again with her uneasiness. "I suppose I'd better get some plates filled and the coffee out there for the guests' afternoon snack."

"Then I should let you work." Ross straightened and took the last bite of his lemon bar then pulled a napkin from the holder on the island and wiped his fingers. "Mom's taking a nap, I think, and I'm going to—"

Before he could finish, Maggie called to Alissa from the other side of the door.

Ross pushed it open, and Maggie smiled at them, holding a large bag imprinted with GARLIC GARDEN.

"So you went to Gilroy, too."

Maggie stepped toward her. "We did, and I couldn't resist buying you a present for your pretty kitchen."

She handed Alissa the gift, and she opened it to find a long garlic braid inside. "Decoration? I can hang it right here, but I'll cook with it, too. These garlic buds are usable."

"I know." Maggie grinned. "And it lasts a long time, the clerk said."

Alissa opened her arms. "Thank you so much. This was very thoughtful."

Maggie embraced her then backed away. "Now I want to have a short nap. Ross is taking me out to dinner." She gave Ross a strange little look then scurried away.

Ross caught the door and paused. "I'll let you get back to work, as I said earlier. I think I'll sit out there and read the paper."

"I have a flavored coffee today. Try it, and let me know what you think."

He agreed and slipped through the swinging door while she watched it sway back and forth a moment and tried to collect herself.

Getting a grip, Alissa placed the bars on a decorative plate and grasped a carafe of flavored coffee then followed Ross into the parlor area. After she set the carafe and dish on the buffet, she glanced toward Ross. He'd leaned back, his nose buried in the *U.S. World News*, and she noticed he'd slipped off his shoes and propped his feet on the crossbars of the table in front of the love seat. He looked relaxed and content; Alissa wished she could feel that way, but her problem with Fern still hung in front of her like a carrot. It had become her driving force.

She ambled into the seating area and straightened the magazines, checked the flowers for freshness—they needed redoing—and picked up a paper plate and empty cup sitting on a table. As she turned, Ross spoke to her from behind his reading.

"I notice you had fewer guests today."

She looked at the back of the newspaper. "This time of year, our guests often check out on Sunday or Monday morning, and then we're busy again starting Thursday night or Friday and through the weekend."

He lowered the paper and looked into her eyes. "Then that gives you some free time to enjoy yourself."

She shrugged. "A little, I guess, but someone still needs to be here."

"What about Fern?"

Fern. A knot tightened in her neck. "My sister's been doing some other things, but, yes, she does come in to help when I need her."

"Are you free this evening?"

His question startled her. "I—I. . . What do you mean?"

He folded the paper and placed it beside him. "I thought maybe you'd like to join us for dinner. We want to go into Monterey to find someplace interesting to eat, and you could help us pick a good one."

"I can do that," she said, hearing a tremor in her voice. She tried to rehear what he'd said. Had he actually asked her to dinner?

"You can join us? Great." He sent her a broad smile.

"No. . .ah, I don't know about that. I meant I can help you find a good restaurant."

His smile faded. "You can't go with us? Mother will be disappointed. She thought it was a good idea."

His mother. Her nervous anticipation was swept away like crumbs beside the buffet. His mother had wanted him to ask her. She heard herself chuckle and tried to stop, but everything seemed so ludicrous.

"Did I say something funny?"

Alissa grasped her decorum and struggled to tame her giddy feeling. "I wasn't laughing at you. I laughed at myself."

He tugged at the collar of his polo shirt. "I'm glad to hear that. No one ever accused me of being humorous."

"But you are, you know. You've made me laugh more than once."

He tipped his head. "Thank you for the unexpected compliment. Let me know when one of those moments happens. I want to cherish it."

She laughed at his silliness, happy for the release from her personal gloom. "How about just now?"

He shook his head, a grin stealing to his face, but it was short lasting. He became serious again. "If you change your mind, let me know. It would make my mom very happy."

"Thanks." She backed up a step, wanting so badly to sit and talk with him about her struggles with Fern, but it wasn't right. People just didn't open their hearts to a customer. "I doubt if I could get help for tonight." She took another step backward. "Maybe another time."

He gazed at her a moment, his look probing, then tossed her an accepting nod, leaned back, and picked up the newspaper again. "I'll be right here."

Alissa strode back into the kitchen, set the coffee mug in the dishwasher, and tossed the paper plate in the trash. She opened a drawer and grasped the scissors she used in the garden then slipped out the back door. Right now she needed some air and time to think, but she also wanted to refresh the parlor flowers.

She headed into the garden and studied the flowers in bloom. The stock was beautiful, and she loved the scent. She gathered a mixture of white, rose, and purple flowers, cutting the stems long for the vase, and then moved to the foxgloves, their tiny trumpets in a deep purplish pink playing off the multihued stock. She thought of the mums, hoping she might find some with stems long enough to work with the ones she'd already cut. As she turned toward them, she faltered.

Ross headed across the grass toward her. "Very nice," he said, eyeing the flowers then gazing into her eyes.

She melted at the sound of his voice. Her mind reeled as she tried to decipher what power this man held over her. "The parlor needed a pick-me-up."

He stepped toward the gazebo. "So do you, I think." He motioned for her to follow.

She eyed the bouquet in her arms, knowing the flowers needed to get into water soon, but despite her excuse, she turned and moved toward the gazebo.

Ross sank onto a bench and patted a seat alongside him. "I know those flowers need to get inside, but I have a question, and I'd prefer to talk in private. Some of your guests have already come back for the afternoon."

Her chest tightened with his admission. *Private?* What did he want to know that needed privacy? If he wanted to know about good restaurants, she could give him some ideas about them in front of the guests, but she sensed his question was more personal. Confused, she sank beside him on the bench. "How did you know I was out here?"

"Lucky guess." He gave her a crooked smile. "I tapped on the kitchen door—I knew you'd gone in and you hadn't come out—and you didn't answer. Then I recalled you'd looked at the flowers earlier in the guest area so I added two and two."

A grin sneaked to her mouth. "You're quite the detective."

"Only when it's an important case."

Important case? She managed not to frown. "Okay, Sam. What's the question?"

"Sam?"

"Sam Spade." She'd say anything wacky to lighten her heart.

"Ah." He rested his elbows on his knees and folded his hands, his head lowered.

His seriousness gave her pause. "Did I do something wrong?"

He tilted his head upward to look at her. "Nothing at all, but something is wrong."

"Your room? I'll talk to the cleaning lady."

"It's not the room, Alissa. Something's up with you. You're not yourself." He gave her a look she didn't understand. "I know we've only known each other for a few days, but that's long enough to see someone's heart, and yours isn't in it today. Something's wrong."

She gave a nod, amazed he'd sensed that, knowing her for such a short time. "Yes, Your Honor, that's true."

" 'Detective,' remember. You don't have to call me 'Your Honor.' "

A grin tugged at her cheek. "It's complex and nothing I should share with a guest."

"I don't expect you to open your soul. I just thought maybe I could help."

She shook her head. "It's something I have to do." Alissa drew in a deep breath, longing to talk with someone. "In short, I had an argument with my sister, and she's quit."

"Quit." His eyes widened. "Then you're in a bind."

"With very tight ropes."

"Any hope of patching things up?"

Alissa turned sideways and placed the flowers on the other side of the bench beside her. "I've asked her to come over tonight and talk."

"Do you know how to make things better?"

"The problem's been a long time coming. Right now all I can do is apologize from the bottom of my heart, ask her forgiveness, and hope we can come to an understanding."

"Sounds like a good plan." He shifted on the bench to face her more fully. "And you can pray."

"I've done that, but you know, I realized today that I've brought some of this on myself. I've been blaming Fern, and I think I'm carrying some old grudges that really need to be tossed in the trash can." She massaged the stress in her neck. "Doing that will be more difficult than admitting it."

He rested his hand on her arm. "It always is, but it's worth the try. And with God's help, things are possible despite our doubts."

"I know." She felt more at ease talking with him than she'd expected. Ross had a tender way about him, his voice gentle, his eyes sincere. She turned her neck back and forth, relieving the tension.

Ross lifted his hand and rested it on her neck. She felt his strong fingers massage her taut muscles while a warm, wonderful sensation whispered along her skin. "Thank you. That was nice."

He lowered his hands. "I hope I wasn't too forward. I can see you're stressed."

Alissa eyed the flowers and the time then gathered the bouquet in her arms.

"Have a nice time at dinner with your mom, and maybe one day I can please her by joining you for dinner."

He placed his hand on her arm again. "It would please me, too, Alissa. Very much."

Astounded at her growing feelings, she rose, holding the bouquet to her chest. "I'd better get these in water." She descended the three steps to the ground. "If you want to go somewhere with good seafood, you could try Passionfish up on Lighthouse Avenue in Pacific Grove, or for steaks, try the Whaling Station in Monterey. I can give you directions." She gave him a wave and headed inside, her heart and mind battling with the feelings she'd discovered so recently.

Inside the kitchen, she paused, and in the hush Alissa prayed. "Lord, help me to understand what's going on with my emotions. Is this You or just passion sneaking from the chambers of my heart? Help me to know the difference. You know this scares me, but I want to put my trust in You."

꒳

In her apartment, Alissa heard footsteps outside her door. When the knob turned, she knew it was Fern. Her sister gave a quiet rap on the doorjamb then swung it open.

"Come in," Alissa said, not needing to since Fern had already stepped over the threshold. "Thanks for coming. It means a lot to me."

A slight frown wrinkled her sister's brow. "You're welcome."

Alissa felt tongue-tied. "How did the appointment go?" Bad question, but it was out.

"I had my hair trimmed." She reached up and touched it.

Relief washed over Alissa as she saw her sister's shorter hair. "It looks nice. I like it." She motioned to a chair. "Have a seat. Can I get you something to drink?"

"No. I'm fine." Fern eased into the chair and finally leaned back. "What do you want to talk about?"

"Us."

The room fell silent, and Alissa tore into her confused thoughts to come up with the right thing to say. All her thinking that afternoon had twisted her stomach into a knot.

"Okay," Fern said, not adding anything else.

Alissa grasped her careening thoughts clashing in her mind and tried to put them in order. "First I want to apologize. I have been critical, and I need to monitor that. You know how important this business is to me, but you're more important, Fern. We're sisters."

Fern's head shot up as if she'd been bopped by a tennis ball. "We are, but I realize this is your business and I'm an employee."

"That doesn't excuse my behavior. We need to decide what's really important to the business and how we can work together without having this happen." Honesty struggled up from the depths of her heart. "I started thinking today about what I've been doing. I keep going into the mistakes you made in the past, I think—but please know I've made many of my own—and I'm not giving you credit for maturity and wisdom. I'm also not doing what I said and forgiving you for losing so much of your inheritance. It's really not my business, and it's not fair to you."

Fern sat quietly, but Alissa could almost see her mind sifting through what she'd said. She finally lifted her gaze. "Thank you." She fidgeted a moment before continuing. "I'll admit I've made mistakes, too. I know it's important to get the registration right. I was careless the other day when I messed up the one for the Cahills. I'm happy you had the room. I would have truly made a problem for you if the room hadn't been available."

Alissa studied her sister's repentant face. "I think the Lord looked over that situation. I'm sorry about the cookies. I pride myself in having only homemade, but I can't expect you to do the baking. You did what you thought was right and bought them from a bakery. I'm sure they were like homemade, but it was my pride."

"I'll try to remember how important it is to you, Alissa, but you know, I've been thinking. Maybe I should strike out on my own. I can't be dependent on you all my life. It will just add to your resentment. I had money, and if I'd been careful, I would still have a savings and finances to fall back on, rather than need income to supplement what I wasted."

What he wasted filled Alissa's mind, but she muzzled the thought. "It's reassuring when you're here. I know you're family, and I can count on you to be honest and to treat people well. You've always done that. Anyway you're my sister."

"But that shouldn't be your purpose in having me here. If I'm not doing the job you want, then I should be asked to leave."

"I don't want you to leave. I think we can work this out. It's good for me to soften my criticism. I handled the cleaning lady who messed up a few things better than I handled you."

Fern's mouth turned upward in a slight grin. "That's because we're family, and we have to love each other."

Alissa rose and put her arms around her sister's shoulders. "We don't have to love each other, but we do."

"We do," Fern said, returning her hug.

"Can we pray together, Fern? How long has it been since we bowed our heads together anywhere other than for a blessing at a meal?"

"A long, long time."

Alissa sat on the arm of the chair and joined hands with Fern. They closed their eyes and bowed their heads, asking the Lord to bless their relationship and to give them wisdom to handle problems before they got out of hand. At the end of the prayer, she raised her head and saw moisture in Fern's eyes and felt tears in her own. She loved her sister, and Fern loved her. With God's help, they could make things right.

Chapter 5

Ross bounded down the stairs, hoping to see Fern helping with breakfast, but when he turned toward the dining area, Alissa was at the buffet. His pulse gave a jolt, sensing nothing had been resolved between them in their talk the past evening.

He stepped behind her and reached around for a coffee mug.

Alissa jumped, and when she looked at him, a smile lit her face. "Good morning. Did you sleep well?"

He gave a perfunctory nod, surprised at her bright smile. "How about you?"

"The best sleep I've had in a couple of days, thank you."

His mind billowed with curiosity, but with other guests sitting at the table, she'd shifted to a more business-like manner. He filled a mug and eyed the fare for the day: cheese melted on English muffins and topped with a strip of bacon. Then he noticed a great-looking fruit cobbler. As he dished a muffin and some fruit on his plate, he heard his mother's voice.

"Good morning, everyone," she said, smiling at those seated as she headed Ross's way. She veered past him and stopped beside Alissa. "Thank you for the wonderful restaurant suggestions. We enjoyed the steak so much. It was very tender." She leaned closer and spoke in a hushed voice. "I'm sorry you couldn't join us. We thought we'd try the other restaurant tonight. Any hope of—"

Ross pressed his hand against her arm, keeping his voice hushed. "Alissa might not have anyone—"

"I'd love to join you. Fern will take over tonight." She gave Ross an arched-brow look followed by a grin.

His mother pressed Alissa's hand in hers. "Wonderful. I'm so pleased." She glanced at Ross. "About seven?"

Alissa nodded and slipped back into the kitchen.

Ross settled at the table and took his first bite. The muffin was excellent, and today he thought he might behave like the big dude who went back for seconds a couple of mornings ago. Before his second taste, his cell phone chimed. Disappointed, he let the muffin drop to his plate and grasped his phone. "Excuse me," he said, flipping it open as he walked into the parlor. "Ross Cahill."

He sank into a chair, hearing the manager he'd left in charge relate a contract problem with one of their largest distributors.

"Give me his number. I'll call him from here. If we need to talk in person, I'll have to drive back for a day." He grabbed a notepad from the registration desk and jotted down the number. "Thanks, Hersh. Is everything else okay?"

He listened to his manager's calm voice.

"Great. I'll get back to you."

After he hung up, he started to make the call then flipped the cell phone closed. No sense in ruining his breakfast totally. He might as well eat first and fight later. Ross slipped the phone back into his pocket and headed back into the dining room. When he'd settled down with his breakfast, his mother leaned closer, a worried look on her face.

"Problems?"

He shrugged. "Nothing a telephone call can't resolve, I hope. I'll call after breakfast." He sank back against the chair, but the food didn't sit well. Problems with distribution could be serious. The product made it to the market through distributors and no other way. Avocados needed to reach stores at their peak—not overripe.

His mother rose to refill her coffee cup and take a little more fruit cobbler then sat again. Ross sensed her watching him, and he tried to relax his expression. "Are you anxious to get to the sanctuary?"

"When you're ready."

"I shouldn't be too long. If it's a problem, then I'll go to Plan B."

"Plan B?"

"Let's stick with Plan A for now, Mom." He slid back his chair and carried his cup to the decanter. "I think I'll take a walk outside and make the call."

His mother gave an agreeable nod, but he spotted concern on her face. The sooner he resolved the situation, the better.

"Are you going to the sanctuary?"

Ross lifted his gaze to an elderly woman seated at the end of the table.

His mother's concern shifted to an amiable smile. "We are once my son's business is finished."

"I'm heading that way. I'd be happy to take you over with me. I just have to get my binoculars, and I'm ready."

"That's so kind." She turned to Ross. "Would that be helpful, Ross?"

He wanted to kiss the woman across the table. "That would be great, if you don't mind."

The woman smiled. "I'd be happy to have someone to go with. I'm Amanda Darling." She shook her head. "I know. It's a strange last name, but my husband was as delightful as the word. He was darling."

"You're a widow?" Maggie asked.

Amanda nodded. "For two years. It's difficult."

"Ralph's been gone three years. We have a lot in common."

Ross felt as if he were an onlooker in the female conversation. "If you're settled, then I'll go ahead and take care of business."

"That would be wonderful, and you can pick me up about—" She eyed her watch.

"No need," Amanda said. "I'll be coming back. Are you on a time schedule?"

His mother waved him away. "None at all. I'm sure my son would be grateful."

Ross leaned over and kissed his mother's cheek then turned to Amanda. "Thank you. Have a great day, Mom, and I'll see you later."

"I'll be back by dinnertime," she said.

He gave her a thumbs-up and headed outside, filled with a sense of freedom. He'd been a dutiful son the past few days, but today with the added problems at the ranch, he could use some breathing space. He strode to the gazebo and slid onto a bench. In the shade, the morning breeze drifted in and ruffled his hair. He pulled the paper from his pocket and eyed the number, but before hitting the buttons, he gave thought to the problem and how he might solve it. He had an ominous sense he was being more positive than he would feel when he ended the conversation.

After thinking it through, he punched in the number and waited. "Chuck Conklin, please," he said when the secretary picked up. Silence reigned over the line except for ghostlike voices far in the distance echoing from other calls somewhere along the cables. Finally a gruff "Hello" cut through the sound.

"Chuck, this is Ross Cahill. I understand—"

Ross's eyes blinked when he heard Chuck's contentious tone that followed.

"I know what our contract says—"

With his mind spinning, Ross listened to threats from his largest distributor. "You know weather conditions affect our crops. Who else has met their contracts this year in California?"

More intimidation followed.

"So what's our solution?" Ross already knew. The guy wanted to raise prices and at the worst time, when his crop had been affected by things out of his control. "We all have to make a living, Chuck."

Ross realized the conversation was going nowhere. He needed to look at the books and see the guy in person. A telephone conversation wouldn't resolve this issue to his satisfaction at all. When Chuck quieted, Ross took over. "I need to talk with the manager and see what we can do to resolve this. We're happy with your service, and I understand you have employees to pay, too. What works best for you, San Luis Obispo or Paso Robles?"

Though he grunted a response, Ross sensed a face-to-face meeting was what Chuck wanted. Chuck had made it clear he expected Ross to either meet the contract or provide him with some compensation. That would mean a new contract, which was what the guy was hoping for, Ross realized. "How about tomorrow afternoon at my office in San Luis Obispo? Say around one."

Chuck agreed, and Ross ended the conversation, knowing he needed to call his manager before giving any thought to contract concessions. He slipped his cell phone into his pocket and rose from the gazebo bench.

The morning held the promise of another beautiful day, and instead of worrying about his business, Ross wished he could head to a park or walk on the wharf, anything but have stress follow him here. The surroundings of Pacific Grove offered nature in all its glory—the rolling waves dashing against the seal-laden rocks, the bay's white foam spreading along the beach, and the colorful monarch butterflies clinging in clumps on the eucalyptus and pine trees. But the beauty didn't linger in Ross's thoughts. Instead his mind settled on his problem and clung to the hope that he could find the wisdom to deal with Chuck.

He trod across the yard, and as he reached the house, the back door opened and Alissa stepped out. "I see you escaped visiting the butterflies today."

"And I'm grateful. A woman at breakfast—Amanda, I think—offered to take Mom to the sanctuary with her. It was perfect timing."

Alissa's smile slipped to a frown. "Perfect timing? What's wrong?"

He patted the pocket holding his cell phone. "Business problems. I have to go down to my office in San Luis Obispo tomorrow for a few hours." He raised his brows. "I haven't broken the news to Mom yet."

Her frown changed to what appeared to be disappointment. "I'm sure your mom will do fine. Amanda's staying with us for at least a week of sightseeing and visiting the sanctuary, so I'm sure your mother will be in good company even if you have to go."

Ross studied her face a moment. "How did it go with Fern?"

"Better than I thought." Her eyes turned heavenward. "Praise God, well, really. I think we were open and honest, and we have a place to start with some long-overdue healing."

"You don't look as happy as you should."

The beginning of a grin touched her lips. "Fern's going to work tomorrow for me all day. I hoped to get away and—"

"And join us for some sightseeing and dinner." Personal disappointment sailed over him.

She nodded. "But I can still go along with your mother. She was the one who—"

Ross held up his hand. "I was looking forward to your coming along, too, Alissa. It's not just my mom." Though feeling ill at ease, he charged ahead. "I enjoy your company. I really like you, and that's unusual for me."

The scowl returned. "Unusual? Why?"

"My business is different from yours. You have to be a people person, so you have skills to be genial and friendly even if you don't want to. My business is business. I deal with produce. Avocados and. . . I don't have to smile at or chat with an avocado."

She chuckled. "I suppose not."

"My life is geared to judging people's honesty and intentions. I'm hesitant with new people, and it carries over into my social life. I'm always looking for an ulterior motive."

"My guests usually don't have those. They're on vacation and want to enjoy the sights."

"That's what I mean. You provide a service. I offer a product. I suppose that's the difference."

She thought for a moment. "What's the problem at your ranch? Anything you can solve by telephone?"

"I tried that." He shook his head. "No go."

She only nodded and lowered her gaze.

The tingle of an idea rose up his back. "If you have the whole day free, why not come with me? I can show you the ranch, and while I'm doing business, you can relax or take a look at the orchard. We could have dinner on the way back. What do you say?"

Her eyes shifted, and a hint of color tinted her cheeks. "I don't know. You're going there for business, and what if it takes longer or you have to stay overnight? Then—"

"That won't happen. The meeting is with one of the companies that distribute our product to the stores. The man won't stay that long. I'm guessing he's harassing more ranches than mine, so he'll be anxious to move on."

"Harassing? Why?"

"Bad weather last spring caused ice damage to some of our crops and slowed the growth of others so we haven't been able to keep up with the guaranteed amount of produce leaving the ranch. But we should have a good harvest from now on, and I have to convince him of that."

She seemed to think it over.

"What do you say about joining me?"

"I'll check with Fern and make sure she has no qualms about my being away from the area for that long. I'll have my cell phone so I can answer most any question. I can't see why—" She paused. "Sorry. I'm thinking aloud."

He slipped his arm around her waist and gave her a friendly hug. "I'm getting used to that."

She grinned, and a deeper flush rose to her cheeks.

~

Alissa slipped out of Ross's car, her hair windblown and her cheeks ruddy from the ride. The morning was glorious, and the warm sun had encouraged her to roll down the window and let the autumn air surround her. The air smelled different in San Luis Obispo. A distance from the ocean, the aura of salty water and fish had been replaced by pungent soil and foliage—rich soil that produced grapes, olives, and avocados.

Her interest grew past the fragrance to the rambling buildings in front of her—long buildings with forklifts and long trailers parked nearby, and CAHILL AVOCADOS painted everywhere. From inside she heard rumbling and the echo of voices.

"My office is in here," Ross said, heading toward a door with OFFICE printed on the glass. He held it open, and she stepped inside, noticing the beige walls and dusky brown carpet—so nondescript she would never find a hint of Ross reflected in the decor. He strode through the small waiting room with a couple of tweedy beige chairs and a desk behind a five-foot counter. In this room, one wall was covered by a huge relief map of land—the orchard, she guessed—and two larger prints of avocados filled the other walls, along with smaller photographs of men standing on long ladders, picking the fruit.

"Are these photos old?"

"A few years," he said, eyeing the one she'd been looking at.

"They must use machinery to pick them now."

He chuckled. "No. They're still picked by hand. I'll show you in a minute."

A middle-aged woman appeared from a doorway and smiled. "Mr. Cahill. Good morning."

He eyed his watch. "I guess it still is morning, Val." He motioned to Alissa. "This is Alissa Greening. I thought I'd show her what we do here."

"Welcome," Val said.

Alissa smiled. "It's nice to meet you."

Ross's voice broke through the greeting. "You know I have a meeting at one?"

Val nodded. "Yes, Mr. Hershel left the information on your desk, and I've copied what you'll need for the meeting."

"Great. I'll take a look." He took a step forward. "Do you have any coffee?"

"Coffee and tea, if you prefer." She looked at Alissa.

Alissa felt as if she were watching a tennis match. She swiveled her head in one direction then another, seeing Ross in a new light—the owner of a big company. Today in this environment, he seemed more like the Ross she'd met the first night he arrived at the inn.

Ross looked at Alissa. "What's your pleasure?"

"Coffee's fine. . .with cream," she added, speaking to Val.

"Coming up."

Val strode back into the room she'd come from, and Ross opened a door and motioned Alissa to follow.

His office was filled with files, a large desk, three chairs in front of the desk, and a credenza beneath some windows. As she moved closer, photographs on the credenza caught her eye. She spotted Maggie with a gentleman she guessed was Ross's father by the resemblance. "This is your father?"

Ross glanced at the photo and nodded his head. "It was taken about a year before he died."

Another photo caught her eye, a picture of a younger Ross with an even younger man. His brother, no doubt. "Is this your brother?" She drew the photo closer, looking for a resemblance. She saw it in the shape of his face and the coloring, but otherwise she saw Maggie's features, except for the eyes. Ross had his mother's sparkling eyes that glinted when he laughed yet couldn't cover the sorrow beneath. Losing loved ones could do that.

Ross didn't respond, and she realized he'd sat in his chair behind the desk and was studying the reports the manager had left him.

Instead of bothering him, she moved on and lifted another photo where the sun filtered through the trees at what appeared to be a picnic. They were seated around a picnic table, smiles as wide as the blue sky above the tree line. From the other photos, she recognized Ross's father and mother, his brother, a younger woman, and an older couple. She looked more closely and noticed Ross's hand on the woman's shoulder.

Her heart tripped as she looked at Ross again. He appeared more relaxed in the picture than he did now. His smile was bright, his eyes glinted, and. . .he just looked happier. A sensation rolled through her, as if she had dug too deeply into something she shouldn't see.

"That was a Fourth of July picnic."

Ross's voice penetrated her guilty rumination, and she jumped.

"Sorry," he said, resting his hand on her shoulder. "I didn't mean to scare you."

She managed to laugh. "I guess the photo took me away for a moment. I recognize your parents and brother."

He took the photo from her hand and pointed. "These are my aunt and uncle. My dad's brother. Those were happier days."

"I'm sure they were."

She waited, hoping he'd identify the woman. "Who took the snapshot?"

"My cousin."

Unable to let her curiosity go. "This is another cousin?"

He didn't speak for a moment, and she knew she should have monitored her nosiness.

"No. She was a friend of mine."

"Oh," she said, trying to add an amiable lilt to her voice.

"Audra was my fiancée, actually."

"You didn't marry her?" She held her breath.

"No. She made other decisions, and I'm grateful now." Nostalgia hung in his voice.

"Really?"

"Really. It would have been a disaster. I wasn't ready to marry then."

Then. But was he now?

"Here you go." Val bustled into his office with two mugs of coffee and handed them to her and Ross. "I can make you a sandwich if you'd like."

"Thanks, Val, but I think we'll grab something at the house in a few minutes." He eyed his watch. "Why don't you explain the relief map to Alissa, and I'll be done shortly. I just want to finish reading some of these figures."

"Sure thing." She turned to Alissa. "You can finish your coffee first."

"No, I'll carry it along." She watched Ross sink back into his chair, his gaze glued to the report, and she followed Val into the outer office.

"I noticed this when I came in," she said, standing beside the woman. "I assume this is the orchard."

"It is. We have many acres, and they're divided by types and harvesting cycles."

Alissa noticed a blend of pride and enthusiasm in her voice as she spoke.

"I'm not sure if you know much about avocados."

"Nothing much," Alissa said, "except it's an ingredient of guacamole."

Val chuckled. "We have a wonderful recipe Mr. Cahill loves. I'll have to give you a copy before you leave."

"He told me about it, and I'd love a copy."

Val nodded. "Let me tell you about avocados. California produces about 95 percent of the nation's crop, and most are grown from right here to the Mexican border. The most well-known variety of avocado is Hass, and that's because it grows year-round, unlike the other varieties."

She pointed to the lower section of the map. "All of this area is Hass. As you can see, Mr. Cahill can provide the fruit on a year-round basis. But he decided to expand some of the land going up the mountain, so that area was terraced. And up here"—she pointed to the top of the map—"is where we grow Pinkerton and Zutano avocados."

Alissa studied the huge map, eager to see the property. "Terracing must be a huge undertaking."

"Mr. Cahill owned the land, but making it workable was expensive."

"What do you think?" Ross said, coming toward them.

"I'm impressed." She turned to face him. "I knew nothing about avocados until Val filled me in."

"Let's look at the packinghouse, and then I'll take you on a ride through the orchard."

"Thanks for the coffee," Alissa said, setting her cup on the counter. "And thanks for explaining a little of the business."

"You're welcome," Val said, lifting the cup and carrying it behind the counter.

"I'll be back before one, Val. Chuck Conklin is expected then."

She gave him a wave, and Ross steered Alissa through the doorway.

The sun, warmer here than in Pacific Grove, heated Alissa's arms as she followed Ross across the dusty concrete to the large metal-and-cement-block building. He pulled open a heavy door, and she stepped inside and stopped. In front of her, forklifts moved along the concrete floor, carrying large bins to an area on the other side of the big room where workers guided the bins into what appeared to be a storage room.

She felt Ross close beside her, his aroma mingling with the scent of fruit and dusty air. "What's going on here?"

"Trucks have brought the avocados in from the field in those bins you see, and the forklifts move them into our cold storage, where they'll sit for twenty-four hours to cool from the outdoor heat and to preserve them." He motioned her to follow.

She glanced into the area where they were moving the bins and felt the cooler air from inside. He led her up a set of stairs where she could look below to see what was happening.

"In this area," Ross said, pointing to conveyor belts, "avocados are separated by a grading belt that determines their size. Those workers over there are checking and sorting to make sure the avocados are all the same size. Then they'll be removed from the bins by the belt, which tips the fruit gently so as not to bruise it."

"This is interesting. I had no idea—"

She felt his hand rest against her shoulder. "You had no need to know until now." She liked the sound of his words— "until now." Until now, things had been so different.

"Come with me," he said, grasping her hand and guiding her along.

His hand felt massive around hers, and she could feel his pulse beating against her palm as if their hearts were beating as one. He stopped too soon, releasing her fingers to point.

"Here's where they are brushed and washed then carefully placed in cartons called lugs. And finally"—he grasped her hand again and this time squeezed it—"this area checks the avocados again for quality—size, condition, cleanliness. Then the lug is sealed over there." He drew her along the walkway. "And they're organized here and stacked onto pallets of sixty lugs each."

"Whew. I'll appreciate my avocado more now that I've seen this."

He grinned, slipped his hand from hers, and wrapped his arm around her shoulders. "You've had a quick lesson in avocados."

"Not totally. I'd love to see the orchard."

He drew her against his shoulder. "And you will after lunch. We're heading for the house now."

She'd never been to a ranch before, and her excitement heightened. Alissa felt alive amid the bustle of workers and the clang of machinery. As they descended, she could again see forklifts moving through a wide doorway toward the cooling area. Her heart pulsed with the joy she felt in being here and even more in being with Ross.

Chapter 6

Ross loved watching the animation in Alissa's face. She'd truly been excited about seeing the packing plant, and he hoped she would enjoy the orchard as much. Although the meeting was here, he almost wished they could make a stop at Paso Robles so he could show her his real headquarters, but for now he believed this was wiser.

He linked his arm in hers as they stepped outside.

"Which way?" she asked.

"We'll take the car." He guided her toward his sedan and opened the passenger door. He saw a questioning look on her face, but he didn't say anything until he slid into the driver's seat. "My house is up that road." He pointed ahead to the blacktop road wending past the trees.

He pulled away, and as he did, Alissa rolled down the window again and rested her arm on the frame. "Are these avocados?" She pointed to the trees along the road.

"No, they're fruit trees—a few for us and a few for the birds."

"The birds?"

"Crabapples and cherries. They love them."

"That's thoughtful," she said. "Do they bother the avocados?"

"Not really. They prefer this fruit."

He noticed her eyeing the peach and orange trees mingled with shade trees as they drove around the bend. His ranch house appeared ahead of them, a solid structure with large rooms, yet so much smaller than his other home. When he'd pulled into the drive, he hurried around to open the door and let her step out. He pulled out his keys and unlocked the side door, and they stepped inside the back hall.

"Go ahead in," he said, slipping off his boots, a habit he'd learned from his mother. "This is the kitchen, as you can see. I have a day lady when I'm here, but otherwise she enjoys the time off. She's not dependent on the money but loves to occupy her time. It works well for me."

Alissa gazed around the room as if taking it all in then wandered through the doorway into the great room, a section of the ranch he'd added with a two-story ceiling with skylights. "This is beautiful, Ross. So airy."

"I enjoy the outdoors, and I felt crushed inside this large room with the low ceiling. It was worth the money, and I added the loft up there." He pointed to his favorite room. "It's my home office. But I have a futon, and some nights, I lie there and look at the stars."

She pivoted, scanning each area of the room, from the fireplace to the seating arranged around the wide windows looking into the orchard then to the loft staircase. "May I go up?"

"You sure can." He followed behind her, her small frame bouncing up each stair, the sunlight glinting in her buttered-toast blond hair.

At the top she let out a cry. "It's wonderful! Is that the orchard?"

He followed and stood behind her at the windows, looking out at the edge of the Hass trees. "Yes, the Hass avocados. That's our largest orchard."

"I know, because they can be picked year round."

He wrapped his arms around her from behind and drew her into his chest. "I'm proud of you. Val must have explained that."

"She did, along with a few other things. I'm a host of knowledge."

Ross pointed toward the rows of trees, aware of her closeness. He stepped away and suggested they head back down. Not waiting for a response, he led the way.

At the bottom of the stairs, he turned to face her one step up, and Alissa touched his arm. "Thanks so much. It's so nice to see where you live and to understand your work."

Her lips were so close, he could almost feel the softness. Needing to control his emotions, he eased back, resting his hands on her shoulders. "I'm glad you enjoyed it. Are you hungry? I am."

"I could eat something." She took the final step to the floor.

"Let's have a sandwich and then take a ride out there." He wanted to get outside soon and clear his head of the emotions racing through him.

He headed to the kitchen and paused inside the doorway. "Help me be creative." He motioned for her to open the refrigerator, and he stood next to her, studying what was inside.

Alissa chuckled. "Do you have peanut butter?"

"It's that bad, huh?"

"I see some bread in here and lo and behold, an avocado."

He walked away and opened his kitchen pantry. "Do you like tuna salad?"

"With avocado? Yes."

"Then we have lunch." Though he didn't use this house often, he kept canned goods stocked in the pantry. The bread looked fresh enough. He assumed Rosa, his day lady, had come in to clean and left it there. He pulled out a can of albacore, found a can opener in the drawer, and took off the lid.

Alissa had made herself at home. She'd taken out the mayo and had already begun to cut the avocado. "All we need is chips, and this would be gourmet," she said, grinning as she diced the fruit.

His smile broadened as he returned to the cabinet and pulled out an unopened can of chips. "I hope these will work."

"Great. Who could ask for more?"

He loved her lightheartedness. "Can you handle paper plates? I live with them."

"Saves us from dishwashing," she said, wiping the countertop.

Ross watched her separate the tuna flakes, dice up a small onion and add avocado, mix in the mayo, and pile it on the slices of bread she'd placed on the plate. "Sorry. No lettuce."

She waved away his apology. "This will be delicious."

He opened the can of chips and dropped a pile onto each plate. "How about a soda?"

She nodded, and he let her choose then beckoned her to follow. He walked down a short hall and opened the side door to the patio. The umbrella table, lacking the umbrella, looked clean enough, and they settled into the chairs.

Alissa had thought to bring the napkins and handed him one, and with her hand so near, he captured it in his. "I'd like to ask a blessing."

"Please," she said, leaving her fingers in his grasp.

He bowed his head and thanked the Lord for the day, the food, and every blessing, and when he raised his head, Alissa's remained bowed.

When she looked up, she grinned. "I had an addendum."

He felt his eyebrows rise.

"A private addendum," she said with a coy look.

He asked God that her prayer concerned something wonderful about their relationship, because that's where his heart was headed.

When they'd finished their sandwiches and nibbled the chips between swigs of soda, Ross rose and tossed away the paper plates and napkins, dropped the cans into the recyclables, then reached for Alissa's hand. "You want to take a look?" He pointed toward the orchards.

"I can't wait."

He strode around the side to the garage and opened the door then motioned Alissa inside. He hit the remote and unlocked the doors of his SUV. "This is the only way to travel on a ranch."

She climbed in, and after he backed out to the road, they continued along the asphalt until a cutoff led him into the orchard. With the windows rolled down, the scent of ripe fruit filled the air. Alissa's smile made the sunny day even warmer. Her short hair ruffled in the wind, and she tossed back her head and laughed like a young girl, with a carefree look that melted his heart.

He drove to the top terrace overlooking the lower trees with his home and the packinghouse in the distance. He slowed then stopped and climbed out and walked to the passenger side. "What do you think?" he asked, opening the door.

She slipped out and stood beside him, the trees blocking some of their view. "It's wonderful, Ross. Really. I feel alive and so happy."

"I'm glad." He longed to take her in his arms, but he recalled the earlier emotions he'd felt and stopped himself. Seeing her in his home had made him long for his life to be complete again. Forcing his mind in less romantic directions, he changed the subject. "Too bad I didn't know you sooner. The avocado festival was in Carpinteria the weekend before we came to your place. It's a huge fund-raiser for local nonprofit groups. They have a poster contest and another one for the biggest avocado and another for the best guacamole recipe." He snapped his fingers. "Remind me to give you that guacamole recipe before we leave. It won a couple of years ago."

"I'll remember," she said. "I love the stuff."

He refocused on the orchard. "These are the Zutano variety. They won't blossom and grow again until later in the season, but below we're still picking."

"I noticed. Those ladders are high, plus the long poles."

"Some ladders can extend up to thirty feet, and the poles can be up to fourteen feet long. Each fruit is picked by hand with a special clipper to assure quality. Bruising ruins the fruit. The nylon bags you saw around their necks hold up to forty pounds. When the bag is full, it's placed in a bin. Those are the large containers you saw coming into the packinghouse."

"Who would think one little avocado took so much work?"

He slipped his arm around her. "Lots of things take work. Think about your inn. It's not easy. You depend on quality service from your cleaning ladies, accuracy and geniality from the person at the reception desk." He felt her wince when he mentioned that job. "The food you prepare, the special amenities that make your inn different from others. Your grounds, the gardens, and gazebo. You have to provide service, charm, and a smile, even when you feel rotten."

She nodded as if she hadn't thought about that. "You make the job sound hard."

"It is, but you enjoy it, and so it's not quite as much work for you." He gestured to the orchard. "This is work and a pain sometimes, but I love it." Work. He glanced at his watch, almost forgetting he'd come to San Luis Obispo for a meeting. "We need to get back. It's getting late."

He grasped Alissa's shoulders and turned her to face him. "May I be honest?"

Her beautiful indigo eyes widened. "Yes."

"This day has been special for me, too." Ross bent down to kiss her cheek. "Thanks for coming with me."

She looked surprised, but she didn't respond for a moment until she grinned. "I loved every minute of it."

Every minute. He hoped that included the kiss.

༄

"And that's it," Ross said, relating the meeting he'd had earlier. "Concessions on both parts. We pay more for two months then back to our original contract, but he guaranteed to give us a discount next year if we exceed our shipping agreement. Give a little; take a little. That's business."

"I'm glad it went well," Alissa said, looking across the bay to Morro Rock, its rugged outcrop soaring above the water. "This is a gorgeous sight."

"It is. I hope you don't mind going back on Highway 1. I know it's nerve-racking, but the scenery is tremendous."

"It is, and I haven't been this way in so long." She thought about her last trip. "I'll enjoy this one more than the last. We took it south on the ocean side of the highway last trip. At least we have the mountain wall going north."

He chuckled. "It does feel safer." He motioned ahead. "I thought we'd look for a place to eat farther up the highway, or would you like to stop here in town?"

"No. I'm not hungry yet. While you were at your meeting, I ate the last few chips in the can. I hope you don't mind."

He chuckled. "You could have eaten anything, and I'd be pleased." He reached over and rested his hand on hers. "You've made my day, Alissa. I'm really glad you came along."

"Me, too," she said, placing her other hand over his and loving the feel of being together.

"I have a place I'll take you then. It's not too far. I think you'll enjoy it."

They settled into silence, and Alissa reminisced about the wonderful day. She'd enjoyed relaxing at Ross's while he went to his meeting. She'd gazed up at the sky, creating cloud pictures, something she never did at home. Afterward Alissa had found a magazine about avocados and skimmed it, learning some new things with the turn of every page. She'd been fascinated by the packinghouse and the orchard and loved seeing Ross's office. Everything seemed beyond what she had anticipated; even the house she thought was rather small for a man with such a lucrative business, she loved despite her previous expectations.

Though Ross had never said he was rich, Alissa knew what it meant to own a produce farm or orchard in California. It meant living more than well, a life she'd never considered possible for her. The thought gave her an uncomfortable feeling. She loved her inn, and though she would never be rich, she had a good life; she asked God's forgiveness for thinking of material goods when they weren't important in the scheme of things.

"Are you sleeping?"

Ross's voice cut into her thoughts, and she looked up. "No, I'm thinking about the day and what a wonderful time I've had. It was so nice to see where you live and work."

The image of his office credenza filled her mind, and though she'd tried to forget the ex-fiancée's part in Ross's life, she couldn't. "Tell me about Audra. What happened?"

"Audra."

He uttered the name then grew quiet.

Alissa panicked, thinking she might have ruined the perfect day with her question. She wanted to retract it, but obviously it was too late. As she listened to the stillness, except for the hum of the tires on the road, she struggled to find how to cover her error.

"It's not an easy question to answer."

Air shot from her lungs. "I'm sorry I asked, Ross. It's really none of my business."

"It's fine, Alissa. You know, sometimes in life things happen beyond our understanding, but I always think God knows best. At least I've realized that through the years. Like death and loss, we don't know exactly why they happen."

His profile tensed, and Alissa wondered if he were thinking of his father and brother.

Ross's demeanor changed. "Now that I look back, I realize Audra and I weren't meant for each other from the beginning. She was a beautiful woman, and my father thought she would be an asset to our family. She had a knack for stepping into the limelight, for entertaining, and for wearing the right designer—so many things I didn't value, but she did them with style."

Alissa weighed his words. "It was one of those opposites-attract relationships."

"Sort of, yes. But the opposite doesn't sit well in the long run sometimes. While I loved the outdoors, nature, and the work I do, Audra detested ranch life. She tried to adjust and rented a condo in Paso Robles, but she much preferred the more glamorous city life—Santa Barbara, Carmel, and Los Angeles."

"I love the quieter life, I think. I'm not a social butterfly."

He chuckled. "More like a monarch?"

"I wasn't thinking about that," she said, grinning at the metaphor. "I can entertain when I must. I love cooking and showing guests a good time. It's my job."

"You are good at that."

"But I'm not into glitz. Not at all."

"We have that in common," he said, glancing her way.

Her heart skipped as she thought about having things in common with Ross. She loved the life here, the outdoors, nature, but she loved Pacific Grove, too, and her inn. It was her security, and it was what gave her confidence and pride in herself.

"Look at the view."

Alissa looked up. As they rounded a bend in the road, the vista stretched unending with rugged cliffs falling to the ocean where waves lashed against their jagged edges, smoothing them in time and spreading white foam to the shoreline. A mist had begun to hang on the cliffs, an ethereal haze that softened the rocks and spawned an unreal aura that seemed to wrap around the landscape.

"It's unbelievable." She viewed the sun as it lowered toward the horizon, its deepening hues melting into the rolling green water, turning it into shades of amber and coral that rippled with black dimples. "It takes my breath away."

"I know," he said, his voice only a whisper.

Shortly, Ross slowed and turned off Highway 1. They stopped at a traffic light, and soon he guided the car through a split rail fence into a parking lot. "This is it. Cambria Pines Lodge. They have great food and a terrific garden. We can stretch our legs there before we finish the drive."

She slipped from the car and gazed at the old building that looked like someone's rambling house with blue and white trim, nestled among the pines and shrubs a short distance from the dangerous stretch of highway.

The dining room had a quaint look with small print wallpaper and white molding. A stone fireplace stood in the corner, and pine furniture added a fitting look to the homey room. They were seated at a small table by the window, and outside she could see the expansive garden Ross had mentioned, with a winding path that wove past a fountain.

She ordered a tossed salad followed by chicken piccata with rice pilaf, and Ross couldn't decide between the grilled fillet with fried onions or the wild salmon. The salmon won out, served with sun-dried tomato, cucumber salsa, and rainbow pasta.

The waitress returned with their iced tea, and when she left, a hush fell over them. Alissa wavered between looking at the scenery outside the window or gazing into Ross's blue eyes. "This is so nice, and I would love to have time to walk outside. Did you see the fountain?"

"They have others. We'll make the time."

"But it gets dark early, and I don't think you want to drive on that highway in the dark."

"I'll be fine. Don't worry." He brushed her cheek. "Now give me your pretty smile and stop worrying about me."

Pretty smile. She hadn't been called pretty by anyone since her mom died. Alissa pulled herself from her thoughts. "You asked earlier about Fern and me."

His face spoke volumes. "It's not my business to ask, but if you ever need a friend to listen, you know I'm here."

"It's one of those long stories like you mentioned with Audra, I guess. Fern and I were never really close. She skittered from one thing to the next. I was quieter. I love to read. Fern liked to argue. I preferred quick resolutions. We were very different. My mom knew that. I had goals early on, and Fern couldn't settle on one thing. She hopped from hobby to hobby then job to job when she was old enough."

"That's what we talked about earlier. Opposites."

"Yes, but it's difficult in families, I think, because we're in a forced-proximity situation."

"True. You can drop a friend who becomes irritating."

She calmed, grateful he seemed to understand.

Ross slid his hand across the terra-cotta–hued tablecloth and rested it over hers. "Has that been your problem with Fern?"

"It worsened when my mother died." She paused, thinking of the anger that had sprouted at that time. "I told you she'd left a small will. We weren't rich, but she had the house and a little savings, mainly from Dad's life insurance and his social security. Mom never worked."

"Some women prefer to be homemakers. My mom, too."

She smiled, sensing more camaraderie with him and Maggie. "The problem arose when my mom left me the house and a smaller portion of her savings, with the rest going to Fern."

"You did tell me that."

"But it got worse. Fern resented me for selling Mom's house to buy the inn. She thought I should keep the family home. Nostalgia, I guess, but I was looking at it from a business standpoint."

"It was wise. The house located on Ocean View Boulevard with the magnificent view will draw in many more guests than a house that's tucked away in the downtown area."

"I know, but I couldn't convince Fern." She felt her hand tighten beneath his, and Alissa tried to relax. "The worst part was—and I don't know if it was spite or just her nature—Fern wasted her money. She bought an expensive car and a complete new wardrobe. She met a man who convinced her to loan him money for this great business deal, and then he vanished. Fern didn't have that much to begin with so she ended up with little left, and I loathed the situation."

"I can understand how bad you must have felt."

She looked into his eyes. "I didn't just feel bad. I was bitter. I saw my mom's skimping and saving and then how Fern tossed her gift away. I couldn't forgive her for that, and I've held it against her all this time."

Ross didn't say anything for a few minutes. His gaze left her to look out the window. Finally he turned back. "It really wasn't up to you how Fern spent or wasted her money. Do you realize that now?"

"I do, but I still begrudge her."

"Then you have to work on that, I guess." His face darkened as the words left him.

Alissa longed to know what thought had shadowed his face. "I'm hoping to do that. I think we have a start. When we talked, I told her the truth, and I think just getting it out in the open helped both of us. She resented my getting the house and selling it. We'd both let each other down."

Ross nodded. "It's easy, isn't it, to let people down. I've done that myself, Alissa, and it's hard to forgive ourselves." He quieted a moment before continuing. "I think that's often the problem. We can forgive others, but we can't forgive ourselves."

Alissa's pulse skipped a beat. Was that it? As the idea settled into her mind, she realized how close to the truth Ross had come. The problem was forgiving herself, and now she had a new place to start. "Thank you."

"Thank me? For what?"

"For being you."

Though her words were interrupted by the waitress, she needed Ross to know how important he'd become in her life. He'd made a difference, such a difference that she didn't know what she would do without him.

Chapter 7

Heavy floral fragrances mingled with warm earth and the distant scent of the ocean. The muted sun hid beyond the ancient pines and cottages, leaving a shadowed walk, and around the bend, Alissa came upon the trickling water of a fountain. As they continued, she read the signs marking the gardens—herbs, succulents, and organic produce served in the lodge's kitchen.

Alissa stopped beside a flower garden, admiring the clusters of colorful blossoms, almost as bright as her life had become since she'd met Ross. "I wish I had a camera."

"I'd love to take your picture here," Ross said, his eyes searching her face. "You look more relaxed and more beautiful than you have since I met you."

Heat rose up her neck. "It's the flush on my cheeks. You're making me blush."

"Then you should blush all the time."

Her pulse skittered along her limbs and fluttered in her temples. Sensations she'd never felt before washed over her—contentment, comfort, joy, untold happiness—but as reality struck her, she feared being hurt. "You're silly."

"I'm being honest."

He slipped his hand into hers, and she knew her pulse pounded against his palm. Alissa had no idea how to control the emotion she felt. She loved it and hated it because it made her feel out of control.

"You shouldn't talk like this," she said, hearing the breathless sound of her voice.

"Why?"

"Because it sounds romantic, and it can't be."

"I don't understand, Alissa."

"First, we barely know each other, and second, our worlds are in different places."

Ross stopped beside a towering tree and drew her toward him so they stood face-to-face in the dappled sunlight. He lifted her hand and pressed it against his chest. "Can you feel this?"

She closed her eyes, and beneath her palm, his heart thumped in a steady rhythm. "I can feel your heartbeat."

"As sure as my heart is beating, you have the same certainty of how much I care about you. I know we've only known each other a short time, but can we question how the Lord works? I didn't want to go to Pacific Grove. I work long hours, and I'm antsy when I'm home without my work. I came here for my mother, as you know, but things have changed. Now I sense God guiding me in a direction I never thought possible."

Alissa lowered her gaze, fearing she would be entrapped by his beautiful eyes. "I'm not saying we haven't connected. I'd be lying if I did. I love your company. I think your mother is a wonderful woman. I hate thinking of your leaving because I know life will slip back into its usual rut. But—"

"Life doesn't have to be a rut, Alissa. I'm not saying we're ready for commitment, and yes, we have things to learn, but I want time to get to know you better. I don't want to go back home and never see you again."

Tears pooled in her eyes. "I don't want that either."

"Then let's agree we won't let go of this great beginning."

A ragged breath fluttered from her. "I'd like to get to know you better. I really would."

He pulled her into his arms, and through her tear-filled eyes, she studied his face and knew he meant every word. As her gaze met his, she watched his lips lower to hers, a tender kiss that was there and gone in a heartbeat, but one she would remember forever.

She buried her head against his chest, thinking of his home and work in San Luis Obispo and hers in Pacific Grove—a hundred miles away. How could two hardworking people get to know each other with those circumstances?

Not wanting to think about the impossible, she straightened, and he slipped his arm around her waist and led her back toward the restaurant from a different direction. A few moments later she faltered, seeing a wishing well surrounded by another glorious flower bed. As they neared, Ross paused while her gaze shifted from the fairy-tale wishing well to his face.

"I don't believe in wishing wells, do you?"

She managed a smile. "No."

He touched her hand. "We both believe in prayer."

Her pulse did a jig. "Yes."

"Then let's both pray, Alissa, that the Lord guides us in the path He has planned for us."

"And that we can hear His wisdom, whatever it may be."

Ross squeezed her hand. "Amen." He pulled a coin from his pocket and tossed it into the well. "God's power is all we need, but tossing in a coin is still fun."

"It's like blowing out birthday candles. No matter what we do, God's in charge."

He sent her a gentle smile that lifted her beyond her doubts. *Thank You, Lord,* she thought, grasping his hand as they headed back to the car.

∿

Ross supported his mother's arm as they followed the guide through the Monarch Butterfly Sanctuary. Since he'd last visited the site, the butterflies had multiplied, and today they hung in heavy clusters on the pine and eucalyptus trees like dried leaves caught among the green branches. Whether he was a fan of butterflies or not, the image was an amazing sight, and it would only have been better if Alissa had been able to join them.

They paused as the young woman continued with her spiel. "As you know, the monarchs travel as far as two thousand miles, but you may not know they can cover a hundred miles a day at a height of up to ten thousand feet. Picture these fragile creatures being driven by instinct back to the same place their ancestors have come for years."

Driven by instinct. Ross understood that feeling. God had created man and woman so they didn't have to live alone and so they could procreate and populate the earth. He'd given up on that idea years ago when his relationship with Audra had crumbled like dried clay. It left a mess with nothing good coming out of it. He'd never wanted to have that happen again, and every relationship he'd encountered tended to leave him with the dried-clay feeling. But Alissa. . . She was different.

The guide's voice surged back into his consciousness. "Let's head this way." The woman beckoned them to follow and continued her talk. "When you think about the short life of a butterfly, you will realize no butterflies here today were here last year. They are guided totally by a genic message that triggers them to follow the same route as their ancestors to arrive here the same time each year. Some scientists think they may rely on the earth's magnetic field and the position of the sun, but some believe it's a gift."

"A God-given gift," his mother whispered.

Ross agreed. The Lord had ways to guide His creatures, from the most fragile butterfly to a husky forty-five-year-old like Ross Cahill, and Ross sensed that God had tucked a message in his heart.

"This way," the guide said. "Be careful—the stone walkway is rough here."

His mother and pointed down a connecting path. "Let's sit there for a minute."

Ross veered her toward the seat he saw in the distance beneath a large pine. As he neared, he eyed the amazing bench in the shape of a butterfly, its back the upper wings and its legs the lower wings with a cross piece that served as a seat. His mother sat, but Ross eyed the delicate sculpture and decided not to chance it.

"Are you enjoying yourself?"

"It's amazing, Mom. Hard to believe those little things make their way here every year."

"But can you blame them?" She grinned. "It is beautiful."

"It's very interesting, and since it's their first time here, how do they know the way?"

"God created the little beings to know. Sometimes we know things, too. It's in our hearts without facts or even common sense."

296

Her words settled in his thoughts, and as she spoke, an orange and black monarch fluttered past, settled on the pine a moment, then spread its wings and flew off. Yesterday he'd seen Alissa spread her wings. Each day she grew more and more a part of his life until—

"How was your day yesterday?"

His mother's voice intruded on his thoughts. He lowered his gaze. "Nice. Alissa enjoyed the packinghouse, and I took her for a ride into the orchard."

"You got back very late."

He tried not to smile. His mother's grilling made him feel like a teenager again. "We stopped for dinner in Cambria."

"Cambria?" Her eyes widened. "You came back on Highway 1?"

"Yes."

"Ross, you know that's a treacherous highway at night. You should never—"

"Mom, I drove it, so I know. I was careful. We decided to walk through the Cambria Pines Lodge gardens, and that took longer than I thought, so it was dusk when we left. I'm home, and I'm safe."

"Yes, but it was pitch-dark when you drove through Big Sur, right?"

"Right." No sense in arguing. He would bow to her lecture, and she was correct. It had been a dumb thing to do, and Alissa had been nervous, too; the kiss in the garden had been wonderful, though, so he didn't regret the stop.

"Please promise me you'll use your head next time."

He leaned over and kissed her cheek. "I promise."

"Thank you." She tilted her head upward and grinned. "You like Alissa."

"She's a very nice woman."

"I know that. She's wonderful, but that's not what I mean."

He drew in a lengthy breath and shook his head. "No. I'm not going there."

She rose and gave him one of her "mother's always right" looks then started down the path. "Never mind. I already figured it out. I've never seen you so attentive to a woman. Not even Audra."

Her words struck him as he stood to follow her. He'd blamed Audra for walking away from him, but perhaps he'd walked away from her emotionally. Her leaving had been a blessing. He'd realized that long ago. Marriage was forever, and his relationship with Audra wouldn't have lasted.

"Look." She pointed ahead.

He jerked from his thoughts and saw his mother hurrying ahead to view an astonishing cluster of monarchs in a nearby tree, their wings open wide, fluttering like petals of orange flowers in a breeze. As he watched her, Ross saw his mother stumble. He darted forward, feeling helpless as she lurched forward, reeling to catch her balance before she collapsed to the ground against a boulder along the path.

"Mom, are you okay?"

Her moan filled his ears, and when he looked at her face, he knew she wasn't okay at all. His heart thundering, he knelt beside her. "Don't move, Mom." He rested his hand against her arm to keep her from shifting. "Where does it hurt?"

She didn't answer for a moment. "My upper leg. Maybe my hip."

The pain in her eyes cued him. Her injury was worse than he wanted to think. "Let me run back, Mom, and get help. Please don't move."

The unnecessary request struck him. Horrendous pain registered on her face. He gave her a pat while fear gripped him. Ross pulled out his cell and dialed 911, praying the fall wasn't as bad as he knew it was.

～

Alissa checked the time again. Ross and Maggie had left early, and she'd thought they'd be back in the afternoon. She'd made more lemon bars, and since they hadn't arrived, she kept a plateful in the kitchen so Ross would be sure to get some.

Trying to distract herself, she checked the buffet one more time then wandered into the sitting room where a husband and wife were relaxing. "How was your day?"

"Wonderful," the woman said. "We spent a couple of hours at the sanctuary, and then we went to the wharf for lunch."

"I'll do anything to keep her from shopping," the husband said and chuckled.

"Most husbands don't like—"The telephone jarred her thought. Alissa gave them an apologetic shrug and turned toward the call. "Butterfly Trees Inn. May I help you?"

"Alissa, this is Ross."

Hairs prickled on her neck at the sound of his tense voice. "What's wrong?"

"Mom fell at the sanctuary."

"Fell?" Her pulse escalated. "Is she hurt?"

"We're in the emergency at Community Hospital of the Monterey Peninsula."

"Emergency?" Her mind filled with questions. "What did the doctors say?"

"Probably surgery. They think it's her hip, but they needed to do X-rays before they know how bad. I'm in the waiting room."

Surgery. Hip. She turned her back on the couple seated nearby, not wanting them to see the tears forming in her eyes. "What can I do?" She knew what she wanted to do. Be with him.

"Pray. That's what I'm doing."

"I'm sending up prayers now, Ross. Was she conscious?"

"Yes, but in a lot of pain. Mom didn't know which hurt worse—her hip or her leg."

Alissa grimaced. "How did it happen?"

"We stopped so she could sit on a bench while the docent went on ahead with the group, and then when we started again, she saw a beautiful cluster of monarchs nearby and dashed off but apparently tripped over a rock or something. She was in a lot of pain, and I called 911. It broke my heart to see Mom in so much pain. She's always so healthy and—"

"Healthy's the key. If she's in good health, then we can hope she'll heal quickly if anything's broken." If Alissa had to choose a break, she'd wish for a broken leg. They healed more quickly. She didn't even want to think of a hip fracture. "When did it happen?"

"Around eleven thirty. We were about ready to leave for lunch, and she wanted to go to the museum afterward."

"You must be miserable, Ross. Keep me posted, okay?"

"I'll call you as soon as I hear something. I'd better let you go, but I thought you'd want to know."

"I'm pleased you called. I was beginning to wonder, and know that I'm praying."

"Thanks. I'll keep you informed."

She heard a click ending their conversation, and she struggled to keep the sadness from her face as she turned back to the guests. "Enjoy the treats." She gave them a smile and headed back into the kitchen.

Once she was through the door, tears rolled down her cheeks. Maggie had become a dear friend, almost like a mother figure, and Alissa couldn't bear to think of her in pain. She paced the kitchen, trying to think of what to do. She eyed the clock again. Surgery would take so long if Maggie needed it, and Ross was alone.

Alissa knew what she had to do—what she wanted to do. She grasped the kitchen phone and punched MEMORY ONE. She clenched her lips together, praying Fern would answer, and when she did, Alissa got herself under control.

"Is there any way you could come over and work tonight?"

"Another date?"

Alissa weighed the sound of the words, trying to decipher between envy, sarcasm, or acceptance. She chose the latter. "Wish it were. Maggie—you remember Ross's mother—fell at the butterfly sanctuary, and she's in emergency in Monterey."

"I'm sorry. Is it serious?"

"Ross is waiting to hear. They took her up for X-rays. I guess it's her hip. I'm praying it's not a break."

"You want to go up there?"

"If you can come. I'm miserable here, knowing he's alone and wondering what's happening."

"I can be there in a few minutes. Get ready."

"Thanks, Fern. This means so much to me."

"That's nice to hear, Alissa. I'll be there in a flash."

Alissa hung up the receiver with Fern's words ringing in her ears. *That's nice to hear.* She thought back, trying to remember how many times she'd never properly thanked Fern or ever said how much her help meant. People wanted to know they were doing a good job.

Chapter 8

Ross took a sip of the strong coffee and closed his eyes. *Surgery.* He hadn't expected it. Since his mother's fall, he'd prayed fervently; the Lord had His reasons, though, and Ross couldn't fight the Lord. Christians often asked, Why me? Why did this happen to so and so? They were such good people. Why a child? Why this? Why that? Questions fell like raindrops, but the answers were a drought. God knew the full scheme of things. All things had a purpose, and Ross would know the answer only when it didn't matter anymore because he'd be with God.

A stream of air whispered from his lips. After Dr. Louden from the ER had let him know it was a hip fracture, he'd allowed him to visit his mother for a moment. The look on his mother's face hung in his mind.

"How do you feel, Mom?" he'd asked.

"Not like jogging."

Her witty response had taken him by surprise. "I don't suppose. You need to have surgery. You know that."

Her eyes searched his. "I know. What I did was so careless. . . and dumb."

"You were excited, Mom. Those monarchs with their wings open looked like flowers."

"They did, and I didn't get a photograph."

He wanted to tell her she'd get there another day, but he stopped himself. She'd know he was only trying to cover his fear. "Maybe I can get one for you."

"Would you?"

Her voice sounded so plaintive that his voice caught in his throat. "I'd do anything for you." He leaned over and kissed her cheek. "Mom, I'll see you when you're out of surgery, and I'm praying."

Her eyes fluttered, and he realized she'd had a shot to make her drowsy. She licked her lips and tried to speak. "Pray. . . ."

"I am, Mom." He backed out of the room and returned to the waiting room where he'd paced. He looked at a magazine. He paced some more. He opened his cell to call Alissa again but had no new information, so he slipped the phone back into his pocket.

Now with the time still dragging, Ross eyed the wall clock and rose again, searching for a new magazine. His stomach growled. He and his mother had missed lunch. *Lunch.* With this sad event, his mom would miss much more than lunch. A few chairs over, he spotted a *Time* magazine and grasped it then turned toward his seat and came to a dead stop. "Alissa."

She walked toward him, her arms open in greeting, and he welcomed her embrace, holding her close and cherishing the feeling of her slender frame in his arms.

"How is she?"

"She's still in surgery."

"Still?"

"It's a hip fracture, but they can't tell the severity until they really take a look."

"I'm so sorry about this. Your mom's such a delight and so excited about her vacation."

"Let's sit." He pointed to the chair beside his, dropped the magazine on the table, and sank into the cushion. "How did you get here?"

"Car."

He gave her a feeble grin. "I know that. I mean, how did you arrange it? You have—"

"Fern came over."

"That was nice of her."

"She wanted me to be with you."

"Really?" Pleased at the changed relationship between Fern and Alissa, he felt his eyebrows rise.

"You know, Ross, I realized today that I rarely tell Fern she's done a good job. I say thanks, but it's one of those perfunctory ones you say to a stranger at the supermarket who lifts the laundry soap off a top shelf for you or holds open a door. I've had expectations, and when she didn't meet them, I told her so; otherwise I said little."

He searched her face a moment, wanting to respond with something meaningful. "Sometimes it takes a tragedy to realize where we went wrong. It's never too late to say thanks and mean it or give her a compliment when she deserves one."

Alissa nodded, her expression thoughtful. "It hit me today that she did a great job while I was gone with you yesterday. She made three reservations. I could read them, and she was very explicit—two people, one room—so I knew she'd marked it accurately."

Her comment triggered a new thought. "She was the one who made my reservation, I suppose."

"She was, and I let her know about it."

"I hope you said something to her yesterday after our talk."

"I did, but not enough. I told her she was doing a good job and how much I appreciated it." She shifted on her hip to face him more directly. "You know what she did? She baked two kinds of cookies and made double batches so we could freeze some. They'll taste fine and save me from baking every day. I've always done that for my guests, except once during an emergency when Fern—" She waved her words away.

"Sounds as if Fern had an innovative idea."

"She did. Why hadn't I thought of doing that? I'm such a stickler for fresh this and that. Cookies frozen right after they cool are still fresh if you use them within the month."

"You don't have to convince me." His stomach growled with the talk of food.

She grinned. "I forgot." She lifted her shoulder bag and pulled out a sack. "I made you a ham and cheese sandwich. I figured you'd missed lunch, and you'll find two lemon bars inside the bag, too."

He held the sack in his hands, emotion knotting in his chest. "Thanks so much. I am hungry, and I hate to leave, even to go to the cafeteria."

"I'd feel the same." She motioned to the food. "Go ahead. Eat. I had lunch."

Ross opened the lunch bag and pulled out the sandwich she'd placed on one of the inn's lacy-looking lilac paper plates. He pulled off the plastic wrap and took a bite. She'd added lettuce and some kind of spicy mayo he'd never had. "It's delicious. What's the sauce?"

"Mayo with chipotle seasoning. It adds a little tang."

"It's great." He took another bite, watching her eyes follow his every move as he chewed and swallowed. "You're a wonderful woman, Alissa."

"Anyone would bring you a sandwich."

"I wouldn't say that, but this has nothing to do with the food, although I appreciate it more than I can say." He reached over and brushed the back of his fingers against her cheek. "I'm talking about you."

She lowered her eyes then drew in a breath. "Thank you."

"Even my mom agrees."

She scooted forward to the edge of the chair. "You were talking about me to your mom?"

"She started it." He slipped his hand over hers.

"Maggie did?"

He nodded. "She asked me if I liked you."

"I hope you said yes."

"That wasn't what she meant. She meant do I *like* you."

Alissa chuckled. "Aha. There's a difference, I suppose."

He noted color rising in her cheeks. "You know there is." Ross couldn't believe he was going in this direction, but it was a wonderful distraction.

"And what did you say?"

"I'm not going there."

A frown swallowed her sweet grin. "Why not?"

"That's what I said to her."

She thought that over awhile then laughed. "I see."

The last bite of sandwich tasted as good as the first, and Ross wadded the plastic wrap and slipped it into the bag before pulling out the lemon bars—bars she'd made for him, and he knew it.

"Would you like something to drink?" he asked, rising to get a fresh coffee.

"No, I brought a bottle of water." She reached into her bag and pulled out the drink.

"What else do you keep inside that thing?"

"I'm not going there either."

For the first time that day, Ross laughed, and it felt great. He ambled to the coffeemaker, poured a fresh cup, and returned, anxious to tackle the lemon bars. But before he did, he heard his name. He spotted the surgeon and motioned for Alissa to follow.

"Mr. Cahill, your mother has a broken hip, but she was very lucky. We were able to put in a pin that will hold it in place without the added complications of a metal plate. Her recovery will be quicker, although I need to warn you—she'll need extensive therapy and be unable to be alone for a couple of months. We recommend a nursing home, and after she's released, she'll still need home care."

His words spun in Ross's head. *Pin. Extensive therapy. Unable to be alone. Months. Home care.* Overwhelmed by the news, he stood in shock, not able to remember questions he wanted to ask. "Can I see her?"

"It'll be awhile. She's in recovery, but once she's awake, the nurse will call you in."

"About how long?"

"Another hour maybe." He stepped back. "Your mother is in excellent health. That makes a big difference. We hope she'll be able to get back to most of her activities in eight months to a year."

The surgeon turned and walked away while Ross stood with his mouth hanging open and watched him go.

Alissa gave his arm a squeeze. "He said your mom was lucky, but you know what?"

"What?"

She smiled. "I say she was blessed. She'll be fine, Ross. Your mom isn't a quitter. She'll fly through therapy and be walking in no time."

"I hope so."

She put the palms of her hands on his cheeks. "You know so."

His heart beat so fast that he could only nod.

꒰

Alissa watched the door throughout the next evening. It was nearly nine o'clock when Ross came in looking tired and miserable. "How is she tonight?"

"Angry that they're trying to get her up already."

"It's important."

"I know, and she does, too. But she's on pain medication, and she's not herself." He leaned against the registration desk. "Actually, they had her walking twice today."

"That's wonderful. When will they move her?"

"In a couple of days. They want to keep an eye on her vital signs. This is a bad time for blood clots and pneumonia. I feel better with her being at Community Hospital."

"But she'll be in good care in a nursing home."

"I suppose." He looked away as if his mind were still at the hospital.

Alissa touched his arm. "Are you hungry?"

"I grabbed something in the cafeteria at four when they took her in for therapy. I'm okay."

She beckoned him into the kitchen. "Have something to drink." She motioned for him to sit at the table then brought out a can of cola and popped the lid. "Here." She crossed the room and brought back a small plate of lemon squares. "What about your work?"

"I thought about that. I'll have to go down for a day or two and make arrangements. I hope Mom understands."

"She will, and I'll take your place. I know that's not quite the same, but I'll make sure I get there each day to visit her."

He gave her a tender smile. "You're too good to me."

"Never." His look sent her heart on a surfer's ride on the crest of a wave.

"I know everything will work out. It's just making plans. Obviously I hadn't expected this to happen, and being away two weeks was bad enough, but now. . ."

He fell silent, and she didn't interrupt the quiet.

Finally Ross gave a one-shoulder shrug followed by a faint grin. "I'll manage."

"Any ideas what you'll do about your mom's care?"

He drew in a lengthy breath. "I don't know. She can't ride home in a car. I'll either have to get an ambulance to take her back home for her therapy, or I suppose I could let her stay here and get through her therapy at least. I'll hire someone to stay with her when she's home."

"I've been thinking." She weighed the words before releasing them. "She can stay with me."

Ross scowled, his eyes questioning.

"I can spare a room. Gratis, naturally. Things slow down this time of year once the weather turns colder, and you know I'm here all day or Fern is. If we're both gone, which is rare, I have competent help that will fill in."

"I couldn't do that."

"Why not?"

"It's a huge responsibility. Why would you want to take on that job?"

Her heart gave her the answer. "Because I think a lot of your mom, and you need help. I know you can't stay here. You have to go back to work, and if I do this, it will help you."

He ran his fingers through his hair. "You're unbelievable."

She didn't think so. It's what people were supposed to do—treat others as they would like to be treated—but this was different. She'd be doing it for two people she'd grown to. . .what? *Like? Care about? Love?* Alissa felt breathless as the questions rattled in her mind. Love was impossible. No one could fall in love in only a few days. That was what fairy tales were made of, or those soap operas. Not real life.

Ross took a swig of the drink, set it down, then fingered the plastic wrap and pulled out a lemon bar. He took a bite, his thoughts seeming miles away. "I'll have to give all of this some thought. I don't have the answers now."

She didn't want to push, so she backed off. He needed time to let things sink in, and she had all the time in the world. "I had a good talk with Fern last night."

He turned toward her as if grateful she'd changed the subject. "Good. Any outcomes?"

"We hugged. I told her I noticed how she'd made every effort to clarify the registration, and I thanked her again for the cookies. She looked shocked when I told her what a great idea it was to bake a double batch—that I'd never thought about it."

"And that surprised her, I suppose."

"I think it did. She said she thought I wouldn't consider them fresh enough, but she did it because she figured I could use a rest."

"How true. We all need a rest." He took a final drink of the soda and set down the can then turned and drew her into his arms.

"I had some thoughts myself, Alissa. Yesterday I realized Audra wasn't the only one at fault in our relationship. I know it always takes two, but I really believed she had been the biggest problem. But something my mother said yesterday made me think."

Alissa held her breath, waiting to hear what it had been, but when Ross said nothing more, she released the air, disappointed. "Mothers can be very wise."

He nodded then tilted her head upward. "Mom said she'd never seen me so attentive to a woman as I am to you. Not even Audra."

A soft gasp slipped from Alissa's throat. "Ross."

"And it's true. You're on my mind all the time, and in a good way. I even find myself smiling when I think of something you said or did."

Watch your heart, Alissa. Warnings shot through her. She knew one day Ross would need to go home, to live his life in San Luis Obispo, and she would live in Pacific Grove. They both had their businesses, their careers, their identities. Their friendship could lead nowhere.

"Did I upset you?"

His voice sounded sad, and it broke her heart. "No. I'm overwhelmed, I guess. I think of you, too, but I said it before. We live in different worlds, Ross, and—"

His mouth covered hers and ended her sentence. The gentle kiss lingered a moment; then he eased back as his gaze captured hers. "Don't think why this can't work, Alissa. Think how it can work. Let's not limit God's power. Do you know what I was thinking today?"

She shook her head.

"Besides you, the one thing that would keep me here is my mother. Do you see how it worked out?"

His comment startled her. "You think God broke your mother's hip to keep you here in Pacific Grove?"

"Not exactly, but if it had to happen, it happened here, here where someone loves her enough to offer to care for her, someone who's only known her for a few days, someone with a heart that's as big as the sky."

Alissa gazed at him, overcome by what he'd said, but she agreed. If Maggie had to have a fall, she thanked the Lord she was there to help.

"You're doing so well," Alissa said, inching her way along the hospital corridor with Maggie at her side clinging to her walker.

"I feel like a turtle."

"But a perky turtle." She patted Maggie's arm. "I know how disappointed you are, but you looked forward to being in Pacific Grove, and now you'll be here even longer than you expected."

Maggie chuckled for the first time since her injury, and Alissa loved the sound.

"Let me tell you a secret," Alissa said, feigning a conspiracy as she spoke in a hushed voice. "I'm trying to convince Ross to let you stay here for a while once you're out of the nursing home."

"Stay here?" A scowl dislodged her smile.

"With me at the inn."

Maggie's head drew back as if she didn't quite believe what she'd heard. "With you? But you don't want all that extra work."

Alissa chuckled. "You sound like Ross." She slipped her arm around Maggie's shoulders. "Our workload slows down in the winter. We have only a few guests, and either I'm there or Fern is. You're in a room on the first floor. It works out so well, rather than having you go back and sit at Ross's with a stranger caring for you."

Maggie seemed to think about it a moment. "I'd like that better, but I couldn't let you do that for free. I'd want to pay you."

"No. Absolutely not."

"For the room at least."

"Not at my prices." She chuckled at Maggie's expression.

"You make me laugh, Alissa, and it feels good." She tilted her head toward her room. "Could we sit for a while?"

Alissa eyed her watch. They'd been walking for about six minutes, and that seemed pretty good to Alissa. She nodded and helped Maggie into a comfortable chair rather than her bed. Alissa tilted up the footrest then sank into another chair nearby.

"I'm being moved tomorrow," Maggie said after a long silence.

"I know, but I think you'll like it better. It's more like a hotel than a hospital. You'll have other people going through therapy for company. It'll be different."

"I keep telling myself that."

"The doctors think you're doing amazingly well."

"That's what they say." She wiggled in the chair as if trying to get comfortable.

Alissa rose and pulled a pillow from her bed. "Do you want this under your leg or behind your back?"

"My back, I think."

She settled the pillow there then returned to her chair. "Ross is coming back from Paso Robles today."

"He called me this morning." Maggie raised her eyes to the wall clock. "He should be here soon."

Alissa glanced at the time. "Any minute."

She looked more comfortable with the pillow, but Alissa had been noticing something in her eyes and wondered what was going on in Maggie's mind. She looked as if she had something she needed to talk about, but Alissa didn't know how to drag it from her.

Maggie finally looked her way. "What are you and Ross going to do?"

"To do?"

"About your relationship."

The desire to deny or to avoid responding pressed against Alissa's mind. "I know you're Ross's mother so you're concerned about him, but to be honest, Maggie, I don't know."

"He cares about you very much."

"And I care about him, but—"

Neither spoke for a moment until Maggie broke the silence. "It's the *but* that worries me."

"It worries me, too. I keep pinching myself to make sure this is real. It happened so fast, a connection so amazing it seems unreal."

"That's how God works, Alissa. Don't doubt Him."

"I keep telling myself that."

"You keep telling yourself what?"

Ross's voice flew from the doorway, startling Alissa and making her wonder if he'd heard the discussion.

"How are you, Mom?" He strode across the room and kissed her cheek, bringing with him the fresh scent of outdoors clinging to his clothing. He slipped off his lightweight denim jacket, revealing a burgundy knit shirt beneath.

He turned. "Alissa."

She nodded.

Maggie's voice halted the uncomfortable silence. "Go ahead and kiss the girl, Ross. What's wrong with you?"

Ross's eyes widened, and he chuckled. "Thanks, Mom."

He leaned down and kissed Alissa's cheek, whispering, "More later."

As he headed back to Maggie, he veered off and dug a packet from his jacket pocket. "Here you go, Mom. This is to prove I keep my promises."

"What's this?" She reached out and took what looked to Alissa like a photo sleeve.

Maggie drew the folder from the sleeve and pulled out the photos as her eyes brightened. "Ross, these are beautiful. Come look, Alissa."

Alissa shifted to her side and gazed at the wonderful shots of the monarchs clinging in huge clumps to the green branches. "They're gorgeous. When did you take these?"

"On the way here." He gave Alissa a wink. "I promised Mom. She has a digital camera, so I stopped by the pharmacy up the road and printed them right there. They're hot off the press."

Maggie hadn't taken her eyes from the pictures. "I love these." She held them against her chest.

"I love you, Mom." He took the photographs from her hand, slid them back into the folder, and set it on her bedside table. "So how are you?"

"Great. Alissa and I just came back from a walk."

"Good for you." He grinned at Alissa. "Thanks. I owe you a good dinner or—"

She shook her finger at him. "You owe me nothing. I'd do anything for this lady."

Maggie smiled. "Did you hear that?"

"Miss Greening, you're getting me into trouble."

His voice sounded playful, and it dawned on Alissa he'd come back from the ranch in a good mood.

"How did it go?"

Ross sat on the edge of the bed. "I have a reprieve. Everything's set for a couple of weeks more; then I'll have to go back. I brought my trusty laptop with me. That'll help, and naturally I have my cell for emergencies. But Hersh is capable, and so is Diaz."

Diaz. She'd never heard Ross mention him, but that shouldn't be a surprise. He had a multitude of employees.

She listened while Maggie and Ross talked about her move the next day, but her mind clung to her discussion with Maggie. She sensed Maggie liked her and accepted her friendship with Ross. She'd even encouraged a kiss, so why would she doubt it? But she knew a mother wanted to protect her son, and

Alissa wanted to protect herself. The more she thought about their relationship, the more impossible it seemed, and she still sensed that Ross had something on his mind that troubled him. Though he tried to hide it, his eyes reflected a kind of inner struggle. Was it guilt or sadness or remorse?

She might never know.

Chapter 9

Ross held open the passenger door as Alissa scooted out and headed inside. Though the worship service had lifted her spirit, she'd noticed that same distant look in Ross's eyes and knew he still struggled with whatever had been bothering him since they'd met.

"I think I'll drive over to the nursing home and spend some time with Mom, but I want to talk with you a moment first if you can spare the time."

Alissa's gaze searched his. "Sure." She looked toward the inn and noticed the curtain shift back. Though she knew Fern had heard them arrive, she hoped her sister would give them a minute alone. She turned and headed to the gazebo, hoping Ross would finally tell her whatever it was that bothered him, but in her heart, she feared the talk had to do with them—that he might give her an ultimatum.

He motioned her toward a bench then sat beside her.

"I understand, Ross," she said before he could say anything. "I've given it a lot of thought."

Ross gave her a curious look. "Thought about what?"

"About us. Isn't that what you want to talk about?"

He looked as if he wanted to grin, but stress muted it. "No, but maybe we should talk about that, too."

He'd thrown her. "I just expected—"

"I'm not giving up on us, Alissa. In fact, our relationship is what brought on the need to talk with you."

Her chest tightened with the seriousness of his voice. "I'll be quiet and listen."

He covered her hand and drew it into his. "Can you take off tomorrow? I'd like to take you south again. I'll talk with Mom today. She's already made lots of friends at the nursing home, and so I'm comfortable with leaving her alone for the day. If we get back early enough, I can still drop by and see her."

"I thought you'd taken care of everything for a couple of weeks." She searched his face, wanting to understand what was wrong.

"Not everything. I'd like you to go with me if you can. . .and if not, there's no sense in my going."

He'd confused her. "What's this about?"

"I want to show you. Think you can make arrangements?"

Faltering between wanting to learn what it was about and not wanting to be hurt, Alissa couldn't find her voice.

Ross rose. "Think about it, okay? I need to head over and see my mother." His voice flooded with disappointment.

She reached for him and caught his arm. "Ross, I'll check with Fern. If not tomorrow, will another day work? I don't know her schedule."

"Whatever you can arrange. I just decided to do this, and I wanted to get it... get to it."

Get it over with. That's what he'd started to say.

Alissa didn't like surprises, and she felt certain this was one she didn't want at all. Yet Ross needed to deal with something, and she seemed a part of it.

He turned away and headed for his car without another word.

"I'll see you when you get back."

He lifted his hand to let her know he heard, but he didn't turn around. The old attitude she'd disliked when Ross arrived had made its appearance again.

What could be so important? Her pulse raced, her mind conjuring up horrendous possibilities.

⁓

Ross tried to draw Alissa out, but she'd been quiet since he asked her yesterday to go with him to his office. He understood he'd been rather cryptic with his invitation, and he'd tried to decide when to tell her why they were making the trip. For too long he'd dealt with the old issues rioting in his mind. If shame and guilt were tangled in his business, then he needed to take care of it. He realized he needed to be honest with Alissa and to make amends. Though it was too late to apologize to his father, his mother would be grateful, and he sensed the Lord would be pleased with his decision.

"Are you upset with me?" He realized he'd jerked Alissa from her thoughts.

She looked at him, confusion filling her eyes. "I don't like surprises. I'd rather know what's going on than to spend the whole trip trying to guess why this is so important. I've been here before. I saw your packinghouse, the orchard, and your home already. It's not that I didn't enjoy myself last time, but I'm edgy."

He drew up his shoulders. "We're not going to San Luis Obispo."

She turned on him as if he were a kidnapper. "I thought you said we were going to your house."

"I did, and we are."

She shook her head and looked out the passenger window. "You're talking in circles, Ross. I don't want to play games."

"This is no game, Alissa. I wanted you to see the place before I explained, but maybe I'm doing it backward. I'm not good with women, I guess."

"Yes, you are when you're acting normal. Since yesterday you've been somebody else."

Maybe he had. "It's a long story, so let me get started. I also have a business in Paso Robles. I'm sure I told you, and that's where I live most of the time."

"What?"

He nodded. "My mom has a place there, too, although I've been thinking about having her live with me now that she's had this accident."

"What kind of business? More avocados?"

"No, and that's been my problem." The memories came crashing back, two bullheaded Cahills, each trying to prove to the other he was right.

"Then what? Just tell me. Is it illegal? Like drugs?"

His heart ached for her fears. Leading her on had been a mistake. "It's grapes."

"Grapes?" She gazed at him, more confusion filling her eyes. "What's wrong with grapes?"

"They're for making wine."

She shook her head as if trying to clear away the cobwebs. "Right, but people eat them, too."

"Mine are wine grapes. They're different."

"Oh."

"Do you see my problem?"

She looked out the passenger window a moment. "Jesus made wine."

"First, I don't make wine—I just grow the grapes. And second, yes, Jesus turned water into wine, but many Christians believe drinking is a sin because it leads to trouble and addiction."

"It can. I know. I don't drink, but some people don't think it's wrong."

"My family does. I do, and my dad was staunch about it."

She shifted beneath the seat belt to face him. "So is this what's been troubling you? Did you and your father have a falling-out?"

"My dad loved me, but he was set against my buying into the wine-grape business. He advised me not to, and he had good reason. Drunks ruin lives."

Alissa gasped and covered her mouth, her eyes filled with understanding. "Your brother."

She startled him. "You know about my brother?"

She lowered her hand. "Your mom told me about him one day."

"Do you know that he—"

"Yes." She closed her eyes. "It was a tragedy."

"So you can see how my dad hated the business, and it did put a barrier between us. He tried to be the same dad, but he couldn't forget what I'd done." Ross released the steering wheel from his left hand and massaged the tension in his neck. "I dropped a wall between us with that decision, and when my dad died three years later, I wondered if I'd been to blame."

Alissa opened her eyes. Moisture clung to her lashes. "No, Ross. I'm sure that had nothing to do with it, but I can understand how it might make you feel guilty. It's just that you and your dad weren't looking at the business in the same way."

"Right. I was looking at the profit. He was looking at it as a moral issue—a faith issue, really."

Alissa remained silent but reached over and rested her hand on his arm.

"It's a lucrative business," he added, "but not when it's started bothering me so much. It's not worth the money or the pain. Lately I realize how often I don't tell people about the grapes. I always say I'm in avocados. I never know when I'm talking to Christians who might be offended. It's gotten worse the longer I've let that happen, and I know I can't go on like this."

"If you're ashamed, then you know you're doing wrong."

He nodded, facing the truth. "I've known this for a while now, but it's my business, and I couldn't see changing it. The equipment costs so much, and trying to change the product wouldn't be worth it. I really want to get rid of the business. I know many people enjoy wine and don't find it a sin. And the Bible says Jesus turned water into wine, as you mentioned, but I don't want to be that person."

"Why now? What's made the difference?"

"You."

She drew back, her eyes searching his. "Me? I never said anything about—"

"Because I didn't tell you, and I've told you everything about me, Alissa, except that. It made me realize I'm doing something I know is wrong. It's not just Roger's death or his addiction. It's my faith. The two just don't go together."

Alissa fell silent, and Ross speculated on what she was thinking. His admission could have turned her against him, or, he hoped, she comprehended his remorse.

"What will you do?" she said finally.

"I don't know what to do. I wish I hadn't made the decision, but I did, so it's too late to alter that. But I can do something. It's what I have to decide."

She nodded and became thoughtful again.

The scenery passed by, and once through San Miguel, he knew they were getting close. Before Paso Robles, Ross veered off on a side road leading up into the hills, where terraced grapevines flourished on both sides of the road. When he came to his sign, PROSPERO VINEYARDS, he took a right and wound his way through the tree-lined road to his house.

When they came through the trees into the circular driveway, Alissa gasped. "This is your home?"

"Welcome to Cahill Ranch."

She sat there as if stunned.

Ross walked to the passenger side and opened the door. "Alissa?"

She turned toward him. "It's gorgeous. All of this is your house?"

He nodded. "My office is a little distance from here."

She didn't move.

"Are you getting out?"

"I'm startled. This has been too much of a surprise for me."

He took her elbow and helped her out, standing beside her as she studied the rambling stucco home with a wide courtyard entrance, the fountain he loved sending water over its spout to the wide basin below. Wind chimes tinkled in the breeze, music to his ears. He loved this place and couldn't imagine ever finding a home as satisfying. "Let's go inside."

Alissa looked at him then gazed at the entrance and took a step forward as if questioning every step.

⁓

"I've never seen anything more wonderful," Alissa said, turning full circle to survey the wide entrance with curved staircases on both sides heading to the upper rooms. Ahead she viewed a great room, its ceiling soaring upward, enhanced by a stone fireplace that rose to the rafters with an expanse of windows on both sides offering a view of the landscape and the foothills beyond.

"I love it here," Ross said, his voice filled with nostalgia.

Alissa stepped forward, questioning her wisdom to tell him what she'd thought when she visited San Luis Obispo. He'd talked about being open, and she decided to do the same. "When I visited your other house, I was surprised it wasn't more elegant. It is very lovely with the cathedral ceiling and skylights. The view is similar to this one, but less scenic. I'd imagined that if you owned an avocado ranch, you would be rich, and the house didn't quite fit the mold."

"I don't fit the mold either." He stepped closer to her and rested his hands on her shoulders.

"This house fits the mold, even if you don't." She grinned, hoping to bring a smile to his face.

"I'll give you the grand tour later, but come with me." He beckoned her to follow.

He led her through a doorway on the side of the great room into a formal dining room and then into the most tremendous kitchen she'd ever seen.

A woman stepped through a doorway across the room, her dark eyes crinkling with her smile. "I heard your voices."

"*Hola*, Carmelita."

"Hola, Mr. Cahill. You're right on time."

"This is Alissa Greening, the woman I told you about."

"*Mucho gusto.*"

"It's nice to meet you, too," Alissa said.

Ross rested his hand on Alissa's shoulder. "Carmelita is my housekeeper and cook."

"I have your lunch almost ready, but if you'd like to go out on the patio, I'll bring some appetizers."

Ross moved toward her and gave her a hug. "You're a gem. *Gracias*." He grasped Alissa's hand and steered her toward a sliding door.

When they stepped outside, she drew in the scent of foliage and the sweet fragrance of grapes. Looking past the landscape, she saw the terraced hills beyond.

"Your vineyard?" She pointed to the neat rows of vines clinging to supports.

"That's it." He motioned toward an umbrella table then pulled out her chair so she sat facing the distant hills. Shadowed by the umbrella, Alissa felt a soft breeze whisper through her hair, and she imagined what it might be like to live in this house. . .and with a housekeeper, of all things.

"I don't travel much since I've owned the inn, so this is a treat. Being served by someone in a private home is unbelievable." She looked from him to the landscape and back. "And you live like this every day."

He nodded. "God has been good to me, even with my mistakes."

"We all falter, Ross." She rested her hand on his. "This is so special for me, and I can't imagine your having to give this up."

His eyes filled with sadness. "I can't either."

"Could you sell the vineyard and keep the house?"

He shook his head. "The house is part of the land. They go together. Whatever I do, the two stay together."

Sadness washed over her, seeing his despondency. Though his decision to buy the vineyard had been one some people might call careless, Alissa understood why he'd purchased it. Besides the income, the area was gorgeous, its rugged landscape an amazing demonstration of God's creation, with the mountains and lush soil and the ocean only a few miles away. She couldn't be angry with him, and his dilemma broke her heart.

"Here you are," Carmelita said, approaching them.

Alissa turned as the woman neared them with a tray. She rested it on the table and set a tall glass of iced tea garnished with lemon and mint leaves in front of her with a bowl of guacamole and a basket of homemade corn chips. Another bowl of salsa filled out the treats.

"This is great," Alissa said to the woman. "Thank you."

Carmelita grinned and dug into her pocket. "I'm supposed to give you this." She handed Alissa an envelope then smiled at Ross and headed back inside.

Alissa eyed the envelope then turned it over in her hand. "What's this?"

Ross chuckled. "Open it."

She undid the flap and pulled out a recipe card. The words PRIZE-WINNING GUACAMOLE were written across the top. "I forgot to get this the last time. This is your recipe, isn't it?"

"It's the one I told you about." He gestured toward the bowl on the table. "Try it."

Alissa reached for a corn chip and dug it into the avocado mixture then took a bite. The taste tingled in her mouth, a delightful mix of the fruit with spices and citrus. She took another bite, loving the flavor of lime and cilantro, the zest of chilies and onion and refreshing bits of tomato. "It's delicious."

"I thought you'd like it, and now you can make it yourself."

"You know I will." She grasped another chip and dipped it into the guacamole.

Ross joined her, and they nibbled the appetizers, avoiding any more sad talk.

The unpleasant topic remained unspoken through dinner. Carmelita prepared chicken flautas with Mexican rice, a tempting mix of grilled chicken, peppers, and onions with cumin and other spices. The meal would have been perfect except for their earlier conversation weighing on her mind.

When they prepared to leave, Alissa admired the lovely home, the second floor with its massive bedrooms and spacious baths and a home office on the first floor, so lovely her own heart ached for Ross's decision.

Alissa felt sad when the topic came up again on the way home.

"I hope you understand why I didn't mention this business, Alissa. As we've become so close, I knew I had to be open with you, and I needed you to understand what's bothering me and how I allowed material things to influence my faith."

She wanted to say something to soothe his regret. "It's easy to do, Ross. I think we all make those horrible mistakes. While we were there, I had thoughts of my own. In a way, I did something similar to what you did. Fern was set against my selling the family property. Mom's house would have been a lovely bed-and-breakfast, and it was closer to the downtown area so it had that good feature, but I wanted to be classier. I knew I could make more money having an inn on the ocean's doorstep, and I set up all those rules for myself—home-baked cookies, afternoon snacks, flowers and fruit bowls in each room."

"But all those things make your place unique. You can't be upset for that."

Alissa pressed her hand against her chest, emotions billowing as she spoke to him with frankness. "The point is, I hurt my sister by making that decision." A sense of sorrow crept through her as she studied Ross. "The difference is, I have time to say I'm sorry and to make amends. You don't."

He nodded. "That hurts even more than selling the property." He lifted his hand and made small circular motions on his temple as if to chase away a headache.

Her temple pulsed, as well. "I can't imagine your going through with this, Ross. I really can't."

"I can't either, Alissa. I really can't."

Chapter 10

Ross stood in the doorway of his mother's room at the nursing home and watched her a moment. She'd made excellent improvements, beyond the physician's expectations, but she still needed care. He'd been spending time dealing with one dilemma after another. First, he needed to find someone to care for his mother or he needed to accept Alissa's offer to care for her. That seemed unfair to Alissa, and he feared his mother would feel abandoned.

Next, he struggled with his property in Paso Robles—his home, his vineyards, his life in that city—and finally, Alissa. His feelings had grown beyond friendship or attraction. He'd fallen in love. The idea seemed preposterous, but as he'd said so often, with God all things were possible. He'd felt the Lord guiding him very soon after he met Alissa. Her values and personality fit his so well, but their careers created a towering wall holding them back from finding a solution.

He could never ask Alissa to give up her inn. It meant so much to her, and he knew she would never ask him to give up his livelihood. God had the answer, but Ross didn't.

His mother glanced toward the door and smiled. "How long have you been standing there?"

"A couple of minutes. You were so engrossed."

She waved the little book toward him. "Crossword puzzles. Alissa brought me this the other day. It certainly helps to pass the time, when they're not torturing me."

"That's called therapy, Mom." He crossed the room and kissed her cheek. "I suppose this box of candy can't compete with that puzzle book."

"Try me." She extended her hand and accepted the chocolates. "No nuts. Good. I prefer the nougat and cream centers."

"That's why I bought them." He pulled a chair closer, slipped off his jacket, and sat beside her. "How was therapy today?"

"Good. I even tackled a few steps. It's a challenge."

He leaned back in the chair. "You know they're sending you home in a few more days. You should be home by Thanksgiving."

"I heard, and I can't wait." She tossed the puzzles onto her bedside table. "Everyone's nice here, but it's still too much like a hospital."

"I think I'll have you stay with me. I'll put a hospital bed in my downstairs office, and I'll hire someone to care for you during the day. I could ask Carmelita, but I think that's—"

His mother held up her hand. "Whoa! Slow down."

Her determined voice surprised him. "What?"

"Did you ask me what I want to do?"

He squirmed, feeling as he had when he was a troublesome teenager. "I want to do what's best for you, and I thought—"

"If my brain stopped working, you'd have the right to make decisions for me. I have that in my living will. But now you can discuss things with me."

He knew he was in for a battle. "What don't you like about my idea, Mom?"

"First, your telling me what I'm going to do."

"Okay." He stopped himself from rolling his eyes. "What else?"

"I don't want to go to your house. That's not home."

He released an exasperated sigh. "If you go to your home, you'll have to have twenty-four-hour care with strangers. I can afford that, Mom, but I thought you'd want to be with someone who cared about you."

"I do want that."

"You want me to move into your house?" He pictured her small condo a few miles from his place. Though staying with her would be inconvenient, he would make the arrangements. "Okay. I can do that."

"You're not the only one who cares about me."

Her comment struck him between the eyes. *Alissa.* "You mean—"

"Alissa offered me a room, and I feel very much at home there. She's a beautiful person, and I enjoy her company."

He stood and walked across the room and back, trying to figure out how to say what he had to say in a nonaggressive way. "Don't you think that's asking a lot of Alissa? She really doesn't know us that well. We're guests in her inn. She's kind, but—"

His mother shook her head. "Are you trying to pull the wool over my eyes?"

"The wool? What are you talking about?"

"You and Alissa are in love. She'll be my daughter-in-law soon enough, and this is a wonderful way for me to get to know her better."

His pulse kicked into high speed. "Who told you we're in love?"

"I have a bum hip, Ross. I'm not blind. Anyone can see—"

"We've never talked of love. Never."

"You don't have to. Look at your sleeve. It's written all over that and your face. The two of you were meant for each other. Don't tell me you haven't figured that out yet."

He sank back into the chair with the truth ringing in his ears. He'd fallen hard and fast, and he had no idea what to do about it.

"Cat got your tongue?" she asked.

"No. I'm just surprised."

She chuckled. "Surprised that your mother can still read your mind after all these years?" She wagged her finger at him. "You were never good at lying,

Ross, and you were never good at hiding your mistakes. I knew when you took a dollar from some change on the table and bought candy. I knew when you told me someone vandalized your bicycle that you and Butchy had tried to do some foolish tricks with it by jumping off a hill. You could have killed yourself."

Ross looked to his right, expecting to see a jury tallying up his "guilty" points. "How did you know all that? And it wasn't Butchy. It was that kid whose father owned the bakery."

"So I got that wrong." She waved it away.

He laughed at the expression on her face.

"I knew you weren't in love with Audra. Not the way a man should be."

A chill rolled down his back. Why had she known and he hadn't?

"Ross, I've never told you this, because I thought if I interfered, you wouldn't listen anyway and would be more set for the marriage. I prayed you would figure it out on your own, and you did. That marriage would have been a disaster."

"You really think so?"

"I just told you I do. But this one—you and Alissa—it's made in heaven, if ever a marriage was."

"We're not married, Mom. We're not even engaged. We've never spoken of marriage for that matter."

"No, but you will, and that's why I want to stay with Alissa. I'll pay for my room and my care. You don't need me to leave money to you. You're a wealthy man."

He opened his mouth and closed it, knowing he'd lost the battle.

"Good. No argument." Her eyes twinkled, and then she patted the arm of her chair. "Now that we have that settled, let's talk about your other problem."

"What other problem?"

"Business, I think. I know you're worried about where you two will live, but just remember the Lord guides your steps. A verse in Hebrews says, 'I will put my trust in him.' That will work out with time, but you have a business problem. Tell me about it."

Air escaped his lungs as he searched her face, wondering when she'd learned to be a mind reader, or was that an attribute God gave mothers?

❦

"Do you see the boxes?" Alissa called through the opening as she stood below the drop-down ladder while Ross rummaged through her attic. She didn't hear anything. "I can come up."

Ross looked over the edge, holding a carton of wreaths. "How do you do this each year?"

She shrugged. "Determination, and I have to for the guests. Anyway, Fern usually helps."

He handed down the cumbersome box then shifted away from the opening. She heard a rustle, and soon he reappeared with another carton. "And *why* do you do this?"

She chuckled at his taunting. "Christmas is coming, for one, and the other, Butterfly Trees is part of the Christmas-at-the-Inn event. It's an honor."

"For whom?"

This time she laughed. She raised her arms to reach for the carton then set it down, while he hurried off for another box. She had five, maybe six boxes filled with holiday decorations, not counting the huge outdoor wreath she kept in a storage area off her kitchen.

When he'd unloaded the boxes, Alissa left one upstairs with the decorations for that floor, and they carried down the others. With Thanksgiving in a few days, the inn was empty for a change, and she was grateful. "Your mom's released on Wednesday?"

"Right," he said, undoing the flaps of a carton and looking inside.

"That gives me two days to get these Christmas decorations up."

"And I can't help tomorrow. I have an appointment."

"Appointment? Down in Paso Robles or—"

"No, it's in this area. I won't be gone the whole day, I don't think."

A local appointment made her curious, but she sensed she shouldn't ask. His business wasn't her business. She let her questions fade and flagged him to follow. "Let's look at your mother's room, and tell me what you think."

He dropped the garland he'd untangled across the chair and joined her. "You really care what I think?"

She knew he was teasing. "This is in regard to your mother, so I hope so." She opened the door of the Painted Lady Room and stepped inside. "Look around and tell me if you think everything is out of the way for her to get around. I removed all the scatter rugs so she won't trip."

Ross grasped her hand and pulled her to him, his look so tender she felt weak. "You're an angel, Alissa."

"No, I'm not. I like your mother. Love her, really. She's sweet and spunky both. I love that in her, and I don't want her to get discouraged. She'll enjoy sitting out in the parlor and talking with guests. They'll think she's my mother. She won't be a problem at all."

"And I'll sleep at night knowing she's with someone who loves her."

"I'm glad. That's what I want for you. I know you have lots of things on your mind."

He nodded, his gaze searching hers until he lifted her chin with his finger and lowered his lips to hers.

Their lips fit perfectly, gentle and sweet like honey on a spoon. He drew her closer, his arms against her back, and she breathed in his woodsy citrus scent she'd learned to love. She'd learned to adore everything about Ross, even his pensive moments when he struggled with his thoughts.

He drew back, his lips so close she could feel the whisper of his breath. "I'm crazy about you."

She wanted to cry out that she felt the same, but her heart and mind wrestled with reason and emotion. She'd prayed, but no answer had come. "You mean so much to me, too. I'm glad your mother's here, because it means you'll be here."

"I could be with you always, Alissa, if you want it to be."

"If we want it to be, but I have no answers, Ross." She drew back, sorry the lovely moment had ended and they were back to reality. "We have careers we've both worked hard for, and I've prayed, but I'm not sensing an answer."

He grasped her hands and pressed them against his chest. "I've prayed, too. We can't find the answer alone, but I believe God has led us to this place in our lives. The other day my mom talked about us, and she said—"

"Your mother?"

A crooked grin stole to his lips. "You know mothers. They think they know everything." He shook his head. "And sometimes they do. Anyway, she reminded me of a Bible verse that's so simple but one we need to listen to. 'I will put my trust in Him.'"

The verse seemed too easy. "I trust the Lord. I really do, but—"

He pressed his finger against her lips. "There's your problem. Trust means no buts. I'm talking seriously for once. We need to trust without the buts."

She rested her head against his chest, feeling safe in his arms, and knew she should feel safe in God's arms, as well.

They stood in the room with the sunlight streaming through the window, and Alissa could see the rugged shoreline outside washed in the waves that pounded against it. The rocks were strong and steadfast, as was the Lord. Today she felt as safe as the seals who lolled there in the sun.

"The room looks great," Ross whispered in her ear. "Everything is perfect. The hallway is wide enough, and Mom will enjoy sitting here in the wingback chair."

His words brought her back, but the word *trust* remained in her heart. "I found a footstool in another room for her. She may want to prop up her feet." She motioned to the blue upholstered ottoman she'd located that nearly matched the blue in the chair.

"You think of everything."

"Speaking of everything, I have work to do." She eased back and headed for the door.

"*We* have work. It'll take you weeks to do that decorating alone."

Happiness wrapped around her, and she felt like skipping down the hallway like a girl.

The tasks began as Alissa hung wreaths in every window and arranged a single candle on each windowsill while Ross set a ladder against the inn to hang the huge wreath that sparkled with miniature lights on the gable of the porch. He festooned the porch railing with garland and ribbons while she moved from room to room with holiday pillows and special wreaths designed for each door featuring a butterfly for which the room had been named.

Enjoying the partnership, she made hot chocolate and carried a mug outside for Ross. Even without snow and the bitter chill of winter found in most states, Alissa felt the spirit of Christmas. Ross tackled his last task, hanging the cluster of bells on the door so it jingled when people came inside.

He lowered the hammer. "I've never done this before."

She felt her nose wrinkle. "You've never hung bells?"

He chuckled. "I've never hung anything. Bachelors don't decorate for holidays."

"What about when—" That would have been a mistake, and she stopped herself.

"Audra?"

She nodded.

"Audra decorated her place and carried on because I didn't. One time she brought me a real pine tree in a pot with a string of lights."

Alissa didn't want to know about the sweet things Audra did. "That was nice."

"She was embarrassed because I was hosting a party for her friends. Audra had Carmelita decorate the dining room table to her specifications. I don't know why I didn't care."

Because you didn't love her. Alissa had watched him lug the decorations out of the attic to the first floor, hang wreaths, wrap garland around the long porch, and hang the bells. He did that for her without her even asking. Her heart stretched with awareness, and she wrapped her arms around his neck. "Thank you for doing this."

"It was fun." He opened the door, listening to the jingling bells. "Now show me what you did."

"I'm not quite finished, but I will be."

"We will be." He curved his arm around her waist, and they headed inside.

৵

"Are you okay, Mom?" Ross slipped the ottoman closer to the chair then pressed his lips to her cheek. "It's good to see you home."

Home. The inn had almost become home to him. Here he found the feeling of comfort and completeness he'd missed for so many years. And here he found Alissa. She'd become his light at the end of a lonely tunnel, and she'd helped him focus on what was important.

"It's good to be here," his mother said, sending him a tender grin. "The only frustration I have is I'd like to help with the cooking for Thanksgiving tomorrow."

"I'm sure you can help with something. We'll see what Alissa needs. You can stand now, and you can definitely sit."

She chuckled. "I'm good at sitting. . .and taking naps."

"Naps help to make you well." He squeezed her shoulder. "But walking is the important thing. Your therapist will be here soon."

"I can walk now, and I'm getting stronger," she said. She gazed toward the window. "I love this view. It's so beautiful, and I'm grateful I had a chance to see the monarch butterflies before I decided to take my last trip."

"Your last trip?" It took him a moment to understand, and he laughed. "You mean your trip over the rock."

She nodded. "That's one trip I don't want to repeat." She pointed through the window. "But this is one I could enjoy often."

"I know." His chest tightened. "I love you, Mom," he said, giving her a wave. "Alissa has me lined up for tree decorating."

"It's about time. I never saw anyone who avoided putting up decorations as you do." She grinned. "I guess Alissa has found the secret of motivation."

He knew she had something on her mind.

"Love does wonderful things."

He gave her a scowl and shook his finger. "We've never talked about that."

"It's about time you did."

He shook his head and stepped into the corridor, very aware that his mother, as always, was absolutely correct.

When he entered the parlor, he saw the bare evergreen standing beside the stair railing, and he knew he was supposed to string the lights. He could smell something wonderful drifting in from the kitchen, and he pushed open the door— no need for guest protocol anymore—and gazed at Alissa. "What are you doing?"

"Making cookies. I need refreshments for the Christmas-at-the-Inn event, and I thought I'd get started."

"You said you were making pies."

"That's next." She scratched her chin with her knuckle and left a white splotch of flour. "How's your mom?"

"Spunky as ever. Her therapist will be here soon, and I hope she isn't too achy afterward." He walked closer and brushed the white dust from her face.

"Do you think she'd like to help out here?"

"She'd love it. Ask her. She mentioned feeling disappointed she couldn't help."

"Good," Alissa said. "I'll see how she feels after therapy."

Her expression changed, and Ross felt uneasy with her look.

"Where did you go yesterday? You usually talk about your business, and you didn't this time."

He knew it. "I visited a ranch in Watsonville."

"Watsonville? That's the 'Strawberry Capital of the World.' Do they have avocados there, too?"

"Watsonville has all kinds of produce. I was visiting a ranch to see how they handle the business. I always learn new things to improve my companies." He'd told her the truth but left out some things. He didn't want to give her hopes he couldn't fulfill.

"Good idea since you're this far, I suppose." She still looked suspicious, but she didn't question him further and slipped a tray of cookies into the oven.

"I'll sit with Mom and wait for the therapist, or if you tell me where the Christmas tree lights are, I'll string them."

"They're in a box near the registration desk. Thanks. I'll come out and help when I get this last batch finished."

He slipped through the door and spotted the box she'd mentioned. As he untangled the long strands of lights, Ross reviewed what he'd heard and seen yesterday in Watsonville. Although he knew nothing about strawberries, he could learn, and buying the farm would bring him closer to Pacific Grove. He'd still have his home in San Luis Obispo when he needed to be down there.

Selling Prospero Vineyards and the ranch cut deep. He could give up the vineyard; he loved his home there, though, and he suspected he'd never find another as special. Still, he wanted to make a change, and this seemed a possibility.

Before he unknotted the third string, Ross heard the doorbell ring. He dropped the strand and opened the door, hearing the bells jangle. "You're the therapist?"

The young woman nodded and introduced herself.

"Glad you found us," he said, pushing the door open. "Mom's right down this corridor."

"Thanks," she said.

He led the way then tapped on the door and heard his mother's voice. Ross pushed it open. "The therapist is here."

The woman walked inside and set her bag on a table near the door. "Hi, Mrs. Cahill. I'm Kim Roland. Ready for a workout?"

His mother quipped a comment, and he chuckled as he turned away. He would rather untangle Christmas tree lights than watch his mom be in pain. Grasping a string of lights, he went back to work. He looped the white lights around his hand and began the task of draping them over the tree branches. The tree looked real, but Alissa had purchased a quality artificial tree, she'd explained, knowing it would last through the lengthy time it would stand in the parlor.

When he neared the bottom, Alissa came in from the kitchen. "It looks great." She motioned toward his mother's bedroom. "How's Maggie doing?"

"I'm not sure, but I haven't heard any screams yet."

She waved his words away with the shake of her head. "I'll check."

She bounced across the room then turned to face him. "Coward." She made a cute face and flitted away.

He looked at the Christmas tree and grinned.

Chapter 11

Alissa stood in the doorway, watching Maggie with the therapist a few moments before she interrupted. "How's it going?"

"Good," the therapist said, introducing herself. "She's really strong for her age, and—"

"What do you mean, for my age?"

Maggie had a twinkle in her eye, and Alissa chuckled at the surprised look on the therapist's face; then the young woman caught on and laughed with them.

"I see you're walking well," Alissa said. "Could you help me with the pies later?"

"Pies? I'd love to."

"Maggie's doing amazingly well, and she can do a lot of things, but she needs to take a few precautions." The therapist gave Maggie a stern look. "No crossed legs and no reaching past your knees or between your legs. When standing, don't lean forward, and avoid sitting on low, soft chairs. Otherwise, if you're not in pain, then go for it."

"I'll be jumping rope in a week or two," Maggie said, her optimism heightening.

"I think it'll be a number of months before you'll be doing that," Kim said, "but you're on your way if you keep doing your exercises." Kim looked toward Alissa. "The main activity is walking. In another week or so, she needs to get outside with the walker. Get used to walking there."

"We'll help with that," Alissa said, smiling and stepping away. She returned to the living room, where Ross had finished the lights and begun stringing garland that looked like cranberries. "Let me help." She grasped the loop of beads, and they passed it back and forth as they wound their way to the bottom.

"Now that's the way to do it," Ross said. "It's easier with two." He slipped beside her and tilted her chin upward. "Many things are. Remember the animals filled the ark two by two."

"I remember reading about that," she said, eyeing the hallway for the therapist. She gave him a teasing frown, and he leaned down and gave her a quick kiss on the end of her nose.

"Let's get serious," she said.

"I was. I'm being very serious."

Though he was being playful, Alissa sensed his comment meant more than decorating the tree. She'd been dealing with her emotions for weeks now, knowing she'd fallen in love; she loved the inn, though, and he loved and needed his work. These were their livelihoods.

With God all things are possible. The words nettled her like a bee sting. She reeled back from the unexpected revelation. Maybe the good Lord had to smack people in the head once in a while just to keep them on their toes. God had an answer. She would have to wait patiently for it.

Forcing her mind away from her thoughts, Alissa delved into decorating the Christmas tree. She loved the Victorian-style ornaments she'd purchased over the years—ones that looked like home-baked cookies, metal designs, crocheted angels, and amazing paper baubles. She'd found cloth balls that looked like patchwork and needlepoint squares at the craft show. She thought now they were finished, but when she looked up, Ross had found some pinecones adorned with paint and glitter.

He held one up, eyeing it. "I could have made this."

"Then I'll get you a booth at the craft show next year."

They laughed, and just as he'd stepped toward her with that mesmerizing look in his eyes, the therapist strode into the room.

"I'll be leaving. I'd like you to encourage Maggie to do her foot pumps and ankle rotations and especially the knee bends." She described how they were to be done safely. "And walking. She can walk around her room and up and down the hallways with her walker. Another month or more on that, and then we'll see how a cane works." Her eyes widened as she turned and glanced over her shoulder. "For an older woman, she's doing extremely well."

"Mother's determined," Ross said. "She'll get well or else."

"Don't let her overdo it—and don't tell her she's doing well for her age. She doesn't like that."

Alissa and Ross chuckled at the same time.

The therapist left, and when Alissa went to check on Maggie, she found her lying on the bed with a quilt over her knees. "I'm going to take a little nap. Can we do the pies later?"

"Absolutely. You're not holding me up at all. Ross and I are decorating the tree."

Maggie released a soft chuckle. "If you only knew him a year ago, Alissa, you'd know he is a different man." She gave Alissa a tender look. "Thank you."

Alissa watched Maggie close her eyes, letting what she'd said soak in. *A different man.* She recalled when he first arrived at the inn, the night he checked in late, and he was very different then. He'd arrived like a chrysalis, and he'd opened up to become a magnificent butterfly—an emperor butterfly—just like the name of his room.

Gathering her thoughts, she returned to the parlor. Ross had disappeared, and she figured he was upstairs. She headed for the kitchen, and when she opened the door, she found him inside preparing hot chocolate.

"I hope you don't mind. I hung those pinecones, so we're finished, and this tasted so good earlier. I thought we could just sit for a while and enjoy the tree lights."

"I don't mind at all, and I'll steal a few of those Christmas-at-the-Inn cookies."

"Great." He motioned to the doorway. "I want to get something in my room. I'll be down in a minute to finish."

Alissa placed the cookies on a plate then set it and the mugs on a tray, but before she could carry them into the parlor, Ross appeared and took the tray from her. She held open the swinging door and followed past the tree while Ross set the tray on the low table.

Alissa settled on the love seat, admiring the old-fashioned Christmas tree with a hand-crafted angel on top. The metal ornaments glittered with tiny white lights. They'd attached a few clip-on candle ornaments with lights inserted so the Christmas tree had the look of a Victorian tree with real candles burning.

"Since it's almost Christmas, I thought—"

Alissa chuckled. "You sound like a little kid. Christmas is a month away."

"You'd hardly know it with all these decorations, so let's pretend it's Christmas."

She shrugged, not sure why it made any difference. "Okay. It's Christmas."

"Good," he said, pulling a bag from beside a chair. "Merry Christmas." He handed her the bag and settled back.

"What's this?"

"Open it, and you'll know."

She studied the unmarked sack, trying to image what it could be. Laughing at herself for dallying, she unwound the top and looked inside. "It's from the bazaar, isn't it?"

He grinned. "You liked it, and so did I."

She drew out the metal rod holding the lovely copper and black monarch butterfly. "It's beautiful, Ross. Thank you." She leaned over, kissing his cheek.

"That made it all worthwhile—the smile on your face and the kiss."

She rose and studied the Christmas tree. "I think I could stick it in the branches for now, and it'll look like an ornament."

"Sounds like an idea." He stood and helped her find the perfect spot then manipulated the stick through the branches while trying not to knock off any ornaments. When he finished, they stood back and admired the lovely decoration.

Alissa returned to her seat and grasped her hot chocolate. "Let's make a toast to a job well done," she said, lifting her mug.

"I'd rather toast to us."

Ross lifted his drink, and they clicked their mugs together; instead of bringing Alissa joy, though, the toast reminded her of their difficulty.

"Cheer up," Ross said, slipping his arm around her shoulder. "Answers will come. I know they will."

"I wish God would give us a little hint of how it can work out. You're not in a position to leave your businesses. They're successful because you run them with your wisdom and love. It's the same here. This place is my dream, and I—I don't know."

"You don't know about me?"

His expression looked strained, and her chest hurt from holding back her emotion. "It's not that. I think we should be friends. Good friends, and leave it at that. I don't want to be hurt."

"Neither do I, but friends? You mean I can't hold you in my arms. I can't kiss your sweet lips. Is that what you mean?"

She didn't know how to respond. Desperation swept over her, and she saw the same in Ross's eyes.

He set his mug on the table and leaned closer to her. "Do you care about me, Alissa? I mean, really care? Forget we've only known each other for a few weeks. It doesn't take a lifetime to find someone when God is the guide."

She faced him, trying to control the tears pushing against her eyes. "Do you have to ask?" She slid her mug onto the coffee table. "You know you've been the focus of my days. I feel empty when you're not here, and the only thing that helps is that I know you'll be back because I'm holding your mother captive."

Ross grasped her hand. "You didn't agree to keep my mother here because of that, did you?"

She flexed her palm upward at his joke. "Scout's honor. I've grown to love your mom, and I—I care about you. It's good for all of us. And your visiting is the bonus."

"What if we could be together every day? What if—"

She pressed her finger against his lips, unable to bear his pleading. "Don't." She closed her eyes, wrestling with the myriad of questions and thoughts bound inside. "What we have right now is wonderful. We're dearest friends. We enjoy each other's company. We laugh, we tease, and we have good talks. We share a faith. What more do we need?" Alissa knew what she needed, but all she had was an elusive dream that had no future.

"We need each other, Alissa. I didn't realize until meeting you that I want a real home and family. I want you to be part of that."

She sat a moment, hoping to find some way to sway him—to sway herself. "So do I," she whispered.

He shifted closer and drew her into his arms. "Then let's work this out. We can find a way. The answers are there if we want this bad enough."

She nodded, hoping he was right. She'd lived without love for so long. Alissa knew she could continue the same way, but now that she'd tasted the gift, could she let it go? "We need time to let things work."

"Until then I want us to remember that 'all things work together for good to them that love God.' Don't forget that."

"I won't."

"Tomorrow is Thanksgiving, and let's use that day to thank Him for our finding each other."

She managed a smile, and he leaned closer and pressed his lips to hers. She thawed in his arms, her cold fears fading and her prayers rising, and when Ross drew back, Alissa caught her breath. "If I don't get busy on the preparations, we'll be thankful tomorrow for a toasted cheese sandwich." She slipped from his grasp with a laugh. "You wouldn't want that, would you?"

He opened his arms. "If we could stay here forever, I wouldn't care."

"Phooey!" She skittered away, hoping the playful mood stayed with her. The dark feelings she'd had reminded her that life these past weeks had been unbelievable.

༄

Alissa put the last of the turkey in the freezer, though she'd left some in the refrigerator for sandwiches and a casserole. She put on the coffee and pushed open the swinging door. "Who's ready for dessert?"

She heard a playful groan coming from Ross. "I suppose I can force myself to have a piece."

She strode into the parlor. "How about you, Fern? Maggie?"

"I'll have a piece," Fern said.

Maggie nodded. "Just a sliver. The meal was delicious, but I want to see how my pies turned out."

"They look delicious. I'll whip the cream."

"Let me help," Ross said, jumping from the love seat and heading her way.

"He just wants to lick the beaters," Maggie called.

Fern laughed, and Alissa did, too, delighted Maggie had felt well enough to make the pies yesterday and had been so spirited today. She couldn't recall a time when her life had seemed so full.

Ross slipped in behind her and pushed the swinging door closed. He drew her into his arms and pressed his lips against her forehead. "This is a day to be thankful for. Mom's in fine spirits and is looking so good. Fern has been great, and we've come to somewhat of an agreement"—his smile inched to a scowl—"haven't we?"

"We have. I'm just scared. I don't want to get my heart broken."

"Neither do I, so I'm trusting in you, me, and the Lord."

She relaxed in his arms.

He shifted one arm and pulled up the edge of her lip. "There, that looks better. I see a smile."

She burst into laughter and sprang away. "No foolishness. We're here for the pies."

She grasped the cream then opened the freezer and pulled out the bowl and beaters. "You're in charge of the whipped cream while I cut the pie. Do you know how to hook in the beaters?"

As she lifted one, he pulled it from her fingers. "I had freshman home economics in high school. I'm a whiz."

She kept an eye on him while she pulled out the plates and cut the pie. When it was time for the sugar, she sprinkled a tablespoonful into the cream and let him finish the job.

"Done," he said, turning off the motor. "Look at this. Stiff peaks."

"Great job." She laughed as he pulled out the beaters, took a big lick off one, then pulled out the other and handed it to her.

She joined him as they gobbled up the delicious whipped topping. When she looked at him, she chuckled. He had white splotches above his lip and on his cheeks.

"You don't look any better, my dear." He turned her to face the toaster and lifted it for her to use as a mirror.

He was right. She grabbed a napkin and wiped her face then gave him a spoon to add the topping while she poured the coffee. Eventually they carried the drinks and dessert into the parlor while Maggie sat on a kitchen chair, her walker by her side, waiting patiently.

"I thought you'd decided to eat in there," Maggie said when they arrived.

"We had a whipped-cream battle," Ross said, handing her a piece.

Alissa handed Fern her piece and set the coffee mugs by each spot then dug into the pumpkin pie. She took a bite then another, feeling her eyes widen. "Maggie, this pie is outstanding. What did you do?"

"It's the orange zest. It really makes a difference."

"I guess."

"I thought pies were supposed to taste like this," Ross said, giving his mother a wink.

When they had finished, Alissa gathered the dishes while Ross helped his mother into the bedroom. Fern followed Alissa, and they piled the dishes into the dishwasher and cleaned up the kitchen.

"If you don't need me," Fern said, "I think I'll say good night to everyone."

"You've done enough. Thanks for helping clean up."

"This was great." Fern opened her arms, and Alissa gave her a big hug.

"It was nice, and you're always welcome."

"I feel welcome," Fern said, giving her an extra squeeze. "Love you."

"I love you, too," Alissa responded before Fern went into the parlor to say good night to Ross and Maggie. When she finished, Ross left the room while Alissa pulled the shades and helped Maggie get ready for bed, wrestling off the surgical compression stockings and helping her with her nightgown. After Maggie was tucked in, Alissa left her to sleep.

The day had been wonderful, and she hoped the evening would go as well. They'd avoided talking about anything that would put a damper on the day. Their dinner blessing had been one of thanksgiving, and each had added a personal prayer of thanks. Fern's thanks had warmed Alissa's heart, and Maggie had thanked God for bringing Alissa into her life. She couldn't have asked for a better Thanksgiving.

Ross had spread out on the love seat, taking up the seat, so Alissa sank into a chair, studying his handsome face made more handsome by his loving spirit. He'd become a blessing in her life. They sat in silence for a while until Ross straightened and beckoned her to sit beside him.

"I didn't tell you earlier, but I'm leaving in the morning to go to the ranch. I have some things I need to handle, and I think you'll do better without me here during the Christmas-at-the-Inn event."

"You'll be gone that long?"

"It's not that long. I'll be back a couple of days after the event is over. Mom's doing well, and she doesn't need me, and you won't have to explain me to all the visitors."

"What do you mean, explain you? I'd love you to be here."

He shook his head. "Fern always helps you, and since I have things to attend to, it makes sense for me to go now."

"Is something wrong at the ranch?"

"No, everything's great. I talked with Hersh down in San Luis Obispo. Things are going smoothly, and Diaz says everything's fine, but I have paperwork and things to handle. I'll be back."

"I know. I have your mother hostage."

He laughed, and she managed to chuckle, too, but for some strange reason, she felt concerned about his leaving. Their talk the day before had been serious enough to affect them both. Each had hopes, but each had fears. At least she did, and if Ross were honest, he'd have to admit they had big decisions to make.

๛

"Thanks, Fern. I appreciate your coming back this morning to help clean up."

Her sister wiped another punch bowl cup and placed it in the box. "You're welcome. I knew you were tired last night after all your visitors from the Christmas-at-the-Inn event, and that's why I suggested we do it today."

"The two days went well, I thought."

Fern clasped another cup. "Very well. That cranberry apple punch was excellent. I think the lime slices added an extra zing."

"I thought so, too."

"And you really had a nice group," Fern said, placing the punch cup in the storage box.

"Ticket sales were good, as usual." She raised her shoulders in a sigh. "Looks like we're finished. I'll just run a dust cloth over the parlor. I saw some cookie crumbs."

"I'll do that. You take a break."

Alissa eyed her sister. "Why? You've helped enough. Everything's in good shape."

"Then why do you look so tense?"

Alissa raised her shoulders. "I'm not really tense. I'm—"

Fern shook her head. "Okay. Then you're uptight, agitated, stressed. You pick the right word."

Alissa felt helpless. "I suppose I am." She rested her elbow on the kitchen island and her cheek against her fist. "I have too much on my mind."

"Ross and what else?"

She heard a hint of satire in Fern's voice. "Ross and. . .Ross."

Fern snorted. "So what does that mean?"

"I don't know. I'm wondering why Ross left so abruptly and for so many days. He's been here faithfully since his mother's accident, and he left following a difficult discussion we had."

Her sister moved closer and stood beside her. "He proposed, and you refused?"

She could hardly speak. "Not exactly, but he talked about our future, and I don't see a future for us. It's too difficult. My work is here, and his is there."

"It's not on the moon, Alissa. It's a couple of hours away."

"I know, but—"

"I thought for sure you two were in love. Are you telling me it's one-sided?"

"No. It's not that."

Fern straightened and walked across the room then turned. "You're not making sense."

Alissa nodded. "I'm not making sense to myself." She raised her elbows from the counter.

Fern moved closer and rested her hands on Alissa's shoulders. "Love means giving and taking. It means compromise. I can't believe that if you truly love each other, you can't find a way to work through these problems."

Alissa pulled away, irritated at her sister's remark. "It may sound easy to you because this isn't your business. You didn't give up anything for this bed-and-breakfast, and I—"

"Hold on." Fern's eyes narrowed. "I didn't give up anything? I beg to differ. Our mother gave you our family home so you could have this place. You sold it. You took our family memories—the only thing we had left of Mom and Dad—and sold them to strangers because you wanted a classier place. You asked me to help you here when you needed someone, the pauper sister who'd lost money because of a scam artist she fell for. Even before you knew he was a crook, you begrudged my relationship with him, and you never let me forget it with your I-told-you-so attitude. Now you're telling me I never gave up anything."

Tears filled Alissa's eyes. "I never knew you felt that way about the house,

Fern. I thought you resented Mom's giving the place to me and not to you."

"Never. I was proud you had a dream. I looked forward to being a part of it with you, but you never let me. Only after I messed up did you ask me to work part-time, and you know what happened then. I never did anything to your liking." She held up her hand to keep Alissa from speaking. "But we've talked that through. It's forgiven, and I hope soon forgotten. I love this place. I'm proud of what you've done. When you need me, I'm here. I'd be happy to help fill in so you could spend more time with Ross." She lowered her hand and moved closer, her voice softening. "Alissa, I want you to be happy. At least one of us should be."

Alissa couldn't answer. She buried her face in her hands and wept.

Fern backed away and kept her distance for a while then drew nearer and wrapped her arm around Alissa's shoulders. "I love you, and I'm sorry I made you cry."

Her words of love brought Alissa another sob, and she buried her face against Fern's shoulder. When she'd contained her tears, she raised her head. "I love you, too, with all my heart."

"Aren't we silly?" Fern said, shaking her head.

The look on her face made Alissa chuckle, and in a moment, they were back in each other's arms but this time laughing.

When they had parted, Fern put her hands on her hips. "You've worked hard. The place looks wonderful, every room decorated. You still have cookies for the holidays. Ross should be here tomorrow. Maggie is doing well, and I'm here. Take a break. Go for a ride and think good things. And let me reassure you, Ross is a wonderful man. If he had to go away for a few days, he had good reason, and he'll be back, loving you as much as he did when he left. So go."

"Go where?"

Fern shrugged. "What place do you love around here? Take a walk on the pier. Go to the lighthouse. Visit Lovers' Point." She chuckled. "Maybe not there. Wait until Ross is back."

"Asilomar. I'll take a walk on the beach. I could use some fresh air, and I love it there."

"Good, and cheer up while you're at it."

"I'll put on some running shoes. I haven't had any good exercise in a while."

"You'd better get it now because soon you'll have the Christmas visitors, and then you'll be busy."

"Thanks, Fern, and I really mean that."

"I know you do. Now get out of here. I'll take care of Maggie when she wakes from her nap. She's doing so well that she astounds me."

Alissa grinned. "Me, too, but not as much as this talk. You and I needed to have these talks years ago. I can't believe how people waste time harboring worries and grudges."

"Listen to yourself, Alissa. You're talking about wasting time. You have a man who's let you know he cares about you, and you're worried about Butterfly Trees Inn. This place will survive longer than you're here on earth."

Alissa stood a moment, her sister's words wending their way into her brain. *Wasting time.* That's what she'd been doing for too long. She loved her inn, but she cherished Ross. Which was more important? She didn't have to answer. The truth was in her heart.

As she approached the beach, Alissa's thoughts drifted from her conversation with Fern to a conversation she'd had with Ross. He'd said trust had no buts, and yet she'd continued to allow that word to permeate her thoughts and decisions.

The beach spread out before her as she slipped from the car and walked down to the sand. *Lord, clear my mind today just as the fresh air clears my lungs. Help me breathe in the truth.* As the words left her, something fluttered past. A dried leaf? A monarch butterfly? Life sometimes fluttered past, and if she didn't keep her eyes open, she'd miss something wonderful.

Her feet sank into the sand as she made her way toward the beach, and her eyes were dazzled by the sun glinting off the waves. She thought again of the monarch butterflies. Butterflies' lives were so short, but the Lord had given monarchs seven or eight months longer to live, long enough for them to make the journey back to their ancestors' winter home. Alissa had faith that God provided for the birds and the butterflies, as the Bible said, and He would provide for her, as well. Her heart leaped with the realization.

Why had she feared? Why had she put buts on every option? All she needed was faith and to wait patiently on the Lord's will.

∽

Ross grinned as he headed down Highway 1. He'd been able to wrap up his business and even added a few things to his list, and he was still arriving in Pacific Grove a day early. He couldn't wait to see Alissa's surprised face.

Her face. He'd prayed and prayed the last few days that Alissa would see things as he did. He'd taken a leap of faith and made changes in his life, and it was almost too late to turn back. If Alissa let him down, he'd be hurt beyond belief. Still he'd resolved more than one issue since he'd left on Monday.

The radio played a love song, and Ross's pulse did a jog. He'd turned into a real romantic since he met Alissa. She'd grabbed his heart within a few days and hadn't let go. He whistled along with the tune, grinning to himself as he hit the town of Marina. Seaside was the next city then Monterey and Pacific Grove.

He tried to imagine what Alissa had been doing all morning. For the past two days, he knew, she'd been busy with the Christmas-at-the-Inn event. He'd avoided calling her, not wanting to lie if she asked him about his activities. Keeping secrets from her was difficult. He'd learned quickly she was a woman who wanted details.

The music cut off as a newscaster's voice interrupted the program. "Pacific

Grove police are warning residents and guests to be alert for a possible mountain lion believed active in the beach tract and Asilomar area."

Beach tract and Asilomar. His brows tugged together with concern. He couldn't imagine Alissa being on the beach today following the inn event when she'd have cleaning up to do; however, an active mountain lion could wander around the beachfront homes, and he suspected she hadn't bothered to turn on the TV or radio.

The newscaster continued. "If you come upon a mountain lion, do not run. Face the animal and look into his eyes. Move slowly and make yourself appear as large as you can by standing on your tiptoes or spreading a jacket wider. Mountain lions will not attack if they believe they are in danger. These animals usually attack the head or neck, so avoid crouching, bending over, or sitting in lion country, especially if you are alone. These animals have been considered protected mammals in California since 1990, so their population has grown in the last eighteen years."

Though he'd hoped to surprise Alissa with his early return, Ross tossed the idea aside and pulled out his cell phone. He punched Alissa's speed dial number, his ear pressed to the receiver.

"Butterfly Trees Inn."

A charge of disappointment struck him. "Fern, this is Ross. Could I speak to Alissa?"

"Sorry, Ross. She's not here. She didn't take her cell phone either, because I see it on the registration desk."

"Is she shopping? I thought she'd be there today."

"We cleaned up the place, and your mom is napping, so she decided to get some exercise on the beach."

His heart flew to his throat. "The beach? Which one?"

"Is something wrong?"

"Which one?"

"She mentioned Asilomar."

"No."

"What's wrong?"

"A mountain lion's been spotted in that area."

"What should I do, Ross?"

"I'm on my way. You stay put. I'll head over there."

"I'll be praying," Fern said, her voice tense.

"Thanks. So will I."

Ross flipped the cell closed and tossed it on the passenger seat. "Lord, please keep her safe. There's a lot of beach, and I might be silly here, but I can't take chances. I love this woman. You know that because You can see into my heart. Thank You, Jesus, for Your protection."

He gripped the steering wheel and pressed his foot firmer against the accelerator. If he got a ticket, so be it. Then he'd have a police escort. . .at least he hoped.

When he hit the beach tract, he watched the road but glanced along the shoreline, his heart thundering. Maybe he was being foolish. Of all the people in the world, why would Alissa be the one to be on the beach at the very moment a mountain lion had also decided to wander along the shoreline?

The road curved, and he spotted the lighthouse and slowed. Traffic had thinned, so he took his time, even pulling off the road to scan the horizon. Fern had mentioned Asilomar, so he stepped on the gas and made his way to the Asilomar area. He parked on Sunset Drive, as close as he could get to the water, then spotted Alissa's sedan and knew he was in the right place.

Ross made his way toward the beach, his eyes shifting from right to left in search of a possible mountain lion. When he reached the crest of a grassy area, he spotted a lone figure running along the mile stretch of sand. *Alissa!* He recognized her shape and her buttery blond hair glowing in the early afternoon sun. She paused and stretched her arms upward, jogging in place.

He opened his mouth to call but thought better of it and stood at the higher point to scan the area. Below him on a lower crest, he saw a movement, or had it been sand swirling in the breeze? *No.* He narrowed his eyes. Something sand-colored moved forward. *The mountain lion!* Ross watched as the lion crouched in the mix of sand and grass, facing Alissa.

With his heart racing, Ross tried to remember what the newscaster had said. Although he knew the rules for encountering a dangerous animal, his senses had frozen and his mind reeled with fear. Recollection hit him. Convince the lion Alissa wasn't prey, but how could he do that? As his gaze darted toward Alissa, he noticed her sink Indian-style into the sand. *No!* His stomach churned. She'd chosen the worst position she could be in. As he snapped his head toward the lion, it crouched lower to the ground and began inching forward.

Alissa, please stand. Lord, give her an instinct to stand. She remained seated, still, her head bent forward as if in thought or prayer. *Stand up, Alissa.*

God, help me. As the prayer left him, the answer came. His only course of action was to draw the lion's attention to him. He could reach his car faster than Alissa. He closed his eyes and began to slip off his jacket; then in the loudest voice he could summon, he screamed toward the lion.

Chapter 12

A man's cry jarred the silence. Alissa pivoted her head and saw a man slipping off his jacket. *Ross.* What was he doing? He raised it over his head, whirling it in the air. She followed the direction of his eyes, and her knees weakened. A mountain lion was heading for Ross!

Her pulse escalated, leaving her breathless. Had it been heading for her? She could only guess. She rose slowly and headed upward toward the grassy knoll but kept her distance. Ross stood between her and the animal.

Ross yelled again as he moved forward, flapping his jacket. The lion settled into a crouch.

Alissa whispered a prayer. "Lord, please. No." Her breath left her as she made her way up the hill, trying to be unobtrusive yet ready to draw the lion to her rather than seeing Ross lose his life to save hers.

Ross bellowed again, and the cat raised its head, its back twisting as it turned and sped away from them across the grass.

"Ross." Her voice penetrated the sound of the surf, and he turned, bounding down the sand dune to meet her. She flew into his arms and buried her face in his chest. Her fear released in hot tears.

Ross's body trembled beside her, their emotion at high pitch. "Thank You, Lord," he said, rocking her against him. "I couldn't believe what I saw. I can't believe I could have lost you."

"How did you know I was here?"

He eased back to look at her. "I heard a police report bulletin on the radio about a mountain lion spotted in this area, and I began to worry it would wander too close to the inn, so I called. Fern told me you were here."

"You weren't supposed to come until tomorrow."

He released a pent-up breath. "I know. God works in amazing ways. I planned to surprise you. My business was finished, and I couldn't wait to see you."

"You did surprise me," she said, trying to make light of the horrible experience. "I've never seen a mountain lion. I know they can come this far, but I've never seen one."

"We've had a few at the ranch, but they've always been scared off. They don't want to fight humans. They want food." He brushed his hand along her hair. "The problem is you sat on the sand and lowered your head. They go for the head and neck. I panicked."

"No, you saved me."

He tucked his arm in hers. "Let's get to the car. I want to call the police and tell them what we saw, and then we need to talk."

Her legs still trembling, Alissa leaned on Ross as they made their way to her car. Ross stopped and made the call and then took time to call Fern. After he told her Alissa was fine, he handed Alissa the telephone to finish the details, but before she hung up, Ross took back the cell phone.

"We'll drop off her car, but we won't come in if that's okay. I want to take Alissa for a ride."

A ride? The reality of what had happened exploded in her senses. Alissa wanted to calm down. She wanted to go home and take a shower.

Ross clicked off and turned to her. "I hope it's okay. We need to talk now."

"Here on the beach?"

"No. Let's get out of here. This place is making me nervous. I don't know where that cat went, and I can't concentrate while I stand guard."

She nodded, realizing his suggestion made a lot of sense. "But I can't go anywhere fancy."

"Nothing fancy," he promised.

Ross started the car and made his way to Ocean View. Alissa parked her car then settled into his. She studied his profile, speculating on what could be so important. It probably had to do with the time he spent at his ranch or maybe another lecture about not walking alone on the beach.

Ross slipped his hand in hers, his expression uneasy. "I still can't believe what I saw. I'm glad you didn't see him and try to run. He would have been on you in a nanosecond."

"Don't say that. You're scaring me."

"Alissa. It's true. I watched the cat's tail twitch, and he crouched then inched forward toward you. I could have lost you, and I'm not willing to do that."

"Lost me?" She shook her head. "I can't believe I was so dumb, and you endangered your own life for me."

"For *us*. I couldn't bear the thought of anything happening to you." He drew her into his arms and rested his cheek against her hair. "It wasn't stupid. You didn't know a mountain lion had gotten so close to the city. It's always wise to go jogging with someone. Never alone."

"But I wanted to think. I needed time alone to make decisions." She felt his hand twitch in hers. "They were good thoughts, Ross."

"Good?"

She nodded. "I'm trusting in God's guidance, and I'm trying to make wise decisions."

"Tell me." His gaze searched hers for a moment before he straightened and shifted into reverse.

Alissa glanced away. "You first."

Ross released the brake and rolled to the end of the driveway. "Let's wait until we get there." He backed out onto Ocean View and shifted into drive.

Alissa didn't speak, confused as to where they were going and why.

Ross passed Forest Avenue, and when he reached Seventeenth Street, he drove into the parking lot and turned off the motor.

Her hands felt clammy. "This is Lovers' Point Park. Is this where you wanted to go?"

He nodded, slipped from the driver's seat, and came around to open her door. "I thought this was a good place to tell you what's been on my mind."

Lovers' Point. She felt swept away by his words. She'd spent a couple of hours thinking on the beach and had been struggling with her thoughts before that, but her talk today with Fern had made all the difference. As if the Lord had whispered in her ear, the answer came, as sweet as nectar to a monarch butterfly.

Ross wrapped his hand around hers and led her to a quiet place on the grass away from another couple a long distance away. He spread his jacket on the ground, and they sank onto it, close to each other's side.

Ross entwined his fingers through hers. "You want me to go first?"

Alissa nodded, almost afraid to hear what he had to say.

"I found a buyer for Prospero Vineyards."

Her head snapped toward him. "You what?"

"A neighboring vineyard has wanted my land for years. We've been in competition, but we've still remained business friends. He's offered me an overwhelming price."

Her pulse tripped through her veins. "What will you do?"

"I still own the avocado ranch, and that brings in a great income, too, Alissa."

"I hope you didn't do this because of me."

"You know I didn't. I did it for me, and for my fathers—both of them."

"Both of. . ." It took her a moment to understand. "You'll be blessed, Ross. It bothered you, and when we feel we're doing something not to the Lord's liking and stop it, then He will reward us."

He squeezed her hand. "God's tremendous gift of salvation is all the reward I need."

"What will you do now?" Her spirit sank, picturing his loss. "Move down to San Luis Obispo, I suppose."

He captured her gaze and grasped her other hand. "That depends on you, Alissa."

She let his words sink in.

"Say you're ready to give our relationship a chance."

"I do want to."

His excitement appeared to heighten. "I want to take you someplace tomorrow if you're willing. It's important you see this."

Alissa lifted his hand in hers and kissed his knuckles. "I've been doing a lot of thinking, Ross. When you left a few days ago, I had a horrible feeling of emptiness. I missed you, and I thought I'd pushed you away with my negative attitude. Your mom is always so upbeat, and she talks as if she thinks we're already a couple."

"She does."

His quick agreement made Alissa chuckle. "And I don't want to disappoint her."

The brightness in his eyes faded.

"Or disappoint myself," Alissa added, wanting him to know how she felt.

"You scared me for a minute. I don't want you basing any decision on what my mom wants."

Alissa slipped her hands from his and clasped his cheeks. "Do you really think I would?" She leaned forward and brushed her lips on his.

He looked surprised and drew her closer, lengthening the tender kiss.

"Fern thinks like your mom."

"Really?" His gaze drew her in, and a faint grin curved his lips. "Are you telling me you're willing to make this work?"

"I'm telling you. . .I am."

"Alissa." He opened his arms and drew her into them, kissing the top of her head, her forehead, and the tip of her nose. "I promise you we can make this work, because I know in my heart this is God's will. Everything has worked out too smoothly to be otherwise."

She smiled at him. "Do you want to know what I've been thinking?"

"Please."

"I thought about the butterflies and how God guides them, and I realize God will surely guide our steps, too. Another thought came to me after that. Fern loves the inn. She's willing to work longer hours and give me time away, and I've been thinking about that. Since she and I have talked, I see where I've gone wrong. I discouraged her in many ways. She continued to work at the inn because she needed the money, but what she really hoped was to be part of the business with me and help me make the inn a success."

Her heart skipped as she faced her admission. "Can you believe when I was thinking of what God wanted of me, I heard a verse from Ecclesiastes in my head, 'Better is the end of a thing than the beginning thereof: and the patient in spirit is better than the proud in spirit'? The beginning part of the verse was easy to understand, but when I thought about the last part—'the patient in spirit is better than the proud in spirit'—I blamed Fern for the pride, and it was me all along. I was prideful of the gifts God had given me rather than thankful for His blessings. I just ran along with my head in the clouds, doing everything and treating my sister like hired help—maybe worse, because she's my sister and I should have shown her love."

"But things are different now."

A weight flew from her shoulders. "I want Fern to manage the inn for me."

Ross's face brightened with a broad smile. "That's a great idea. Tremendous! You've been thinking all of this since I left?"

"Yes. Since you left. I didn't want to lose you, Ross, and I asked myself which was more important—the inn or you—and I decided."

He sat beside her, his face expectant, waiting for her to finish, and she couldn't wait to tell him.

"I want you with all my heart."

"Thank You, Lord," Ross said, looking at her with love in his eyes.

"But now I feel bad because I've put you under all this stress. You could have kept—"

"Alissa, without trying to, you motivated me to do something I should have done a long time ago. I love this area. It's far more beautiful than San Luis Obispo, and you'll still want to be part of the inn."

"I would still love to help out here. I love this place."

"I know. So believe me when I say God is in charge. What's happened is His will and not something we thought of by chance." He brushed his finger along her cheek. "Ask Fern if she can take over tomorrow just for the morning. We'll be back. I want to show you something."

"Can you give me a hint?"

"It'll be more fun if you wait."

She stuck her lip out in a playful pout, but her heart leaped with happiness.

⁓

"Close your eyes." Ross hoped to distract Alissa before she looked at the view.

She frowned. "Why?"

"Because I asked you to." He put his arm around her shoulders. "It's a surprise."

"I hate surprises."

"You'll love this one."

She stared at him without blinking, and though Ross figured they would have a standoff, she finally closed her eyes.

"Now keep them closed." He moved the car forward into the circular driveway and parked. "Keep them closed."

"I heard you the first time," she said in a tone he recognized as irritation trying to sound lighthearted.

He walked around the car and opened the passenger door. "Step out, and I've got you."

She felt the door handle and slid from the car, grasping his arm.

"A few steps and you can open them."

Shifting her in front of him, his arms around her from behind, Ross told her to open her eyes. He felt her draw back when she saw the house. "What is this?"

"It could be my new house in Watsonville."

"Watsonville?" She spun around to face him. "Watsonville is less than thirty miles from Pacific Grove."

"That's right. Would you like to see inside?"

"I can't wait. Is the house inland, or can you see the ocean?"

"Come along, and you'll see." He took her hand and drew her up the short incline to the front of the house, its broad windows looking out over the landscape, the rolling hills and strawberry fields, some of which he would own soon.

"I love the big windows." She glanced over her shoulder to look at the view. "It's lovely, but it would be extra special if it had an ocean view."

Ross could see her disappointment so he didn't respond. He unlocked the door, and Alissa stepped inside.

"Ross, it's huge, and it's empty."

"But not for long if I buy it."

She hurried through the broad foyer into the living room with its elegant fireplace and built-in cabinets on each side of the mantel; then she made her way into the formal dining room and into the bright kitchen with golden oak cabinets and counters. "It has a huge island. I love this. You could make wonderful meals here."

"I could?" She'd never tasted his mediocre cooking. "You mean Carmelita."

"Would she come with you?"

"I wouldn't move without her."

He took her hand and led her across the kitchen to the family room. "Now what do you say?" Seated on a hill, the landscape had its own small pond, and in the distance, the ocean spread out before them.

"Ross, this is unbelievable." She turned full circle. "I love all these windows where you can see the ocean, and this stone fireplace is out of this world."

"Carmelita has great quarters with a bedroom, sitting room, and bath beyond the kitchen. There's another suite where Mom can stay on the first floor, and upstairs are four bedrooms, each with a bath."

"What about an office for you?"

"There's a room that attaches to the garage with a door that goes out to a huge deck. Come and see."

She followed him, her mouth agape as she looked into every closet and opened every door. "I think it's a tremendous house. I really do."

"Could you live in a house like this, Alissa?"

She paused and turned to face him. "Who couldn't? It's wonderful with lots of room for guests."

He drew her closer, his arms around her waist, his heart in his throat. "And children. I think this house needs the patter of little feet."

"I have little feet." She lifted her foot and wiggled her tiny shoe.

"I'm serious."

Alissa gazed into his eyes, a look so sad it hurt him. "Isn't it too late for children?"

He nestled her closer. "Not if God's in charge. Forty-year-old women have children, and remember—a little one doesn't have to be my own flesh and blood to be my child. I'm leaving that decision to the Lord."

"Then I will, too," she said, a faint flush rising on her cheeks.

"Alissa, today is amazing. I love you with all my heart."

Her eyes searched his. "I love you, too, from the very bottom of my being. I never thought I'd say that, but it's so easy."

His chest tightened, longing to proclaim to the world that God had led him to this wonderful woman. "I've loved you forever."

"Forever?" A grin spread to her lips. "We've only known each other weeks."

"When God creates your soul mate, you've loved her forever. You only have to wait until He brings that special one into your life. It happened the day I met you."

He gazed at her sweet mouth, her lips waiting to be touched, and he lowered his mouth with a kiss he would remember always.

❧

Alissa spotted her sister with her handbag over her shoulder before she had a chance to talk with her alone.

"I think I'll get going," Fern said. "I checked a few things upstairs. The new cleaning girl is doing a good job, and I took care of a couple of reservation letters. They're ready for the mail in the morning."

"Fern, stay for dinner. When we were on our way home, Ross picked up some steaks to grill for us."

"Steaks? What's the occasion?"

Alissa glanced into the backyard through the kitchen window and saw Ross and Maggie deep in conversation. She assumed Ross was telling his mother their news; now she longed to shout it from the rooftop, but before she did that, she wanted to talk with Fern. "He's celebrating buying some new property and a few other changes in his life."

"Is that what he took you to see this morning? You were quiet about that, and I didn't want to ask."

"Yes. He's buying a strawberry farm in Watsonville."

"That's close to Pacific Grove." She stepped closer. "That's good news then."

"It is, and I hope this is some more good news." She closed the distance between Fern and herself then rested her hand on her sister's shoulder. "I want to ask you a favor."

Fern's face flickered with a question. "What kind of favor?"

"The kind I hope you'll accept. Let's sit for a minute." She patted a nearby kitchen chair and sank onto another one.

Fern rested her handbag on the table and sat, a frown growing on her face. "Is something wrong?"

"Everything is right, Fern. I've fallen in love with Ross, and I want to spend time with him. It's difficult to do that with all of the responsibilities here, so I wanted to ask you if you'd consider managing the inn. It would mean so much to me. You belong here as much as I do. It was our family home that bought this place, and I feel as if it's part yours anyway."

Fern's eyes had widened, but she hadn't uttered a sound.

"What do you say, Fern?"

"I'm speechless."

"I suppose you need time to think. That's arrogant of me to expect a decision so—"

"Alissa, stop."

Fern startled her, and she did just that. She pressed her lips together.

"I'm startled, but I'm thrilled—first because you've found the man of your dreams, and second because I would love to work here at the inn. Nothing would make me happier."

"Really?"

"Really."

Alissa rose and dashed to her sister's side, kissing her cheek.

Fern rose, and they embraced as the back door opened and Maggie came in using her cane. She looked rosy cheeked, and the grin on her face let Alissa know Ross had told her. Ross followed with the steaks on a platter. They both had surprised looks on their faces, from seeing Fern in her arms, Alissa guessed.

"I hope you're staying for dinner, Fern," he said, sweeping the platter beneath her nose. "You can't pass up a Cahill-grilled steak."

She chuckled. "If you insist. Anyway, how can I pass up the celebration?"

Ross did a double take from Alissa to Fern, and she knew he'd misunderstood.

Alissa chuckled. "I told Fern about your latest business deal."

"Ah," he said, looking pleased. "Are the salad and potatoes ready?"

Alissa nodded.

"Then let's gather around the table for a blessing."

They were seated and joined hands. When her fingers touched his, Alissa felt something fall into her palm, and her heart soared.

"Heavenly Father," Ross said, "we thank You for every blessing You shower on us, and we thank You for vacations that lead us on journeys we never expected. We ask You to bless this food and bless each of us here. And, Lord—" He paused a moment and released her hand.

Alissa understood. She opened her palm and gazed on the gorgeous glowing diamond set in gold filigree. She let out a gasp, and the two women looked up, their mouths dropping open; then they both smiled.

Before they looked at the ring, Ross continued. "Father, we ask You to bless Alissa and me with Your grace and love. You've brought us together in an amazing way, and we thank You for the love we have for each other, for our families, and for You. We pray this in Jesus' name."

Amens rose heavenward as Fern and Maggie leaned closer to watch Ross slip the lovely gem on Alissa's finger.

Everyone talked at once as they admired the ring and asked question after question while the food got cold, but Alissa didn't care. All she could hear was Ross's voice earlier in the day saying, "I've loved you forever."

She would love him forever and to eternity.

Epilogue

The Next May

Alissa couldn't believe how her life had changed since the evening a man and a woman arrived at Butterfly Trees Inn and she thought they were a May-December married couple. When she pictured the scene, she chuckled, now that she'd grown to love the man she'd assumed was Maggie's husband.

Maggie had become a second mother to Alissa, and though she wished her own mother could be with her for this special day, her joy couldn't be diminished. Today she would become Ross Cahill's wife. Two single people on separate journeys who met that amazing night as only the Lord could have planned.

Ross had jumped into the wedding plans like a colt in spring. They'd selected the Asilomar Conference Center. Alissa loved the fieldstone pillars and dark brown cedar-shake building, nestled amid the pines, with its sweeping porch and a view of the bay. It was not only a lovely setting, but also a reminder of the day she had faced the mountain lion and made the wisest decision of her life. Today she faced no lion. Instead she would face the man of her heart.

She and Ross had visited the facility to view the wedding chapel then selected the chapel hall for their dinner, and they even topped off their plans by choosing to honeymoon on the grounds in one of the center's lovely guest rooms, so close to home yet far away from their everyday lives. They could stroll the beach or walk the boardwalk across the sand dunes and watch the sunset on the bay, never alone anymore but always together as one.

Fern came through the kitchen doorway, wearing her blue dress, the color of a summer sky, and looking especially attractive with her new hairstyle. She'd changed since Alissa had given her more rein at the inn, preparing for her to take over. Fern had begun to care about herself, and it showed in her manner and in her appearance. Alissa praised God for opening her eyes and giving her another chance to make amends with her sister. Fern had moved into the inn the week before and taken over Alissa's quarters, while Alissa became a guest in her own house. She loved the new sense of freedom.

Though Alissa knew she could do the housework at the new home in Watsonville without Carmelita, she loved that Ross wanted her to have a housekeeper and wanted to give Carmelita a home. Alissa knew she could cook if she wanted and give Carmelita well-deserved time for herself. Having help in the huge house would allow Alissa free time to work at the inn for Fern, and it would give Alissa more time to be active in church and the community. It hadn't taken her long to realize, too, that being Ross's wife meant an active social life she would enjoy with him at her side.

Since Ross had moved to his new home, life had changed. They were only a short distance apart, and they'd begun to feel even more like partners as they planned their future. He'd asked her to select some new furniture for the house in Watsonville. Though she loved what he would bring from Paso Robles, she added a few pieces to make the place their own—including a gorgeous piece of artwork of the Pacific Grove beach, painted by a local artist. She would never be homesick looking at the lovely seascape with the waves dashing on the steadfast rocks.

Her life had been so much like those rocks. She'd stood firm in her faith, no matter how life's disappointments and troubles had dashed her hopes, and God had sent her a man with the same conviction.

"I can't believe this day is finally here, and I'm so happy for you," Fern said, standing back and shaking her head. "You look absolutely lovely in that dress."

"Thanks. It is beautiful," Alissa said, catching a glimpse in the mirror of the beaded bodice with the delicately draped neckline adorned with seed pearls. She smoothed the skirt of her gown, a swirl of beads along the sculptured skirt. A veil seemed unnecessary, and instead she'd selected a low crown of pearl and translucent beads, the same style that graced her dress. She gazed again at her magnificent diamond that glittered in the afternoon sun, shooting red and blue colors like fireworks. "I've wanted to show this gown to Ross so many times, but I stopped myself. He'll see it today, and that will make the wait worthwhile."

Fern drew closer and kissed her cheek. "The wait was worthwhile, wasn't it?"

Alissa knew the wait Fern alluded to. Waiting for marriage had allowed her to meet the man God had planned for her and one who was far more wonderful than she could have dreamed.

"It's time, I think. We'd better go," Fern said, beckoning her as she moved to the doorway.

Alissa made her way to the car and fell silent, overwhelmed by emotion, as they drove to the Asilomar center.

The scent of pines and warm grass greeted her as she stepped from Fern's car. They hurried inside past the large stone portals of the entrance, and she made her way to the area where she would wait to be called for the wedding.

Maggie had already arrived and stood inside, the small room beside the box with the florist logo. Alissa knew it held Fern's and her bouquets.

Maggie opened her arms, and Alissa hurried into her embrace, emotion heightening as the minutes ticked past.

"You look so beautiful," Maggie said, stepping to the table and opening the florist box.

Alissa gazed at the woman she'd grown to love. "You look wonderful, too, and I'm thrilled to see you walking as you used to. I think of it every day. It's a miracle."

"I know," she said. "I was very blessed." She turned to Fern and lifted her bouquet from the box, a blend of white and pale rose-colored flowers tied with a sky blue ribbon. "Perfect. Look how it matches your dress."

Fern eyed the ribbon and her gown, agreeing the color seemed exact. She grasped the blossoms and lifted them to enjoy the scent.

"And now the bride," Maggie said, lifting a bouquet of white and pale pink lilies with tendrils of stephanotis trailing from a bed of greens. She handed the flowers to Alissa as a tap sounded on the door.

Fern opened it then closed the door again. "They're ready."

Alissa drew in a lengthy breath and followed Maggie and Fern from the room to the chapel hall where church friends, guests from San Luis Obispo, and even some from Paso Robles sat on white-draped chairs, waiting for the special moment.

Music from the Steinway grand piano across the room floated on the air, and Alissa watched as Maggie was assisted to the front and seated. Fern went first, looking lovely in blue, and Alissa lingered a moment, gazing at Ross, as rugged and handsome as any man could be with a heart that went on forever. When she took her first step, her gaze met Ross's, and his azure eyes drew her to him as if she were floating on a cloud.

Side by side, they listened to Pastor Tom's voice, praying for their life together, speaking the vows they repeated, and reminding them of the lifelong commitment they were making to the Lord and to each other. They exchanged rings, and Alissa waited for the glorious announcement that they were man and wife.

"Before we finalize these vows," the pastor began, "I ask you to follow the bride and groom outside where we will complete the ceremony."

Alissa's pulse skipped. *Outside?* She looked at Ross, confused and concerned, but he only grinned and took her arm. Her mind swirled with questions.

Ross took her arm and led her down the aisle between the rows of chairs, through the chapel hall, and out into the warm spring afternoon. A light breeze rustled the skirt of her gown, and the sunlight glinted from her diamond as she followed him onto the grass. Alissa gazed around the area for a surprise, but she found none. Nothing made sense.

Ross only smiled and patted the hand that was still clasped around his arm, and when the people gathered with them, Pastor Tom began again.

"In Genesis, we read how God created man and woman, saying man should not be alone. And in Noah's day, the Bible tells us Noah followed God's orders, gathering together pairs of all creatures that breathed to enter the ark. The Bible says, 'There went in two and two unto Noah into the ark, the male and the female, as God had commanded Noah.' Noah brought on board every kind of bird and everything with wings.

"Today we send Ross and Alissa onto their own ark on the sea of marriage, two becoming one where they will find shelter under God's wing."

Pastor Tom stepped back then motioned to a crate on the ground behind him that Alissa hadn't noticed. "Psalm 139 reminds us that God is always with us in every situation. 'If I take the wings of the morning, and dwell in the uttermost parts of the sea; even there shall thy hand lead me, and thy right hand shall hold me.'

"Today you will witness a special understanding of God's amazing promise to all of us, but especially as God shares this promise with Ross and Alissa. Standing here in Pacific Grove, we recall the monarch butterfly that travels miles and miles to reach safe ground for the winter, totally by God's design. We know as Christians we, too, must trust in God to reach the safe ground of our lives. Seeing the monarchs return brings us joy. With this release, you will witness the joy and unutterable emotion of the first moments in the new life of"—he spread out his arm toward Ross and Alissa—"Mr. and Mrs. Cahill."

A cheer rose as Ross drew Alissa into his arms, but instead of a kiss, he turned her toward Pastor Tom, who had knelt beside the box and lifted the lid.

Alissa let out a cry of joy as hundreds of butterflies—painted ladies, monarchs, and others—fluttered into the sky, their wings in colors of blue, teal, tawny browns, and orange. She watched their wings catch on the wind and lift high, just as her dreams and hopes had been caught on the wings of God's promises. Yet one lovely monarch fluttered near and rested on Alissa's bouquet. "Butterflies," she said with tears in her eyes. "Ross, look. God's sent us a special blessing."

Ross's gaze captured hers. "He has, Alissa. My wife. My love. My own lovely butterfly." His lips lowered to hers for a moment, a day, a lifetime that she would never forget.

Author's Note:

While reading *Butterfly Trees*, you read about Alissa's cookies, including lemon bars, and Ross's special guacamole. I thought I would share Ross's recipe with you. If you'd like the lemon bar recipe, visit www.gailmartin.com, and you'll find it under the tab GAIL'S KITCHEN.

PRIZE-WINNING GUACAMOLE

Guacamole, which originated in Mexico, is a dip made from avocados. Make sure you check the ripeness of the avocados by pressing gently on the outside of the fruit, feeling for a little give. If the avocado gives too much, it is overripe.

Ingredients:
   2 ripe avocados
   ½ purple onion, minced (about ½ cup)
   1–2 serrano chilies, stemmed and seeded then minced
   2 tablespoons cilantro leaves, finely chopped
   1 tablespoon fresh lime or lemon juice
   ½ teaspoon coarse salt
   dash of freshly grated black pepper
   ½ ripe tomato, seeded and pulp removed, chopped

Preparation: Cut the avocados in half. Remove seed and scoop fruit from the peel; place in a mixing bowl and use a fork to mash the avocado. Next add the chopped onion, chilies, cilantro, lime or lemon juice, salt, and pepper, and mash some more into a somewhat smooth paste. Keep the tomato separate until ready to serve. Cover with plastic wrap directly on the surface of the guacamole to prevent discoloration caused by the mixture being exposed to the air. Refrigerate until ready to serve. Just before serving, add the chopped tomato and mix.

Serve with tortilla chips. This serves 2–4 people.

A Letter to Our Readers

Dear Readers:

In order that we might better contribute to your reading enjoyment, we would appreciate your taking a few minutes to respond to the following questions. When completed, please return to the following: Fiction Editor, Barbour Publishing, Inc., P.O. Box 719, Uhrichsville, OH 44683.

1. Did you enjoy reading *Monterey Memories by* Gail Gaymer Martin?
   ❏ Very much—I would like to see more books like this.
   ❏ Moderately—I would have enjoyed it more if _____
   _____
   _____

2. What influenced your decision to purchase this book?
   (Check those that apply.)
   ❏ Cover   ❏ Back cover copy   ❏ Title   ❏ Price
   ❏ Friends   ❏ Publicity   ❏ Other

3. Which story was your favorite?
   ❏ *And Baby Makes Five*   ❏ *Butterfly Trees*
   ❏ *Garlic & Roses*

4. Please check your age range:
   ❏ Under 18   ❏ 18–24   ❏ 25–34
   ❏ 35–45   ❏ 46–55   ❏ Over 55

5. How many hours per week do you read? _____

Name _____

Occupation _____

Address _____

City _____ State _____ Zip _____

E-mail _____